USA TODAY bestselling author **Rita Herron** wrote her first book when she was twelve but didn't think real people grew up to be writers. Now she writes so she doesn't have to get a real job. A former kindergarten teacher and workshop leader, she traded storytelling to kids for writing romance, and now she writes romantic comedies and romantic suspense. Rita lives in Georgia with her family. She loves to hear from readers, so please visit her website, ritaherron.com.

Debra Webb is the award-winning *USA TODAY* bestselling author of more than one hundred novels, including those in reader-favourite series Faces of Evil, the Colby Agency and the Shades of Death. With more than four million books sold in numerous languages and countries, Debra's love of storytelling goes back to childhood on a farm in Alabama. Visit Debra at www.debrawebb.com.

Also by Rita Herron

Redemption at Hawk's Landing
Safe at Hawk's Landing
Hideaway at Hawk's Landing
Lock, Stock and McCullen
McCullen's Secret Son
Roping Ray McCullen
Warrior Son
The Missing McCullen
The Last McCullen
Cold Case at Camden Crossing

Also by Debra Webb

In Self Defense
Finding the Edge
Sin and Bone
Body of Evidence
Dark Whispers
Still Waters
Bridal Armor
Ready, Aim...I Do!
Colby Law
High Noon

Discover more at millsandboon.co.uk

HOSTAGE AT HAWK'S LANDING

RITA HERRON

THE DARK WOODS

DEBRA WEBB

MILLS & BOON

First Published in Great Britain 2019
by Mills & Boon, an imprint of HarperCollins*Publishers*
1 London Bridge Street, London, SE1 9GF

Hostage At Hawk's Landing © 2019 Rita B. Herron
The Dark Woods © 2019 Debra Webb

ISBN: 978-0-263-27405-9

0319

MIX
Paper from
responsible sources
FSC® C007454

This book is produced from independently certified FSC™
paper to ensure responsible forest management.

For more information visit: www.harpercollins.co.uk/green

Printed and bound in Spain
by CPI, Barcelona

HOSTAGE AT HAWK'S LANDING

RITA HERRON

To my fabulous daughter Elizabeth for always loving
and helping others.

Love you, girl.

Mom

Chapter One

"I found your father."

Dexter Hawk tensed. Detective Frank Lamar's words echoed over the phone line as if boomeranging off the mountains.

Steven Hawk had left the family ranch and abandoned Dex and his family eighteen years ago, shortly after they'd lost their sister, Chrissy. No one had heard from him since.

Dex had taken advantage of his PI skills to search for him, and asked his friend Detective Lamar to help. Lamar was several years older than him, but had taken Dex under his wing a long time ago, becoming his mentor.

"Dex?" Detective Lamar asked. "You there?"

Dexter released the breath he was holding. He'd waited a long damn time for this phone call. But judging from the tone of Lamar's voice, the news wasn't what he wanted to hear.

"Yeah. Where is he?" Dex finally asked.

"Briar Creek," Lamar said.

Briar Creek? Only thirty miles from Hawk's Landing. Had he been nearby all this time? Or had he moved around, then decided to finally come home? "Did you talk to him?"

"He's not talking, Dex." A tense second passed, filling Dex's head with dread.

"I'm sorry," Lamar said gruffly.

Sweat beaded on Dex's forehead. His father was dead. Lamar didn't have to say the words. His apology said it all.

Dex heaved a breath, his chest straining for air. "I have to see him."

"You can do that at the morgue," Lamar said. "I've already called an ambulance."

"No, don't move him. I'm coming there." He snagged his keys from the end table and rushed outside to the SUV he'd bought when he'd donated his pickup to the ranch for the hands.

"What happened?" Dex asked as he climbed in and started the engine.

"Looks like an accident. Pickup truck ran off the road." A hesitant pause. "Dex, there's really no reason—"

"I mean it, Lamar. Do not move him," Dex said between clenched teeth. "I'll be there ASAP." He had to see him for himself. Had to know exactly what had happened to the man who he'd once ridden piggyback and who taught him to ride and fish. Had to know why he'd just up and left and never even called. Birthdays and holidays had passed. Years of worry and wondering and…grief.

His phone vibrated from the console. He gave a quick glance. Harrison, his oldest brother. For a brief second he wondered if Lamar had called him, but he'd sworn Lamar to secrecy about his desire to find their father, so he let the call go to voice mail. He wouldn't destroy the peace and happiness his mother and brothers had recently found until he knew for certain that this dead man was his father.

His family had no idea he'd made it his mission to find him. Not that he had some wild fantasy about a happy reunion with their long-lost patriarch, but Dex's anger had festered for years. He'd practiced what he'd say to his old man for so long that disappointment swamped him.

Now he wouldn't even get the pleasure of telling him off. Memories of his childhood bombarded him as he drove.

His father playing horseshoes with him and his brothers in the backyard. The camping trip where they'd told ghost stories while they huddled in their tent to escape the rain. His father teaching him how to tie knots and rope cattle.

He turned onto a side road that wove past farmland and neared the small town of Briarwood. Briar Creek was known for flooding during heavy storms, but the land looked dry now, and the water low.

He spotted Lamar's unmarked police car on the side of the road around a curve, an ambulance behind it. He parked a few feet behind the ambulance, then climbed out, the summer heat oppressive. Dusk was settling in, the sun was fading and gray clouds were adding a dismal feel.

A drop-off on the left side led from the shoulder of the road to the creek. A black, rusted pickup had nosedived into the water.

Gravel skittered beneath his boots as he descended the hill and approached it. Lamar was speaking to the medics, his craggy face beaded with perspiration. When he looked up at Dex, his expression was grim.

"We're ready to move him," Lamar said.

Dex held up a hand. "Just give me a minute." He swallowed hard. "Please."

A heartbeat passed before Lamar replied. "All right. Just don't touch anything."

Dex hiked over to the truck with Lamar on his heels. The front of the pickup was submerged in about six inches of water, the passenger door ajar. The driver was slumped forward, his head against the steering wheel. The scent of whiskey assaulted Dex, obviously from the empty liquor bottle on the seat.

Disgust slammed into Dex. Had his father turned into a drunk?

With gloved hands, Lamar lifted the man's head away from the steering wheel. Blood streaked his face and arms, his nose was crushed, and a jagged scar ran along the upper right side of his forehead. Gray streaked the man's shaggy hair and beard.

Dex inhaled a deep breath. He hadn't seen his father in eighteen years. Anger and resentment had obliterated memories and images of him until he had a hard time picturing him in his mind.

He remembered that he was a big man, and this man was big. Was he looking at him now?

He cleared his throat, forcing back emotions. He was a PI; he had answers to find. "What made you certain this is my father?"

Lamar rubbed a hand over his sweaty face, then lifted a bag holding an ID. Dexter peered at the ID through the plastic. The name on the driver's license was Steven Hawk.

"I found these in the dash, too." Lamar held up another evidence bag, and Dex's chest tightened. Photos. One of him and his brothers and sister when they were little, then another of his father and mother on their wedding day. His mother still kept the same picture on her dresser in her bedroom.

"I'm sorry, Dex," Lamar said.

Dex blinked hard. He damn well would not cry, not in front of Lamar. And not for the man who'd walked out on him and his family and never looked back.

But denial also reared its ugly head. "I want DNA for confirmation."

"Of course," Lamar said.

Dex studied the dead man's features, struggling to make this bloody face belong to the man he'd loved and idolized.

But an image of his father laughing when Dex had fallen from his horse into a mud puddle surfaced and moisture blurred his eyes. A second later, he saw his father's strained expression as he searched the woods for Chrissy, then the anger in his eyes when the sheriff had treated him like a suspect. But it was his mother's tearstained cheeks the morning after his father hadn't come home that still haunted him.

That was the final blow that had nearly crushed her.

Lamar waved the medics down the hill to remove the body from the truck. Dex noticed a business card on the floor by the seat, snatched the card and jammed it in his pocket. Maybe something on the card would lead him to answer the questions that kept him awake at night. Like where his father had been all this time.

Had he forgotten about his family? Found happiness with another woman?

Had he even thought about them?

Emotions pummeling him, he turned and strode back up the hill. Lamar would let him know when the DNA results were in. Then he'd have to break the news to his family.

Not tonight, though. Tonight he'd grieve alone.

He fingered the card in his pocket as he climbed in his SUV and pulled out the wooden nickel he always carried.

His father's voice echoed in his head. "Don't take any wooden nickels, son."

Dex had taken that meaning to heart. He'd never accepted anything at face value and always investigated things himself.

The name of a homeless shelter had been scrawled on the card.

Maybe someone there could tell him more about his father.

Six weeks later

MELISSA GENTRY SIPPED HER evening tea as she ducked into her small office at the Lend-A-Hand Shelter outside Austin. The evening meal was complete. Tonight the volunteers had served over a hundred dinners, shared stories and camaraderie with the transients who'd wandered in and passed

out personal hygienic supplies and water bottles to everyone who'd shown up. The summer heat was stifling, the
danger of heat stroke and dehydration always high during
the summer months.

The staff was busy clearing the dishes and cleaning the
kitchen, while a few of the short-term residents who'd committed to a plan to get back on their feet gathered in the
common room for a game of cards.

She glanced at the newspaper as she took her break, her
heart clenching. The Hawk family was back in the news.
Last year, they'd found their long-lost sister's body, tying
up the mystery of what had happened to Chrissy Hawk
nearly two decades ago.

Then a few months ago, a human trafficking ring had
struck Tumbleweed, drawing the attention of the FBI and
brother Lucas Hawk. The head of the ring had forced a local
plastic surgeon to change his face so he could create a new
identity, and lawyer brother Brayden Hawk had helped the
feds take down the trafficking ring.

But her attention was focused on the photograph and current headline. Dexter Hawk, the third brother, and the man
who'd stolen her heart her first year of college, stood by a
grave with his family as they said goodbye to Steven Hawk,
his father who'd disappeared shortly after his daughter had.

Some had speculated that he'd run off because he'd hurt
Chrissy, but that theory had been rectified when the family
learned that Chrissy had been killed by a man with a de-
velopmental disability. The more likely scenario for the father's abandonment was that guilt and grief had eaten at him
until he'd left. Couples rarely survived the loss of a child.

Sympathy and envy swelled in her chest. That family
had suffered so much, yet they stood together in loving
support by Mr. Hawk's grave.

All her life, she'd craved a family like that. But working
at the shelter had taught her that you had to play the cards

you'd been dealt in life. So she'd made a family with the volunteers and the drifters who wandered in for food and comfort and a helping hand.

Voices and noises echoed from the front, the sound of arguing forcing her to leave the privacy of the office. She walked down the hall, then poked her head into the doorway of the gathering room to assess the situation.

While she empathized with those in need, instincts warned her to stay alert for trouble. Some people fell on hard times and were humble and wanted help. Others suffered from mental issues, drug addictions and PTSD. There were also criminals who took refuge in shelters and on the streets to escape the law.

She stole a look at the man who'd joined them a few days ago. Jim Smith. He was quiet and secretive, and kept to himself. The dark intensity in his expression suggested something was wrong, that he was on the run from something—or somebody.

She and April Stewart, the director of the shelter, had discussed consulting the local police, but Smith had given them no reason to. If they called the cops on everyone who made them nervous, they might as well shut down.

On the surface, Smith looked rough. He had a long scar on the side of his face, walked with a limp and he was missing the end of the third finger on his left hand. But he'd been polite and respectful to her and April. They'd encouraged him to share his story, but so far he hadn't opened up.

He didn't appear to be mentally ill or an addict. Perhaps he'd recently lost a loved one or his family. Deep grief often forced people to retreat into depression to the point of losing their homes.

Two of the men at the card table were squabbling, one of them accusing the other of stealing his King of Hearts. Smith stepped in, calming them both by clarifying that the card was on the floor.

Melissa smiled. Sometimes Jim surprised her by show-ing a softer side. It made her even more curious about his background and how he'd ended up at Lend-A-Hand.

She cradled her tea mug in her hands as she bypassed the kitchen and made her way to the common room.

The card game ended, and a few of the men headed outside to wherever they wanted to go for the night, while others retreated to the bunk room. The kitchen volunteers waved good-night and hurried out the back door. Smith grabbed a cup of coffee, sat down at the table and started scribbling something in a small notepad, which, she'd no-ticed, he did a lot. She wondered what he was writing.

She locked the front door, but a noise from the back made her jerk around, and she rushed to make sure one of the volunteers hadn't returned and needed her. Or it could be Samuel, the night volunteer arriving.

But just as she reached the hallway, the door to the back burst open. Melissa startled and called out Samuel's name, but a man in dark clothes and a mask grabbed her and shoved a gun to her head.

She opened her mouth to scream, but the man tightened his hold around her throat. "We don't have money or drugs," she managed to say in a choked whisper.

"Shut up." He shoved her forward, and she stumbled and bumped the corner of the wall. He pushed her harder, his voice a growl in her ear. "Where is he?"

Fear clawed at Melissa. "Who?"

"Smith," the man snapped.

"I'm right here."

Melissa's eyes widened as Smith stepped into the door-way, his hands held up in surrender. His dark brown eyes met hers, worry and an apology that she didn't understand etched in the depths.

Then Smith shot an angry look at the gunman. "Let her go and I'll do whatever you want."

Chapter Two

Melissa clenched her jaw. She didn't know why this gunman wanted Jim, but her protective instincts for the drifters at the shelter kicked in. She'd taken self-defense classes, and was tempted to jab her elbow into the man's stomach, then jerk his arm up so hopefully he'd drop the gun. But common sense warned her that if she made a mistake, she'd end up dead and so might Jim Smith.

She couldn't live with his death on her conscience.

The brute with the gun tightened his hold, the gun barrel pressing against her temple. "You'd better back off, Smith, or the little lady gets it."

Tension radiated from Jim's body as he went ramrod still. "It's me you want. Let her go and we'll take this outside."

The man shook his head and shoved her toward a chair in the corner. "Tie her up, then we talk."

Melissa bit her lip to keep from crying out as she sank into the metal folding chair. As much as she wanted to fight, she had to consider the other men in the back. The intruder pulled a rope from his pocket and tossed it toward Jim. He snatched it, then shocked her by swinging it like a cowboy and throwing it toward the gunman like a lasso. The movement caught the gunman off guard, and Jim charged the brute.

The man grunted and the two of them slammed against the wall as they wrestled for the gun. Footsteps sounded from the back, and two of the homeless men, Gunther and Dwayne, rushed into the doorway. She shouted for them to stay back.

Jim threw the intruder to the floor and jerked the man's arm up. The weapon went off, the bullet hitting the ceiling. Jim knocked the gun from the man's hand, and it skidded across the floor. Melissa ran for the weapon, but the shooter snagged her leg as she passed him. She tripped and went down hard, her knee slamming into the wood floor.

Jim rolled twice, then reached the gun and snatched it. The brute jumped him, and they struggled, but the gun went off again. Melissa covered her mouth to stifle a scream as the gunman collapsed on top of Jim.

Was Jim hurt?

A second later, he shoved his attacker off him. Blood oozed from the gunman's chest, and he made a choking sound, then gurgled blood.

Jim pushed himself to stand, the gun in his hands, the other man's blood soaking his shirt. The shooter's body jerked and spasmed, then he suddenly stilled, eyes wide and blank.

Jim looked over at her, his jaw clenched. "Are you all right?"

She nodded, too stunned to speak. He gestured toward Gunther. "Call 9-1-1."

Gunther nodded and rushed toward the phone the men were allowed to use on the counter in the corner. Melissa swallowed, and struggled to stand on shaky legs. She had to know why the man wanted Jim.

But he jammed the pistol into the back of his jeans and ran for the side door. "I'm sorry, Melissa," he murmured, then he unlocked the door and disappeared.

Outside, a siren wailed. The police. Jim had left just in

time to avoid them. Why? She would have vouched that he'd acted in self-defense.

And that he'd saved her life.

DEX CLIMBED IN his SUV and flipped on the radio as he left the homeless shelter near Tumbleweed. Damn. Another drifter had gone missing. That was three in recent months.

The director had reiterated what he'd heard at the two other places he'd visited: the homeless who took refuge at the shelters didn't stay long. The center had no control over where the men went and rarely was informed of their destinations when they left.

Worse, none of the men wanted to talk to him. They seemed wary, even suspicious of his intentions. He'd tried to assure them that he was concerned that someone might be preying on transients, but the only thing he'd accomplished was planting fear in the men's eyes.

Grief still made his chest ache. The damn DNA had confirmed that the man found at Briar Creek was his father. He and his family had mourned and buried him beside Chrissy.

But questions over where his father had been and what he'd been doing for eighteen years gnawed at him. What had happened to drive him to alcohol and the streets? Chrissy's disappearance had been horrible for all of them. But his mother hadn't walked out on her sons or buried herself in a bottle.

Had his father seen the news about Chrissy's body being found, and been driven over the edge by grief?

Dammit, there was nothing he could do to bring his father back. But in his search for answers, he'd stumbled on another mystery.

Even if his father's death wasn't connected to the other missing men, Dex was determined to make sure a predator wasn't taking advantage of these homeless men when they were already down. If nothing else, he'd find the truth in honor of his father.

A newscast broke into the country music on the radio as he headed toward the small apartment he rented over his PI office in Austin.

"This late breaking story just in. A man was shot and killed tonight at the Lend-A-Hand Shelter outside Austin. Assistant Director Melissa Gentry stated that a gunman broke into the facility just as the shelter was locking up for the night and held her at gunpoint. According to Ms. Gentry, one of the men at the shelter jumped the gunman to defend her, and the gun went off. The gunman died onsite, then the other man disappeared."

Dex's heart pounded. Melissa Gentry. Her name was a blast from the past. A blast of happy memories and a time when he'd allowed himself to enjoy the company of a good woman. Although when he'd found himself falling in love with her, he'd broken it off. Well, technically he hadn't exactly done that. He'd walked away like a coward.

Maybe he was like his old man...

Melissa was sweetness and kindness and way too damn good for the likes of him.

He'd known that she'd wanted to be a social worker, so hearing about her job at Lend-A-Hand fit.

The reporter segued to another story, and he veered to the side of the road, plugged the name Lend-A-Hand Shelter into his GPS, then pulled back into traffic and drove toward it.

The thought of a man holding a gun to Melissa made his blood turn cold. He wanted to see for himself that she wasn't harmed. And if she knew anything about the other missing transient men.

If someone was targeting them, tonight's shooting might be connected.

MELISSA WAS STILL trembling as the police roped off the shelter as a crime scene. Detective Frank Lamar from the Austin PD was in charge, delegating a female cop named Nikki Whalen to question the men at the shelter. Melissa could barely control her anger. These men had fallen on hard times, yet now they were being treated as suspects.

She'd given her statement. Told the truth. Assured the detective that none of the other men were involved in the shooting incident, but he'd quickly silenced her with a warning to let him do his job.

Questions about Jim Smith needled her. If he wasn't hiding from the law, why had he run?

A noise from the front door jarred her from her thoughts. Detective Lamar strode to the door to speak to the officer in charge of securing the scene.

"What's going on, Frank?"

Melissa paused to listen. A male voice. Angry? Concerned?

"I want to talk to Melissa."

Melissa tensed. The man…his voice sounded familiar. She hadn't heard it in ages, but…it sounded like Dexter Hawk.

"This is a crime scene. I can't let you come in," Detective Lamar said bluntly.

Melissa hurried to the door and nudged up beside the stocky cop. He was about her height, but his voice and demeanor were intimidating. By design, probably.

"Melissa?"

Her heart pounded. It *was* Dexter.

"Dex?"

The cop looked back and forth between them, his bushy eyebrows furrowed. "You two know each other?"

"Yes," they said at the same time.

"Well, hell." The cop scraped a hand down his chin.

Dex took a step forward. "Lamar, you know I've been investigating the missing transients since we found my father. This incident could be related."

"It's not," the detective said brusquely. "You saw Dr. Hudson's autopsy report. Your father's death was an accident, Dex. Accept it and move on."

"I wish we could have used Dr. Weinberger from Tumbleweed," Dex said. "I know him and trust him."

"Hudson is a good ME," Lamar said.

Melissa twisted her hands by her sides. Apparently Dex and this detective knew each other, too. PI to cop, or were they friends?

"Go home, Dex, and let me handle this," Detective Lamar said.

Melissa made a snap decision. She hadn't seen Dex in almost ten years. She wanted to tell him how sorry she was about his father. To ask him why he thought his father's death, the missing transients and the shooting might be connected.

"Excuse me, Detective," she said, giving the cop a gentle push as she reached for the door. "I need some air."

He started to protest, but she slanted him an icy look. Ever since he'd arrived at the shelter, he'd made her and the residents feel as if they'd done something wrong. "You can't make me stay inside," she said simply. "Not unless you're going to charge me with something."

The man's thick lips pressed into a tight line. A breath laced with the foul scent of cigarettes wheezed out, then he stepped aside. "Just don't leave the county without telling me," he said. "I might need to ask you some more questions."

She gave a quick nod, then pushed past him and out the door. The odor of blood and death inside the shelter was making her nauseous.

She quickly dragged in a breath, then looked up to see

Dex's handsome face. Worry darkened the depths of his eyes as he gently took her arm and led her down the steps to a cluster of trees. She was still shaking so badly that her legs nearly buckled.

"Ahh, Melissa." A second later, Dexter pulled her up against him, and she leaned her head into his chest.

DEXTER WRAPPED HIS arms around Melissa, his heart racing. Although he hadn't seen her in years, he'd never forgotten how wonderful she felt in his arms. He stroked her back, and inhaled the fragrance of rosewater, the fragrance that had taunted him in his sleep every day since they'd parted ways.

His nights had been filled with dreams of her to the point that he'd thought he'd never get over her.

She clung to his chest, her shaky breathing doing a number on his emotions.

Maybe he *hadn't* gotten over her. He sure as hell hadn't let any other woman in his life or heart since. No…he'd been too damn afraid of loving to put himself out there and chance getting hurt. Watching the heartbreak his mother had suffered when his father left had taught him a lesson.

He hadn't deserved Melissa anyway. Not after he'd told his sister to get lost that night. And then she had. *Forever.*

Still, he couldn't help himself. He rubbed Melissa's back again, savoring the feel of her in his arms for another minute. She was alive. She appeared unharmed, at least physically.

Time to do his job and talk. Not lose himself traipsing down memory lane.

"You okay, darlin'?"

She nodded against him and gave a deep sigh. "Thanks." She patted his chest, then eased from his embrace and lifted her chin. "Sorry."

"No apologies," he murmured, his chest squeezing with

emotions again. Damn, she had that effect on him. The thought of anyone hurting her made him want to pound something.

He swallowed hard, forcing his mind back on track and his eyes away from her beautiful face. The sight of that unruly dark auburn hair that had driven him mad when he'd run his fingers through it taunted him to touch it again.

He had to resist.

"I saw the story about your father. I'm sorry," she said softly.

Dexter ground his teeth, the pain back. "I want answers," he said honestly.

"He died in an automobile accident?"

He nodded. Thankfully, the paper hadn't revealed that he was inebriated at the time. "I found a card from another homeless shelter in his truck."

She tucked a strand of hair behind one ear, a frown marring her heart-shaped face. "He was living in a shelter?"

"I don't know," Dexter said. "But I've been visiting some of them to see if anyone knew him. I'm curious as to what he was doing all this time." And why he never came back.

Lamar's voice as he spoke to the officer guarding the scene echoed from the front stoop, jerking Dex back to the reason he'd come.

"You were involved in a shooting tonight?" Dex asked.

Her face paled, and she wrapped her arms around her waist as if to hold herself together. He wanted to draw her back into his arms.

But if he did, he might never let go.

Something he'd have to do. He'd walked away from her before because she deserved better.

She still did.

Chapter Three

Melissa rubbed her arms to erase the chill invading her. Dex's warm embrace reminded her of feelings that had never really gone away.

Dex exhaled. "What happened here?"

"We were locking up for the night when this man burst in the back door. He had a gun and grabbed me, said he wanted Jim Smith."

"Did he say why?" Dex asked.

She shook her head. "No, it happened really fast. He pushed me toward the common room, then Jim appeared. Jim offered to trade himself for me, then the gunman told Jim to tie me up. He tossed him a rope. Smith grabbed the rope, then charged the man with the gun."

Detective Lamar stepped outside, his voice carrying in the slight breeze that stirred. "I want an APB out on this man. Name is Jim Smith. Approach with caution. He's already killed one man tonight, and is armed and dangerous."

Melissa tensed at the detective's tone. She crossed the space to him as he hung up. "Detective Lamar," she said. "Jim isn't dangerous, at least not in the way you're suggesting. He acted in self-defense. He wasn't armed when he came here."

Dexter had followed her over to the cop, his arms crossed as he listened.

"How do you know Smith didn't have a gun?" the detective asked. "Did you search his belongings?"

"Well, no," Melissa admitted. "But I didn't see any signs of a weapon. In fact, he was almost gentle at times. He tried to talk the gunman down, then he wrestled with the man and the gun went off." Her voice cracked as the memory returned. "He was a hero, not the enemy. He saved my life." And she wanted to thank him for it, not see him hunted down like an animal.

"You certainly are defensive of him." The detective narrowed his eyes. "Exactly how well did you know Mr. Smith?"

Anger shot through Melissa at the insinuations in the cop's voice. "He was a welcome guest here just like all of the other men who seek housing with us at Lend-A-Hand."

"What was his story?" Detective Lamar asked. "Did he have a family?"

Melissa bit the corner of her lip, a habit she had when thinking. "I don't know. He'd only been here a couple of days and didn't share much about himself."

"What *did* he share?" the detective asked.

Melissa searched her memory banks. "Nothing really. He was quiet, and kept to himself. But he was always polite at mealtimes and respectful of the other men and our volunteers."

"So you're defending a man you know virtually nothing about," Detective Lamar said flatly. "His name sounds fake. He could be a criminal hiding out."

She had considered that. "I don't think that's the case."

Detective Lamar raised a brow. "What *do* you think?"

Dex cleared his throat. "Lamar, why don't you lay off? Melissa told you all she knows. It's her job to help the men who come here, not interrogate them."

Officer Whalen, who'd been questioning the men inside, stepped to the door. "I'm finished here."

The detective shrugged. "You get anything useful?"

Officer Whalen shook her head. "No one seemed to know anything about Smith. General consensus was that he didn't want to talk. One guy thought Smith was hiding something. Another said Smith hinted that he didn't have family. But Smith didn't elaborate so we don't know if he was married, divorced, had kids, or if he did, what happened to them."

"What about a job?" Detective Lamar asked.

The officer shook her head. "Didn't mention one."

The detective turned back to Melissa. "Did he tell you what kind of work he did?"

He'd thrown that rope lasso-style, like a pro. Maybe ranching? Then again, most men in Texas knew how to rope and ride. "I'm afraid not." She lifted her chin. "Instead of investigating Smith, why aren't you looking into the dead man on the floor in the shelter? He's the one who broke in here and put a gun to my head."

DEX COULDN'T DRAG his eyes from Melissa and that tangled mass of hair. She had a heart of gold. But was she naive? Was Smith a criminal, using the shelter to hide from the law? Or...perhaps he was in trouble and the gunman was a bad guy chasing him?

Various scenarios bombarded him. Smith might have owed the man or someone else money. The shooter could have had a personal vendetta against Smith for some transgression against him.

"Listen to me, Ms. Gentry," Lamar said. "We have to close down the shelter until we're finished processing it. The men staying here will have to leave, at least temporarily."

Melissa's eyes flickered with unease. "How long will we have to be closed?"

"I can't say for sure. I'll let you know when we release

the space and you can use it again. Meanwhile, I'll have Officer Whalen escort the men outside."

Lamar went to speak to Whalen, and Dex gave Melissa an understanding look. Knowing Melissa, she'd worry about the men they'd have to turn away.

"If you find a place for the men to stay tonight, I'll provide transportation," he offered.

Melissa's look of gratitude suggested he'd read her correctly. She was more concerned about Smith and the men at the shelter than she was about herself. "Thanks, Dex. I will do that. I don't like the idea of putting anyone out when it's so hot."

Melissa removed her phone from the pocket of her jeans and stepped aside to make a phone call.

Lamar walked back to him, his expression grim.

"Don't you think you were a little hard on her?" Dex asked, annoyed at his friend.

"I'm just doing my job." Lamar grunted. "How do you know her?"

Dex didn't intend to share details of their relationship. "We met in college."

"I didn't think you went to college," Lamar said.

Dex gritted his teeth. He had gone but not finished. Brayden was definitely the most educated of the Hawk men. Still, he loved his work. "I did, but just one semester. College wasn't for me. I did take business classes at a local school though before I hung my shingle."

Lamar worked his mouth from side to side. "I take it you and Ms. Gentry were…involved?"

Dex shrugged. "It was a long time ago. But I can vouch for her. Melissa's the most honest, caring person I've ever met."

"Caring enough that she'd cover for Smith?"

"You heard her story," Dex said. "You can believe her."

He gestured toward the inside of the shelter. "Dr. Hudson in there?"

Lamar nodded. "They should be bringing the man's body outside to transport to the morgue any minute."

Dex shoved his hand in his pockets. "What do you know about the gunman?"

"Not much, yet. Name on his ID is Clark McTruitt." Lamar shifted, putting his body between Dex and Melissa as if he didn't want her to overhear what he had to say. "He had a PI license on him, Dex."

A tense minute passed. "He was a PI? Where?" He would recognize his name if he worked out of Austin.

"Amarillo." The door opened and two medics carried a stretcher with McTruitt's body encased in a body bag on it. "He obviously had reason to come after Smith," Lamar said. "Finding out more about Smith is key."

Dex agreed with him on that. "I'll go to McTruitt's office and see what I can dig up."

Lamar's deep frown of disapproval coincided with a firm shake of his head. "Listen, Dex, this is a homicide investigation. I have to play it by the book." He slanted him a warning look. "If I need you, I'll let you know. Otherwise, go home and be with your family, and let me do my job."

Dex clenched his jaw as Melissa strode toward the homeless men being escorted from the shelter. She could have died tonight.

That thought sent fear crawling through him. He didn't give a damn what Lamar said.

There was no way he could walk away without answers.

MELISSA DIDN'T KNOW why the detective rubbed her the wrong way, but he did. She had been defensive of Jim Smith, but rightfully so. Although she had wondered about his past and what he was hiding from, he'd saved her life and she owed him.

She phoned her friend at Another Chance Shelter about forty miles away and explained the situation. The volunteer had enough beds open for the men to stay with them for a few nights if needed.

Several of the men went their own way, although three agreed to move to another facility.

She had a soft spot for Gunther and was glad he accepted the offer. He'd had a hard life. Had been injured in the Gulf War. With a bad leg and PTSD, he'd lost his job when he'd become addicted to pain meds. And he had no family.

An awkward silence filled the car as Dex drove them to the shelter. When they arrived, he parked, climbed out and met her at the passenger side. The men congregated a few feet away, the night taking its toll in the way they spoke in hushed tones about what had happened with the gunman.

"Wait here while I introduce them to the volunteers," Melissa told Dex.

Dex hesitated, shifting on the balls of his feet. "Actually, I wanted to go with you, ask if anyone in there knew my father."

He removed a photo from his wallet. She'd expected to see the picture he'd shown her when they'd met in college, but this photo was of an older man, the one he must have buried.

"Did you ever meet him?" Dex asked.

The pain in his voice ripped at her heartstrings and reminded her that Dex had been lost when they'd first met. She'd wanted to save him, but later realized she couldn't save everyone. She'd learned that with her own father when he'd died with one hand around the bottle, the other holding a pistol.

He hadn't cared enough about her to stick around. That had hurt the most.

Water under the bridge.

She had to move on, do what she could to help others.

She studied the photo, mentally tapping into the decade of homeless men she'd met on the streets or in various shelters, but she didn't recognize the one in the picture. "I'm sorry, Dex, but I don't recall seeing him anywhere." She squeezed his hand, a warmth stirring inside her that triggered emotions she'd once felt for this strong, hurting man.

Dexter clenched his jaw. "All right. But I'd like to ask inside."

She nodded in understanding.

Sadly, she'd heard similar stories from other families before. One family member left, leaving the others full of questions, pain and guilt. God knows she'd had her share of that over her own situation.

It was a complicated problem and could only be dealt with one family at a time.

Heartbreak City, if she let herself get too involved. The reason she needed to keep her distance from Dex. She had her own demons to slay.

And she'd barely survived the first time he'd left her.

She didn't want to revisit that kind of pain again.

DEX JAMMED HIS hands in his pockets. A faint breeze stirred, bringing the scent of cigarette smoke and the hushed voices of the homeless men.

Melissa rolled her shoulders, fatigue showing on her face. "Let's get the men settled."

She texted her friend that she'd arrived, and he followed her to the door. A few minutes later, the men accepted cots in the back of the shelter, and she and Dex stood talking to Edgar, the volunteer.

"I heard what happened," Edgar said with a worried look. "I'm so sorry, Melissa. Are you all right?"

"Yes," Melissa said. "But it's a reminder of how quickly someone can break in."

Dex showed Edgar the recent photograph of his father and another shot of him around the time he'd disappeared.

"I'm sorry, sir," Edgar said. "But he hasn't been here."

"You're sure?" Dex asked.

"Edgar has a near photographic memory," Melissa said.

Dexter eyed the man. He was late forties, wore big chunky brown glasses, had a wide nose and a missing front tooth. The way he picked at his fingernails indicated nerves, maybe a habit from living a hard life himself. Everyone had a story.

He just wanted to know what his father's was.

Melissa lapsed into silence as he drove her back to Lend-A-Hand. When they reached the facility, she snagged her keys from her purse. "Thanks for driving us to Another Chance."

"No problem." He spotted a beat-up minivan in the parking lot and guessed it was hers. Melissa had never valued material things. "I'll follow you home," he offered.

"That's not necessary." Her voice took on a stiff ring.

He knew she was shaken, but he wasn't ready to let her out of his sight. "Melissa, you could have been hurt tonight." Killed, but he couldn't allow himself to voice that awful thought aloud. "I'll see that you get home safely, so don't argue."

Melissa rubbed a hand over her eyes. She was obviously so exhausted she simply nodded and slipped from his SUV. Just as he thought, the beat-up minivan belonged to her.

She jammed her keys in the ignition, the engine taking three tries to sputter to life.

Anger that she sacrificed so much for others mingled with worry that she might have died doing just that.

She deserved so much better. To have diamonds and pearls. At least a car that didn't look as if it had been rolled twice.

He glanced back at the shelter before he pulled from the

parking lot. Melissa was no doubt worried about the men she'd had to move tonight. But worry for her raged through him. He didn't like the fact that Melissa put herself in danger by trying to help them. Tonight's incident proved the facility wasn't secure.

The thought of losing her bothered him more than he wanted to admit as he followed her through the streets of Austin. His gut tightened when she veered into an area consisting of transitional homes. A couple had been remodeled, but most looked as if they were teardowns. The street was not in the best part of town, either, and was known for shady activities, including drug rings and gangs.

Her house was a tiny bungalow with a sagging little porch and paint-chipped shutters, and sat next to a rotting shanty where two guys in hoodies hovered by the side porch, heads bent in hushed conversation as if they might be in the middle of a drug deal.

He gritted his teeth as he parked and walked up the graveled path to the front porch. She paused, her key in hand. A handcrafted wreath said Welcome Home, which for some reason twisted his gut even more.

Melissa had never had a real home, while he'd grown up on the ranch with family and brothers and open land.

She offered him a small smile. "Thanks for following me, Dex."

"I'll go in and check the house," he said, itching to make sure that at least her windows and doors were secure. From his vantage point now, it looked as if a stiff wind would blow the house down.

She shook her head. "That's not necessary, but I appreciate it." She ran a shaky hand through her hair. "I'm exhausted. I'm going to bed."

She opened the door and ducked inside without another word and without looking back. An image of her crawling into bed in that lonely old house taunted him.

He wanted to join her. Hold her. Make sure she was all right tonight.

But that would be risky for him.

Still, he couldn't shake the feeling that she was in danger as he walked back to his SUV.

Chapter Four

Melissa closed the door, shutting Dex outside and hoping he left immediately. She had come close to allowing him to come in. But if she had, she might have asked him to stay all night.

And that would be a mistake.

It had taken her months to get over him when he'd walked out of her life in college. She'd dreamed about him for even longer. Worse, she'd compared every date she'd ever had to Dex and no one had come close to measuring up.

Eventually she'd just stopped dating. Had accepted the fact that marriage wasn't for her, that her family was the people she served. They needed her.

Worse tonight…the shelter she'd given so much of her heart and time to was a crime scene.

She dropped her keys and purse on the side table, flipped on the light and scanned the living room. The faded blue couch and rocking chair that had come with the rental house were simple, the walls decorated with a few flea market finds from the owner. Nothing that held any sentimental value to her. And certainly nothing fancy. But she didn't need fancy things.

Just a safe haven to lay her head at night.

Not having personal items made it easier to pack up and move on when she felt the urge.

And she was starting to feel that urge. She'd already been at Lend-A-Hand nearly a year, longer than most places.

Nerves clawed at her stomach. She could have died tonight. And she had watched a man lose his life. She'd seen bad things before, but never death so close-up.

With the temperature soaring outside, she opted for a glass of wine over her cup of nightly hot tea and carried it to the bathroom. She filled the tub with bubble bath, undressed and climbed inside to soak away the stench of blood and death that permeated her skin.

Dex's handsome face flashed behind her eyes. Once they'd shared a bath, had loved each other the way young lovers did.

She wasn't young and innocent anymore, though.

And she couldn't entertain fantasies of Dex again. For all she knew, Dex might be involved with someone else.

She had to focus on work, which made her wonder about Jim Smith. Why had that PI been willing to hold her at gunpoint to get to Jim?

THE NEXT MORNING Dex met his family at the main house for a big country breakfast his mother had prepared. Honey and Harrison and their baby, little Steven, were already there, the baby cooing from the high chair where he banged a spoon on the tray.

Lucas and Charlotte arrived as he did, Lucas steadying a very pregnant Charlotte as they joined the family in the large dining room off the kitchen. Brayden and Mila and Mila's little girl, Izzy, were talking to the foster girls their mother had taken in after they were rescued from the human trafficking ring that Lucas had broken up.

As chatter, laughter and hugs floated between the family members and the ones who'd joined the family, a warmth spread through Dexter. For years after Chrissy disappeared, the family had suffered from guilt and the uncertainty of what had happened to her. Learning she was dead had been a blow, just as learning about their father had been. But at least they had closure.

Love for his family overcame Dex as he thought about Melissa. When they'd dated, she'd confided in him her feelings about losing her mother, about her father moving them from place to place. They'd lived in shelters all her life.

No wonder she was at home there.

It still wasn't fair. She deserved to have more.

"Let's eat," his mother called over the noise.

The next few minutes were hectic as everyone grabbed a plate and served themselves from the buffet. Platters of sausage and bacon, eggs, grits, homemade biscuits and roasted potatoes made Dex's mouth water. One by one, they found seats at the giant farmhouse table the brothers had built to house their growing needs, then his mother tapped her spoon on her coffee mug to indicate it was time for a prayer. The family joined hands and bowed their heads, the voices quieting as their mother gave thanks for all they had.

As the prayer ended, the conversation began again.

The baby squealed as his mother drizzled a biscuit with honey, then tore it into small bites and put it on the tray. Izzy sidled next to the baby and began to talk to him, and the foster girls joined at the opposite end, jabbering about the pool his mother had decided to build so they could cool off in the hot summer.

Charlotte was excited about putting the finishing touches on the nursery for their baby girl who was due any minute. Brayden stood and gestured that he needed everyone's attention.

He motioned for Izzy to join him and Mila, then grinned at Izzy. "You want to tell them, sweetie?"

Izzy bobbed her little head up and down. "I'm gonna be a big sister!"

The family cheered and stood, hugging and congratulating the couple. Dex slapped Brayden on the back. He still couldn't believe his little brother was married and had a stepdaughter. And now he was going to add another child to his new family.

Pulling away, Brayden asked with a grin, "When are you going to settle down, man?"

His mother looked at him, and Dex shrugged. "Not going to let anyone tie me down."

Lucas pounded him on the back. "Because you haven't found the right woman."

Dex chewed the inside of his cheek as an image of Melissa taunted him. She was beautiful and sweet and the most selfless person he'd ever known. She'd invaded his dreams and fantasies since college. She would love his family and would fit right in.

But…losing his sister and father had nearly destroyed him. If he gave his heart to Melissa, she might crush it, too.

So he simply laughed off his brothers' teasing. As they finished breakfast, he asked his brothers to join him in the study. Their mother didn't allow work talk at the table.

Harrison eyed him with a frown. "What's going on, Dex?"

Dex crossed his arms. "Did you hear about the shooting at the Lend-A-Hand Shelter last night?"

"Yeah," Harrison said. "Someone broke in and one of the homeless men shot him."

Lucas pulled a hand down his chin. "Police are looking for the shooter. They suspect he was using an alias, that he was on the run from the law."

Brayden raised an inquisitive brow. "Why are you asking, Dex?"

"I know the woman who runs the shelter," Dex admitted. "Went to college with her years ago."

"You dated her?" Brayden asked.

Dex cursed himself. Why had he shared that he knew her? "Yeah, but that's not the point. She claims Smith wasn't dangerous, that the shooter broke in and put a gun to her head."

Harrison scowled. "What else do you know about Smith?"

"Nothing really," Dex said. "But the shooter was a PI, name was Clark McTruitt."

"Maybe McTruitt knew why Smith was on the run and that he was dangerous."

"But why hold a gun to Melissa?" Dex asked.

"Melissa?" Brayden said with a tease to his voice.

"That's her name," Dex said, irritated. "Anyway, after we found Dad, I asked around at a few shelters to see if anyone had seen him."

"Dex," Lucas said with a warning note to his voice. "Dad abandoned us. No need to ask anything else."

Harrison's jaw tightened. "He's right. You have to let it go."

Brayden twisted his mouth to the side. "Did you find out anything?"

Dex shook his head. "Not yet. But in visiting the shelters, I discovered that three other transients have gone missing the past six months. That started me thinking—"

"That maybe Dad's death wasn't an accident," Brayden said.

Lucas made a sound of disgust. "He was drunk. Loaded, according to the medical examiner's report."

"Transients go missing all the time," Harrison added. "That's nothing suspicious, Dex. It's their nature. They roam from place to place. These three may have just moved on to another shelter."

"Not to any that I've found," Dex said. "And now a PI breaks into this one and tries to kill another homeless man. Don't you think that warrants an investigation?"

Harrison sighed. "Do you have any evidence suggesting all this is related?"

"Or is this just your imagination looking for problems that aren't there?" Lucas asked.

Anger seized Dex. Granted, he'd been the hothead of the bunch, and had seen his own share of trouble. But sometimes his instincts had been right.

Like it or not, he had to follow his gut.

And that gut told him something was wrong.

MELISSA RUBBED HER hand over her bleary eyes as she sipped her morning coffee. Nightmares of the break-in and shooting had plagued her all night. The feel of the gun against her head…the blood spattering… Smith's shocked face as he stared at her afterward, pain and regret and worry in his expression.

When she'd finally drifted back to sleep, she'd woken up an hour later because she'd thought she'd heard a sound outside. She'd imagined someone breaking into her house. This time she'd been shot and was dying.

A wariness spread over her like a gloomy fog. She was going to turn thirty this year. She was too young to die, especially alone.

Maybe she did want more than work and saving others. Maybe she wanted to carve out a little bit of a life for herself. She'd just been afraid of getting hurt again the way she had with Dex.

She finished her coffee and poured another cup, then phoned April. April offered to contact the volunteers about the center being closed.

"I'll call the detective and see if he'll release the shelter for us to go in and clean up today," Melissa promised. "Then I'll let you know."

She ended the call, then punched the detective's number. The call went straight to voice mail, so she left a message. A knock sounded on her front door just as she finished.

Maybe the detective had come to update her? Or interrogate her again? She hoped it wasn't bad news about Jim Smith, that some overeager cop hadn't gunned him down.

Another knock sounded, and she headed toward the front door to answer it. She checked the peephole, always wary that a stranger might come knocking thinking she was the drug dealer they were searching for. There were at least two on the street that she was aware of.

Her breath caught. Not the detective or a stranger. Dex.

For a moment, she drank in the sight of his handsome face. He wore his cowboy hat, jeans and boots, and the brooding expression that made him look even more mysterious and sexy.

She took a deep breath and opened the door, her heart stuttering as their gazes locked.

"You didn't sleep, did you?" he asked in a gruff voice.

Awareness of his sexuality jolted her nerves. He'd always been intuitive and been able to read her. Maybe that was the reason he'd walked away. He'd sensed she was getting too close, starting to imagine a lifetime with him.

"Not much," she admitted as she motioned for him to come in.

"I'm sorry." He stopped in front of her, his breath huffing out. His six-two frame towered over her. He had big broad shoulders and muscles that had probably made every woman's mouth water when they met him.

She didn't want to think about how many there'd been.

"It's not your fault," she said softly. "But I couldn't stop thinking about Jim and if he was okay. That detective talked like they'd shoot first, then ask questions later."

"You really thought he was a good guy?"

Melissa bit her lip. "Yes. Sure he had secrets. But not everyone who does has a criminal past. Some have just suffered life, and are trying to manage the best they can."

"Like my father," he said, a trace of bitterness to his voice.

Sympathy filled her. "I don't know, Dex. I'm really sorry you didn't have a chance to talk to him and sort things out."

"Me, too." He closed his eyes for a moment, and she realized he was still wrestling with pain and guilt.

She wanted to comfort him. But she clenched her hands by her sides instead. She'd run him off once by becoming too emotional.

She wouldn't do it again.

DEXTER PROMISED HIMSELF he wouldn't make this visit about him and his father, but Melissa had a way of getting to the heart of the matter.

And into his heart.

Focus, man.

"I should have stayed last night," he said.

Melissa shook her head. "Don't be silly, Dex. I'm fine. Now why did you come? Did you hear something from the detective?"

Dexter shook his head. "Afraid not. I'm on my way to McTruitt's office to see if someone there can explain why he was hunting Smith."

"You're investigating this for Detective Lamar?"

"No, but I like mysteries." Or rather, he couldn't let them go until they were solved. He'd always been that way. Always would.

He removed a card from his pocket and offered it to her. "I wanted you to have my number in case you needed something."

Melissa took the card, their hands brushing. She immediately jerked back as if she felt the same tingle he had.

Then she lifted her chin and reached for her purse. "I'm going with you."

"You don't need to do that."

She pressed her hand to his arm. "Yes, I do. I want answers, too, Dex. I can't get into the shelter right now anyway, and I'm going crazy sitting around."

He conceded with a brief nod. No use arguing with Melissa. She might be tenderhearted, but she was also stubborn as hell.

Loud, arguing angry voices from a neighbor drifted their way as they walked to his SUV. Dammit, he didn't like this street or Melissa living here alone.

They rode in silence to McTruitt's office, a faded brick structure in a strip center outside of Austin. Except for a tattoo shop and fertilizer store, the other spaces were deserted, the exteriors run-down.

He parked in front of the building, scanning the property. A black sedan sat in the back parking lot. No one inside. It was too early for the tattoo parlor and the fertilizer store to be open.

A light glowed through the window, indicating that someone was inside. Maybe a secretary? Or McTruitt could have a partner? Damn. He should have done some research on him the night before.

But thoughts of wanting Melissa had distracted him.

He reached for the door to get out. "Wait in the car."

"No, maybe I can help." The silence thickened as they walked up to the building. The door was closed, but Dex saw a flashlight beam moving in the back.

Not a secretary. A man was tossing the place.

He pushed his hand in front of Melissa and murmured

for her to go back to the car. But before he could, a bullet shattered the front window and sailed past his head.

Melissa screamed and ducked. He pulled his gun and shouted for her to get down.

Chapter Five

Melissa ducked to the side of the window, glass spraying as it shattered.

"Stay down!" Dex shouted.

She pressed herself against the front wall, her chest heaving as she tried to catch her breath. Dex pulled a gun from his back pocket and fired through the hole in the window.

Inside, footsteps pounded and noises echoed as if someone was turning over furniture. Dex motioned for her to stay where she was, and he inched closer to the window and looked inside. Banging, then a man's voice, and another bullet whizzed by Dex's head.

Melissa screamed as he ducked to avoid being hit. He covered her head with his arms to shield her as another bullet flew past and more glass rained down on the front stoop.

She clung to Dex, the two of them hovering low until a few seconds later, the sound of an engine rent the air. The black sedan in the back parking lot shot around the side of the building, roared past, then flew onto the street.

Dex jumped up and gave chase, firing at the car's tires, but the vehicle screeched forward and disappeared.

Melissa stood on shaky legs as Dex ran back to her. "Are you all right?" he asked breathlessly.

She nodded, the realization that she'd been involved in

two shootings in two days sending shock waves through her. "Are you?"

"Yeah." He removed his Stetson, scrubbed a hand through his shaggy hair, then set the hat back on his head with a grunt. "I couldn't get the license plate."

"What's going on?" Melissa asked, trying to piece together what had happened.

"I don't know, but I'm damn well going to find out." He wiggled the doorknob on the front door, and the door squeaked open.

As soon as they entered, Melissa could see that the office had been ransacked. The space consisted of a small entryway with a desk and a door leading to the back. Through the doors, they found the main office, a large space with an oversize metal desk, filing cabinet and rolling desk chair. The filing cabinet drawers stood open, papers were scattered all over the desk and floor as if files had just been dumped, and the space on the desk where a computer should have been was empty.

"Either he had his laptop with him or someone took it," Dex mumbled.

Melissa scanned the disheveled room. "What do you think they were looking for?"

Dex shrugged. "Who knows? Something to do with one of his investigations."

"You think it was the person who hired him to find Jim Smith?"

"That's possible. With McTruitt dead at Smith's hands, whoever that was might not want his name to come out."

"Or his motive," Melissa said. "Do you think McTruitt was sent to kill Jim?"

Dex's dark gaze met hers. "Maybe. If he had a file on Smith here, that would help." Dex walked over to the desk, pulled on a pair of gloves and started rummaging through the scattered papers.

Melissa shifted, but stooped down on the floor to help search. He tossed her a pair of latex gloves, and she yanked them on. The fact that the person shooting at them might have already found that information and taken it was a real possibility.

But maybe they'd interrupted the intruder before he'd found it, and she and Dex would turn up something helpful.

DEX GRITTED HIS TEETH. He should call Lamar, but first he wanted to look around. He scoured through the papers on the desk, searching for any signs of suspicious activity, specifically anything with Jim Smith's name on it or notes referencing the reason McTruitt was looking for Smith—and why he'd held Melissa at gunpoint to get to him.

According to Melissa, Smith hadn't pulled a gun on McTruitt. It was the other way around, which meant that McTruitt either thought Smith was dangerous, or whoever had hired McTruitt to find Smith wanted him badly enough to tell him to use force.

Or…what if he'd been hired to kill Smith?

Ordering a hit would mean someone had motive.

There were pages of notes on old jobs, mostly cheating spouses, a couple of runaway teens, a case of a stolen dog, and other miscellaneous cases, nothing big or criminal.

"Do you see anything?" Melissa asked.

"Nothing on Smith. You?"

She shook her head and stood, then walked over to the wall and studied a photograph of McTruitt with a group of fishing buddies. Dex glanced at it, then strode to the filing cabinet and shuffled through the files.

The man may have had a computer, but he kept files alphabetized old-school style, with scribbled handwritten notes inside. Again, nothing on Smith.

On a whim, he checked the H section, hoping that the man had information on his father, but no file for Hawk.

He started to close the file cabinet drawer, but a business card was stuck in the edge, so he yanked it out.

It was a card for a cattle auction site run by a rancher named Vance Baxter. Dex frowned. He'd heard of Baxter. The man's business was booming. He worked with an expert breeder to raise prize studs.

He wondered why McTruitt had the card in his file, but didn't see how it related to Smith or his own father. Still, he jammed it in his pocket.

Time to call Lamar and tell him about the shooting.

"We'd better step outside." Dex took Melissa's arm. "I have to report this to the police. I don't want him to know we were snooping around in here."

Melissa nodded. "You and Detective Lamar are friends?"

Dex shrugged. "He took me under his wing a few years ago. Since then, he's thrown a few cases my way when he hit a dead end and manpower on the force was spread thin."

Melissa frowned.

"You don't like him, do you?" Dex asked.

Melissa shrugged. "I guess I'm not as trusting of cops as some."

He narrowed his eyes. "Bad experience from the shelter?"

"And growing up." A haunted look passed through her eyes, but she clammed up. Dex wanted to ask more, but Lamar answered the call.

"I came out to McTruitt's office," Dex said. "Someone was here and ransacked the place, and they shot at me and Melissa."

Lamar exploded with a string of expletives. "I'll be right there. And for God's sake, don't touch anything, Dex."

Dex bit back a smile. "Of course not, Lamar. We're waiting outside."

Melissa was watching him with avid curiosity when he hung up. "You don't trust him?"

"I didn't say that," Dex said. "But I'm not going to be shut out of this case. If the attack on Smith has anything to do with the other missing transients, I intend to find out."

A FEW MINUTES LATER, Melissa stood with Dex on the steps to the building as the detective stalked toward them. Anger slashed his craggy features as his gaze traveled from Dex to her.

She forced herself to remain expressionless. She'd learned not to show fear or to react to the men who came to the shelter or she couldn't be effective, and she refused to let this man intimidate her.

"What the hell are you doing here?" Detective Lamar growled.

Dex planted his feet apart in a wide stance, his arms crossed. He looked intimidating himself. "You know why. I want answers about my father—"

"Your father drank himself into a car accident," the detective said with a note of sympathy to his voice. "Why would you think his death is connected to this Smith man or McTruitt?"

A muscle ticked in Dex's jaw. "I don't know. Maybe it's not. But it seems odd to me that I found a card for a shelter in Dad's truck, then other transients have gone missing, and now this shooting at another shelter." Dex narrowed his eyes. "Something is going on, Lamar. You have to admit that."

The detective rubbed a hand down his chin and sighed. "What I think, Dex, is that you still haven't gotten over the fact that your father left, and that you're trying to make something where there isn't anything."

Dex shrugged. "Maybe so. But you know I'm like a dog with a bone. I don't quit until I get answers."

"Then trust me to do my job. If I find out anything related to your father or that these incidents are connected, I'll bring you in."

Dex shifted, his jaw tightening. Detective Lamar angled his head toward Melissa. "And you. What are you doing here?"

Melissa forced her voice to remain steady. "I want to know why this PI wanted Jim bad enough to put a gun to my head."

"She has a point," Dex interjected.

The detective heaved a breath. "I'm looking into that, but what I don't need is two civilians interfering." He gestured to Dex. "Your friend was almost shot last night, and now you come here and are shot at again. This is dangerous, Dex. Take Ms. Gentry home and keep her out of this so she'll be safe."

Melissa curled her fingers into her palms and dug her nails into them, a trick she'd learned to control her reaction in confrontational situations. "I asked to come with him," she said firmly. "Now why don't you try to find out who shot at us?"

The detective's brows shot up. "I plan to do that, Ms. Gentry. But it would make my job easier if I'm not distracted by worrying about the two of you."

Melissa started to retaliate with a retort, but Dex took her arm. "He's right, Melissa. Why don't you wait in the car?"

Melissa bit her tongue. She didn't like taking orders from either man.

She'd been taking care of herself all her life. She couldn't stop now.

DEX COULD HANDLE a reprimand, but not in front of someone else, especially a woman he cared about.

Cared about?

Why had he thought that? He'd known Melissa a long time ago, but there was nothing between them now. Except his protective instincts kicked in full force when she was around. And he sure as hell didn't want to be shut out of this investigation.

He and Melissa both wanted answers. Answers that he would find.

He brushed her back with his hand. "Melissa, please…?"

For a brief second she looked as if she was going to argue, but then she glanced back at Lamar, and nodded. He clenched his jaw as he watched her climb into his SUV.

Lamar was texting on his phone when Dex turned back to him.

"Tell me exactly what happened?" Lamar asked.

"Like I said on the phone, someone was inside when we arrived." He gestured toward the parking lot. "I spotted a black sedan in the back."

"Any other vehicles around?"

Dex shook his head. "No. The place was dark inside, except for a flashlight beam. That's how I knew someone was in there."

Lamar studied him. "Then what?"

"I looked in the window to see who it was, but then someone started shooting." He walked over to the window and pointed out the broken glass. "Melissa and I ducked to avoid being hit, then I saw movement inside."

"Was there one person or two?" Lamar asked.

Dex chewed the inside of his cheek. "One. At least I didn't see anyone else."

"How about the car? Anyone inside it when you got here?"

Dex shook his head again. "No. It was empty."

Lamar scribbled something in his pocket notepad. "Did you see what the shooter looked like?"

"Afraid not. Like I said, it was dark inside. And he ran out the back."

"License plate on the car?"

"No." Dex felt like a failure as an investigator. Dammit, he wished he could offer more concrete information. But he'd been too busy dodging bullets and worrying about protecting Melissa to chase the bastard.

Lamar examined the window and peered through the broken glass. He dug a bullet casing from the window edge. "You said he shot at you. Did you fire back?"

Dex didn't want to answer, but he had to. Lamar's people would find two different types of bullets when they searched inside.

"Dex?"

"Yeah." He removed his weapon from the back of his jeans and held it out to Lamar. "I fired twice. You can check."

Lamar's gaze met his. "Did you hit him?"

"I don't think so. I was just trying to warn him off."

Lamar scoffed. "You know I could haul you in."

"But you aren't going to," Dex said. "Because technically I fired in self-defense. And you, my friend, don't want to waste time when it'll go nowhere."

Besides, he hadn't really crossed the line.

He would, though, if necessary, to find out the truth about Smith and what was going on with these shelters.

MELISSA WATCHED THE interchange between Dex and Detective Lamar, her curiosity piqued as to how the two of them had met and become friends.

Her phone buzzed, and she checked the number, expecting it to be her coworker April. Instead the name of the director at another shelter appeared. Candace Fuller from Retreat. She'd once worked closely with Candace and they still had coffee on occasion.

She quickly connected the call.

"Melissa, I heard about the shooting. Are you all right?"

"I'm fine," Melissa said, then explained what had happened. "The police are looking for Smith, but I don't think he's dangerous. He saved my life."

"I'm just glad you're okay." Candace paused. "There's another reason I called."

Melissa tapped her fingers on her leg. She didn't like the worry in her friend's voice. "What's wrong?"

"A man named Bill Small at Retreat thinks something has happened to one of his friends. He claims he disappeared."

"Did you report it to the police?" Melissa asked.

Candace sighed. "Yes, but they don't seem concerned."

Sounded typical. A crime scene van pulled into the parking lot, and she saw Dex heading toward her.

"Why does Bill think something happened to his friend?" Melissa asked.

"He saw the story about some other missing homeless men, and said his friend expressed concern over them, too. He disappeared the next day."

Melissa's breath stalled in her chest. "Is Bill still at Retreat?"

"Yes."

"I'm with a private detective right now, Candace. We'll stop by and talk to Bill."

Chapter Six

Thirty minutes later, Dex parked at Retreat, his curiosity aroused by what Melissa had told him. Lamar's last words echoed in his head.

"Let me do the police work. And leave Melissa out of it or you're going to get her killed."

His friend had always cautioned him about overstepping, but today his warning had sounded different. Almost like a threat. As if he didn't stay out of it, Lamar would see that his PI license might be revoked? That he'd lock him up for interfering?

He didn't give a damn. No one stopped Dexter Hawk when he was on a mission.

"Tell me about this shelter," Dex said as they walked up to the entryway.

"Because of its location, it's one of the busiest," Melissa said. "I worked with Candace for a short while until a position opened up at Lend-A-Hand."

'Why did you make the move?"

Melissa shrugged. "I just saw a need," she said quietly, but didn't elaborate, making him wonder if it was one of the shelters she'd lived in as a child. Her father had dragged her around Texas, dumping them wherever and whenever he pleased.

"They house close to a hundred people here at any time,"

she said. "We work with the court system and advocates for domestic violence and abuse to find places when needed for women and children, but there are a lot of men in need, too. This one stays pretty full most of the time." She hesitated at the door and pressed the intercom buzzer for entry.

Dex swallowed hard as he scanned the property. It was set off from the street in a wooded section that shielded the cement block building from passersby on the road and was surrounded by a tall metal fence. For the residents' protection or for the people who lived nearby in the housing projects that had been built a half mile from the shelter? Probably both.

The volunteer buzzed them in, and Melissa led the way. A young blonde about Melissa's age greeted them and hugged Melissa, murmuring concern about the shooting the day before.

"Candace, this is Dexter Hawk," Melissa said as the women pulled apart. "He's a private investigator and a friend."

Candace gave him an assessing look. "Hawk, that name sounds familiar."

Dex offered her a smile. "My family owns a ranch in Tumbleweed. You may have read about my brother Lucas, who shut down a human trafficking ring recently."

"That's right," Candace said. "And your other brother is a lawyer."

"There are four of us," Dex said. "My oldest brother, Harrison, is sheriff of Tumbleweed."

Melissa cleared her throat. "Dex is looking into the man who saved my life yesterday. He's also been investigating the disappearance of a couple of other homeless men who've gone missing."

"You suspect foul play?" Candace asked.

Dex shrugged. "It's too early to tell. But if someone is preying on these men, I want to find out who and why."

"Can we talk to Bill now?" Melissa asked.

"Of course." Candace led the way through a small entry into a large dining area where men sat finishing breakfast and drinking coffee.

She and Melissa stopped to chat with several of them, and Dex spoke to a few men, although they looked wary of him and didn't have much to say. Maybe they thought he was law enforcement although he was dressed in jeans and his cowboy hat.

Seeing so many needy men made him wonder if he should talk to his brothers about hiring a couple as ranch hands. Something to check into. Although the safety of his family and the foster girls took priority. Still, if they grew the cattle side of the business, they'd need more hands.

Candace paused at a long table near the door to the kitchen where an old-timer in grimy overalls sat alone. She and Melissa exchanged looks of concern as Candace stood by the table. The young woman laid her hand on the man's shoulder and leaned over to speak to him.

He gave a little nod, then looked up at Melissa. A tentative smile softened the harsh age lines bracketing his mouth, which tightened when he spotted Dex.

"It's okay," Candace said softly as she introduced him as Bill Small. "Melissa and Dex are here to help find out what happened to your friend. I need you to tell them your story."

Bill glanced into his cup of coffee as if it would give him answers, then pushed out the chair beside him, inviting Melissa to sit down. Dex walked to the opposite side of the table and claimed a chair across from Bill, then accepted a cup of coffee from Candace.

"You a cop?" Bill asked with a wary look.

Dex shook his head. "A PI. My father lived in a shelter and recently died. That started me looking at the shelters for answers about him, then I learned that several men had gone missing."

Bill's expression softened. "Sorry about your daddy."

Dex nodded. He couldn't escape the grief. "Me, too. And I'm sorry about your friend."

The simple exchange calmed Bill. He took a sip of his coffee, wiped his mouth on a paper napkin, then set the cup down. "His name was Harry Willis. I think something bad happened to him."

"What makes you think that?" Melissa asked.

Bill drummed crooked fingers on the table as if trying to put together his words. "Harry was kind of a loner, about my age," Bill said. "But he had a daughter."

"Did he keep in touch with her?" Dex asked.

Bill shook his head. "Not really. But he recently learned she had a baby. He wanted to see that kid more than anything. He was saving up money to send to his girl, hoping she'd let him visit."

Melissa murmured a sympathetic sound. "Did he go see her?"

Bill raked a hand through his thinning white hair. "Naw, at least I don't think so. But one night he showed up here with a wad of cash."

Dex frowned. "Did he say where he got the money?"

"Said he did a favor for someone, and they paid him. But that worried me. He wouldn't say who it was or what he did."

"Could it have been a drug deal?" Melissa asked.

Bill shook his head. "Harry didn't do drugs, and would never have sold 'em."

Money was a powerful motivator. "Not even for money to send his daughter?" Dex asked.

"No way," Bill said firmly. "His son OD'd when he was only nineteen. That's what drove Harry to the streets. The guilt."

Dex understood about guilt.

"So what happened after you talked to him about the money?" Melissa asked.

"Next day he said he was going to mail it to his daughter. Left to walk to the post office but never came back."

Silence, thick with tension, stretched between them for a full minute. "Maybe he decided to take it to his daughter in person instead of mailing it," Dex suggested.

Melissa's gaze met his. "Or someone could have stolen it from him."

The implication that he'd been killed for the money rang between them, but neither voiced it aloud.

Dex mentally made a plan. First, he'd check with the daughter to see if she'd heard from her father.

If she hadn't, he'd check police reports and the morgue in case Harry had shown up in jail…or dead.

MELISSA HATED THE thoughts running through her head, that Harry might be dead. The men who needed their help moved around constantly. She and her father certainly had. Sure, they became friendly with others staying at the shelter, but usually not for long.

The center's goal was to help them rejoin the work force, and take charge of their lives. They facilitated family reconciliations through counseling, assisted in arranging financial assistance, and offered programs to aid in mainstreaming the men back into society.

If someone moved of their own accord, it was usually because they didn't form attachments or weren't ready to accept the help offered. Pride, depression, mental illness, addictions, physical injuries or illness, emotional trauma, past criminal activities, imprisonment and PTSD were contributing factors that landed the men on the streets and were obstacles to recovery.

"Did he have any friends that he might go to or turn to for help?" Melissa asked.

Bill scratched his chin. "Said he never stayed anywhere long enough to make friends. Got antsy if he was in one place too long. He used to work odd jobs on ranches across the state when he was younger. But arthritis kicked in and joints hurt too bad for physical labor."

Melissa gestured around the room to the other men who were dispersing. "Did you ask to see if anyone knew the nature of the job Harry did?"

"Sure did. Ms. Candace talked to them, too. But no one knew anything about the money or where it came from."

"You said he liked to move around," Dex cut in. "Other than the money, what makes you think he didn't panic about seeing his daughter and move on to another city?"

Bill pushed away from the table and stood, then picked up his coffee. "Come on, I'll show you."

Melissa and Dex followed Bill as he carried his cup to the counter and left it to be washed. In the bunk rooms, he went to the back wall and the bed at the end.

Bill squatted down and pulled an old duffel bag from beneath the bed, then set it on the cot. "This was all Harry had to his name." His sad eyes met Melissa's, then he removed a photograph and showed it to them. "This was the only picture he had of his daughter. Was taken when she was five. Harry never would have left without it."

Melissa's heart squeezed. Bill was right. Most people kept a memento of their past life that they clung to and carried with them wherever they went. Her father had held on to a pocket watch that had belonged to his own father. She'd kept a picture of her mother that her father knew nothing about. It was in her wallet now.

"There's something else." Bill carefully placed the picture back in the bag.

"What?" Melissa asked.

"The day he left, I saw someone watching him. A car, a black sedan, was parked down the street. When Harry started toward the post office, it pulled out and drove real slow behind him."

Melissa's gaze locked with Dex's. The man who'd shot at them at McTruitt's office had been driving a black sedan.

DEX'S SUSPICIONS KICKED up a notch at the idea of the same black sedan following Harry as the one at McTruitt's office. It was possible it was a different car, but everything Bill said made him wonder if Bill was right to suspect his friend had fallen prey to foul play.

He gestured toward the duffel. "Do you mind if I look through that bag?"

Bill glanced at Melissa, who nodded that it was okay, and Bill moved aside to give Dex access. He handed Bill the photo. "Hold on to that. I wouldn't want it to get damaged."

Bill's look of gratitude warmed Dex's heart. He'd just won the man's trust and respect. Bill ran his finger over the picture with a sad smile as Dex searched the bag. The larger section held assorted clothing. One outer pocket contained chewing gum, a fast-food wrapper from a burger joint and an empty water bottle. A small section in front held a few toiletries. He dug deeper into the inner pocket and discovered a slip of paper with a name on it.

Sally Layton.

"Was Sally the daughter's name?" he asked Bill.

Bill nodded. "Yeah."

A business card was tucked inside the folded scrap of paper. Dex flipped it over and saw it was a card for a large animal vet.

Dr. Bart Huckleberry. He specialized in large animal medicine and worked closely with an expert cattle breeder.

Why would Harry have a card for the vet in his pocket?

He tapped it on his hand. "Did Harry mention anything about a vet to you?"

Bill shook his head. "No, why?"

"I found this card in his bag. Maybe the vet is connected to the job he did."

Bill shrugged as if he had no idea.

"I'll talk to him." Dex tucked the clothing back in the bag, but stuffed the business card in his pocket.

Sympathy tinged Melissa's expression, and she patted Bill on the back. "Let us know if you hear anything from Harry. And we'll do the same."

Bill cradled Melissa's hand between his. "Thank you so much for listening to me and trying to help."

Melissa gave the older man a hug. "Of course."

Admiration for Melissa and her role in helping these homeless men mushroomed in Dex's chest.

Bill extended his hand, and Dex shook it. "Thank you, too, Mr. Dex."

Dex cleared his throat. "We'll do everything we can to find your friend." He just hoped they found Harry, and that when they did, he was still alive.

Chapter Seven

As he drove away from the shelter, Dexter couldn't shake the feeling that Bill's friend might be dead. Needing to verify the facts, he veered into the parking lot of a place called the Barbecue Pit.

"Let's get a late lunch," he said as he snagged his phone. "I want to see if I can locate Harry's daughter before we visit the vet."

"I could eat," Melissa said softly, reminding him that she loved burgers and barbecue and wasn't one of those picky women who only ate rabbit food.

The popular café boasted the best brisket in Austin, and was decorated Western-style, with a metal pig beneath a rustic wagon wheel, surrounded by beef cattle made from metal and wire.

"I know learning about your sister and your father was difficult," Melissa said as they settled at a booth in the corner. "How's your family doing?"

Dex pushed the menu aside. He knew what he wanted.

Time with Melissa.

Dammit, he couldn't have that. He had to focus.

"Everyone's hanging in there," he said gruffly.

The waitress appeared, and he paused so they could

order. Melissa asked for a pulled pork sandwich and iced tea while he ordered the pork plate and coffee.

"Of course we were hoping to find Chrissy and Dad alive, but after eighteen years, I guess we'd all prepared ourselves for the fact that might not happen. The sad thing is that Chrissy's death was really accidental. The guy who killed her was mentally challenged and infatuated with kids. He just wanted to play with her, and got too rough when she tried to leave." The waitress brought their drinks, and he sipped his coffee. "Unfortunately, the guy's mother covered for him to protect him. That was a mistake."

"He did the same thing to some other children, didn't he?" Melissa asked.

Dex nodded, the guilt back.

Melissa covered his hand with hers. A tingle of warmth shot through him, making him shift in his seat. He'd always liked Melissa's touch. Her hands were so gentle. Soft. Filled with tenderness and love.

A love he didn't deserve. Chrissy wouldn't have died if he'd watched her that night.

"I realize you blamed yourself," Melissa said in that uncanny way she'd always had of reading him. Maybe that was the reason he'd left her. He didn't like anyone seeing his vulnerabilities.

"But I hope you've let that go, Dex. You were all just kids. Siblings argue and fight. Your sister obviously adored all of you, or else she wouldn't have followed along. That night was just a series of unfortunate events." She squeezed his hand, and he had to force himself not to turn his palm over and clasp hands as if they were a couple. "Like you said, it was an accident," she said softly. "Your sister wouldn't have wanted you to blame yourself."

She was right. On an intellectual level he knew that. But his heart and conscience refused to let him off the hook.

MELISSA SENSED DEX was still beating himself up over his little sister's death as they dug into their food. She wished she knew how to help him move past it.

She wiped barbecue sauce from her mouth. "Your mother took in some of the victims of that human trafficking ring, didn't she?"

Dex nodded and shoveled up a forkful of coleslaw. "Yeah, it's been great for everyone. Mom struggled after Chrissy disappeared. Then when Dad left, I think she blamed herself because he abandoned us. The house was quiet, sad, for a long time."

"Even with four boys in it?" Melissa asked.

Dex chuckled. "Well, maybe it wasn't always quiet. But my brothers and I bore the brunt of guilt over the whole thing. We kind of all shut down for a while, retreated into ourselves, tried not to make trouble and upset her even more."

Melissa gave him a sympathetic look. "You mean *you* behaved?"

Dex chuckled. "For a little while. But then I couldn't help myself. I was angry and took it out on everyone. I started breaking all the rules."

Dex's mischievous, daredevil attitude had drawn her from the beginning. He was a bad boy, yet he had morals and fought for the underdog. A potent combination.

Ignoring the seed of desire sprouting inside her, she finished her meal while he excused himself to make a phone call to his brother Lucas. Maybe his brother could locate Harry's daughter and she could tell them if he was all right.

"HER NAME IS Sally Layton," Dex told Lucas. "She's the daughter of a homeless man who might be missing."

"Hang on, I'll see what I can find."

Dex paced by the men's room as he waited. Dammit, he needed distance from Melissa. Talking to her, being with her again, stirred old feelings that he thought he'd left behind in the dust.

"I found her," Lucas said as he came back on the line. "She's a nurse at a clinic near the main hospital. I'll text you her address and phone number."

Dex thanked him and hung up, then waited on the text. When the address appeared on his screen, he called the clinic but Sally wasn't at work. He returned to the table and paid the bill, then he and Melissa drove to the woman's house.

Sally lived in a neighborhood with small ranch homes that appeared to have been updated.

"These are nice," Melissa said.

"They remind me of the homes Harrison's wife, Honey, renovates. She bought a bunch of older places in Lower Tumbleweed and has completely revived the town." Melissa should be living in a cute little house like this, not in that dump where she was now.

A station wagon sat in the driveway, and a flower bed filled with impatiens in various colors brightened the neatly kept yard. The front porch boasted two rocking chairs, making the place look homey and inviting.

They walked up to the house in silence, and Dex knocked. Footsteps, then a voice sounded inside. A few seconds later, the door opened. A petite blonde carrying a baby stood at the door, rocking the infant in her arms.

Melissa's expression softened as she looked at the infant, a hint of yearning in her eyes. Dex shifted, wondering why she'd never married and had a family herself. Although the thought of her with another man didn't sit well in his gut.

"Sally?" Melissa said.

The young woman nodded and glanced between the two of them. "Can I help you?"

Dex gestured for Melissa to take the lead, and she explained about their visit with Bill.

Sally's eyes widened. "You've seen my father?"

"I'm afraid not," Melissa said softly. "I work at a homeless shelter called Lend-A-Hand. Earlier, we spoke with a man named Bill at another shelter."

Pain wrenched the young woman's face. "My father is in a homeless shelter?"

"He was," Melissa said.

"His friend Bill is worried because Harry left and hasn't come back. Have you seen or talked to him recently?" Dex asked.

The baby started fussing, and Sally lifted the child and patted its back, soothing it. "Not in months. I kept hoping he'd contact me." She pressed a kiss to the infant's head. "Sari is two months old today. I wanted Dad to meet his granddaughter."

Melissa smiled. "Bill said that Harry had just earned some cash and that he was going to send it to you. He wanted to see you and the baby."

A sliver of hope sparkled in the woman's eyes, but worry quickly replaced it. Or maybe it was disappointment. Dex knew what it was like to wonder where your father was and why he'd left.

"But I haven't heard from him." Her voice cracked. "He probably just changed his mind. It wouldn't be the first time."

A heartbeat passed, then Melissa squeezed Sally's hand. "Did you know he carries a picture of you wherever he goes?"

Tears moistened Sally's eyes, but she blinked them away and shook her head.

"Dad blamed himself for my brother's death, but it

wasn't Dad's fault. I tried to reconnect with him, but Dad started drinking and disappeared."

"I'm so sorry," Melissa said softly.

Dex removed a business card from his pocket and offered it to her. "Please call me if you hear from him."

Sadness tinged Sally's expression. "If you find him, please tell him that I love him, and that I want him to come home."

Compassion filled Dex, and he nodded, his throat too thick to speak.

Melissa reached out and stroked the baby's head. "She's beautiful."

"Thanks," Sally whispered. "I just hope Dad gets to meet her." A tear trickled down Sally's cheek and Melissa hugged the young woman.

"I hope so, too," Melissa said. "We'll keep in touch."

Sally hugged the baby tighter and closed the door. Melissa wiped a tear from her cheek as they walked back to the car, and they settled inside in silence.

He hoped to hell Sally's search had a better ending than his had.

MELISSA TWISTED HER hands together, her nerves on edge as they drove toward the vet's office. So many sad stories of families torn apart. Tragic circumstances, folks wandering around homeless and alone while the people they left behind struggled with grief and fear and guilt. She wished she could give them all a happy ending, but she'd learned a long time ago that she couldn't. She'd expected to become immune to the pain, but each story got to her.

Dex's face looked strained as he drove. No doubt he was probably thinking about his own father and how he and his family had wanted him to return. They'd waited eighteen years only to find him dead in a DUI accident. That had to be a hard blow.

Dex veered off the main road down a bumpy country one with acres of farmland spread out on both sides. A rustic wooden sign bearing the name Huckleberry Animal Hospital dangled from a post as Dex steered the SUV toward the clinic.

It was situated about thirty miles outside of Austin on farmland equipped with emergency facilities, as well as barns and stables for livestock if the animals needed housing for treatment. A mobile unit and attached trailer used to travel to farms and ranches was parked by the main office.

"Do you think Harry is dead?" Melissa finally asked, breaking the strained silence as they bounced over the ruts in the road.

"I don't know," Dex said. "The bodies of the three men recently reported missing haven't been found, so they may still be alive. Lamar could be right, and I'm looking for trouble and connections when there is none."

"But you may be onto something," Melissa said. "We have to find out, Dex."

"I won't argue with that." His mouth twitched. "Can I ask you something?"

Melissa tensed. She refused to admit he'd broken her heart. Maybe he'd walked away and hadn't given her a second thought. She didn't want to know if that was the case. It hurt too much to think the feelings she'd imagined between them had been completely one-sided. "Depends on what it is."

"Fair enough." He parked by the mobile unit and cut the engine. "Did you and your father stay at Retreat when you were young?"

Melissa averted her gaze, afraid he'd see too much. There was agony in her heart when she remembered roaming from one place to another, sleeping in the car, or a park, or an alley. And the shame.

She'd always been so ashamed.

"No," she said honestly. "It's reserved for single men."

He nodded in understanding. "How about Candace? Did you two meet through work?"

"Yes and no. We met in college when we were both volunteering at a women's shelter. We instantly bonded over shared goals." She rubbed her finger over a silver charm on a chain around her neck. "We've been close friends ever since, although she married last year, so we haven't seen each other quite as much lately."

"Doesn't her husband worry about her working at a men's shelter?"

Melissa laughed softly. "Yes, but he loves her, and he knows that her work is a part of her, that she's passionate about it. I think it's one reason he fell in love with her. How could he ask her to give it up?"

Dex's dark eyes flickered with some emotion she couldn't define. "You're right. He couldn't."

A second later, he opened his car door and slid out. Melissa joined him, and they walked side by side up to the vet's office, a long building that looked as if it was once a barn that had been converted. A tin roof topped the dark red painted building. Dex was scanning the property as if anticipating trouble, and she did the same.

In the distance, she spotted two horses galloping across a field, but no cattle. A small herd of goats roamed the field to the right, and a gray cat lay sleeping on the front porch of the brick ranch house. The driveway to the house was empty.

The area seemed unusually quiet, as if no one was around. Maybe Dr. Huckleberry was on a call.

Except his mobile unit was parked in front.

Perhaps he had a second one or only took the mobile unit when necessary. Routine calls might not require all his medical supplies. Or heck, he could just be running an errand.

Dex knocked, then called out for the doctor as he opened the metal door. "Dr. Huckleberry?"

Silence greeted them as they entered, then the scent of strong cleaning chemicals hit her. The cement floor looked fairly clean, an office with a desk to greet clients facing the door. It was empty. Did Huckleberry have a secretary? An assistant?

Dex strode past the desk through a double door, and Melissa followed, an eerie quiet enveloping her as they checked two exam rooms, a surgical unit and a room that served as the pharmacy. A locked glass case held medical supplies and drugs. Everything appeared to be intact.

They walked through a hallway to find a small office in back. A metal desk and filing cabinet were the only pieces of furniture. The office was empty, as well. A calendar on the wall marked the days, an appointment book lay on the desk and the bottom desk drawer stood slightly ajar.

Dex gave it a quick glance and scanned the desk, but didn't touch anything. A photograph on the wall showcased the vet receiving an award. The man was probably in his midforties, with a stout frame, a thick beard and chunky hands.

Dex gestured toward a back exit leading out to the barn. The sound of a dog barking met them as he opened the door.

A big gray shepherd-mix dog greeted them, its head cocked. Melissa froze, giving the dog time to sniff her and recognize that they didn't pose a threat.

"Shh, buddy, it's all right." Dex leaned over to pet the dog, his hand halting in midair. He muttered a curse, then shot her a look that indicated something was wrong.

Melissa inched closer, and Dex gestured toward the dog's nose. Melissa sucked in a sharp breath. Blood.

Dex rubbed the back of the dog's head. "Show me what happened, buddy." He pulled his gun and motioned for her to stay behind him as they followed the shepherd across the back of the property.

SENSES HONED FOR TROUBLE, Dex gripped his gun at the ready as he hurried behind the shepherd. They passed a small barn, which appeared empty at the moment. The dog barked again, then turned to see if Dex was following.

"I'm right behind you, bud," he said, then picked up his pace as the dog broke into a run.

Melissa raced behind him. Dry brush crunched beneath his boots as he passed a stable and veered toward a second barn. The sound of cows mooing echoed from the building, then another sound that made his pulse jump.

An angry bull stomping, banging and snorting. He held his hand up, warning Melissa to wait while he checked out the situation.

The dog barked at the open door to the barn, pawing at the dirt and turning circles. "You stay here, too," he murmured to the shepherd as he inched inside the building.

Stalls on both sides of the barn flanked a hallway. He eased down the hallway, glancing into each stall in case someone lay in wait. Two cows were housed in separate stalls on the left. The angry bull was on the right at the end. The sight of something dark that looked like blood on the rough wood floor caught his eye, and he stooped to examine it.

Definitely blood.

His senses became more alert. He couldn't afford to be caught off guard and walk into an ambush.

The stamping and snorting grew louder, and the wooden slats on the stall door vibrated as the angry animal pounded the locked stall door.

Dex had a healthy respect for cattle and horses. He could handle both. But both could be dangerous. A few attempts at bull riding in a local rodeo had taught him the power of the beast.

He approached slowly, and peered over the stall edge. One bull. The angry animal huffed and dug his hooves into the dirt where a man lay, facedown. His clothes were ripped to shreds and drenched in blood.

"Dex?" Melissa called.

"Call 9-1-1," he shouted.

Although judging from the man's slack body and the amount of blood loss, they were too late.

Chapter Eight

Melissa gasped at the sight of the man on the stall floor. "Oh, God… Is that the vet?"

"Yeah, looks like he was gored to death by that bull."

Her mind was reeling as she pulled her phone from her pocket, punched 9-1-1 and backed away from the stall. The operator answered, and she explained what they'd found. "We need an ambulance and the police."

Her back brushed something hard, then someone grabbed her from behind. She shrieked and dropped her phone, then a cold hand clamped over her mouth.

Panic shot through her, and she kicked and clawed at the man's arms.

A bullet suddenly whizzed by her head. It had come from behind her. Then another.

She kicked the man again, then bit down on his hand as hard as she could. He cursed and yanked his hand away for a second, but slammed his fist against the side of her head, and she saw stars.

Dex leaned against the wall to avoid being hit by the bullet. Her captor dragged her toward the door while the shooter fired again. Dex fired back and hit the shooter, who dropped to the floor with a grunt. But a bullet from the second shooter pinged by her head.

The man holding her gripped her tighter and pulled her

near the door. Dex fired again, and the man shoved her into the stall. He spun around to fire at Dex, but Melissa jumped him from behind.

He tried to shove her off, but she jabbed at his eyes. More gunfire in the barn. She prayed Dex was all right. Meanwhile she had to fight for her life.

The man tried to pry her hands from his face. She struggled to stay on his back, but he was strong and threw her to the floor. Her head hit the back of the stall, and the world spun. But she spied a cabinet with medical supplies in the corner and scrambled toward it.

The man lunged toward her. She grabbed a hypodermic just before the man reached for her neck.

She gripped the hypodermic and jabbed upward, driving it into his belly as his hands closed around her throat.

He squeezed her neck, choking her. She kicked out and pushed at his arms, determined to free herself, but he dug his meaty paws into her throat again, cutting off the air to her windpipe.

She clawed at him, but his hold tightened and a dizzy spell overcame her. Her vision blurred, then everything went black, and her hands fell limp to her side.

She fought to remain conscious, but the darkness was sucking her in, pulling her into an endless tunnel where she kept falling and spinning. As hard as she tried, she couldn't grab hold of anything to hang on to.

DEX INCHED FORWARD, plastering himself against the barn wall to avoid another bullet. Dammit. One man was down. He thought he'd hit the second, but the bastard hadn't given up.

And where the hell was Melissa? In that stall on the end by the door? Sweat beaded on his skin. He couldn't see her, and he didn't like it.

Another shot. Anger propelled him forward. He aimed

his gun at the stall where the shooter had taken refuge, firing bullets through the slats. A grunt echoed from the inside, and he raced to cross the distance, firing another round as he glanced inside.

The man was finally down. Blood soaked his shirt and spattered the wall and floor. He darted inside, grabbed the man's gun, then checked his pulse.

Dead.

Now, he had to get to Melissa.

He loaded another magazine into his weapon, then slowly crept toward her. It was too quiet ahead. Had the man managed to drag Melissa outside?

Fear made him hurry, and he checked left and right, maneuvering closer. A noise echoed from the stall, and he jerked around in front of it, his gun aimed.

The bastard who'd attacked Melissa lay on the floor, unmoving. So did Melissa. She looked pale and limp, a hypodermic on the floor beside her open hand.

Dear God, she had to be all right.

He raced into the stall, quickly dropped down beside the man and checked him for a pulse. Low but thready. He was alive but didn't appear to be stirring.

Keeping one eye on the bastard, he rushed to Melissa, knelt and pressed two fingers to her neck. Precious seconds passed. Finally a pulse.

He muttered another prayer, then gently brushed his hand against her cheek.

"Melissa, come back to me."

Slowly, her chest rose and fell.

Heart hammering, he brushed her cheek again. "Talk to me, darlin'."

A flutter of her eyelids. Her breath quickened, and she emitted a soft gasp.

He slid one hand below her head to raise her to an incline position, murmuring soft words of comfort. Yet the handprints on her neck made him want to curse and kill the man on the floor beside her.

"It's all right, I'm here," he murmured softly.

Her eyelids slowly opened, then closed. She lifted one hand and reached for his arm. He wrapped his arm around her, holding her and rocking her back and forth while she slowly regained consciousness.

A siren wailed outside.

She blinked again, her voice raspy as she whispered his name.

"I'm here, darlin'." He held her close, his chest aching as he waited on the ambulance to arrive.

Melissa could have died today. And yesterday. Who was the bastard on the floor and the dead man in the stall?

They had to be working for someone, but whom?

Someone who knew he and Melissa were asking questions? Someone who didn't want them to find answers...

MELISSA SLOWLY RETURNED to reality. Her head was throbbing from where she'd hit it against the wall, and her throat felt raw.

But she was in Dex's arms, and that felt right.

The last thing she remembered was gasping for air and wondering if Dex had been shot.

She blinked, struggling to clear her vision. Dex's handsome face slowly slipped into view. His strong jaw rough with a constant five o'clock shadow. His dark serious eyes.

"Melissa, that hypodermic? Did he inject you?"

She shook her head. "No, I jabbed it in his chest." She gulped. "Did I kill him?"

Dex shook his head, then glanced at the cabinet of medical supplies. "That was probably a tranquilizer that the vet used." He cupped her face between his hands. "But if you had killed him, it would have been all right. He tried to kill you."

"What about the other shooters?" Melissa asked.

Dex's jaw tightened. "Both dead."

The sound of the siren wailing drew closer. Dex heaved a breath.

Melissa clutched Dex's arm as he helped her stand. Her legs felt weak, and she was trembling, but the fresh air revived her as they stepped from the barn. She clung to him as they made their way across the space between the barn and main clinic, where she sat down on a bench.

A police car raced up and screeched to a stop, gravel spewing. An ambulance roared up on its tail. Detective Lamar unfolded his legs from the front of the police cruiser.

Two medics exited the ambulance and jogged toward them. Dex waved them over to her. The detective scowled at her and then at Dex.

"What the hell is going on with you?" Detective Lamar growled. "Everywhere you go, bodies are piling up."

Dex muttered an apology. "I drove out to talk to the vet and found him dead. Then three men came out of nowhere and jumped us."

"Where are they now?" Detective Lamar asked.

Dex shifted, removed his Stetson, raked a hand through his hair, then settled his hat back on his head. He had a habit of doing that when he was stalling. "In the barn. Two dead. Melissa fought off the other and managed to inject him with some drug. I think it was probably a tranquilizer."

Dex gestured toward the stall holding the unconscious man.

"Get him first," Detective Lamar ordered. "And I want to talk to him as soon as he regains consciousness." The detective wiped sweat from his brow. "Now I need to see Dr. Huckleberry."

Dex pressed a hand to the detective's chest. "Wait, it's dangerous, Lamar. Let me coach that bull into another stall before you go in."

The medic began to examine Melissa as Dex led the detective and the second medic deeper into the barn.

When the female medic was satisfied that Melissa's breathing was normal and there didn't appear to be permanent damage to her throat, she joined the others to assist with the injured man.

Melissa traced her fingers over the bruising on her neck, grateful she'd survived. A slight wind picked up, stirring the hot summer air, and she coughed as she inhaled dust.

Her eye caught sight of something red sticking out from the corner of the doorway. She stood and went to see what it was.

She stooped down to pull at it. It was a red bandanna. She tugged it from the splintered wood where it had caught and examined it.

It looked exactly like the bandanna Jim Smith had been carrying.

IT TOOK DEX finessing and time to steer the bull into the neighboring stall so Lamar could examine the vet. While he handled the animal, Lamar examined the two dead shooters.

Dex joined him just as Lamar was digging through the pocket of the first dead man. Blood stained his body, clothes, the wall and floor.

Lamar snapped pictures of the man, the bullet holes and bullet casings in the wall and stall, along with the 9mm weapon still clutched in the dead man's hand, then examined the second man.

"So what do you think happened with the doc?" Lamar asked Dex.

Dex chewed over theories. "These men killed Huckleberry, then put him in the stall with the bull to make it appear accidental." Dex explained about his conversation with Bill regarding Bill's friend Harry as he showed him to Huckleberry's body.

"I think you're grasping at straws trying to connect Huckleberry's death to the missing homeless men. Huckleberry worked with prize bulls and a breeding expert. These men could have planned to steal drugs, or maybe they thought he kept some of the bull's seed here."

That was feasible.

"Did you touch anything?" Lamar asked.

Dex shook his head. "I used work gloves to rope the bull and move him." As much for his own protection as to keep his prints off the place.

The bull was still stomping and butting his head against the wood slats next door. Lamar startled, a dark scowl growing on his face as he photographed the bloody scene, then stepped inside.

"I don't see bullet casings like I found with the other two dead men," Lamar said as he examined the barn walls. "Considering the fact these men were armed, it seems logical that would be their murder weapon of choice."

"So you think I'm wrong?" Dex asked.

"Too soon to say. But it's possible Huckleberry got trapped with the bull and the animal killed him."

Dex didn't believe for a minute that Huckleberry's death was an accident. "What about the shooters?"

Lamar grunted. "Like I said, maybe they were thieves." He scrutinized the stall again. "I suppose one of them could have drugged the vet, then threw him in here with the bull. I'll make sure the ME runs a tox screen."

Drugging Huckleberry and then putting him in the stall made sense. If Dex hadn't shown up, the men might have gotten away with their plan, too.

Lamar crossed the stall, then squatted down beside the vet. The man lay on his side, clothes torn, body mauled. Lamar looked at his chest, then rolled him to his side to examine his back. He was looking for gunshot wounds, cause of death.

"No bullet wounds. He's not in full rigor, either, so he hasn't been dead long."

The female medic appeared behind them. "The medical examiner and crime scene techs are here. We're ready to transport the surviving man to the hospital."

"How is he?" Lamar asked.

"Vitals are stable, but he's still unconscious." She angled her head. "No ID on him. Do you know who he is or if he has family?"

Dex shook his head.

"We'll run both men's prints and DNA." Voices echoed from the front of the barn, then the medical examiner walked toward them, followed by two crime techs.

Dex leaned against the stable door, anxious to learn the identity of Melissa's attacker. When he regained consciousness, maybe he'd talk.

"I'm going to check on Melissa."

Lamar cleared his throat. "You two need to stick around for a few more minutes. I have to take her statement."

Dex nodded and went to see Melissa. She was still sitting on that bench, looking lost and shaken as she watched the ambulance pull away. But when she saw him, she lifted her chin, the fight returning to her eyes.

"You okay?" he asked as he approached her.

"Yeah. Do you know who those men were?"

"Not yet." He noticed the red bandanna in her hands. "Where did that come from?"

An odd look flashed across her face, and she stuffed it in her pocket. "It's nothing."

Dex narrowed his eyes. Why did he sense she was hiding something?

Voices from the barn and then footsteps brought their

conversation to a halt. Lamar strode toward them, talking in a hushed tone to the ME.

"I'll let you know the results of the autopsy as soon as I finish," the ME told Lamar.

Lamar thanked him, then stopped in front of him and Melissa. "Ms. Gentry, I need you to tell me what happened here today."

Melissa looked wary, but explained about Bill's concerns over Harry. "Bill thinks that someone hurt Harry because of some cash Harry had."

"How much are you talking?" Lamar asked.

"He didn't say," Melissa said. "Harry was also secretive about how he earned it. He left for the post office to mail the money to his daughter, but she never received it. Bill thought someone in a black sedan was following Harry when he left the shelter."

"What makes you think that Harry has something to do with Dr. Huckleberry?"

"We found a card with his name on it in Harry's things," Dex said.

Lamar made a low sound in his throat. "Everywhere you two go, people are dying, Ms. Gentry. If you don't stop poking around, you're going to get killed." He paused, his expression grave. "Now, go home and let me handle this investigation."

Dex didn't comment. But Lamar knew Dex wouldn't back down because of danger.

"What about the homeless men, about Harry?" Melissa asked. "Are you going to investigate what happened to them?"

Lamar crossed his arms. "As a matter of fact, I have been doing that. I believe your friend Jim Smith is responsible, and McTruitt was onto him. That's why Smith killed McTruitt and ran."

Chapter Nine

Melissa stiffened, the fact that she'd found that bandanna and kept it taunting her. She should show it to Detective Lamar. But it really meant nothing. It might not even belong to Jim Smith.

Lamar seemed so certain Smith was a bad guy. What if she was wrong about him, too? What if he *had* been running from the law?

"What makes you think Jim is killing homeless men when he was one of them?" she asked.

Lamar scratched his chin. "I can't share details of an ongoing investigation. But let's just say that I found evidence McTruitt had gathered that points in that direction."

"Why would Smith kill the homeless?" Dex asked.

Lamar slanted him an irritated look. "Like I said, I can't share details yet. But I do believe he had you fooled, Ms. Gentry."

Melissa's chest squeezed as she remembered the protective glint in Jim's eyes when he'd ordered McTruitt to let her go.

"If McTruitt was following the law and thought Smith was dangerous, then why did he pull a gun on me?" Melissa asked.

"I don't know the answer to that," Lamar said. "Except

that he wanted to get Smith out of the shelter and that was the fastest way to do it."

"I just don't think Jim's a cold-blooded killer," Melissa said.

Lamar's look softened. "I'm sorry, Ms. Gentry, but you're wrong. At this point, he's considered a wanted felon, so if you're withholding information or know where he is, you can be charged with conspiracy to commit murder."

Melissa's eyes widened.

"Lamar, ease up," Dex said in a gruff tone. "Melissa spent time with Smith, so maybe she has insight we don't."

Lamar raised a bushy brow. "Listen, Dex, you and I both know that people can be deceptive. Con men are experts at choosing personality types that will buy into their acts." He tilted his head toward Melissa. "I'm sorry, ma'am. You seem like a caring, trusting woman. Unfortunately, that's exactly the type con artists prey on."

Melissa twisted her hands together. The detective was right.

Self-doubt assailed her. She'd attended workshops on the topic and had been taught to not let down her guard. She had been educated in signs to watch for to protect herself and the others who sought help at the shelter.

Had she been wearing blinders around Jim Smith?

TENSION STRETCHED BETWEEN Dex and Melissa as he drove back toward her house. He sensed she was struggling with Lamar's allegations against Smith, so he stopped for an early dinner at a pizza joint a few blocks from Melissa's.

They agreed on a half-veggie, half-meat-lover's pie. He ordered a beer and Melissa joined him. She'd never been the fussy type, and enjoyed a cold one with him on occasion.

Melissa's silence worried him. But they both needed time to assimilate the conversation with Lamar. Questions nagged at him. If Smith was killing the homeless men, what was his motive?

Had he persuaded them to do something illegal for him, then killed them to keep them quiet?

And how did it relate to the vet and his death?

Lamar had suggested greed for bull sperm or prize bulls might have gotten Huckleberry killed. Stealing those and reselling could bring big money—a motive.

If Smith killed McTruitt because the PI was onto whatever scheme he was running, was Smith working with the shooters today?

His father's face flashed back. He'd been living in a shelter. Could his death have been something other than a DUI accident?

Or was he straining for an explanation that didn't exist because he didn't want to believe his father had been drinking and driving?

Melissa pushed her plate away. "Dex, are you okay?"

He gave her a wry smile. "I was going to ask you the same thing."

Melissa gazed down into her drink. "I'm just trying to make sense of everything."

"So am I," Dex admitted. "I keep trying to connect my father's death to all of this because of the shelters." He set his hat on the chair beside him and raked a hand through his shaggy hair. "I saw the empty liquor bottle on the seat beside him. The ME confirmed that his blood alcohol content was off the charts, that he probably passed out and lost control, then his truck nosedived into the creek."

"But you don't believe that's what happened?" Melissa asked.

Dex shrugged. "How can I know, when I have no idea where my dad has been or what he's been doing?"

"Was he a drinker when he lived at home?"

Bitterness had driven Dex to banish memories of his

father for so long that now he struggled to recall details of life with him. "Not really. He had a beer occasionally, but never more than one. Even when Chrissy first went missing and he was really upset, he didn't drink. He was determined to find her, and went out for hours and days at a time spearheading search parties. He promised my mother he'd never give up until he found her."

Melissa squeezed his hand. "I'm sorry, Dex. That must have been a horrible time for your family."

"It was. But it was even worse when he abandoned us."

"He didn't leave a note or contact your mother afterward?"

"Not even once," Dex said.

An awkward silence stretched between them, his heart aching with the memories.

"It's possible the stress caused him to have a psychotic break," Melissa offered. "Or that your father was so overwhelmed with guilt and grief that he couldn't face the family."

"None of us blamed him," Dex said. They'd all been too busy blaming themselves.

Melissa squeezed his hand again. "Maybe not, but he was the father, the patriarch of the family. Most likely he thought it was his job to protect all of you. And when he couldn't, he felt like he'd failed."

The bitterness in Dex's chest wavered. He could understand those feelings. "Maybe. But he should have stuck around for my mom. Losing Chrissy and then him, I don't know how she survived and raised us."

Melissa offered him a smile. "She sounds like an incredibly strong woman."

A myriad of emotions tightened Dex's throat. "She is."

Melissa ran her fingers through her hair. "I always thought I was a good judge of character," Melissa said softly. "Now I'm questioning myself. What if I only saw good in Smith because that's what I wanted to see?"

"He did save your life," Dex said. "I can understand why you'd want to see the good in him."

Her troubled gaze locked with his, tension simmering between them.

"I probably should have told the detective about this." Melissa pulled that red bandanna from her pocket and laid it between them on the table. "I found it caught in the corner of the barn door."

Dex narrowed his eyes. "I don't understand. I thought you said it was nothing."

"It might be nothing." Melissa sighed. "But I think it belonged to Jim Smith."

Dex stiffened. "If that belongs to Smith, then he was at the vet's office. Lamar might be right. Smith could have killed Dr. Huckleberry."

MELISSA WINCED AT the accusation in Dex's voice. "He wasn't the one shooting at us," Melissa said. "It was those other men."

"They could be working together," Dex pointed out.

"I suppose it's possible, but I just don't believe Jim would hurt anyone. There has to be another explanation."

"Melissa," Dex said, his voice hardening. "Maybe you have been fooled by him. If he's involved like Lamar suspects, and he's using these homeless men and killing them, he may be responsible for Harry's disappearance."

Melissa tossed the idea around in her head.

"I'm going to check the medical examiner's report on my father's death, too. Smith could have killed him, then made it appear as if he drank himself into an accident."

Melissa jerked her gaze up to meet his. She hated the

pain she saw there. If there was anything she could do to ease it, she would.

But believing his theory meant Jim Smith was a cold-blooded, calculating killer.

She took a deep breath. "If you really think that, then give Detective Lamar the bandanna."

Dex stared at the cloth for a moment, indecision playing across his face. Then he stuffed it in his pocket. "Lamar ordered me to stay out of his way, so I'll have Lucas see if he can lift prints." He paused. "Do you have anything that belonged to Smith that I can use for comparison?"

Melissa rubbed her temple. "He was always writing in these little notepads. He may have left one in his room. Although the detective may have taken it. I can look when I go back into the shelter."

The waitress arrived with their check, and Melissa reached for her wallet, but Dex shook his head. "I've got it."

"Dex—"

"It's just pizza and a beer," Dex said.

Melissa thanked him and gathered her purse, then they walked outside to his SUV. Night had fallen since they'd entered the restaurant, the heat still oppressive. Another night that the shelter was closed meant another night men were without a meal or a bed and a roof over their heads.

Memories of going to bed hungry and sleeping in an alley that reeked of urine and trash taunted her as Dex drove back to her bungalow.

"Hopefully the detective will release the shelter tomorrow," Melissa said. "Then I'll hunt for that notepad."

"Smith's pad may contain information on his plans," Dex said.

"True." Maybe it had proof that would clear Smith of suspicion. For some reason she couldn't put her finger on, he felt like a father figure to her. She didn't want to believe that she'd been wrong about him.

Or that he was a murderer.

DEX FOLLOWED MELISSA up to the door. "I'll check inside to make sure it's secure."

"That's not necessary, Dex," Melissa said.

He gritted his teeth. The fact that she kept defending Smith irritated him. If Smith was guilty, he could come after Melissa and try to use her.

"Humor me," he said gruffly. "You've been shot at several times the last two days. We don't know if we were just in the wrong place, or if someone is watching you, or us."

Fear darted across her face, then she unlocked the door.

"Do you own this house?" he asked as he followed her into a small foyer with hardwood floors that desperately needing refinishing.

"No, it's a rental." Melissa dropped her purse on an accent table near the door. "I don't stay in one place long enough to buy."

On a sofa table behind the faded blue couch, Dex noticed a photograph of a child he assumed was Melissa standing beside an older man. He was thin and dressed in shabby clothes, and so was the little girl. She had one tiny hand in her father's and the other wrapped around the handle of a battered little red suitcase. Her big blue eyes looked haunted and incredibly sad.

"This is you and your father?" he asked.

Melissa nodded. "Yeah, the cook at the shelter where we were staying took the picture before we left one morning. My dad used to say we were going on another adventure. When I was really little, I believed him. But as I got older, I realized we had to keep moving because we either had no money, or our time at the shelter where we were currently staying had run out."

Dex's gaze met hers. Some people would have felt sorry for themselves, or had a chip on their shoulder. Not Melissa. Her mature acceptance raised his admiration even more.

He scanned the open living room and kitchen and was surprised to see unpacked boxes standing in the corner. "Did you just move in?"

"No, I've been here almost a year."

He studied her. "But you haven't unpacked?"

She shrugged. "I move a lot, so why unpack? Besides, I don't have much anyway."

He was so close to his family, and had lived on or near Hawk's Landing all his life. He couldn't imagine not having a place to hang his hat and call home.

She gestured around the room. "Everything looks fine. No one inside."

"Let me check the rest of the house." Someone could be hiding in a closet.

She looked wary, but didn't argue as he examined the windows. They were locked, but the wood was rotting, the locks flimsy. One windowpane was cracked, which would make it easy for someone to break it and get inside.

A small hall to the side of the kitchen led to a door and a wooden deck that overlooked an overgrown yard. The yard backed up to an alley between streets that looked shady.

Not a safe area.

The door lock was rusty. Anyone with a hairpin could break into that damn door. His boots clicked on the floor as he returned to the kitchen and found a hall bathroom and one bedroom. Melissa's.

A blue-and-white quilt, which looked as if it had been homemade, covered the iron bed.

"One of the ladies at the shelter gave me that quilt when I was young," Melissa said behind him. "It's the only thing that I've kept."

His lungs squeezed for air. Melissa had had a rough childhood but had devoted herself to helping others.

But someone had nearly killed her today.

He crossed the room and surveyed her windows. Same shabby locks. A quick look in the closet revealed nothing but a row of blouses and jeans. No fancy shoes or dresses.

A suitcase sat in the doorway of the closet as if waiting for her to leave again.

"Satisfied?" Melissa asked he walked back to the doorway.

"You need better window locks, and a dead bolt on the front and back door."

"I'll be fine, Dex."

"Do you have a gun?" Dex asked.

Her eyes widened. "No."

"Hang on." Dex hurried outside and returned a minute later with a rifle. "Do you know how to use one of these?"

"Yes, but I'm not sure I could shoot someone."

He gripped her hand and put the rifle into it. "If someone breaks in, you have to defend yourself."

Her face paled.

Dammit, he hated to frighten her, but the thought of leaving her alone was driving him crazy with worry. "Just put it in the closet in case you need it. Please."

She bit down on her lip, then nodded and placed the rifle on the top shelf of her closet.

The strangle marks on her throat taunted him as she faced him again. Anger blended with other emotions he didn't want to think about or name.

He lifted his hand and brushed his fingers across her neck. She sucked in a sharp breath. "Dex?"

"Does it hurt?"

Emotions flared in her eyes. Fear and...an awareness of the two of them standing close together. He breathed in her sweet scent. Rosewater.

Heat flared between them.

Her lips parted on a sigh, and he couldn't help himself. He cupped her face in his big hand and closed his lips over hers.

He needed to feel her in his arms and remind himself that she'd survived tonight.

Chapter Ten

Even as Melissa told herself to pull away from Dex, she leaned into the kiss. His arms slid around her, comforting and strong. His body was hard yet warm, stirring a need in her that had lain dormant since the last time she'd been with him.

His lips felt tender yet a hot hunger laced his kiss, and she wrapped her arms around his neck, savoring the feel of his mouth on hers. He took at the same time he gave, tracing her lips with his tongue until she welcomed him inside.

He threaded his fingers through her hair and groaned. That gruff masculine sound of need aroused her even more. She sighed and raked her hands down his back, and he pulled her hips into the V of his thighs. His hard length nudged her heat, a reminder of the closeness they'd once shared and the emotions being with him had unleashed.

Once she'd given him her body, he'd had her heart.

It would be the same again if she allowed herself to succumb to this passion.

Passion had never been the problem. The passion had always been there, potent and breathing life between them, making it difficult to think about anything but touching and feeling.

It was committing to more that had nearly made her crumble.

She wouldn't crumble this time because she wouldn't allow it to get that far.

Still, she didn't pull away. Lord help her, but she was weak. And it had been so long since anyone had held her.

He deepened the kiss, their lips and tongues dancing together in a sensual rhythm that belonged only to them, as if they had been made for this. For each other.

Dex moved against her, pulling her closer to the sofa, and she complied and raked her hands across his back, clinging to the hard muscles and planes of his broad body. He trailed kisses down her neck and throat, and she tilted her head back on a sigh, offering him access to tease her. And he did. His soft tongue lashes along her skin made her tingle all over.

But just as he reached for the button to her blouse, his phone buzzed. They both startled, then he leaned his head against hers, their ragged breathing echoing in the air between them.

She closed her eyes, willing herself to be strong, to resist the temptation to beg him to forget the phone and make love to her.

He didn't answer it right away. He seemed to be struggling just as she was.

They might be in trouble, have already gone too far.

The phone buzzed again, a harsh reminder of the fact that he was here because he was working a case involving her.

Not to declare his love.

"I'd better get this."

She nodded against him and inhaled a sharp breath as he pulled away. Needing distance and space, she rushed to the bathroom. The woman in the mirror didn't even look like her. Her face was flushed, her hair disheveled, her eyes flaring with need.

Her chest heaved for a breath, her body humming with

unsated desire. But it was the stark loneliness in her expression that scared her. She hadn't realized how much she'd wanted to be part of a couple, a family, until she'd met Dex years ago. Or how much she could miss someone when they were gone.

She didn't want to feel that aching emptiness again.

A tear slid down her cheek. No, she could not go back to loving and being left behind. That was the story of her life.

Determined to regain control, she splashed cold water on her face. Dex would leave when he finished investigating. And she would be fine.

Her heart would remain intact.

After all, he couldn't break it if she didn't give it to him.

DEX SILENTLY CURSED as he watched Melissa retreat into her room. She'd needed comfort tonight, but he'd let his own needs interfere and had nearly gone too far.

It couldn't happen again.

His phone buzzed again. He walked to the window and looked out, then checked the number. Officer Whalen, who worked with Lamar. He quickly connected. "Dexter Hawk."

"Detective Lamar asked me to let you know that we've released Lend-A-Hand so they can clean up and reopen."

"Thanks. I'll pass that information on to the assistant director." Melissa would be happy about the news. "Is there anything you can tell me about the evidence Lamar has against Jim Smith?"

Her exasperated sigh followed. "Mr. Hawk, I'm afraid I can't share information in an ongoing investigation. Perhaps you should speak to Detective Lamar yourself."

Except his friend wasn't in a sharing mood.

Melissa reappeared from the bedroom and stepped into the kitchen as if avoiding him. Her look was wary, and she'd pulled her hair back into a ponytail.

Yeah, he'd definitely gone too far.

The officer hung up, and Dex closed the curtain, then shoved his phone in his pocket. "Lamar released the shelter as a crime scene."

Relief flooded her face. "Good. I'll go over tomorrow and inform the volunteers."

Dex cleared his throat. "Melissa, I'll arrange a crime scene cleanup crew. They're experts at getting out blood."

She winced. "We don't have a budget to pay for cleaning or repairs," Melissa said. "The volunteers and I will handle it ourselves."

"I'll foot the bill," he offered.

"I can't let you do that," Melissa said softly.

Dex squared his shoulders. "Doesn't the center take donations?"

Her gaze met his. "Of course we accept donations."

"Well, consider it a donation, then." He slanted her a grin. "I've dug a few bullets from walls in my time. And I'm pretty good with a hammer."

She laughed softly. "That doesn't surprise me. But I know you're busy with work."

He shrugged. Nothing took priority over protecting her. "I need to know what happened to Harry and these other homeless men."

"I understand." She rubbed her neck, drawing his attention back to the fingerprint marks on her throat where she'd nearly been strangled.

Anger rose inside him again, followed by the temptation to pull her into his arms and kiss those bruises.

The phone had stopped him before. He had to exert self-control now.

"I know you're tired. I'll leave and let you rest." He walked toward the door. "I'll pick you up in the morning and drive you to the center to evaluate the damage."

She agreed, and he opened the door. But that picture

of her with her father and that damned little red suitcase taunted him. God, he hated to leave her alone in this dump.

But if he stayed, it would be impossible to keep his hands to himself, so he headed to his SUV.

Dark clouds hovered above, threatening a storm. Rain might cool things, but tonight the air felt steamy.

He scanned the neighboring property, his instincts alert. Two guys in hoodies hovered near a dumpster a block away.

Worry for Melissa mushroomed inside him, and he slid into his SUV, backed out of the driveway, then drove down the street. A rough looking man next door saw him and darted down the alley.

If whoever was behind the shooting learned where she lived, he might send someone else after her. If it was Smith, hell, the man could have followed her home at any time while he stayed at the shelter.

Unable to shake the feeling that she might still be in danger, he parked two doors down from Melissa across the street and decided to watch her house.

MELISSA PACED THE confines of the small house, scrutinizing the interior as Dex must have seen it. Shabby was the word she'd use. Worn and outdated furniture, mismatched kitchen appliances, a beat-up wooden floor and curtains that should have been replaced ten years ago.

She'd done nothing to make it her own. Except for the lone photograph of her and her father, she had no personal items of any kind. No collections or special art or mementos.

Her family consisted of the volunteers and workers at the shelter and the people who sought refuge at Lend-A-Hand.

Material things didn't matter. People did. All she needed was a place to lay her head at night.

That was all she'd ever known.

It had to be enough.

Dex's masculine fragrance lingered in the air, teasing her with what-ifs. What if she could have love and a family, a child, of her own? What if she had a home where she could display family pictures of her baby and the memories they made?

What if she stayed in one place instead of moving around as if on the run herself?

On the run from what?

She'd wondered that about Jim Smith and so many others that joined them at Lend-A-Hand and the other shelters where she'd worked the past decade. Yet she'd never realized how much she was like them.

She moved around so she wouldn't get too attached.

She pressed her fingers to her lips, remembering that kiss. She would be lying if she didn't admit that she wanted it again. That for a second when she'd closed her eyes, she'd fantasized about making love with Dex and waking up in his arms the next morning. And the morning after.

Thankfully, though, he'd left. Tomorrow they'd go to the shelter and get back to business. No more heated kisses.

She walked to the bedroom and glanced at the suitcase she kept in the corner. The urge to pack and find a new start seized her.

But she couldn't leave until she understood what had happened with Smith. And Harry. And if other homeless men were being targeted.

Too antsy to sleep, she snatched her purse and keys and decided to go to the shelter. Jim Smith had constantly written in those little notebooks. But he hadn't had time to retrieve them after the shooting.

Maybe they held something that would help Dex solve the case.

She slipped out the side door and locked it, then rushed to her minivan. It was just as battered as the house. But it served its purpose. It got her around and was big enough to transport supplies to the shelter and from donation centers to alternative housing when necessary. That usually meant a positive step for a person or family. They'd obtained employment and were moving into a home or apartment of their own.

She glanced to the neighbor's drive, grateful it was dark and the driveway empty. She hadn't shared with Dex her anxiety over the guys next door. She was almost certain they were dealing drugs, but she had no proof. At this point, she couldn't afford to anger them or they might retaliate against her.

She pulled onto the street and drove toward the shelter, keeping alert as she maneuvered the roads. She'd never been paranoid, just careful. After the last two days, she'd be crazy not to be.

Darkness enveloped her, the night a reminder that the house she lived in might need updating, but she had a roof over her head and she was grateful for it. There were others out there less fortunate, sleeping on park benches, or alleys or in their cars.

She turned onto the narrow road leading to Lend-A-Hand, veered into the back parking lot and parked. It seemed odd to see the place dark, closed, empty.

Hope brightened her dismal mood. Tomorrow they could reopen. She scanned the exterior for signs of trouble, then grabbed her flashlight and slid from the van. She clenched her keys as she approached the back entrance, unlocked the door and slipped inside.

The scent of blood lingered. Or maybe it was embedded in her memory. She paused and forced herself to remember that the police had cleared the shelter. It was time to move forward and prove that she wouldn't shut down this place because of one incident.

She eased the door closed, listening for sounds of an intruder, but an eerie quiet reverberated through the space.

She fought off her fear and allowed pleasant memories to return. Thanksgiving, when they'd served turkey and dressing, then Christmas, when they'd given wrapped packages of socks and hygiene supplies as gifts. Like a family, they'd worked together to prepare a warm holiday feeling.

Not wanting to alert anyone of her presence in case a vagrant or questionable sort was watching, she used her flashlight to shine a way to the bunk room. She forced herself not to go into the common room where the shooting had occurred.

Smith had occupied a cot in the back left corner of the bunk room, so she passed the other cots, shining her light on the floor. A coin in the corner caught her eye, a battered comb, and a bus ticket stub. All fallen between the cracks of the cots.

She reached Smith's, and shined the light across the mattress. The blanket still lay neatly folded as he'd left it. He had always been neat and orderly. She checked the floor beneath the bed, then raked her hand between the sheet and blanket, and underneath the mattress.

Suddenly a creak of the floor made her freeze. She clenched the flashlight, braced to use it as a weapon if necessary.

But a cold hand grabbed the flashlight, then another hand covered her mouth and the man jerked her against the wall.

Chapter Eleven

Melissa's heart pounded as the man tightened his grip. She'd escaped death twice lately—was this going to be the end for her?

She dug her nails into his arms, struggling to get free.

"I'm not going to hurt you," the man growled in her ear. "Just be still and don't scream, and I'll let you go."

Melissa froze again, the voice registering. Jim Smith?

"Do you understand?" he said in a low voice.

She nodded, her breathing rasping out as he released her. She whirled around, squinting in the darkness.

Yes, it was him. Jim Smith.

The scar on his face made him look menacing in the dark.

Detective Lamar's accusations rang in her head. "What are you doing?" she cried. "And why did you run? I told the police you saved my life."

"It doesn't matter what you told them," Smith said, his voice laced with frustration. "That cop is gunning for me."

Melissa narrowed her eyes. "What does he have against you?"

Smith paced in front of the beds, his limp pronounced, his agitation obvious. "I don't know."

"Please let me call him. We'll explain what happened together. I was a witness."

"You already did that and he's still after me," Smith said. "I'm serious, Melissa. I think that cop wants me dead."

Melissa shook her head in denial. "That can't be true. Why would he want you dead?"

Smith's jaw tightened as his gaze landed on the bruises on her neck. "He's a dirty cop," Jim finally said.

Chilled, Melissa rubbed her arms. "Why would you say that?"

"Because he tried to kill me," Smith said.

"What? When? Where?"

"At that vet's clinic."

Melissa inhaled sharply. "You were there?"

He nodded. "But I didn't kill the vet. I swear. He was dead when I arrived. I saw someone dragging him toward the barn. I hid, but Lamar appeared out of nowhere and shot at me."

Confusion clouded Melissa's mind. "Detective Lamar was there before Dex and I arrived?"

He nodded. "I'm telling you—he's dirty. And he's setting me up."

"None of this makes sense," Melissa said.

Smith wiped his hand over his eyes. "I know. I've been trying to figure out why he'd frame me for murder, but I don't have a clue."

"Then let me call my friend Dexter," Melissa pleaded. "He's a private investigator—"

Smith shook his head. "I saw that Hawk guy with the detective. Melissa, if they're friends, then you can't trust Hawk."

Melissa's breath caught. She hadn't trusted very many people in her life.

But Dex was the one man in the world she did trust. Occasionally he might cross the line, but he fought for justice.

Still, what if Jim was right and Lamar was dirty?

DEX'S IRRITATION HAD mounted as he followed Melissa to the shelter. Why the hell had Melissa driven here tonight? They'd planned to come together in the morning.

Dammit, didn't she know how dangerous it was to be here alone at this hour?

The interior was dark, but her flashlight beam glowed through the window. Had she simply wanted to see the damage to the place without him hovering over her?

If so, why hadn't she turned on a light?

He slid from his truck and eased up to the side of the building. The light from her flashlight was coming from the back, maybe the bunk rooms?

He crept closer and inched along the wall, then peered through the window.

Cold fear seized him. A man was inside the room with her. He leaned closer. A male voice, one that sounded angry.

Had she stumbled on a vagrant who'd drifted in? Or did she know this man?

He peered closer, trying to discern the man's face. A sliver of moonlight illuminated a deep jagged scar on his cheek, and a nose that had been broken at least twice. He was tall but thin, tattered clothes hanging on his frame as he paced. His left leg must have been injured because he limped as he paced. Thick shaggy silver hair made him look like he was in his fifties maybe sixties, and he was missing a finger on his left hand.

Was it Smith?

Had Melissa intentionally come here to meet him?

According to Lamar, Smith was armed and dangerous. Dex pulled his gun. He couldn't take any chances, not with Melissa's life.

Moving slowly, he eased into the side door and inched down the hall, his gun at the ready. The voices drifted to him, Melissa's soft and hushed, the man's low and rough.

He couldn't quite understand what they were saying. Except he did hear Melissa call the man Jim.

It was Smith, dammit.

He gripped his weapon tighter, bracing himself to barter for Melissa's life.

He crept to the doorway, then raised his gun and aimed it inside as he stepped into the entry to the bunk room. Just as he did, the man's hand came up, a gun clenched in it.

"Don't come any closer," Smith growled.

Dex planted his feet firmly, his stance a statement that he didn't intend to back down. "Let her go," Dex said coldly. "If you want a hostage, take me instead."

Their gazes locked in a standoff.

Melissa stepped between them, her hands raised. "Both of you put your guns down. We all have to talk."

"He was holding a gun on you," Dex snapped. "Why should I listen to anything he has to say?"

"He didn't have a gun on me," Melissa said. "We were just talking."

"That cop is framing me," Smith said bluntly. "How do I know you aren't helping him, that you aren't here to kill me?"

Dex hardened his jaw. "Every criminal claims he was set up."

"I'm not a criminal," Smith said.

"You ran from the law," Dex muttered. "You wouldn't do that if you weren't guilty of something."

"He's not a cold-blooded killer," Melissa interjected before Dex could argue. "He saved my life, Dex. When he took that gun from McTruitt, he could have hurt others at the shelter, but he didn't."

Melissa turned to Smith before Dex could speak. "And Dex is not going to shoot you. He's a good guy, Jim. I trust him. So can you."

Smith's gaze moved from Melissa to Dex, skepticism darkening his eyes. "But he's buddies with that detective."

"Believe me, Jim, Dex just wants justice." She pinned them both with a disgusted look. "Now put down your guns, *both* of you."

Dex and Smith stared at each other for a long moment, the tension thick.

Dex shifted as Melissa gave him an imploring look. "You do trust me, don't you, Dex?"

His lungs squeezed for air. He did trust her. But he didn't trust Smith or any other man where Melissa was concerned.

Smith cleared his throat. "I trust you, Melissa." He slowly lowered his gun, then eased it onto the cot nearest Melissa.

Dex inhaled and did the same. "All right," he said as he stepped away from his weapon. "Now we all know Smith is not your real name. Who the hell are you?"

MELISSA BREATHED A sigh of relief as the men relinquished their weapons. For a moment, she'd feared they'd go at it, if not with guns, with fists. The testosterone and anger in the room was a visceral force.

Dex stepped toward the wall, flipped on a light and seemed to study Smith. "Who are you?" Dex repeated.

Jim's face paled. "That's a question I can't answer."

"Can't or won't?" Dex growled.

"Can't," Jim said in a gruff tone.

Dex crossed his arms. "What does that mean?"

Melissa shot him a warning look. "Jim, tell us what's going on and maybe we can help you."

He glanced back and forth between the two of them, then sank onto one of the cots and scrubbed a hand over his face. He looked wary and exhausted, as if he hadn't slept since the shooting. Maybe he hadn't.

She softened her tone. "Please talk to us."

He cut his gaze toward Dex. "Why? So he can call his dirty cop friend to arrest me?"

"Because we all want the truth," Melissa said. "Dex has been searching for his father who disappeared almost two decades ago. Recently he found him, but he was dead. He traced him to a homeless shelter where he learned that several homeless men have gone missing the past few months."

Jim's brows climbed upward. "I don't understand."

"Me neither," Dex said. "But I think someone is preying on homeless men." Dex paused, voice cold. "Detective Lamar thinks that person is you."

"Me?" Jim flattened his hand on his chest. "Why in the world would he think that?"

"I don't know," Melissa said. "Dex?"

Dex shrugged. "Maybe you should start with who you are and why Clark McTruitt was after you."

Silence fell across the room, filled with Dex's mistrust.

Melissa softened her tone. "Please, Jim, talk to us."

He made a frustrated sound. "I wish I could tell you who I am. My real name. But I don't know what it is."

"Don't bother feeding us some story," Dex said sharply. "Either tell the truth or I will call Detective Lamar."

Jim lifted his head, resignation in his eyes. "I *am* telling you God's honest truth. I have amnesia."

Melissa traded a look with Dex, questions echoing between them. Finally she broke the strained silence. "What happened? Were you in an accident?"

Jim rubbed the back of his head. "A head injury."

"How did you get it?" Dex asked.

Jim stared at the floor, at his boots, his hand tracing a line over his head where a scar must have settled in his hairline. "The last thing I remember was being on some farmland near a bunch of rocks. Someone attacked me and hit me in the back of the head. I blacked out. When I came to, I was disoriented and confused. I didn't remember anything, but my head was hurting and I was bloody. I started walking and eventually found the road." His voice cracked. "Some trucker picked me up and dropped me at a free clinic where they stitched me up. I went from there to a shelter near the clinic, and I've been wandering around ever since trying to figure out what happened, and who I am."

Melissa's heart ached for the man. If his story was true, Jim had been the victim of a violent attack.

And whoever had attacked him might still be after him.

Dex locked his teeth together. Melissa was buying Smith's story, hook, line and sinker. He straddled the fence. The man sounded sincere, but amnesia?

It was possible, he supposed.

It was also downright convenient.

"Why was McTruitt after you?" Dex asked again.

Smith raised his gaze, his look flat. "I have no idea. But he's not the first person who's tried to kill me over the years. That's one reason I've stayed on the move."

"Did you have any ID on you when you regained consciousness?" Dex asked.

Smith shook his head. "No, nothing."

"How long were you out?" Dex asked.

Smith shrugged. "I don't know." He touched his hair again. "The blood had dried on the back of my head so it must have been a while."

"How long ago was this?" Melissa asked.

Smith frowned. "Years. Maybe fifteen, sixteen." He rubbed his head again. "Maybe longer. I…sometimes my memory slips. I've lost days, even weeks at times."

"That must be awful," Melissa said softly.

"Where exactly were you were attacked?" Dex asked.

Smith worked his mouth from side to side. "Some farmland or a ranch, I think. It was rugged, miles from a road." He pulled an arrowhead from his pocket and showed it to

Dex. "I found this on the ground beside me. There were a lot more arrowheads there, too."

Memories teased at Dex's mind. He and Chrissy searching for arrowheads on Hawk's Landing. She'd loved finding the arrowheads with him. She'd wanted to go hunting for them the night he and his brothers were supposed to watch her. But he hadn't been in the mood. Then he'd told her to get lost.

The guilt made it hard to breathe again.

Melissa cleared her throat. "Jim, you're always writing in those notepads. What's in them?"

Smith released a wary sigh. "Notes of places I go, people I meet. I keep hoping something will ring a bell and trigger my memories to return."

"What have you learned?" Dex asked.

Smith shook his head. "Not much, except that someone wants me dead."

If that were true, there had to be a reason. Several scenarios popped into Dex's mind. Smith had crossed someone the wrong way, he was party to a crime or a witness—and that person wanted to make sure his memories stayed buried.

Chapter Twelve

Dex studied Smith's body language. He'd learned to read people. Typically, if they were lying, they had a tell.

So far, he hadn't detected one with this man. "Where was this shelter where the driver dropped you?"

"About a half hour from here. Doc said I had a concussion and told me to rest for a few days."

"How long did you stay there?" Dex asked.

Smith shrugged. "A couple of weeks. Thought my memory might come back, but nothing. Then I kept getting this antsy feeling like someone was watching me. That's when I left. Been doing that ever since."

"Did you see someone or notice a particular car?" Dex asked.

Smith shook his head. "Not anyone I could identify. But sometimes I'd see a dark car following me." He rubbed the back of his head again. "Maybe I was paranoid because of my head injury, but I figured if someone left me for dead and found out I survived, they might come back and finish the job." He hesitated, voice shaky. "I got shot at outside Dallas once. And then in Austin another time." He wrung his hands together. "And then that guy broke into Lend-A-Hand and put a gun to Ms. Melissa's head."

"And you defended her?" Dex asked, tensing.

Smith rubbed at his leg as if it was hurting. "Had to. The

man wanted me. I couldn't let him hurt Ms. Melissa. She's the kindest person I've ever met."

Dex couldn't argue with that. "How about the man who gave you a ride when you first regained consciousness? Do you know his name or where he lives?"

"No. I was pretty out of it that day. Had a killer head-ache and was so confused I didn't know where I was or where I was going."

"That sounds awful," Melissa said softly.

Smith offered her a tentative smile. "You can't imagine. I feel like I've got a big hole in my head. For a while I won-dered if I had family, had hoped someone was looking for me. I searched for pictures in the paper and the news, but never saw any." He gave a low whistle. "I figured if I was a wanted criminal, my picture would be all over the news, too. But it never showed up anywhere."

"Which leads us back to the question—why would someone want you dead?" Dex asked.

"Beats the hell out of me," Smith muttered.

"Did you check the news for crimes that happened around that time?" Melissa asked. "Maybe you witnessed one."

"I checked," Smith said. "But there weren't any major stories. And nothing rang a bell."

Melissa glanced at Dex for answers, but he had none. "Listen, Smith," Dex said, "if you really want to know who you are, I have an idea."

His look turned skeptical. "What?"

"Let me run your prints. If they pop in relation to a past crime or a missing persons' report, it'll give us your name."

Smith shook his head. "That detective friend of yours will lock me up. I'm telling you—he's dirty."

Dex gritted his teeth. He'd known Lamar for nearly two decades. How could he believe a stranger over his friend?

Yet he'd seen Lamar cross the line before. Both times he'd planted evidence that had helped convict his collar.

But both times he'd been certain the perp was guilty and dangerous, and he hadn't wanted the suspects to escape on a technicality.

What kind of evidence did he have against Smith? Lamar hadn't wanted to share with Dex…

"I'll have someone else run the prints and Lamar won't know," Dex offered. Lucas could handle it without involving the Austin PD.

Smith reluctantly agreed. "I guess if I have done something bad, it's time I face it and pay up. If not, maybe I'll finally figure out who I am, and why someone wants to kill me."

"Let me make a call." Dex stepped into the hallway, phoned Lucas and explained the situation.

"You're harboring a fugitive?" Lucas asked in an incredulous voice.

Dex silently counted to ten. "Not exactly. Melissa claims he only acted in self-defense, and Smith insists that Lamar is framing him."

Lucas grunted. "Why would Lamar do that?"

"That's what I'm trying to figure out. Anyway, after hearing Smith's story, I'm beginning to wonder myself."

"What *is* his story?" Lucas asked.

Dex relayed everything Smith had told him, and his suspicions that someone was using homeless men, then killing them.

Lucas hissed. "You've certainly made connections where no one else has."

Dex didn't like the patronizing tone in his brother's voice.

"I may be wrong," Dex said. "But, if I'm not, a predator is targeting the homeless because they don't think anyone will notice or pay attention. Even when they're reported missing, the cops don't prioritize the case because—"

"Because by nature of being without a home or family, the men move around," Lucas said matter-of-factly.

"Right. Just indulge me, Lucas. If we discover Smith has committed a crime, I'll bring him to you myself."

Lucas released an exasperated sigh. "All right. What do you want me to do?"

"Simple," Dex said. "Run his prints without alerting the Austin police. If we learn his identity, we'll go from there."

"And if he is a criminal, you'll turn him over."

"Yes." That was a promise he'd keep. Although he had a feeling Melissa would fight him on it.

And if Smith wasn't a criminal, it was possible that he was a victim just as the other missing homeless men were.

MELISSA'S HEART HURT for Jim Smith. She couldn't imagine what it was like to go through life not knowing who you were or where you came from or if you had any family. Although if he did have family, surely they would have been looking for him. Unless they thought he was dead…

Then again, she'd worked in the system long enough to know that when a family filed a missing persons' report, the police investigated—for a little while. Then other cases took priority, leads went cold and enthusiasm waned.

Eventually the family members accepted the loss, especially if they thought their loved one had left of his or her own accord. Missing children were a different story. Families never really gave up looking for them or hoping for their safe return.

"Why did you come here tonight?" Jim asked her.

Melissa traced a finger over her neck, a chill invading her. "After what happened at the vet's clinic today, I couldn't sleep. I remembered that you kept notepads and came here looking for one. I thought you might have jotted down something important."

Smith patted his shirt pocket. "I usually write down anyone I talk to, especially if I think they might give me useful information."

"Did you know a man named Bill Small or Harry Willis? They were staying at the Retreat Shelter."

He wrinkled his brow. "I haven't been to that one."

Her stomach twisted with unease. Was he holding back?

"Jim, I went to bat for you with Dex. Please be honest with me."

He removed a pad from his pocket and flipped it open. He tapped a page where he'd written the vet's name.

"One night at an old warehouse, I heard some of the men talking about that vet, how he took care of stud bulls. When I regained consciousness years ago, I had a card in my pocket with the name of a cattle breeder on it. I thought if the vet worked with that breeder, he might remember me."

"That's the reason you were at Dr. Huckleberry's today?" Melissa asked.

Smith nodded.

"What happened when you got there?" Melissa asked.

"Those gunmen were dragging the vet's body into the barn. One of them said something about taking care of Harry, then the other guy saw me and fired. I ran for cover. I guess that's when I dropped the bandanna."

"Did you recognize the men or their voices?"

He shook his head. "No, I wish I had. But that detective showed up and fired at me, too, and I had to get the hell out of there."

Dex appeared at the doorway with a scowl. Judging from his expression, he'd overheard their conversation. "I thought you said you didn't have any ID on you when you regained consciousness."

"I didn't," Smith said. "This was a business card." He

removed it from his pants pocket and offered it to Dex. "It had the name of a cattle breeder on it. I thought it probably didn't mean anything, but went to talk to him."

"What happened?" Dex asked.

"It was a dead end. The man claimed he had no idea who I was. Said he passed his cards out all the time. I could have picked it up at a ranch or restaurant or rodeo."

"But you kept the card all this time?"

Smith nodded. "I don't know why. But it was all I had to go on."

Melissa saw the wheels turning in Dex's mind. "What is it, Dex?"

"That breeder's name was on a flier in the vet's office." Dex drummed his fingers on his thigh. "It might not be related, but I'm going to question this guy myself."

Jim stood. "I'll go with you."

"No." Dex held up a warning hand. "I'm sticking out my neck for you with my brother. You need to lay low. Stay here and out of trouble. If the police discover Melissa is allowing you to stay here, she'll be arrested for harboring a fugitive."

"I don't want to get her in trouble," Smith said.

"Then let me do the grunt work." Dex took the card from Smith. "One way or the other, I'll get to the bottom of this mess."

DEX HOPED HE wasn't making a mistake in trusting Smith. But he did trust Melissa, and if there was any truth to Smith's story—and to his allegations against Lamar, which Dex did not want to believe—he couldn't stop digging.

He'd give that card to Lucas and see if he could lift a print. If Smith was in the system and dangerous, he'd get the man away from Melissa.

"I'll leave my car here and ride with you," Melissa offered.

Dex shook his head. "It's been a harrowing day, Melissa. Go home and rest. I'll let you know what I learn."

Melissa looked hesitant but agreed, and Dex insisted on walking her to her car.

"Thank you for trusting me and listening to him," Melissa said as he opened her minivan door.

He tightened his jaw. Trust didn't come easy. The one man he'd completely trusted had abandoned him and his family. And now this man he barely knew was making allegations that Lamar, the man who'd mentored him, was dirty. "Just be careful around Smith. Don't let your guard down, Melissa."

Melissa squeezed his arm, tension simmering between them, a reminder of the kiss they'd shared earlier and where it might have taken him.

Dammit. He missed having her in his arms. Although he'd been with other women over the years, no one triggered his emotions the way Melissa did.

But most of all, he missed her sweet smile. If heaven had angels, Melissa Gentry was one of them.

He didn't deserve an angel.

"I'll follow you home and make sure your house is secure." But this time he wouldn't go inside. That would be too dangerous. Too tempting.

"You don't have to do that, Dex. I've been taking care of myself my entire life."

That made him even sadder. She not only took care of herself. She took care of everyone else.

It was time someone took care of her for a while.

"I'm following you," he said bluntly.

Her gaze locked with his, heat flaring.

But she didn't touch him again. She climbed in the minivan, closed the door and started the engine. He hurried to his SUV. He glanced back at the shelter just before he pulled away, and saw Smith hovering in the shadows, watching.

Something about that man disturbed him. Made the hair on the back of his neck stand up.

He needed to figure out what it was. If he was lying and using Melissa and him, he'd put an end to it.

No one would hurt Melissa while he was around.

Chapter Thirteen

Dex conducted another quick search of Melissa's house after he followed her home. Satisfied she was safe for the moment, he hurried away before he succumbed to temptation and asked if he could spend the night.

He paused in the driveway, grabbed his laptop and researched Emmet Wilson. The cattle breeder had an impressive website detailing his expertise and breeding techniques, complete with photographs of prize cattle he'd bred and testimonials from ranchers who'd used his services.

All positive, which made him wonder if the man only allowed positive reviews.

Dex skimmed for details. Wilson utilized natural services along with artificial insemination, genomic-enhanced EPDs, or Expected Progeny Differences, timed estrus synchronization, embryo transfer and sexed semen. He'd also been working with the newest tool, gene editing.

The man owned a large ranch about forty miles from Austin. Night had set in, and the country roads were deserted as he passed small farms and houses on his way. At one time when he was little, his father had talked about expanding his herd at Hawk's Landing. Dex and his brothers had ridden with him to an auction house and watched as his father bid for the best deal.

Dex had been infatuated with the auction process and

the speed with which the bids were made. His father had studied the cattle from the auction catalog in advance so he was prepared to make the best choice for the ranch.

He was on the verge of expanding the herd when Chrissy went missing. But he'd put those plans on hold while he spearheaded the search parties day and night.

When he hadn't come home that last morning, his mother had assumed he was still out searching. Dex's father had been obsessive about not giving up and had spent long hours combing different parts of the ranch and area by the swimming hole.

By day two, his mother was frantic that something bad had happened to him.

She'd called the sheriff who'd issued a bulletin for his father and his truck, but nothing had turned up. No phone calls. No message or word. No sign of him anywhere.

Emotions flooded Dex, the memories as painful and vivid as if it had happened yesterday.

He blinked and scrubbed a hand over his eyes, then spotted the sign for Wilson's Breeding.

He veered onto the narrow, paved road that led to the main area of the property. A traditional ranch home sat on a hill overlooking the barns and stables spread across the land.

Dex parked in front of the house. As he left the truck and headed to the front door, the sound of cows mooing drifted in the hot air. Once his father left, his mother had slowly sold off their stock. She and her teenage boys couldn't keep up the business, and none of their hearts were into the ranch.

Lately, with the addition of the foster girls, he and Brayden had added horses, and had offered riding lessons to the teens.

The door opened, jarring him back to reality. A short robust man with graying hair and reading glasses perched on the end of his bulbous nose stood in the entry.

"Mr. Wilson?" Dex asked.

"Yeah. What can I do for you?"

Dex removed the business card from his pocket and handed it to the man. "By now, I'm sure you heard about the shooting at the Lend-A-Hand Shelter."

Wilson pushed his glasses up with a crooked thumb. "Yeah. Some guy named Smith. Heard the police are looking for him."

"That's right." Dex studied the man but Wilson showed no reaction to Smith's name. "Smith had his card with you. He said he came to see you a while back. He claims he has amnesia and thought you might know his name."

Wilson cut his eyes to the side and seemed to mull over the information. "I do recall some fellow stopping by saying he didn't know who he was, but that was a long time ago."

Dex nodded. "He also claims someone is trying to kill him." He showed Wilson a photo on his phone. "This is Smith. Maybe you can take another look and something will ring a bell."

Bushy eyebrows raised, Wilson leaned forward and studied the picture. "Can't say it does. But I meet a lot of folks in my business. I could have met him at an auction and don't recall it. Or he could have picked up my card at one. I also visit the rodeos and I work with a vet named Dr. Huckleberry. He keeps cards in his office to hand out to interested clients."

Frustration filled Dex. He was getting nowhere.

"Did you talk to Dr. Huckleberry?" Wilson asked. "Maybe he knows this guy Smith."

Dex shifted. "Actually, I went to see him earlier, but I'm afraid he was dead."

Wilson's eyes widened. "Huckleberry is dead? God... How?"

Wilson's reaction seemed sincere. "He was in the stall with one of the bulls and had been gored. But two men were there and shot at me, so it's possible he was murdered, and they put him in with the bull to cover it up."

The color drained from Wilson's face. "Good Lord. Poor guy." He scratched his chin. "Do you have any idea who'd do such a thing?"

Dex shook his head. "I was hoping you could tell me that."

MELISSA WAS ACCUSTOMED to living alone, but the rental house felt empty now. She missed Dex. His masculine scent lingered, taunting her with the fact that their earlier kiss had almost led to the bedroom.

She phoned April to inform her that they could get in the shelter the next day to reopen. April offered to relay the news to the other volunteers and to Another Chance Shelter. The men she and Dex had transported there could return to Lend-A-Hand if they wanted.

Melissa rolled her shoulders, her muscles aching. The red marks on her throat were turning dark purple now.

Shivering with the memory of her attacker's hands around her neck, she undressed and showered, letting the warm water soothe her frazzled nerves.

She closed her eyes, savoring the scent of rosewater in her body wash, and scrubbed her body and hair clean. Willing the water to wash away the haunting memories of nearly dying twice, she stood beneath the spray until the water started to turn cold.

Finally, she dried off and pulled on a T-shirt and pajama shorts, then padded to the kitchen and made a cup of hot tea. She needed to sleep and to forget about how close she'd come to death.

Dex could distract her…

Her suitcase caught her eye, but she fought the instinct to pack and run. She couldn't leave yet. Not until she knew what had happened to Bill's friend Harry, or who Jim Smith really was. Or if the shootings and the vet's death and the missing homeless men were connected.

Dex wanted answers about his father, too. She wanted them for him.

Then she would leave town and find a place to start all over again like she had so many times before.

A place where she could permanently put her fantasies about Dexter Hawk behind her.

"Mr. Wilson, do you have any idea why someone would want to kill Dr. Huckleberry?"

Wilson fidgeted and glanced past Dex. "I have no idea. Everyone I know liked the doc."

"Were you two friends?" Dex asked.

Wilson shrugged. "More like business acquaintances. He treated my animals. I respected that and paid him well for it."

"Did he have any enemies?"

Wilson blinked rapidly and shoved his glasses on the top of his head, making his graying hair stick out. "Not that I was aware of. He was married once, but his wife ran off a couple of years ago." He arched a brow. "You think she'd do something like this?"

"I don't know," Dex said. "Was their relationship tumultuous?"

Wilson shrugged again. "Huckleberry worked all the time. She got lonely, entertained herself elsewhere if you know what I mean."

So she'd cheated on him. But that would have given the vet motive to hurt her, not the other way around. "How about financially?"

"Hell, she wanted everything, but he fought her."

"That's certainly a theory the police will investigate," Dex said, although he couldn't imagine a woman dragging her husband into a stall with a raging bull. Then again, she could have hired those men to kill her husband, and he and Melissa showed up at the wrong time.

He made a mental note to ask Lamar about the man's will and if his wife had an alibi. He could check into her financials.

"Or, hell, maybe someone broke in and wanted to steal drugs," Wilson suggested.

"That's another possibility," Dex agreed.

"Did Dr. Huckleberry keep bull sperm at his place?" Dex asked.

Wilson shook his head. "No, the seed we use is locked away tight and secure."

Dex retrieved the recent picture of his father. "Mr. Wilson, one more question. Do you recognize this man?"

Wilson examined the picture. A shake of his head accompanied his response. "Don't know him. Like I said, though, I could have met him at an auction. They draw a crowd."

Dex swallowed disappointment, then assessed the photo of his father taken twenty years ago. "How about this man?"

Another look, then Wilson's gaze rose to his. "Don't think so. Why? You think these men have something to do with Dr. Huckleberry's death?"

"Maybe," Dex said. "Although they didn't kill him. These two photos are of the same man. And he's dead."

"Who is he?" Wilson asked.

"My father, Steven Hawk. He went missing about eighteen years ago. I'm trying to find out what happened to him."

Wilson looked confused at the change of topic. "Are you one of the Hawks who own that big spread, Hawk's Landing?"

"Yes, sir, that's my family."

Wilson grunted. "Sorry I can't help you out more with

your questions. But if your family needs any breeding or studs, let me know."

Dex bit back a retort. Wilson might claim he knew nothing, but even under fire, he was pushing his business. Still, he seemed nervous about the vet's murder.

Did he know more than he'd admitted?

MELISSA HAD STRUGGLED with insomnia since she was little. Living on the streets and in shelters had taught her to always keep one eye and ear open for trouble. Dangers lurked everywhere.

Bad men. Drug addicts. Pimps. Thieves. Vandals. Pedophiles.

She hadn't known at the time what that last word meant, only that some men liked little girls. Even inebriated, her father had kept her close for protection.

It was the one honorable thing he'd done.

She tried to put memories of those nights aside as she crawled into bed. But they plagued her in the night.

She was five-years-old. She clenched her raggedy doll to her chest as she stumbled along after her father. He hugged his brown bag to him like it was his lifeline, sipping from the bottle inside.

He called it his liquid courage. Said he needed it to get through the day.

She hated the stinky smell, and the way it made him forget things sometimes. Like where they were going or that they hadn't eaten all day. That he got sloppy and fell and sometimes they didn't make it to the shelter. They'd sleep in the park, which she didn't mind as much as the dirty alleys where it smelled like rotten food and nasty beer and pee.

She saw men relieving themselves as if the alley was their toilet, and always covered her eyes. She didn't like the way they looked at her, as if she was doing something wrong, not them.

A grungy man in an army-green coat unzipped his pants and smiled at her as if he was going to show off his thing. She turned her face into her daddy's sleeping body and hid her eyes, burrowing into him as tight as she could get.

The next day when she'd told him about it, he'd gotten mad. Then he'd dragged her to a shelter and left her by herself. Said little girls didn't belong on the street.

She'd cried and begged him not to leave her with strangers, but he'd shaken off her hands and walked away.

That night she'd lain on the cot alone and stared at the ceiling, willing him to come back. She'd heard noises outside, loud voices. Arguing.

The walls shook and the door bust open...

SHE JERKED AWAKE, trembling, her senses on edge. A noise. She heard it outside.

The window rattled. A banging. Wood creaking.

Fear bolted through her.

Someone was trying to break in.

Chapter Fourteen

Dex decided to stop by the hospital before heading home. The doctors should have had time to treat Melissa's attacker.

Maybe he'd be awake by now.

Normally he'd trust Lamar to call him. But with Lamar's warning, he didn't expect to be looped in on the investigation until Lamar was ready to tie it up.

He drove straight to the hospital and parked, then went inside to the ER. He recognized one of the nurses and approached her.

She was in her midforties, with a passel of kids at home. The plump, tenderhearted woman treated all of her patients as if they were her children, too. She'd assisted the doctors in stitching him up a couple of times when he'd been injured on cases.

He quickly explained that he'd witnessed the shooting and fudged slightly, implying he was working with the police. "Was the man moved to a room?"

She checked the records. "Yes, third floor."

"He was unconscious with no ID when he was admitted," Dex said. "Do you know his name now?"

She shook her head. "Afraid not. A detective named Lamar put a detail on his room. Haven't you talked to him?" she asked with an eyebrow raise.

"At the crime scene, yes," Dex replied. "But I had a couple of other leads to look into so haven't spoken to him in the last hour." He thanked her with a smile. "I'll go upstairs and see if the man has regained consciousness."

Her phone was buzzing on her hip, and she gestured to it, so he headed toward the elevator. A siren wailed outside, and an ambulance rolled up, sending nurses and doctors scurrying.

He slipped into the elevator and rode it to the third floor, then got off.

Dex checked the room numbers and veered to the right. Voices echoed from the nurses' station on the corner, and people rushed down the hall. A Code Red blasted over the intercom, and a nurse wheeled a crash cart toward the door where nurses and doctors had gathered.

His instincts kicked in, and he picked up his pace. A guy in scrubs rushed past him, heading toward the elevator. Dex moved on, his pulse hammering as he neared the room.

The code was in Room 312, the room where his John Doe was.

A uniformed officer stood at the door, on guard, his face strained as a doctor ushered him out of the way.

"What's happening?" Dex asked as he reached the officer.

The officer shrugged, his stance tense. "Don't know. I went to take a leak, came back, and the prisoner was struggling for air. I pushed the call button and all hell broke loose."

Dex tensed as he watched the nurses and doctors scrambling to try to save the bastard. One doctor was doing CPR, his movements steady. The nurse with the crash cart rushed in, pulled out the paddles and shocked him. The man's body jerked, but the steady beep of the machine beside him indicated he had no pulse.

More voices. The doctor ordering them to do it again.

Another shock. Then another. Then another, each time

more intense. The man's body jerked and fell back against the bed, no sign of breathing or life.

A nurse checked the clock. Read the time. Looks were exchanged. Then the doctor put the paddles aside and pronounced the man dead.

Dex cursed beneath his breath. That bastard might have had the answers he needed.

But now he was just another body added to the count. They were piling up fast.

And he was no closer to learning the truth.

MELISSA CLENCHED THE sheets and listened. Outside, the wind was silent. No storm.

The noise...the back door rattling. Someone trying to turn the doorknob.

Her lungs squeezed for air.

What if it was another shooter connected to the vet's death?

Slowly she reached for her phone on the nightstand. She pressed 9-1-1 as she slipped from bed, and ducked into the closet.

"9-1-1, how may I assist you?"

"This is Melissa Gentry. Someone is trying to break into my house." She quickly gave the operator her address.

"Please stay on the line—"

Melissa shoved the phone into the pocket of her pajama bottoms and snatched the rifle Dex had given her from the closet. Her fingers trembled as she gripped it.

The noise grew louder. The door rattling. She tiptoed into the hallway. A few steps toward the kitchen and she stared at the back door. The knob was definitely turning.

Through the glass in the upper part of the door, a shadow hovered outside, jiggling the doorknob.

Fear nearly paralyzed her. Would the police get here in time?

She pressed her back against the wall, forcing herself to remain still so the intruder couldn't see her through the glass.

Suddenly the window shattered. She trembled and raised the rifle.

A gloved fist shot through the broken glass, clearing shards of glass, then he reached inside and tried to unlock the door.

She stepped closer, close enough she thought the intruder could see her through the opening. He was a big guy, broad shoulders.

She aimed the gun dead center at the man's chest. Then she cleared her throat. "Go away or I'll shoot!"

She held her breath, praying he'd back down. But the door burst open and the man lunged at her. She tried to get off a shot, but he jerked her arm up and the round hit the ceiling. Plaster rained down and she struggled to hold on to the weapon, but he slammed her backward against the wall. Her head hit the wood so hard that the world spun.

Calling on moves she'd learned in a self-defense class, she brought her knee up and aimed for his crotch. He dodged the blow and clawed at the rifle. Another bullet dislodged and hit the wall. She screamed and shoved at him, but he was too strong.

He growled and backhanded her across the face. Her head snapped back, and her control on the gun slipped.

He snatched the rifle from her hands, then flung her across the room. She grappled for control, but her head hit the corner of the wall, and she slid to the floor.

She blinked through blurry eyes and tasted blood.

But she couldn't give up. She crawled to her knees, desperate to see what he looked like. Burly. A beard. Shaggy hair. Dark clothes. A scar across his cheek.

He aimed the rifle at her.

Her life flashed behind her eyes. She'd done good by helping others.

But she wanted more. She wanted love. A family of her own. A real home that she'd never had.

He took a step closer, his menacing expression sending a shiver through her.

Dear God, she didn't want to die...

DEX WANTED TO slam his fist against the wall. Everywhere he turned, he hit a dead end.

"Was anyone in the room with the prisoner before he coded?" Dex asked.

The officer shrugged. "Just the staff. A nurse earlier. The man seemed fine. Just sleeping." He paused and rubbed his chin as if thinking. "Later, a male nurse came in. Put something in the guy's IV. I figured it was pain meds."

Suspicions rose in Dex's mind. That IV could have held something that killed the man.

The doctor appeared at the doorway, wiping perspiration from her damp forehead. "I'm sorry, Officer. He didn't make it."

"What happened?" Dex asked.

The doctor narrowed her eyes at Dex. "Are you family, sir?"

Dex shook his head. "No, but—"

"I can't discuss this with you," the doctor said. "Either get his family here or I'll talk with the detective in charge."

The doctor's phone was ringing. She answered it, then rushed to a room across the hall.

The officer guarding the room stepped aside to phone Lamar. Dex turned to the nurse. "Did you find out his name?"

She shook her head. "There'll be an autopsy. Maybe the ME can give you insight into his identity."

And an exact cause of death.

The image of the male in scrubs he'd passed rushing toward the elevator surfaced, and Dex hissed. If those scrubs were a disguise, the man could have slipped something in that IV to cause the suspect to have a heart attack.

Inside the room, the doctor had covered the suspect with a sheet and the machines had stopped beeping, the silence eerie.

A minute later, the officer returned, his face stoic. "Detective Lamar said you need to stay away from here."

Dex worked his mouth from side to side. "I just want answers."

The officer attached his phone back on his hip. "Maybe so. But he asked if you'd been in to visit this man. Said you had reason to want him dead."

"Lamar implied that I killed him?"

"Not in those words."

Anger churned inside Dex. Lamar knew him better than that. But this officer? "You've been here since he was brought in?"

"Yes."

"Then you know that I haven't been inside the damn room."

Furious, Dexter walked away. But he dialed Lamar as he rode the elevator. Lamar answered immediately.

"What's going on?" Dex asked. "You think that I did something to the John Doe in the hospital. I wanted—"

"Whoa," Lamar said. "I never said anything of the sort."

"Well, your officer implied it."

A grunt echoed back. "You know how cops are, Dex. Always questioning everything."

"Well, someone may have killed the guy, but it sure as hell wasn't me. I passed a man in scrubs rushing past the elevator as I headed down the hall toward our prisoner. The officer said a male nurse gave the prisoner drugs through an IV. He assumed it was pain meds, but what if someone was disguised as a nurse and killed him?"

"Can you describe this nurse?" Lamar asked.

Dex pinched the bridge of his nose, struggling to recall details. "Probably thirties, clean-shaven, medium build. I didn't get a good look at his face. Talk to your officer. Maybe he can add something."

Lamar mumbled something Dex didn't quite catch. "I'll talk to the officer about it. And I'll make sure the ME conducts a thorough autopsy and reports directly back to me."

"Also, I found out that the vet was divorced. You might want to look into her and see if she was included in Dr. Huckleberry's will."

"Dammit, Dex. I don't need you to tell me how to do my job." Lamar paused. "Hang on. I have to answer this call."

The elevator doors opened, and Dex stepped into the hallway, then walked outside.

Lamar returned on the line just as Dex reached the parking lot.

"Listen, Dex, 9-1-1 just received a call from your friend Melissa." A siren wailed. "I'm headed to her house now."

Dex bolted for his SUV. "I'll meet you there."

He jumped inside his vehicle, started the engine and sped onto the road. He shouldn't have left Melissa alone. What if someone had gotten to her this time and he lost her for good?

MELISSA STARED INTO the man's cold eyes, willing him not to kill her. "Why are you doing this?" she asked. "Why kill me? I don't even know you."

His expression darkened, and he tightened his grip on the rifle. He was younger than she'd thought before. Maybe thirties. He looked rough, too, like he hadn't shaved or had a bath in days. And a knife was sticking out of his pocket.

"If you want money, take whatever I have. It's not much, but it's yours."

He kept the rifle aimed on her, but he quickly scanned the hallway.

"Or if you need help, I'll help you. I work at a shelter," she said, hoping to reach him on some level. "I can offer you a bed to sleep in and food, and if you want, I'll help you find a job."

He barked a laugh. "Shut up, lady."

Her head was starting to throb from the blow he'd given her. "I really want to help you," she said softly. "Please put the gun down."

The rifle wavered slightly, and she thought he was about to lower it. But a siren wailed outside, then flashing blue lights twirled and danced through the window.

Rage and panic shot through his eyes, and he snatched her arm. A loud pounding echoed from the front door.

Then something slammed against the side of her head. The rifle?

She grasped for control. But pain ricocheted through her temple and she felt herself falling into the darkness.

Chapter Fifteen

Dex sped onto the highway and wove through traffic. Although it was nearly 11:00 p.m., locals and tourists were still leaving restaurants and bars. The music scene in Austin drew crowds and fueled the economy. He had his favorite haunts, too.

He'd like to take Melissa to them sometime.

Fear for her made sweat break out on his forehead, and he pressed the accelerator and maneuvered past cars, then turned down a side street to avoid more congestion.

Lamar was on his way to Melissa's. She'd managed to call 9-1-1. Hopefully that was a good sign.

It had to be. The thought of anything bad happening to her felt like a knife tearing into his gut.

He whipped the SUV toward Melissa's street, his pulse hammering at the sight of the police car. Lamar had beaten him here.

He swerved into the drive, scanning the property for trouble in case Lamar needed help. He quickly checked his weapon, but kept it tucked into his belt as he slid from his vehicle and approached the house.

The front door was closed, a light burning from the back of the house. Praying Melissa was safe, he hurried toward the rear side door. It stood ajar, a thin stream of light glowing from the interior.

He inhaled sharply and crept up the stairs, still alert in case Lamar had walked into an ambush and needed backup. He paused at the door to listen for voices or signs of violence, but inside it was quiet.

Too quiet.

With one hand on his weapon, ready to pull it, he inched forward, then peered through the open doorway. A creak of the floor made him hesitate, then suddenly the barrel of a gun appeared in his face.

A second later, Lamar whirled in front of him.

"Whoa, it's me," Dex growled.

Lamar cursed and lowered the gun, his face half hidden in the shadows. "Hell, Dex, you just about got yourself shot."

"I thought you might need help," Dex snapped.

"Sorry." Lamar wiped a hand over his face. "Didn't hear you."

"Where is she? Is she okay?" He didn't wait for a response. He pushed past Lamar to look inside and halted.

A rifle on the floor. Blood splattered on the wall. Melissa's?

Please, God, no.

He inched forward. A look to the left. A man's body was sprawled on the floor, blood pooling beneath his chest, his eyes wide and vacant.

"I got the bastard," Lamar said.

"What about Melissa?"

Lamar gestured toward the right.

Melissa lay on the floor, too, blood seeping from her forehead.

"I called an ambulance," Lamar said.

Dex barely heard Lamar. His heart was hammering so loud the blood was roaring in his ears.

He crossed to Melissa and knelt beside her, then checked for a pulse. He held his breath, waiting. Praying.

Finally he felt it.

She was alive.

For a second, he dropped his head forward and said a prayer of thanks. Swallowing against the emotions clogging his throat, he gently stroked a strand of blood-tinged hair from her cheek. "You're going to be okay, darlin'."

He lifted her head and pulled her in his lap and pressed a kiss to her cheek. "Hang in there. I'm going to take care of you. No one is going to hurt you again."

He hugged her, clinging to her as if she might die if he let go.

Finally, the sound of a siren. The ambulance arriving.

He cut Lamar a look and saw his friend watching him with interest. Typically he didn't wear his emotions on his sleeve. He'd learned to silence them, banish them around other people. Look cold. Hard. Tough.

He couldn't help himself now. He was terrified.

And for the first time in his life, he didn't care if anyone saw it. "What happened?" he asked.

"She was unconscious when I arrived," Lamar said. "Bastard was standing over her with a gun. He fired at me, but I hit him first."

Dex nodded. "Thanks. I owe you."

Lamar's gaze met his, dark and troubled. "Just doing my job."

Maybe so. But he'd saved Melissa tonight. Dex would forever be indebted to him for that.

MELISSA FELT AS if she was floating in an endless sea of black. Something hard was hammering at her skull, beating at her to stay down. To give up and let the emptiness swallow her so the pain would stop.

Instinct whispered for her to fight. She had something important to do. Someone to see. A life to live. Dreams to follow.

All the things she'd never had awaited. She reached out her hand and tried to latch onto them, but they slipped between her fingertips and floated away like dust in the wind.

Voices echoed from the distance. Far away, but occasionally a word sifted through. A familiar gruff voice murmuring her name.

"Melissa, come back to me, darlin'."

Darlin'? Who called her darlin'?

She blinked, desperate to see the man. His tone sounded worried. Tender. Almost loving.

She wanted to be loved so badly. Her mother hadn't loved her enough to stick around. And then her daddy hadn't, either...

A warm hand brushed her cheek. Masculine fingers. A touch that made her struggle harder, drawing her back toward the light.

"Melissa, darlin', you're going to be okay. The paramedics are here."

Paramedics?

She must be hurt. Was she in an accident?

Memories tugged at her mind. What had happened? She'd come home, she was asleep. Was dreaming. Then the noise. Someone breaking in.

Her heart jumped to her throat, and she trembled.

"Shh, I've got you."

The male voice, so soothing. Comforting. Then big arms pulled her up against a broad chest. Hard but safe.

She blinked, determined to see his face. To tell him not to leave. That she liked his arms around her and his voice in her ear.

More voices. Footsteps. A door shutting. The man's arms slipped away.

She cried out for him not to leave. She was scared, although she didn't know of what. Dying?

Or of the man who'd broken in? Yes, a man. He'd

grabbed her, thrown her against the wall. He aimed the rifle at her.

He was going to shoot her.

She screamed, her body jerking as she opened her eyes. The gun was gone. The man was, too.

Dex was holding her, whispering her name. A tear slid down her cheek. "Don't leave me," she managed in a raspy whisper.

"I won't," he said in a husky voice. "I'll be right beside you."

But he released her, and two men lifted her onto a stretcher. She closed her eyes, the darkness drowning out the light again.

DEX BREATHED A sigh of relief that Melissa's vitals were stable. She might have a slight concussion and needed a couple of stitches on her forehead at her hairline, but she would be all right.

He'd been so damn grateful when she'd opened her eyes and looked at him that he'd nearly cried like a baby.

A sarcastic chuckle rumbled inside him. Lamar would have liked that. He'd always teased Dex about women, said when Dex fell, he'd fall hard.

Dex had laughed and blown off the comment. He'd insisted that would never happen to him.

But Lamar might be right. Melissa might be the one to do him in.

"I'll be right behind you and meet you at the hospital," he whispered to her as the medics secured her in the ambulance and closed the door.

Lamar had been taking pictures of the crime scene and body. Dr. Hudson, the ME from Austin, arrived on the heels of the ambulance, and joined Lamar.

Dex studied the dead man. "Does he have ID?"

Lamar checked the man's pockets. "Nothing in the shirt pockets." He checked his jeans. "Nothing there, either."

"I didn't see a car outside," Dex said. "How the hell did the bastard get here?"

Lamar worked his mouth from side to side as if contemplating the question. "Probably parked on another street and snuck in on foot."

True. The alleys connected side streets and offered hiding places for all kinds of nefarious activities.

Dex scanned the hallway and space around the body. "Did you find a phone?"

Lamar patted the man's clothing, then lifted the body slightly to check beneath him. A shake of his head indicated no phone, either.

Who the hell traveled without ID these days? Maybe another homeless person? But why attack Melissa?

"No drugs on him, either, but he could have been looking for cash or valuables to steal and sell," Lamar suggested.

That was a possibility, especially in Melissa's neighborhood. But why did he sense the break-in was connected to the case he was working?

Dex glanced at the ME. "Doc, what killed the bastard in the hospital?"

Dr. Hudson's brows furrowed. "He was just transported to the morgue. I haven't had time to perform the autopsy yet."

The poor doc must be working overtime these days.

The ME knelt by the dead man, speaking low into a mic attached to a recorder as he examined the body.

Dex was still trying to piece together what had happened tonight. "Melissa was unconscious when you arrived, Lamar?"

"Yeah, I told you that. The intruder turned the rifle on me. I had no choice but to shoot him."

Lamar snapped a picture of the rifle. "This belong to your friend?"

Dex shook his head. "I gave it to her for protection."

"Good God, Dex. You know people who aren't experienced with guns often get killed by having the weapon turned against them."

Dex nodded. But the thought of Melissa being unarmed seemed even more dangerous. "Look where she lives, man. She's nearly been killed twice this week. She needed protection."

Lamar shook his head as if he still didn't approve.

"What about him?" Dex asked. "Was he armed?"

Lamar lifted a bag containing a hunter's knife. An image of the man holding that to Melissa's throat sent a chill through him. The jerk could have slit her throat in seconds.

Dr. Hudson rolled the body to the side and shined a small flashlight on his back. "One bullet to the chest. No exit wound. Bled out."

Lamar indicated his service revolver. "My weapon. The bullet will match. It'll all be in the report."

A knock sounded at the door, and one of the crime workers poked his head in. "Sergeant Eames and Officer Rafferty reporting."

Lamar met them at the door and explained the scene. The investigators booted up and entered. Officer Rafferty headed to the bedrooms to search for evidence, although judging from the broken glass in the window, the man had entered through the back doorway and Melissa had met him in the hallway. Scuff marks and blood marred the floor and walls leading toward the living room, but the fight had ended in the hallway.

"I'm going to the hospital to check on Melissa," Dex said.

He didn't want her to wake up and be alone.

Maybe the guy who'd attacked her had said something

before he'd knocked her out. Something that would reveal his motive.

And if he was working for someone, maybe he'd given her a name.

MELISSA SLOWLY MADE her way back to reality. The doctor at the ER examined her and stitched her head. Two stitches. It wouldn't leave much of a scar.

Not that she cared that much about a little scar. She'd almost died.

She gripped the sheet as the nurse left the room. A second later, Dex walked in, his face a mask of anger. But his look softened as he approached her.

"Melissa?"

"I'm okay," she said softly. "I just want to get out of here."

"The doctor said you might have a concussion. You should stay the night for observation."

Tears filled her eyes. She hated hospitals, had seen too many sad stories of people from shelters who went in and never came out. "Please just take me home."

A muscle ticked in his jaw. "You're not going back to your house tonight. If the doctor releases you, I'll take you to Hawk's Landing."

Melissa had heard about the ranch from Dexter years ago. And then the stories in the press. She'd even seen pictures Dex had shown her. It was a beautiful place.

And his mother had turned it into a refuge for girls in trouble.

Dex traced a finger along her hand, his breathing ragged. "I know you probably don't want to talk about it right now. But I need you to tell me what happened tonight."

Emotions crowded her chest as memories of the night returned.

"This man, he broke in," she said in a low whisper. "What happened to him?"

"Lamar shot him. He said he found him with my rifle aimed at you." His voice cracked. "He saved your life, Melissa."

So now she was beholden to the detective.

But images of the man threatening to kill her returned. Then the look in his eyes when she'd pleaded for her life.

For a moment, she'd thought he intended to put down the gun. Leave her alone. Run.

But then…the siren. And he'd hit her and she'd blacked out.

After that, she had no idea what had happened.

Dex leaned forward, his thumb brushing the bandage where the doctor had stitched her up. "Did he say anything before he knocked you unconscious? Was he looking for money? Drugs?"

"No," she whispered. "I offered him money, but he told me to be quiet. I tried to persuade him to let me help him. Then the siren wailed and he…maybe he panicked. That's when he hit me."

Dex's gaze locked with hers. "I'm sorry. I should have been with you."

"It wasn't your fault, Dex."

"Maybe it was. I'm the one asking questions. If I hadn't been hauling you all over the place with me, you'd be safe."

She hated the guilt in Dex's voice. He didn't deserve that.

She reached for his hand, determined to reassure him. "Please get me out of here. Then we can talk."

She'd do everything possible to convince him that he had nothing to feel guilty about.

When she'd been on the brink of death, thinking of him had given her a reason to live.

Chapter Sixteen

Melissa's head throbbed as Dex drove, but she was so grateful to be leaving the hospital that she dared not complain, or Dex would have her admitted. Still, she closed her eyes and rested, although it was difficult to rest with the attack still fresh in her mind.

A half hour later, Dex passed under a sign for Hawk's Landing. She studied the property through the window. Moonlight glinted off the fields and pastures, the acres rolling out in an endless sea of green.

"This is beautiful," she murmured. "I can't imagine growing up with all this open space."

"It was pretty amazing," Dex said. "Until Chrissy disappeared."

That terrible event had marked his life.

He gestured toward a big farmhouse. "That's the main house where Mom lives with the foster girls."

"It's lovely," she said. "It looks homey."

"Mom has made it that way." Dex pointed out the horse stables, barns and cabins on the property. "Harrison and Honey live in that one," he said. "Honey helped design their house. She also worked with Charlotte and Lucas to design theirs and recently helped Brayden and his wife, Mila, build."

"I read about the project Honey undertook in Tumbleweed. She sounds amazing."

Dex nodded. "You know she grew up with nothing, though. Had a bad childhood. Her father was known as the town drunk."

Melissa's gaze locked with his. "Are you implying that we'd have something in common?"

A small smile tugged at the corner of his lips. "I think you'd like her. And Charlotte. She runs an art therapy program for troubled girls."

"I read about that when her studio was attacked." Melissa shivered. "Did you help your brother shut down that trafficking ring?"

"All my brothers and I had a hand in it." Dex sighed. "It was rough seeing what those girls went through. But at least now they have a chance at a life."

Like she tried to give the men hope at Lend-A-Hand.

Dex parked in front of a log cabin that backed to a wooded area. A front porch held a porch swing, and a hitching post for horses was built to the side.

"I have a small apartment in Austin, but I thought you'd like it out here better. It's peaceful and away from the city."

"You have a place in Austin, too?"

He nodded. "Above my PI office. But it's pretty bare. Only one bedroom." He parked and cut the engine. "Anybody could track me down at my office. The ranch is more secure. Harrison installed that security gate and cameras when Mom decided to foster the girls."

Melissa unbuckled her seat belt, but her legs felt shaky as she slid from the SUV. Dex hurried around and took her arm.

"You can lean on me," he said, his voice gruff.

"Thanks. I do feel a little unsteady."

"The doc said to watch you tonight. If you feel sick, you have to tell me."

In spite of the throbbing inside her skull, she managed a weak smile. "I'm fine, Dex."

The sound of horses neighing echoed from the pasture nearby as they made it up the porch steps. A slight breeze stirred the trees, a welcome relief from the summer heat. Dex unlocked the door, and Melissa felt as if she'd come home.

A log cabin quilt hung on the wall over a dark leather couch with a crocheted afghan tossed across the matching leather chair by the stone fireplace. The living area and kitchen were one big room with a vaulted ceiling and exposed beams. Picture windows flanking the fireplace offered an expansive view of the ranch.

"This is stunning," she said softly.

"Thanks. It's home."

Something she'd never had. He'd seen her unpacked boxes, the suitcase perched in her room, ready to be packed up so she could leave at a moment's notice.

He escorted her down a short hall to a bedroom on the right. "I promised the doc I'd make sure you rested. The guest room has its own bath, so make yourself at home." He pointed out the linen closet. "Clean towels are on the shelf. I don't have many guests, but I think there's soap, too."

How many women had he brought here? She hadn't asked if he was involved with anyone.

Maybe she didn't want to know.

She suddenly realized that she was still wearing the scrubs they'd given her at the hospital. The paramedics had bagged her clothes to give the detective so he could log them into evidence.

She gestured to the scrubs. "Do you have a T-shirt I could sleep in?"

His gaze skated over her, and her skin tingled. She'd slept naked with him ten years ago. The thought of crawling in bed with him again made her body hum with desire.

But the pain in her head and the scent of blood from her attacker sobered her.

She wasn't here to make love to Dex.

He'd brought her here for protection because someone had tried to kill her.

DEX EXCUSED HIMSELF and returned a minute later with a dark gray T-shirt emblazoned with the name of the ranch on it.

"It'll probably swallow you whole," he said as he handed it to her.

Her fingers brushed his as she took it from him. "It's perfect. If you don't mind, I might rinse off in the shower."

"Of course. Do you want a drink, or some tea?"

"Better not have a drink on top of the painkiller they gave me. Maybe hot tea?"

"You got it."

The temptation to ask if she needed help tugged at him, but he bit back the words. Dammit, she'd been beaten by one man tonight. She didn't need him asking anything from her.

He went to make the tea while she disappeared into the bathroom. The shower water kicked on, and he forced his mind away from images of her naked and wet. Instead, he decided to work.

He booted up his computer and ran a search on Dr. Huckleberry. Glowing testimonials praised the doctor's reputation and care of his patients. Comments about an auction house and rancher named Vance Baxter also were interspersed.

Dex entered Baxter's name and the auction house and found comments about the rancher and his business. Nothing shady. And no complaints.

That struck him as odd. Every rancher or breeder dealt

with dissatisfied or disgruntled people. Breeding and the cattle business were big money. Money not everyone had.

A prize bull's seed was coveted and worth a small fortune.

The teakettle whistled, and he stood and turned off the gas burner. He set a mug on the counter with a tea bag ready for Melissa, then returned to his desk. He tapped his fingers on his thigh, the mystery of the missing homeless men still bothering him. He searched for the name Harry Willis, but he didn't show up in the system. Harry didn't have a record. Or a driver's license. Or any property.

Not surprising.

Curious, he tapped into missing persons' reports and searched for anything about the homeless men.

His pulse hammered. There were more than he expected. Six in the last twelve months ranging from Austin to Amarillo to Fort Worth. That was on top of the three he'd already noted that were recent.

Jim Smith's face flashed back, and he ran a search on the name. Dozens of hits. It took him a good half hour to scroll through them all. None matched the Jim Smith he'd met.

Smith claimed he'd had amnesia for years. But he hadn't mentioned exactly when he'd been attacked.

Dex rubbed his hand over his chin. Six missing homeless men didn't seem like that many, he supposed. He decided to expand the search, going back five years. Twenty-two names appeared. Many from the same areas as the recent missing men.

It would take time to review all these reports.

The bedroom door opened, and he closed his laptop for the night.

Melissa appeared in the doorway, looking small and vulnerable with her bruised face and those damn stitches. She also looked sexy as hell in his shirt.

He wanted to rip it off and make love to her.

But feeding his needs would be wrong.

So he walked to the counter, poured hot water into the mug, then dunked the tea bag into the cup. "You still take sugar?"

"You remembered?"

He nodded. There were so many things he remembered about her. One of them was how her voice had sounded purring his name when he was inside her.

Their gazes locked, and heat rippled between them.

For a second, he was afraid to move. Afraid he'd lose control and kiss her.

"You need to go to bed," he said instead. "The doc ordered you to rest."

Her face paled. "I know. But I'm not sure I can sleep."

He didn't think he could sleep, either.

"Come on, I'll tuck you in."

She laughed softly. He took her hand and walked her to the bedroom, then set the tea on the nightstand and turned down the covers.

She ran a hand through her damp hair, then looked up at him with such longing in her eyes that his body hardened.

Then she lifted her hand and pressed it against his cheek. His breath caught, the ache in his chest stirring full force.

Her eyes darkened. She released a sigh that echoed with need. Heat rose between them, and she pulled his face toward her, parted her lips and closed her mouth over his.

MELISSA HAD NO idea what had come over her. She never made the first move with a man. But she'd seen the hunger in Dex's eyes, and had remembered thinking she was going to die, and couldn't resist.

She didn't want to be alone tonight. She wanted Dex's lips and hands on her, to feel the beating of his heart beneath her hand and the whisper of his breath against her neck as he lay entwined with her.

She deepened the kiss, drawing his face closer to her, and he slid his fingers into her hair just the way he used to do. Need and desire bolted through her, and she ran her hands down his back, raking fingers over corded muscles that stirred her arousal even more.

He made a low sound in his throat, then teased her lips apart with his tongue and deepened the kiss. Their tongues mated and danced in a sensual rhythm that seemed so perfect it was as if they were made for one another.

He stroked her back and wrapped his arms around her, their bodies brushing together. She reached for the buttons on his shirt, desperate to rake her fingers across his bare chest.

But he curled his fingers around her hand and stopped her, then leaned his head against hers. Their ragged breathing echoed in the charged silence.

Insecurity seized her. "Why did you stop? Is there someone else?"

"No," he said in a raw whisper. "But you just came from the hospital, Melissa. I'm not about to make love to you when you may have a concussion."

"I feel okay," she said, although the throbbing in her temple was growing more intense.

He chuckled. "You feel more than okay to me, but you need rest. And that's what you're going to get."

She wanted to pout, but he sounded so sweet and worried that emotions threatened to send her into a crying jag.

Afraid her feelings for him were written on her face, she averted her eyes and tugged the covers over her. He tucked her in as if she was a child. It was such a protective, loving gesture, one she'd never had from her parents, that a tear slid down her cheek.

"Ahh, Melissa. Are you in pain?"

She shook her head and traced a finger along his jaw. "Stay with me for a while, Dex."

He brushed her hair away from her cheek, the sexual heat returning. A myriad of emotions brimmed in his eyes, too. Ones she didn't understand. Ones she refrained from asking about.

Because she feared the answer.

That he'd tell her he could give her one night of loving. Then he'd walk away like he had before.

She didn't want to hear that right now.

But he didn't speak. He stretched out on top of the covers and pulled her into his arms. She snuggled against him, one hand on his chest so she could feel the heat of his body and the beating of his heart.

Hers belonged to him.

It terrified her. But she realized now that it always had.

HE WAS IN TROUBLE. Deep trouble.

Melissa Gentry was boring a hole in his hardened heart and climbing in.

He slowly stroked her hair, willing himself to stay strong and keep his hands off her, which was damn near impossible.

Finally she drifted to sleep. The bruises on her face and her neck looked darker tonight. Stark against the moonlight shimmering through the window.

Fury railed inside him at the fact that someone had physically hurt her.

She sighed in her sleep, her breathing growing steady. Thank God she'd survived.

He needed to watch her. Wake her a couple of times and make sure she didn't have a serious head injury.

Although she'd looked at him with such desire that he'd almost forgotten about the case and why he'd brought her here.

He couldn't forget. Protecting her was his job at the moment. When he figured out what was going on, though, they'd part ways. They'd have to.

He could not lose himself in a woman.

You already have, buddy.

Body wound tight with anxiety, he eased her hand from his chest. Dammit, he missed her sweet touch.

But he didn't deserve her.

He eased off the bed, gently settling her head against the pillow and making sure she was covered. Then he tiptoed from the room.

He needed to work. Too late to call Lucas, though. Besides, Charlotte was due any day now. She needed him.

Still, he texted him about the business card and prints and told him that he'd leave the card in an envelope on the table by the door so Lucas could swing by, pick it up and carry it to the lab.

Unable to sleep, he walked into the kitchen for a drink.

But as he bypassed the arrowhead collection on the wall by the door, nostalgia hit him. Memories of him and Chrissy hunting for the arrowheads. They'd made up stories about how the arrowheads ended up on Hawk's Landing.

A noise echoed from the bedroom, and he hurried to check on Melissa. She was still sleeping, but had rolled to her side.

The need to hold her seized him, but he returned to the den.

He slid in front of his laptop, booted it up and checked hospitals and morgues for Harry Willis. Nothing popped.

Then he decided to search records of missing homeless men that had been reported, this time dating back fifteen years.

His pulse jumped. Several more names appeared. Two that were close to Tumbleweed. Two that occurred around the time his sister went missing.

Sheriff Dunar, the sheriff who'd investigated his sister's

disappearance and then his father's, had been notified of the missing men.

He studied the names, then poured himself a beer and went outside to think. Tomorrow he'd talk to the former sheriff and see what he'd learned about the men.

If someone had been preying on the homeless eighteen years ago and had continued all these years, they were dealing with a serial predator.

It was time to stop him before he killed again.

Chapter Seventeen

Dex checked on Melissa several more times during the night. Satisfied she was all right, he finally snatched a couple of hours of sleep himself, then rose and made coffee. He carried his mug to the porch to watch the horses run and to keep himself from crawling in bed with her.

He had to focus. Today he'd talk to that rancher, and Sheriff Dunar.

God, his father had loved this land. Had worked hard to build the ranch. He'd also seemed like such a family man. Granted, he'd worked him and his brothers, and he'd sure as hell disciplined them, but he'd used a gentle hand.

Finding out Chrissy wasn't his father's birth child had been a shocker to him and his brothers. But apparently his father had known years ago, had forgiven his mother, and had loved Chrissy as if she was his own.

Those damn arrowheads were nagging at him. Smith had talked about a rock formation—

"Dex?"

Melissa's voice jolted him from his thoughts. Morning sunlight dappled her beautiful face and cast subtle red streaks in her dark hair.

He wanted to run his fingers through it again.

Oh, yeah, he had it bad.

"There's coffee," he said.

She stepped onto the porch and offered him a smile, gesturing to the mug in her hand. "Thanks. I found it."

She still wore his damn T-shirt, which came to her knees and looked like a dress on her. He wondered if she had underwear beneath it.

She eased into the rocking chair beside him and pushed it with her feet, her gaze traveling across the pasture. A black stallion galloped on the hill, its mane flying in the wind as it ran.

For a moment, they settled into a peaceful lull where he imagined waking up with her like this every day. Sharing morning coffee together on the porch after a long night of lovemaking. Then they'd saddle up and go for a ride to the creek...

And one day there'd be a kid running around in the yard. A little boy. Or maybe a girl. It didn't matter. He'd teach him or her to ride, and they'd go to his favorite fishing spot and then picnic by the pond.

He bolted up from the chair. Good God, what had gotten into him? He'd planned to stay single forever. Had never wanted to be a family man because it hurt too damn much when that family fell apart.

"Dex?" Her voice sounded worried.

"I'll fix us some breakfast."

"I'll help."

"No," he said more brusquely than he'd intended. The last thing he needed was Melissa in his kitchen, planting memories of the two of them cooking their morning meal together. That seemed even more intimate than sharing a bed.

"Last night I did some research after you fell asleep. There have been several more reports of missing homeless men the past eighteen years. I'm going to talk to the former sheriff about them."

She stood. "Okay. If you drive me home, I'll change and go with you."

"No, I should do this alone." He gazed back at the pasture, anything to distract himself from her. "Besides, the cleanup crew is scheduled to come to the shelter. I'll drive you there to meet them."

She agreed, and he left her on the porch to enjoy her coffee while he scrambled some eggs. He needed some distance between them today to get his head straight. She wouldn't be safe until he solved this case.

And he'd never walk away from her while she was still in danger.

MELISSA LIKED WAKING up and having coffee with Dex. Maybe too much. She yearned to do it every day.

He obviously didn't feel the same way. He'd almost looked panicked when she'd joined him, then he'd bolted inside as quickly as he could.

She blinked away tears. This nasty headache and the trauma of being shot at and attacked were making her weepy and...weak.

She couldn't fall into the trap of believing a relationship with Dex would last. It hadn't before. And he hadn't changed.

Had he?

She swallowed disappointment as the answer screamed in her head.

She breathed in the fresh air and scent of grass and wildflowers, and finished her coffee. Today she'd get the shelter back in shape. Then she could start back to work.

Work was exactly what she needed. Focusing on helping others distracted her from silly dreams that would never come true.

Dex poked his head out. "Breakfast is ready."

"Thanks." She stepped inside and joined him at the table,

although an awkward silence fell between them. As soon as they finished, he cleared the table, and she hurried to dress. The scrubs were a stark reminder of what had happened the day before.

In the car, she texted April to inform her about the cleanup crew, then they stopped at her house. The sight of fingerprint dust and blood made her pause as she entered, and a shudder coursed through her as she relived the break-in.

"You okay?" Dex asked in a gruff voice.

She squared her shoulders, determined not to fall apart. "I need to clean in here, too."

"When the crew finishes at the shelter, they can come here."

She valued her independence, but she wasn't a fool, either, so she agreed. She didn't want a repeat of the night before. It might not end with minor injuries this time.

She hurried into the bedroom, stripped the scrubs and dressed in jeans and a T-shirt. A quick exam in the mirror, and she winced at the dark circles beneath her eyes and the bruises on her forehead and neck.

No wonder Dex had avoided her this morning. She looked as if she'd been run over by a truck.

Reminding herself it didn't matter, she grabbed her purse and joined him in the hall where he was waiting. He was studying the place where her attacker had died.

"Something wrong?" she asked.

"I don't know. Lamar shot your attacker in the chest. I was just thinking that from where you were lying, if the intruder was facing you, when Lamar rushed in, he would have been behind the bastard." He made a sound of frustration. "Lamar must have identified himself, and the guy swung around to face him, then Lamar shot him."

"That makes sense," Melissa said.

Dex nodded, although he remained quiet as they drove

to the shelter. When they arrived, he scanned the property and walked her to the door. The cleanup crew hadn't yet shown up, but they went inside. Dex hurried to the bunk room to see if Smith was hiding inside.

But he was gone.

"WHERE DO YOU think Smith would go?" Dex asked.

"I don't know. He's scared." Melissa sighed. "Even without a threat, it's hard for these drifters to stay put. Moving has become a way of life. It's easier than getting attached and having to say goodbye."

His eyes darkened. "Is that the way you feel?"

She shrugged. "Moving is all I've ever known."

Another reason he needed to maintain his control. He'd had too many people walk out on him to chance it again. He'd seen that suitcase waiting and ready.

Hell, after this was over, he couldn't blame her if she did want to move.

The crime scene cleanup crew arrived, and he showed them in, then explained about Melissa's house.

He didn't want to leave her alone, but at least people were here, and it was early morning, so she should be safe.

"I'm fine, Dex. I have some work to do in my office anyway."

"Call me if you need me."

Their gazes locked again, heat and emotions simmering between them.

"I'll be back in a little while." She nodded, and he left and drove to the former sheriff's cabin on the lake.

Harrison had been elected as sheriff when Sheriff Dunar retired. He and his wife had settled into a peaceful retreat in the woods on the river.

Sheriff Dunar's graying hair was patchy, his face thin and drawn. Although his belly suggested he probably enjoyed a beer or two while fishing.

"This is funny," Sheriff Dunar said. "Just saw your brother Harrison a few months ago. And now you're here." He shoved a fishing hat on his head. "I was sorry about your daddy."

Dex swallowed. "Yeah. Thanks."

"Is that why you're here? 'Cause I thought he had an accident."

"He did." Dex explained about the shooting at the shelter and his theories regarding the missing homeless men. "A couple of homeless men also went missing near Tumbleweed around the time Chrissy disappeared. Do you remember those reports?"

Dunar stared out at the woods. "Yeah. Homeless Joe and Creepy Karl," Dunar said. "Never found either of them, but Joe was a roamer. He'd been sleeping on the streets for years. Took odd jobs at different ranches for a while when he was younger. But after he had an accident with a bull, he landed near Tumbleweed."

"You knew him?" Dex asked.

Dunar shrugged. "I saw him around town a few times. Seemed harmless. Think he and Honey Granger's daddy were drinking buddies."

"Who reported him missing?" Dex asked.

"Ethel Wiggins from the Baptist church. She volunteered carrying meals to the needy."

"I'd like to talk to her," Dex said.

"Afraid that's not possible," the sheriff said. "She passed about five years ago."

Dammit. "And Karl? Why did they call him Creepy?"

"He was touched in the head," Dunar said. "Used to string arrowheads together and wear 'em around his neck, then talked to himself all the time. Nothing coherent."

Dex frowned. He and Chrissy had found dozens of arrowheads on Hawk's Landing.

There were arrowheads all over Texas, though. Didn't mean Karl had found any on the ranch.

He folded his hands, thinking. "The report on Chrissy's disappearance indicated that a homeless man was a person of interest."

Sheriff Dunar's bushy brows bunched into a unibrow. "Yeah, but that old man died of liver failure."

A dead end there. Unless someone had killed him and covered it up.

"Are you sure?" Dex asked.

The sheriff folded his arms. "That's what the ME said. Why are you asking about these men? They were drifters. They moved around all the time. And to tell you the truth, once your sister and then your daddy disappeared, they took priority."

Dex had mixed feelings about that. Selfishly he wanted his family to take priority, but…the sheriff shouldn't have ignored these reports, either. "I think someone has been preying on homeless men, and that they've been doing it for nearly two decades and have gotten away with it."

Shock streaked the sheriff's eyes. "What? That's crazy."

Dex shook his head. "Maybe not." It was possible that his father had been one of the victims. Someone could have poured that alcohol down his throat.

He needed to talk to the ME who'd autopsied his father. Make sure there weren't injuries that could have caused him to crash other than alcohol. The booze could have been the killer's way of covering up his crime.

A dark thought crept into his head. His father, the missing homeless men…if he was right, the crimes had begun on this man's watch. Sheriff Dunar had been the only law enforcement eighteen years ago.

What if he'd known what was going on and had kept the truth hidden all these years?

MELISSA AND APRIL spent the morning in the office while the crime scene crew cleaned up the common area in the shelter. April notified the other agencies to inform them that they were open again.

"The volunteer at Another Chance said they haven't seen Gunther in over twenty-four hours," April said.

"Do they have any idea where he went?"

April shook her head. "He said he'd found some work, and that he was going to take it."

That could be a good thing. "What kind of work?"

"He wouldn't say. She heard him talking about cattle to one of the other men, so maybe he'd gotten a job as a ranch hand. But when she asked him, he clammed up."

Melissa rubbed her temple. Her headache was returning in full force. She hoped Gunther had found work and was trying to get back on his feet. But considering what had happened the last few days and Dex's suspicions, worry gnawed at her.

The crime scene cleanup crew finished, and Melissa gave them her home address. "I'll meet you there."

"Mr. Hawk is sending a repairman to fix your broken window."

Yes, that needed to be done.

She thanked them, then left April to finish ordering supplies and straightening the bunk room. Outside, she phoned a cab to drive her home. But a noise from the alley startled her, and she jerked her head around.

A low moan reverberated from behind a trash can. Heart racing, she inched toward the alley.

Another moan. The trash can rattled. Then a bloody hand reached around the side of it and clawed at the ground.

Chapter Eighteen

Fear seized Melissa at the sight of the bloody hand reaching toward her from the back of the trash can. Could be a drug dealer or victim of a crime. Or… Jim Smith. God, maybe someone had killed him and left him in the alley.

She pulled her phone from her pocket, but a voice called for help, and she rushed forward. She couldn't see the man, but blood covered his fingers, and bloody prints marked the wall behind the dumpster.

She inched closer, scanning the area for trouble. Footsteps pounded the pavement down the alley. Pulse hammering, she veered around the edge of the dumpster.

"Help me…" the voice rasped.

A man in ragged jeans and a bloody plaid shirt lay facedown as he tried to crawl away from the wall. Emotions clogged her throat as he heaved for a breath.

Gently she caught his arm and rolled him to his side. Not a stranger or Smith. Gunther.

His face was ghost white, his eyes bloodshot and wide-eyed, his mouth gaping open as he struggled to draw a breath. Blood soaked his chest and both his hands, and pooled beneath his body. A drop of blood seeped from his nose.

She sat down on the ground beside him and pulled his head into her lap, soothing him with gentle strokes along his cheek. With her other hand she dialed 9-1-1. "Send an ambulance. Hurry, a man is hurt badly!" She gave the operator the address, praying Gunther made it.

His body jerked and convulsed, then he spit blood as he tried to speak.

"I'm here, Gunther," she murmured. "Hang in there, help is on the way."

He gasped, choking on garbled words. His bloody hand rose to claw at her arm, but he was so weak it fell to his side, and a moan rumbled from him.

"Please, Gunther, hang in there. You have to tell me who did this so I can make him pay."

Another gasp. A siren wailed close by. Coming closer. The ambulance would be there soon. More noise down the street. Voices. Arguing. Someone running. What was going on?

She scanned the street, praying whoever had hurt Gunther wasn't still lurking around.

The bloody hand clawed at her arm, urging her closer. He was going to tell her who'd done this.

She leaned closer, but his ragged breath puffed out. His eyelids flickered closed, then open, then his eyes rolled back in his head.

Panic made tears burn her eyes. "Gunther, please, hang in there," Melissa whispered.

The siren wailed again. Louder. Tires screeched. Lights twirled in the parking lot of the shelter.

She rocked Gunther in her arms, begging him to stay alive. But another breath rasped out, and it turned out to be his last. He died in her arms.

DEX PHONED BAXTER to verify that he was home before he made the long drive to the man's ranch. The housekeeper informed him that Baxter was at the auction house, so Dex headed that direction first.

He'd done his research this morning before Melissa had woken up. Vance Baxter had inherited his land from his father when Vance was only eighteen. Vance's father died of a heart attack while driving his herd from one pasture to the next, and had collapsed right on their land.

According to his research, Vance's mother fell ill and died a year after she lost her husband. Just as it had in his own family, the ranch went downhill after that.

Four years after Vance's father's death, the property was about to go into foreclosure. But Vance had taken business classes by then, and he managed to sell off a portion of land he wasn't using to have cash to work with. Then he hired Emmet Wilson, to help him fine-tune his stock. Wilson's techniques had garnered Vance a prize stud. Selling the stud's sperm earned him enough profit to expand his herd, and his business took off. A couple of years later, he opened the auction house.

A large sign advertising the upcoming auction schedule hung in front of the auction house. Two trucks with trailers were parked to the side of the main building. A barn and pens for housing the cattle when they were transported here for auction day sat to the left while another building lay to the right.

Dex parked in front. The auction house looked simple and basic, but expensive deals were made in this facility. Vance Baxter had gone from nearly losing his family ranch to accumulating a small fortune. His business practices had earned him respect in the ranching community. If Vance's father had lived, he would have been proud.

Dex knew what it was like to lose your father.

Then Vance had lost his mother, too. Those losses could have crushed him, but they seemed to have driven him to success. It was difficult not to admire him because he was a self-made icon in the ranching community. Ranchers traveled from all over Texas and even from other states to purchase one of his studs.

Although Dex had heard that Vance could be ruthless in business. Maybe his success had gone to his head? Or had he made his fortune by taking advantage of others?

A man in overalls and a cowboy hat strode from the building and climbed in one of the trucks that was hitched to a trailer. His scowl made Dex wonder just what had transpired between him and Baxter. He was leaving with an empty trailer, too.

The sign out front indicated the next auction was at six that night.

Was the rancher returning for the auction?

A couple of workers exited another building to the left as Dex slid from his SUV. A blonde woman with big hair and heavy makeup greeted Dex as he entered the front door. Her ruby-red lips parted into a grin as her gaze skated over him.

"Hey there, cowboy, you here to register for the auction?"

Dex offered her a small smile. Melissa, with her simple clothes and no makeup, was far more attractive than this dolled-up female. "No, I'd like to talk to Vance Baxter."

She checked the calendar. "Do you have an appointment?"

Dex shook his head. "No, but I think he'll see me. Just tell him Dexter Hawk from Hawk's Landing is here to talk to him. I'm interested in his services."

A lie would get him through the door faster than the truth.

The girl excused herself, then returned a minute later with Baxter behind her.

He was in his forties now, tall and lean with a goatee and silver streaking the hair at his temples. Although he was dressed in a Western shirt and jeans, he wore an expensive-looking gold watch and a gold signet ring with the logo for his business etched on it.

"Thank you for seeing me." Dex extended his hand and Baxter shook it. "Dexter Hawk."

Baxter gave a slight nod of recognition. "I met one of your brothers a while back. You own Hawk's Landing, right?"

Dex nodded. "Sure do. We've been hearing about your success for a while now."

The man grinned. "Thanks. Come on back." Baxter motioned for him to follow, and Dex walked behind him through a set of doors, then down a narrow hall to a massive office on the right. Sleek cherrywood furniture mixed with metal bookshelves gave the place a rustic yet classy feel.

Photographs on the wall showcased Baxter accepting numerous awards for his breeding and included pictures of satisfied customers and their purchases—a testimonial for his business obviously meant to impress potential customers and buyers.

"So, Mr. Hawk, my receptionist said you're interested in my services. I thought you and your brothers were focusing on the equine business."

Dex offered a small nod, surprised that Baxter knew that much about him and Hawk's Landing. "Yes, at this point we are. But we're open to expansion. You're familiar with our ranch?"

"You and your family have been in the news a lot lately."

Dex grimaced at that comment.

"I was sorry to hear about your daddy," Vance said, his voice sincere. "A shame after all these years that it turned out that way."

"Yes, it was," Dex said. More than a shame. "You have an impressive operation. Congratulations on your success."

"Staying relevant is key," Vance said. "I try to keep up with the latest science and breeding techniques. So far, it's worked." He lifted a brochure from a stack on his desk and pushed it toward Dex. His chest puffed up with pride as he described his connection with Emmet Wilson.

"If you're interested in expanding the cattle side of your operation, I'm holding an auction tonight. Six o'clock."

"Maybe next time. I'll certainly discuss it with my brothers," Dex said.

Baxter leaned back in his chair and folded his arms, scrutinizing Dex. "So, why are you really here, Mr. Hawk?"

Dex forced himself not to react, although he'd been scanning the room and the man's desk, and he noticed a business card tucked beneath the brochures. The logo and name looked familiar.

The PI, Clark McTruitt.

"If you've followed the news, I suppose you've seen the story about the woman at the Lend-A-Hand homeless shelter being attacked."

Vance's eyes narrowed. "Yes."

"The man who broke in was a private investigator, Clark McTruitt. Did you know him?"

Vance averted his gaze. "Afraid not."

Dex raised a brow. "Really? That looks like his card on your desk."

Baxter gave a shrug. "He could have stopped in a while back. To tell you the truth, I deal with so many people, I forget."

Yeah, right. "So you didn't hire him?"

"Hire him?" Baxter grunted. "Why would I need a PI?"

"I don't know, that's why I'm asking," Dex said.

Baxter straightened, running his fingers over his bolo tie. "Why do I sense you're interrogating me now? What is this really about?"

Dex maintained a neutral expression, although the air in the room became charged with resentment. "McTruitt broke in looking for a homeless man named Jim Smith."

Baxter flattened his hands on his desk. "Again, what does that have to do with me?"

"Smith claims he has amnesia, said he was attacked years ago. He remembers coming to this auction house."

Baxter averted his gaze. "I don't know anyone named Jim Smith. That said, my auctions draw hundreds of people at any one event, so I can't possibly know every one of them."

Baxter knew more than he'd admitted. Dex had to push a little harder. He removed his phone, then showed Baxter a picture of his dead father. "I think my father was homeless before he died. I've also discovered there are more than a dozen homeless men who've disappeared over the past two decades across Texas. Two disappeared around the time my father did eighteen years ago."

Baxter frowned. "What exactly are you implying, Mr. Hawk?"

"I think someone is preying on homeless men." He listed the names of the most recent missing men. "I also think someone hired McTruitt to kill Smith before he could remember what happened when he was attacked."

A calm rage seethed in Baxter's gray eyes. "I wish I could help you, but I can't. Now, it's time you left. I have business to attend to."

"Don't you think it's strange that the vet you work with was murdered?"

Shock bolted across Baxter's face. "Murdered? I thought one of the bulls attacked him."

Dex shook his head. "Whoever killed him put him in that stall so it would appear accidental."

Another tense second passed. "That's horrible. I certainly hope they find out who did that. But I can assure you his death has nothing to do with me." Baxter dropped all pretense of being nice. "I don't appreciate you coming here under the guise of wanting to work with me, Mr. Hawk. If you need to talk to me again, go through my attorney."

Of course he'd lawyer up. That only made him look guilty to Dex.

"Understood, but if you know anything about Dr. Huckleberry's death, or McTruitt, or these missing homeless men, then you need to speak up or you could be considered an accomplice to murder."

Baxter shot up from his seat and gestured toward the door. "Get out."

Dex simply smiled and thanked him, then stepped into the hallway.

His cell phone buzzed just as he passed the receptionist. Her wary gaze indicated she'd overheard their conversation.

His phone buzzed again as he stepped outside, and he checked the number. The ME from Tumbleweed. He quickly connected. "Dexter Hawk."

"It's Dr. Weinberger. You asked me to review your father's autopsy report."

"Yeah. Did you find anything?"

"As a matter of fact, I did. The tox screen was definitely positive, but there was a serious contusion on the back of your father's head that wasn't consistent with the accident. It cracked his skull."

Dex froze by his vehicle. "The back of his head. He hit facedown on the steering wheel."

"Exactly."

"Then it's possible that that blow to the head could have killed him?"

"Yes, it's possible."

Dex's pulse pounded. If it had, then it meant his father's death wasn't a DUI accident.

He was murdered.

Chapter Nineteen

The realization that his father had been murdered echoed in Dex's ears. "Is there anything else you can tell me?"

"Yes. With this much alcohol in the man's system, it suggested he was an alcoholic, but there was no signs of liver disease in the autopsy. In fact, his liver was in great shape."

Dex contemplated that information. "So it's possible that someone forced the whiskey down his throat, then killed him and staged his death as an accident?"

"I can't say with all certainty, but it's possible."

Dex's pulse hammered. Why would someone have killed his father? Was his murder related to the other missing homeless men?

"I'm sorry, Dex, I understand you and your family have been through a lot."

"Thanks, I appreciate your help," Dex said gruffly. "What we want now is the truth."

He ended the call, then dialed Lucas as he got in his SUV and started the engine. Lucas sounded slightly harried as he answered.

"Everything okay?" Dex asked.

"Yeah, but Charlotte was having some contractions. Turned out to be a false alarm. Braxton-Hicks. We just got back from the hospital. But I did pick up that card and dropped it off to have the prints analyzed."

"Thanks, Lucas." He paused, then pushed on. "I asked Dr. Weinberger to review Dad's autopsy."

Lucas sighed. "And?"

Dex relayed his conversation with the ME. "You'll probably think this is a long shot, but there were two other homeless men who disappeared around the time Chrissy and Dad did. I think it's all connected. That Dad was murdered because he knew something about it."

A long pause. "All right, we'll look into it. I'll compile a board with all the facts you've uncovered so far and persons of interest. Send me anything else you've dug up."

His phone was buzzing with another call. Melissa. Dammit, what if something was wrong?

"Melissa's calling, Lucas. Let me make sure she's all right."

They agreed to meet to review the information they'd gathered and pool their mental resources, then he quickly connected to Melissa.

A ragged breath echoed over the line, making nerves coil inside his belly.

"Melissa? Are you all right?"

Another second passed, then a low cry. Fear stole his breath.

"Talk to me, darlin'. What's wrong?"

"It's Gunther…" she said in a raw whisper. "I found him…dead…outside the shelter."

Dexter pressed the accelerator and swung onto the highway. "Hang on. I'm on my way."

Terror for Melissa choked him as he sped toward the shelter.

APRIL JOINED MELISSA outside the shelter while they waited on the ambulance and police.

"Poor Gunther," April said with tears in her eyes. "The volunteer at Another Chance said he was excited about that work. And now…he'll never have a chance to get his life back together."

"I know, it's not fair," Melissa said.

"Do you think he was attacked by a thief or gang?" April asked.

"Dex thinks the other missing men are connected to Jim Smith." Melissa hesitated. "Maybe Jim Smith uncovered what was going on with them, and someone tried to kill him to cover it up."

The ambulance rolled up, a police car on its tail. Medics jumped out and rushed toward her, and Detective Lamar exited his vehicle and followed. "What happened?"

"I came outside to catch a cab to go home, and I heard a noise in the alley." The image of that bloody hand reaching for help flashed behind her eyes. "Then I found Gunther bleeding and…gasping for breath."

The detective tugged his gun belt up on his hips. "You know the victim?"

Melissa nodded. "He stayed here at the shelter. He was…a good guy."

Melissa stepped away from Gunther. April hovered beside her, twisting her hands together.

A second later, the ME arrived and walked over to them. One of the medics stood with a negative shake of his head indicating there was nothing they could do, then addressed the ME. "We'll transport him when you're ready."

Detective Lamar crossed to Gunther, pulled on gloves, then stooped down beside the ME who was conducting his own examination. Melissa strained to hear their conversation, but they spoke in hushed tones.

The detective snapped a few photos on his phone, then made a phone call before turning back to her. "A crime team is on the way. Ms. Gentry, did you hear anything or see anyone else when you came out here?"

"I heard voices farther down the alley. But I didn't

recognize them or hear what they were saying." Melissa massaged her temple. "Then I thought I heard footsteps running."

"This is a busy part of town with bars nearby," the detective pointed out.

Melissa shifted. That was true.

The sound of tires screeching halted their conversation, and Dex sped into the parking lot, jumped out and jogged toward her.

Detective Lamar acknowledged him with a grunt. Concern darkened Dex's eyes. "Are you okay?"

She nodded. Emotions thickened her throat. "I found Gunther in the alley, but…he didn't make it."

Dex scanned the alley, then glanced at the body. "What was the cause of death?"

Detective Lamar jammed his hands on his hips. "Bled out from a gunshot wound to the chest. Close range."

"What caliber of gun?"

The detective pulled a baggie from his pocket and dangled it. ".45. Bullet was a through and through. I'll log it into evidence and see if it matches any from another crime."

The ME strode toward them. "I'll do the autopsy as soon as possible. But I have a couple stacked up in front of him."

Detective Lamar turned to Melissa. "Do you know who his next of kin is?"

Melissa blinked back tears. So many of the homeless died alone with no one to mourn them or give them a proper burial. She hated for Gunther to be added to the list. "He didn't have any family."

"Then he'll be buried by the county," Detective Lamar said.

"No," Dex cut in. "I'll cover the cost of his funeral."

Melissa's heart melted at Dex's generosity. His thoughtfulness and respect for the people she tried to help moved her more than words.

He was such an honorable man.

No wonder she'd fallen for him ten years ago, and was falling for him again.

DEX STUDIED THE scene as the crime workers arrived and began to comb the alleys and trash cans for the murder weapon and forensic evidence.

He was damn glad to see that Melissa was all right. Upset, but at least she wasn't harmed.

She and April retreated inside the shelter to tie up plans so they could reopen, although he wondered if another murder so close to the shelter might make them rethink that decision. He sure as hell didn't want her anywhere near this place.

But telling Melissa that would only cause an argument. She was determined to help others at any cost to herself.

For God's sake, someone had to protect the damn woman.

A plan formed in his mind. He'd arrange for security cameras for the exterior of the premises to be installed. Simply having them in place would deter some criminals from approaching, and the cameras would help capture the goings-on around the shelter. Better security should have been put in place a long time ago.

But these facilities operated on government funds that were slim and didn't leave room for extras.

He had a little money put aside. He'd make it his mission to help if he could.

The ME walked over to where he stood by Lamar and addressed the detective. "When your crime techs finish with their pictures, you can have the body transported to the morgue. I'll be there working."

Detective Lamar nodded. "Shouldn't be long."

Dr. Hudson scowled at Dex. "I heard your ME in Tumbleweed pulled my report on your father."

Dex bit the inside of his cheek. "I did. And he told me something you failed to mention."

Dr. Hudson raised a brow. "I put everything in my report."

Detective Lamar glanced between the men. "What's this about, Dex?"

Dex spoke in a lethally calm voice. "Dr. Weinberger said my father had a cracked skull from a blow to the back of his head. That blow could have killed him, but you didn't mention it."

The ME squared his shoulders, chin jutted up in challenge. "That injury looked old. I didn't find clear evidence to substantiate that it was COD."

"Then maybe you made a mistake," Dex suggested.

Irritation flared in the doctor's eyes. Detective Lamar stepped in. "Dex, don't start throwing stones. Considering the amount of alcohol in your father's bloodstream, and the trauma to the front of his head, Dr. Hudson's conclusions seem spot-on."

One of the crime techs motioned to Lamar, and he hurried over to the dumpster. Dex followed, curious. The male tech, who was knee-deep in the dumpster, lifted a bloody rag from the trash. "Looks like gunpowder residue on the rag. Maybe the killer wrapped it around the gun when he fired to drown out the noise."

Lamar handed the crime tech a bag, and the man slipped the rag inside. "Test it for GSR, prints and DNA. If we find a match, we can catch this guy."

Dex shifted. Maybe they'd finally gotten a lead. But if a serial predator had been killing homeless men for years, why would he be so sloppy to dump a rag with his DNA on it so near where he'd disposed of a body? And why leave this body in plain sight when so many others hadn't been recovered?

Because they aren't all connected. Some of them are just missing transients.

That was the logical answer. And it could be true—but at least *some* of them were related. Dex would bet his PI license on that.

The fact that someone had tried to kill him and Melissa proved they were on the right track.

Lamar angled his head toward Dex. "It's obvious you care about this woman. Why don't you take Melissa home and away from all this?"

"I need answers," Dex said. "Thinking my father died in a DUI accident is eating me up inside."

Lamar gripped his shoulder and gave it a squeeze. "I'm sorry for what your family has been through. Trust me, I'm here for you."

Lamar had rescued Dex when he was in trouble years ago, had mentored him and been a role model. Sure he'd skirted the line, but he never quite crossed it and was relentless in digging for the truth, always solving the case and making sure the victims received justice.

He had to trust his buddy. He wouldn't let him down. "Thanks. I think I will drive Melissa home. She deserves for someone to take care of her for a change."

Lamar's understanding expression indicated that Dex was in trouble where Melissa was concerned. Dex couldn't deny it, either.

He was drowning so deep in her sweetness, he didn't know if anyone could pull him out from under her spell.

Worse, he didn't know if he wanted to be pulled out.

"ARE YOU SURE we should reopen?" April asked. "Under the circumstances, I'm afraid letting people come here will endanger them."

Melissa couldn't shake the image of Gunther from her

mind. "You're right. We should hold off. Will you let the other shelters know?"

"Of course." April hugged her. "Are you going to be okay tonight alone?"

"She won't be alone."

Dex's gruff voice sounded protective, almost territorial. April raised a questioning brow as he approached.

"I'll guard her tonight and make sure she's safe."

Melissa started to argue, but truthfully, she didn't want to be alone. She wanted Dex with her.

"Thanks, April. How about you? Will you be okay?"

April nodded. "I called my boyfriend. I'm going to his place for the night."

"Good." Melissa hugged her again, and then turned to Dexter.

"Come on," he said. "Let's go home."

"The crime cleanup team is at my house," Melissa said. "I was supposed to meet them."

"You aren't going there now." He removed his phone from his belt and sent a quick text. "They'll take care of things and lock up. Tomorrow we'll talk about installing security cameras at the shelter and your house."

She didn't argue with that, either. At this point, anything to ensure the safety of the men and volunteers at the shelter was important.

She and April agreed to talk later, and Dex walked her to his SUV. His jaw was set tight, the silence thick as they drove back to Hawk's Landing.

When they arrived at his cabin, he ushered her inside as if he thought someone might be on their tails.

Pain radiated from him as he faced her in the kitchen. Something had happened to upset him. Something he hadn't told her yet. "Dex? What's wrong?"

"The ME's report on my father. Dr. Weinberger says he suffered blunt force trauma to the back of his head."

"I don't understand," Melissa whispered. "You mean in the accident?"

"No. He hit face forward on the steering wheel." Dex pulled her to him, his voice a husky whisper. "I think he was murdered."

The agony in his voice tore at her heart, and she couldn't help herself. She loved him so much.

She pulled him into her arms and held him, soothing him as his body shook with emotions he didn't want her to see. A second later, he murmured her name, then closed his mouth over hers.

Chapter Twenty

Melissa deepened the kiss, tugging Dex so close she felt his hard chest against her breasts. He wrapped his arms around her and teased her lips apart with his tongue, his hands skating down to her hips. He drew her into the V of his thighs, and his hard length brushed her belly through his jeans.

Need rose inside her, memories of the times they'd been together in the past returning to taunt her. She knew his touch, his kiss, the way he felt inside her.

She wanted that feeling again.

He stroked her back, then brushed her hair aside with one hand and planted soft tender kisses along her throat. Erotic sensations splintered through her. Today had been tense, sad, painful.

She wanted Dex to erase that pain. And she wanted to ease his suffering.

He lifted his head suddenly, as if sensing her turmoil. His eyes searched hers. Anguish streaked his face. He'd just learned his father was murdered.

That was eating at him, resurrecting his grief and anger, which would drive him until he found his father's killer.

She tunneled her fingers through his hair, raking a strand from his forehead. "I know you're hurting, Dex. I'm sorry about your father."

Regret flashed in his eyes. "And I'm sorry about Gunther."

Fresh tears blurred her eyes. She didn't know if she was crying for Gunther, or Dex, or because she was so in love with this strong man that she could barely breathe.

Intense emotions overcame her, and she kissed him again.

"Melissa," he murmured as she trailed her fingers down to unbutton his shirt.

"I need you, Dex," she whispered.

A low moan erupted from his throat, and he swung her up into his arms, and carried her to his bedroom. The masculine furnishings were so like Dex that she immediately felt safe and warm. He shoved the quilt back and eased her onto his bed.

Hunger darkened his eyes, and he parted his lips, his breath ragged. "I need you, too, Melissa."

She licked her lips and reached for him and he came into her arms. They tore at each other's clothes, hungry for each other's touch, inhibitions floating away as the blissful memory of making love to Dex washed over her.

Dex tossed his jeans to the floor, and looked down at her with the kind of passion that made her body tingle all over. She was naked and aching for him, and she ran her finger over his broad chest, telling him with her eyes how much she wanted him.

A wicked smile curved his mouth, and he crawled above her and angled his head for another kiss. Deep, hungry, it seared her to her soul.

She threaded her fingers into his hair, kissing him back with all the love in her heart. The kiss seemed to last forever but not long enough. It would never be enough.

Need built as he planted kisses down her throat again, then he tugged one bare nipple into his mouth and suckled her. A shiver rippled through her, and he teased the other nipple with his fingers until she clawed at his back.

She wrapped her leg around his, stroking his calf with

one foot as he moved above her. His thick length teased her thigh. Heat flared in every cell in her body.

He was relentless in tormenting her and trailed hungry kisses from her breasts to her belly.

She wanted him inside her.

But he shoved her legs apart with a groan, then dove his tongue inside her heat. He licked and sucked at her secret places until the tendrils of an orgasm began to rock through her.

"Dex," she moaned.

He rose above her, yanked on a condom, then thrust inside her. Melissa wrapped her legs around his hips, clawing at his back as he drove himself deep inside her. One thrust, two; he built a rhythm as their bodies joined together.

DEX WANTED TO prolong the pleasure, but making love to Melissa ignited every need in his body. Desire and passion swamped him as she lifted her hips and allowed him to move deeper inside her.

Her whispered moans of pleasure and kisses reminded him of how precious her touch could be. She was lightness to his darkness, a sweet balm to his aching soul.

She raked her hands down his bare back, clinging to him as he pumped inside her, and arousing him to the point of no return. Erotic sensations exploded through his body, and he murmured her name as his release claimed him.

She joined him, riding the waves of pleasure again, and crying out as another orgasm rocked through her.

His heart raced, his body shuddering against hers. He cradled her in his arms and rolled them to his side, holding her close and kissing her hair as the pleasure slowly subsided. A quick trip to the bathroom to dispose of the condom, and he crawled back in bed with her.

His desire hadn't subsided at all, though. Instead it possessed him with an intensity he'd never experienced.

He wanted her again. And again. And again.

Tonight, tomorrow…maybe always…

The thought sent a bolt of fear through him. He'd never felt this way about a woman. Had always loved 'em and walked away.

No…he'd never really loved them. He'd had sex; no love was involved.

Melissa snuggled next to him with her head on his chest, and emotions filled him. Tonight, with her, was not just sex.

The thought of anyone hurting her twisted him inside out.

She whispered his name on a breathy sigh, and he hugged her closer, then kissed her deeply. Melissa looped her arms around his neck and climbed on top of him. Hunger stirred in him as her hair brushed his chest. She tortured him with more kisses, then slid down his body, trailing love licks down his chest to his belly.

His stomach clenched, his sex hardening again.

He reached for her arms to roll her over, but she used one hand to stroke him while she ran her tongue down to the tip of his sex. Raw hunger heated his blood.

He moaned her name, and she closed her lips around the tip of him, then tormented him with her fingers and her tongue until another orgasm built.

He'd forgotten how insatiable Melissa had been. But he didn't intend to leave her behind. He pulled her above him, settling her hips on top of him and gripping them to guide her on his thick erection. Her warm wet center drew him in, and he groaned, hunger begging him to take her hard and fast. She matched passion at every level, the soft mounds of her breasts screaming for him to touch them.

He cupped them in his hands, massaging her weight, then teased her turgid nipples with his fingers and tongue until she moaned with pleasure. She lifted her hips, pulling away from him, then lowered herself again, impaling herself on him. Over and over.

Her body hugged his throbbing sex, milking him as she rode him up and down. Passion built again, and he clutched her hips, then thrust deeper and deeper until she called his name in a rush of blinding pleasure that sent them both over the edge. She clung to him while the sensations ebbed and flowed, their breathing erratic but slowly settling into a steady rhythm that filled him with a kind of peace he hadn't felt in a long time.

When they'd made love years ago, the passion had been intense, but he'd been too afraid to allow emotions into the mix. Too focused on the pain of his past and what he was going to do with his life.

Melissa had a way of soothing that pain. She made him want to think about a future.

A future that involved more than work and solving cases and running from someone who might care for him.

She made him want to take a chance on love. On them.

His throat clogged with emotions, robbing him of his words. He couldn't make any declarations or promises to her until his life was in order. Until he knew who killed his father and who'd been preying on the homeless men.

It was the only way to keep Melissa safe. And keeping her safe meant more to him than anything.

CONTENT IN DEX'S ARMS, Melissa slept like she hadn't slept in ages. She was safe and cared for, and in a place that felt like home.

Sweet images of living with Dex filled her dreams, images of a beautiful wedding on the lawn of the ranch. She wore a long white antique gown, and Dex looked handsome in his duster jacket and cowboy hat. April stood beside her as maid of honor, and Dex's family watched as he held her hand and declared his vows. A tender kiss, then a party to celebrate with his family, then he swept her into his arms and took her home. They made love long into the night, and every night after that, their love growing stronger each day.

Thanksgiving came, and Dex helped her serve meals at the shelter, then Christmas with presents for everyone in need. Then holiday dinners with the Hawks, and a little dark-haired boy with big eyes who followed Dex around like a doting puppy.

She finally belonged somewhere. Was putting down roots. Had stowed her suitcase in the closet to stay. She added some feminine touches to the house, and decorated their son's room. A map on the wall showed the places she'd moved to, while another map of the ranch hung beside it, a reminder that she was finished running.

She'd hand-painted a Home Sweet Home sign that hung over the sofa and planted flowers in the bed in front of the cabin.

Then she was pregnant again, this time with a little girl. Dex was holding her and rubbing her belly, whispering how much he loved her and their family.

Nothing could ever tear them apart.

A loud knocking jerked her from her sleep. Confused and irritated to have her perfect life interrupted, she closed her eyes and ignored it. It was probably down the street.

But reality intruded. No, she wasn't at her bungalow. She was at Dex's. In his arms.

He rolled over with a groan, irritated, too. He dropped a kiss on her cheek, then slid from bed. "I'd better see who that is."

Morning sunlight streamed through the window, a reminder that her blissful night was over. Gunther was dead. Dex's father had been murdered.

And her dream had been just that—a dream.

DEX STUMBLED FROM BED, still groggy from sleep and hating to leave Melissa. She'd felt so damn good next to him and in his arms that he wanted to stay there forever. The knocking that woke him grew louder. He yanked on a pair of jeans and a T-shirt and padded barefoot to the front door.

"Dex, it's me, Lamar."

Maybe he had news. He opened the door, anxious to hear what his friend had to say.

"You're here early. It's must be important," Dex said.

Lamar's stern expression confirmed that it was. He stepped into the cabin, his shoulders squared.

"You want coffee?" Dex asked.

Lamar narrowed his eyes at Dex, taking in his state of dress. "Sure. And you're definitely going to want some."

Dex stepped over to the kitchen and started a pot to brew. Behind him, he felt Melissa's presence and glanced sideways to see her standing in the doorway. Her hair looked rumpled, but she'd dressed. "Something wrong?"

A vein bulged in Lamar's forehead. Not a good sign. "I have to talk to you about your father's death, Dex. Maybe we should do it in private."

Dex shook his head. "You can say whatever you have to say in front of Melissa."

A flash of irritation in Lamar's eyes indicated he didn't approve, but he shrugged and laid a folder on the table.

He waited until Dex poured mugs of coffee for everyone and Dex and Melissa gathered at the table.

Dex's stomach clenched. "So what is it?"

"You're right, Dex. Your father was murdered."

Dex steeled himself against a reaction. "What changed your mind?"

"I have proof," Lamar said.

"What kind of proof?"

Lamar opened the folder, then laid a medical report on the table. "The DNA from that bloody rag matched Smith's."

Melissa gasped. "That can't be true."

"Forensics doesn't lie," Lamar said bluntly. "And neither do these." He removed several photographs and spread them across the table. "I had our tech pull pics from security cameras around the city and she found these."

Lamar gestured to a set of pictures showing Smith at the vet's, then near the stall where the man was gored by the bull. Another pic showed Smith standing over Gunther with a gun.

Melissa shook her head in denial and rubbed her hand over her eyes.

Two more photographs showed Smith with Harry Willis. Then there was a picture of Harry's dead body.

"His body was found last night in a wooded section not far from the vet's farm. Just like your friend Gunther, Ms. Gentry, he was shot."

Pain wrenched Melissa's face.

Then Lamar produced another set of photos. Photos of Smith with Dex's father.

In the first one, Smith and his father were in an alley. The next one showed the two of them hunched over a fire built in a garbage can. Then one of Smith by the pickup truck his father had crashed.

Smith was holding a liquor bottle in his hand, exactly like the one that had been on the seat beside his father's dead body.

Chapter Twenty-One

Dex's mind raced as he struggled to assimilate what he was seeing with Smith's story. Had it all been lies? Was his amnesia an act?

"I still don't believe it," Melissa said. "Jim doesn't seem like a cold-blooded killer. He kept to himself, but he made friends with the other men at the shelter."

Dex couldn't contain his fury. Smith had killed his father; that was cold-blooded to him. "Stop defending him, Melissa."

"He made friends with them so he could use them," Lamar said curtly.

"What are you talking about?" Melissa asked.

"I have a theory," Lamar said. "Smith paid the men a small amount of money to buy cattle at auction at a low price. That way the deals couldn't be traced back to him. Then he had Dr. Huckleberry fake papers showing that they were stud quality, and turned around and sold them for major bucks."

"And he killed the homeless men so they couldn't reveal their connection to him or what he was doing," Dex interjected.

"Exactly."

"If he made all this money as you suggest," Melissa said, "then why was he staying at the shelter?"

"To hide out," Lamar said.

"But Jim claims he was injured, that he lost his memory," Melissa argued.

"A story he concocted to cover his tracks," Lamar said.

"You think Baxter was in on it?" Dex asked.

Lamar began stacking the pictures back inside the folder. "There's no proof that he was. I think it was all Smith's scheme."

Dex rubbed his forehead. "So who took these pictures, and why didn't he or she stop the murders?"

"They were sent in anonymously," Lamar said. "My people are trying to track down the source."

"I want to show the photographs to Lucas. Maybe he can help us find out if Baxter was involved or who took them."

Lamar nodded, then addressed Melissa. "Do you know how to contact Smith?"

Melissa folded her arms around her waist. "No. He doesn't have a cell phone."

"That you know of," Lamar said. "He probably uses burner phones so they can't be traced."

Melissa shrugged. "I never saw him use one."

"You saw what he wanted you to see, Miss Gentry." This time Lamar's tone sounded sympathetic. "I'm sorry. But these types of people prey on innocent and trusting souls like you."

Dex clamped his teeth together. Lamar was right.

Melissa glanced at Dex. "You can drop me at the shelter. If he comes there, I'll call you."

"That's not a bad idea," Lamar said. "We could stake out the place and catch him when he shows up."

"No." A mixture of anger and fear hardened Dex's tone. "It's too dangerous."

Sympathy blended with Lamar's brusque, businesslike tone. "If you want to catch the man who murdered your father, this is our best chance, Dex."

"Trust me, Dex. He won't hurt me," Melissa said.

"It has nothing to do with trust," Dex said bluntly. "He's a killer, Melissa. There's no way we're using you as a pawn. If he knows we're onto his scheme, then he might turn on you."

DEX'S STEELY LOOK warned Melissa there was no use in arguing with him. She understood his concerns. And the detective had made a good case against Jim Smith.

But her instincts whispered that they were wrong.

Maybe she was a fool. A sucker. But something about Jim had gotten under her skin. The way he'd protected her when McTruitt had put that gun to her said he wouldn't kill innocent, vulnerable men for money.

It hurt that Dex didn't trust her. Although his emotions had to be in a tangle because this investigation was personal. How could she blame him?

He'd learned that the father he'd wanted to reconcile with for nearly twenty years had been murdered. And Lamar presented evidence that Smith had killed him.

"Stay here and get some rest," Dex told her. "Lamar and I are going to see Lucas. Maybe we can figure out a plan to catch Smith." Her earlier offer hung in the air between them. He didn't intend to change his mind.

"I need to go home," Melissa said.

"I'll take you after we finish at Lucas's."

She nodded, and decided to grab a shower while he was gone. Dex and Lamar headed outside, and she went to look out the window. The sun streaked the lush green pastures, and two beautiful black stallions galloped on a hill in the distance. Hawk's Landing was so serene and picturesque that it could have been a postcard advertising for Texas.

She studied Dex's furnishings again. The crocheted afghan over the couch, the stacked-stone fireplace that ran from floor to ceiling, the pictures of his family on the mantel. She walked over and studied each of them. She recognized his brothers from the news in the last year, and picked out Honey and Charlotte and Dr. Mila Manchester.

Dex's mother was surrounded by several teenage girls who, thanks to her loving care, looked bubbly and happy, not traumatized and beaten down from their ordeal with the human trafficking ring.

Each of the men in the family fought to protect and serve in their own way. They wore their badge of justice like an honor. Yet, instead of hardening their attitudes, they valued families and helping others.

She'd always yearned to belong somewhere, to have a family. But as much as she loved Dex, he'd left her before, and he probably would again.

Maybe if she could help find his father's killer, he could finally find some peace in his life. That could be her parting gift before she moved on. And it was time…

She padded to the bathroom, stripped and turned on the shower. The warm spray felt heavenly, yet as the water cascaded down her skin, she closed her eyes and could still feel Dex's fingers on her body, teasing and tormenting her and bringing her pleasure. She'd never forgotten his touch.

She never would.

When the water grew cool, she slipped from the shower and dried off, wishing she had another change of clothes, but these would have to do. Her cell phone was ringing as she finished dressing.

Expecting April or Dex to be calling, she rushed to answer it.

"Hello."

"Melissa, this is Jim."

Her heart stuttered. "Hey. Listen, that detective was here. He has pictures of you and Dex's father and he's saying that you killed him."

"I didn't," Jim said. "But pieces of my past have been coming back. I think they may be important."

"Tell me more."

"Some are about the place where I was knocked out, where I lost my memory."

"What do you remember about it?"

"Everything's still foggy," he said. "I'd like to go back to the place. I think it might jog my memory."

"Do you know where this place is?"

His breath rattled out. "Actually, it's near Hawk's ranch, on the border of it and the Native American reservation."

Melissa inhaled sharply. If he went to the place and remembered who'd assaulted him, maybe he could tell them who was behind the missing homeless men.

"I'm on the ranch now," Melissa said. "I'll go with you."

"That could be dangerous, Melissa."

"I don't care, I believe you're innocent and I want the truth. Dex deserves it, too. Although coming here will be dangerous for you. That cop is looking for you."

"I have to do this," Jim said. "For myself. I…have to prove I'm not who that detective says I am."

"Then come by and get me."

A tense heartbeat passed. "Are you sure?"

"Yes."

"I'll be there in five minutes."

"I'll be waiting outside." She hung up, grabbed her purse and rushed outside to watch for him. Hopefully he'd arrive before Dex returned. If not, she'd have to think of some way to convince Dex to listen to what Jim had to say.

DEX AND LAMAR met Lucas in his study where Lamar laid out the evidence for Lucas to see.

Lamar explained about the DNA on the bloody rag and relayed his theory as Lucas studied the pictures.

"DNA is damning," Lucas said. "And these photographs certainly do look incriminating."

"I talked to Baxter," Dex said. "He denies any wrongdoing, but seemed nervous when I questioned him."

"He should be nervous," Lucas said. "If we prove cattle were misrepresented at his auction house, word will spread and his reputation will be ruined. He'll probably face lawsuits, and possibly charges."

"Let's not get ahead of ourselves," Lamar said. "At this point, we just need to find Smith and force him to confess."

"You already have every law enforcement agency in Texas looking for Smith," Lucas said.

Lamar explained about wanting to use Melissa to draw Smith out, but Dex vetoed the idea again.

Lucas walked over to the whiteboard he kept in his study, flipped it over and gestured to the information he and Dex had collected regarding the case. Lucas had filled in the blanks with the names and dates of all the missing men he'd discovered in police reports over the past twenty years along with the histories of a few of the men and their families.

The dates that two of the men disappeared were only months before his father abandoned them. Could his disappearance have been connected to the missing men?

If he'd learned something about them, why hadn't he gone to the sheriff?

And why hadn't Smith killed him eighteen years ago instead of waiting until now?

"Did Smith indicate where he might go?" Lamar asked. Dex shook his head.

"What exactly did he tell you?" Lucas asked. "Other than the story about having amnesia? How and where did he lose his memory?"

Dex replayed their conversation in his head. "On some

land, near a rock formation. He said that when he regained consciousness, there were arrowheads everywhere."

Lucas drummed his fingers on his desk. "Dex, that sounds like that formation on the edge of our property. The one that borders the land owned by the rez."

Dex nodded. "You're right. I remember us hiking out there with Dad when we were little. He brought us some arrowheads he found there. That's what sparked my interest, and then Chrissy and I started collecting them."

"If Smith lost his memory there, he might return," Lucas suggested.

"Or if he's been hiring guns to cover up his scheme," Lamar cut in, "maybe that's their meeting spot."

Dex's heart pounded. "You're right. I'll check on Melissa, then we'll drive up there."

Lucas pinched the bridge of his nose. "Charlotte had some more Braxton-Hicks contractions last night, so I don't want to leave her alone. Let me take her to the house to stay with Mom, then I'll meet you at your cabin and we'll ride together."

"Sounds like a plan," Dex agreed.

Lamar's phone buzzed with a text, and he stepped outside on the porch and responded to it. When he finished, Dex hurried to Lamar's vehicle. Lamar started the engine and sped toward Dex's cabin.

Dust drifted in the air near his drive as they rounded the curve. Dex spotted an old black pickup heading away from the cabin in the opposite direction.

Lamar noticed it at the same time. "Is that one of your hands?"

"I don't think so," Dex said. "Stop at the cabin."

Lamar sped down the drive and swung the police car to a halt. Dex jumped out, sprinted up the steps and through the front door. "Melissa, are you here?"

His pulse clamored as he raced through the house. Melissa's coffee mug sat on the kitchen table, but her purse was gone. He checked the bedroom, then the kitchen again and found a note on the counter near the coffeepot.

Dear Dex,
I know you don't trust Jim, but I do. I'm going with him to the rocks to see if it will jog his memory. He wants to know the truth the same as you and I do.
Love, Melissa

Dex punched Melissa's number, and it rang several times, but she didn't answer. Dammit.

He raced back outside. Lamar was waiting by the car, a cigarette in his hand. Odd, he thought his friend had quit.

"She's gone," he said as he jumped back in the passenger side. "Let's go."

Lamar stubbed the cigarette on the ground and climbed in, a scowl deepening the frown lines on his face. "Where?"

Dex gestured toward the road. "To the rocks. Smith was in that truck and Melissa's with him."

MELISSA RODE IN silence as Jim drove from Hawk's Landing onto the bordering property, just over the line onto the reservation. The area was miles and miles from the houses and buildings that the natives inhabited, deserted, and out of sight from the highway.

A frisson of nerves rippled through her. If Jim was lying and wanted to hurt her, this would be a perfect place to do so. No one would find her.

But one look at his troubled expression, and a calmness overcame her. So far, her instincts hadn't failed her at the shelters. She wouldn't ignore them now. He didn't plan to hurt her. He wanted her help.

Jim parked beneath a cluster of trees, between a cactus

and a boulder that shielded the truck from the road. He turned to her, his dark gaze serious. "I was here."

He gestured toward the rock formation. "Over there." They sat for a long moment in silence while he seemed to be reliving a memory of the past.

His breathing grew unsteady, and he opened the truck door and got out. Melissa watched. She had to be patient and not pressure him to remember.

Quietly, she slid from the truck and followed him.

Just as he'd said, the rocks were shaped like an arrow. Gravel crunched beneath her shoes, and she looked down and saw dozens of arrowheads on the ground. Dex had a collection on his wall.

Suddenly Jim made a low sound in his throat, then placed one hand on the top of the rocks. His face turned ashen.

She inched forward to see what he was looking at and froze. Dear God. There were mounds of dirt lined up on the other side of the rocks.

Mounds that looked like graves.

Chapter Twenty-Two

Dex texted Lucas and asked him to meet them at the rocks. Fear for Melissa warred with anger. Why hadn't she called him to tell him about Smith?

Unless the man had taken her against her will…

But her note indicated that she'd gone of her own volition.

Hell, Smith could have held a gun on her and forced her to write the note.

Lamar kept a pair of binoculars in his dash, so Dex grabbed them and used them to track the pickup truck as they crested the hill. Smith had parked between a boulder and cactus, hidden. Of course, he was in hiding. He knew good and damn well the cops were after him.

And he had Melissa with him.

Lamar slowed and approached to the left, then parked off the side of the road at the bottom of the hill but far enough away that Smith couldn't see them. The detective pulled his gun as he eased from the unmarked squad car.

Dex joined him, but held up a finger signaling they had to talk. "Lamar, we have to approach with caution. If Smith is armed, we could spook him and he might hurt Melissa."

Lamar glared at him. "Listen, Dex. I'm in charge here. You are to let me take the lead."

"Right." But Lamar didn't care about Melissa personally the way he did. "Please, I just don't want her to be hurt."

Lamar's gaze met his, understanding in his eyes. "I know you're in love with her. I'll do all I can to keep her safe." He gestured toward the rocks. "Now, let's go get your father's killer."

Adrenaline spiked as they crept through the bushes toward the rocks. When they reached a small hill that offered a view of Smith and Melissa, he used his binoculars to see if Smith was armed.

"No weapon," Dex muttered.

"Don't get comfortable. He could have it hidden," Lamar said.

Dex peered through the binoculars again and focused on Melissa's face. She looked pale, nervous, as if she was afraid.

Had Smith threatened her? Was he using her as a hostage?

Smith walked a few feet around the rocks, then stooped down beside a mound of dirt. He ran his fingers over the mound, stirring dust, then picked up an arrowhead and studied it.

Melissa remained frozen, shock streaking her face.

Dex inched forward, straining to get a better look. There was another mound beside the first. Then another.

"Dammit," Dex muttered. "Those mounds—"

"Are graves," Lamar said. "We have him now. Smith led us straight to the bodies of some of his victims."

MELISSA COUNTED FIVE mounds of dirt. Five graves. Had Jim known they were here?

He reached into his pocket, and her breath caught. Did he have a gun? Could she be wrong about him?

She started to back away. Her phone was in her purse in the truck. She could call Dex.

But Jim didn't make a move toward her. His hand slid from his pocket. Instead of a gun, he held a small object, maybe a coin? He rubbed it between his fingers as he stared at the graves. His eyes looked vacant, lost in thought, his posture rigid and tense.

A slight breeze stirred the hot air. She inhaled dust as it swirled around her feet. Jim stooped down and raked at the dirt near one of the graves. What was he doing?

"I was here," he said in a low voice. "This is where it happened. Where I lost my past."

Melissa clenched her hands together. "What else do you remember?"

He angled his head toward the sun, squinting, then at the rocks as if struggling for details. Then he looked at the object in his hand and studied it.

"I came out here to meet someone," he said. "About a deal. Then I found these graves. And then…something hard slammed into the back of my head."

She sucked in a breath. "Someone knocked you out because you found the graves. Did you see who it was?"

He shook his head, his expression tormented. "But I knew something was wrong before he hit me. Before I found the graves. That's the reason I came out here."

A noise, rocks skittering behind her, jerked Melissa's attention to the space to the right of Jim. Dex was perched behind a boulder holding a gun.

"You knew where those bodies were buried because you put them there," Dex growled.

Smith swung his gaze toward Dex, his fingers stroking that coin. But it wasn't a real coin, it was wooden.

"No," Jim said. "I don't think that's what happened. I… I figured out that something was wrong—"

"What are you talking about?" Dex asked.

Jim lifted the wooden coin. Dex's eyes widened. "A wooden nickel. My daddy always told me…"

"Not to take any wooden nickels," Dex finished at the same time Jim muttered the phrase.

Jim nodded. "But I did. I realized I had."

Melissa's head swam as she tried to follow the conversation.

"What do you mean?" she asked softly. "Someone gave you that wooden nickel?"

He shook his head again. "No, the saying, it means don't let anyone cheat you. But I did." He paused, then his eyes lit up as if remembering something. "I bought a bull, thought it was a prize one, but when I went to register it, I learned it wasn't. I'd been conned."

"Someone conned you or you were the one doing the con?" Dex asked.

"I was conned. I went to the auction house to confront the auctioneer and overheard some men talking." He paused, then pinched the bridge of his nose in thought. "They were talking about how they did it."

"You mean how you did it." The detective suddenly appeared beside Melissa, his weapon aimed at Jim. "You came up with the idea. You paid homeless men to buy them cheap at auction, then forged papers to make the bulls look like stud quality and resold at a higher price." Detective Lamar heaved a breath. "Then you killed the men who helped you and buried them here just like you killed Steven Hawk and Gunther and Harry Willis and Dr. Huckleberry to cover your tracks."

The detective stepped forward, clenching his gun tighter. "Now, put your hands up. You're under arrest."

Jim raised his hands, but a challenging look glinted in his eyes. "You can take me in, but I remember what happened now. I didn't kill these men, but I know who did."

"You can give your statement when we get to the station," Detective Lamar snapped.

Dex moved from behind the rock where he'd been standing. "I want to hear what he says right now." Dex aimed his weapon at Smith. "Did you kill my father?"

"No," SMITH SAID. "I didn't kill anyone. I told you I was attacked."

"Tell us what happened," Melissa said softly.

Dex held his breath while he waited on Smith to explain. The man kept rubbing that wooden nickel, stirring childhood memories for Dex.

Smith claimed he'd been attacked in this spot, on the border of Hawk's Landing and the rez. Had his father stumbled onto what Smith was doing eighteen years ago?

Dex slid one hand into his pocket, his fingers running over the wooden nickel his father had given him. The wooden nickel…the saying…it was exactly what his father used to tell him.

Questions clanged around in his head. Questions that made no sense and seemed too coincidental to believe.

But they planted themselves in his mind anyway. Had Smith stolen the wooden nickel from his father?

Dex narrowed his eyes. "When exactly did you lose your memory?"

Smith looked down at the wooden nickel, then back at Dex, then at Lamar. "Ask your friend. He was here."

Stunned, Dex narrowed his eyes. "What the hell are you talking about?"

"Ask him," Smith said sharply.

Dex glanced at Lamar. Something akin to panic streaked his face, then Lamar suddenly bolted to the side, grabbed Melissa and shoved his gun to her head. "I'm sorry, Dex. It wasn't supposed to happen like this."

Melissa shrieked, and Dex's pulse jumped with fear. For a brief second, he couldn't move. Couldn't speak.

Smith claimed Lamar was dirty. But Lamar had been his friend…his mentor…he'd stood by him at his father's funeral…

God…all these years he'd stayed in touch with the family. Had promised that he'd never stop looking for their father.

"Lamar, tell me it's not true." Emotions thickened Dex's throat as a possible scenario formed in his mind.

"I'm sorry, Dex," Lamar said, his brows furrowing. "I really am. I never meant for it to happen, but I was young and desperate for money. At first, it just seemed like an easy way to make some cash. All I had to do was to turn a blind eye to what Baxter was doing."

"So Baxter was behind the scam?" Dex said.

"He was trying to save his ranch," Lamar said.

"And the man who broke into my house," Melissa said. "Was he working for Baxter?"

Lamar nodded."Yeah, he was supposed to take care of you."

"Why did you kill him?" Dex asked. "To cover up for Baxter?"

"Damn fool was about to leave without finishing the job."

"So you've been working for Baxter all this time," Dex said.

Lamar shrugged. "When I first realized what he was up to, I was going to arrest him, but then he offered me a lot of money to keep quiet. It was just cattle. The men who were buying it could afford it. No one was supposed to get hurt."

"But he used homeless men and then killed them," Smith cut in.

Lamar glared at Smith. "By the time I figured that out, I was in too deep. He threatened to take me down with him. I couldn't let that happen. I was in my twenties, I couldn't spend my life in prison."

"So how did my father play into it?" Dex asked. "Did you try to kill him, too? Or did you threaten to hurt us if he talked? Is that why he left? To protect my family from you?"

MELISSA TRIED TO loosen the detective's grip around her neck, but he wrapped his arm tighter around her throat, and she felt the cold barrel of the gun dig into her temple. One slip of his finger and she'd be dead.

Betrayal darkened Dex's eyes. Jim stood stock-still, his posture braced to fight. But he was holding back just as Dex was.

"Please don't do this," she whispered to the detective. "Dex is your friend."

"I'm sorry," Detective Lamar murmured. "But I can't go to prison."

Lucas Hawk appeared from behind a boulder and inched up beside Dex, his weapon drawn. "That's exactly where you're going."

"No, I'm not," the detective barked.

"I knew the minute I saw those photographs that they were fake," Lucas said. "You had them photoshopped to frame this man." He pointed toward Jim. "Because you're the one who knocked him out years ago. You're the reason he lost his memory."

At least Lucas believed Jim.

A muscle ticked in Lucas's jaw. "Drop the gun, Lamar, and let Melissa go."

Lamar shook his head and dragged her backward toward the rocks. "Come any closer and I'll kill her right here."

Melissa's gaze met Dex's. She didn't want to die.

Chapter Twenty-Three

Rage at Lamar coiled inside Dex. This man had pretended to be his friend, but he'd lied to him to cover up his criminal activities. He'd conspired to murder numerous men and was framing Smith for it. Just how far did his deception go?

"You killed Gunther, didn't you?" Melissa cried. "Why? He was trying to get his life together."

"He was coming to tell you what was going on," Lamar said. "I warned him not to, but he wouldn't listen. Damn old man had a conscience."

Dex cleared his throat. "And the man in the truck, my father, you killed him for the same reason?"

Lamar nodded. "You should have stopped asking questions then," Lamar said. "I thought you'd finally have closure."

"All I wanted was the truth. But you lied to me and pretended to be my friend."

Lamar tightened his hold on Melissa. "Like I said, you should have let it go, Dex."

Dex hardened himself to the man who'd mentored him. He had Melissa's life in his hands now. Dex would do anything to save her.

"You aren't going to murder her in front of me and an FBI agent," Dex said. "Then you'd have to kill us all."

Indecision flashed on Lamar's face, then panic, and Dex

realized that Lamar would do whatever necessary to save himself. What were a few more lives added to the death toll he'd already racked up?

"You won't get away with this," Lucas said. "I've already called for backup and spoken with my superior. You're going down, Lamar. The best thing you can do is to cut a deal with us."

"A deal?" Lamar scoffed. "You mean prison time."

Lucas shrugged. "If you testify against Baxter and give us the names of everyone involved in this operation, you might escape the death penalty."

"Baxter's men would find me, even in jail," Lamar said.

Lucas glanced over his shoulder. "At least release Melissa. Backup will be here any minute. No need in taking any more lives."

Lamar shielded himself with Melissa's body and took another step backward. "You aren't the only one who has backup. If you want your family—and I mean all of your family—to be safe, then arrange for a helicopter for me to leave the country."

Dex's blood ran cold. "What do you mean—all of our family?" Dex asked.

"Baxter has men at your ranch house right now," Lamar said. "No one is safe until I fly out of here."

"You've taken them hostage?" Dex asked, incredulous. Who *was* this man?

Not his friend. He was a liar and a cheat and a murderer.

"This is what you did before," Smith said. "You threatened to hurt them if I talked."

Lamar whirled on him, the gun still pressed against Melissa's temple. "You were never supposed to remember."

"But I do," Smith said. "I remember everything now."

Dex and Lucas exchanged a look. Turmoil darkened Smith's eyes as he looked at the two of them.

"I remember who I am," he said. "I was searching for

Chrissy when I stumbled on these bodies. Then I put it all together about the raw deal on the bull."

The blood roared in Dex's ears. "What do you mean? You were looking for Chrissy?" The wooden nickel, the rocks, the arrowheads…

His head spun…could it be true? Could this man be—

"You're our father," Lucas said, voicing the thoughts running through Dex's mind. He shot Lamar an accusatory look. "You faked the DNA report on the man in the pickup to make us think it was our dad," Lucas said to Lamar. "How did you manage that? Did you pay off the ME to fake the autopsy, to say the DNA matched?"

"I didn't have to. I managed to get my hands on Sheriff Dunar's initial files and planted false DNA in there for Dr. Hudson to use for comparison. He really believed the man in the truck was your father."

"That man was just another missing homeless man." Lucas paused. "Good thing, I had my people run Smith's DNA." He pulled his phone from his pocket and held it up. "I just got the results a few minutes ago. It was a match to Steven Hawk's."

Dex's heart was pounding so hard he could barely breathe.

Smith was…his father?

And Lamar had tried to kill him years ago.

And again in the past few weeks just as Smith—his father—had said.

Rage and a sense of betrayal seized Dex.

He hadn't recognized his father because it had been nearly two decades since he'd seen him. And with the silver hair and the scar and missing finger and limp…

Lamar had painted Smith as the dangerous one. And Dex had trusted and believed Lamar…

Instead of caring for his family, Lamar had cozied up to them. He'd pretended to continue the search for Dex's father, but he'd only wanted to make sure he was never found. Or that he never remembered the truth.

"You hired McTruitt to kill me?" Smith—his father—said.

"Damn you. You were getting too close to the truth," Lamar shouted.

"It's over, Lamar," Dex said. "The killing has to stop. You've hurt our family enough."

Lamar was shaking his head, but he looked defeated. Dex crept toward him, determined to get Melissa away from him.

"Don't come any closer," Lamar growled.

Dex stooped slowly and laid his gun on the ground. "I'm not armed." He stood upright, holding his hands in the air in surrender, then took another step. "Let her go and take me as your hostage. Lucas can make the arrangements for the chopper, and I'll fly out with you to make sure you escape." He angled his head toward Lucas. "My brothers won't shoot at you as long as I'm with you."

"He's right," Lucas says. "You should take him. It's your only way out, Lamar."

Melissa shook her head at him, mouthing no. He ignored her. No question in his mind—he'd trade his life for hers any day.

"Let her go." Dex inched closer, and Lamar shoved Melissa forward, then aimed the gun at Dex.

His father grabbed Melissa and pulled her behind the rocks. Lucas remained still, his hand on his phone. "Stay calm, Lamar. I'm calling to arrange for the chopper."

"Then you have to call the goons off our family," Dex snarled.

"When I see the chopper and we're inside," Lamar snapped. "Not before."

Lucas spoke low into his cell. His expression remained

stoic as he lowered the phone. "Done. It'll be here in a few minutes."

Lamar wiped sweat from his brow, his breathing shaky as he kept the gun on Dex. Dex was not about to let him get in a chopper or allow his family to be killed by Baxter's men.

Smith was still holding Melissa behind the rocks, so Dex signaled Lucas that he planned to make a move. A muscle tightened in Lucas's jaw, and he gave a slight nod.

Dex didn't hesitate. He quickly jabbed his elbow into Lamar's side and stomped on his instep. Lamar bellowed and jerked to the side, then Lucas fired.

Dex twisted around and saw Lamar clutch his shoulder where he'd been hit. But Lamar was quick to recover and was lowering his gun hand again. No time to waste. Dex threw himself at Lamar, and knocked the gun from his hand.

"Go save the family!" he shouted to Lucas. "Help him, Dad! And get Melissa out of here!"

"On it!" Lucas yelled. "Harrison and Brayden are on the way."

Dex and Lamar rolled on the ground, trading blow for blow. Lucas tossed his handcuffs toward Dex. They hit the ground a few feet from them. Gravel crunched.

Lucas, his father and Melissa scrambled down the hill toward Lucas's vehicle.

Lamar shoved his knee into Dex's chest and rolled him over, but Dex snatched a rock from the ground, bucked Lamar off him and threw him to his back. Then he climbed above him and raised the rock, ready to smash Lamar in the face.

Lamar heaved for a breath, fear in his eyes as he stared up at Dex. "Go ahead," Lamar growled. "I'd rather die than be locked up."

Dex wanted to kill him for what he'd done. Lamar had

deprived his family of their father for nearly two decades. Had tried to kill him and stolen his life. He'd lied to Dex and pretended to be a family friend.

All so he could keep his dirty secret safe.

All for money.

Pure hatred and contempt railed inside Dex. His hand shook. He wanted Lamar to pay for what he'd done.

Lamar shot him a challenging look, then grabbed Dex by the throat, trying to choke him.

Dex dropped the rock, jerked the man's hands off his throat, then punched him in the face so hard blood spurted from Lamar's nose. He'd broken it. Good.

Lamar sputtered, blood gushing. Dex capitalized on the moment, snagged the handcuffs, shoved Lamar to his stomach and handcuffed him. Lamar was cursing and fighting, but a kick to his kidneys quieted the fight from him. Lamar groaned in pain and curled on his side, then passed out.

Dex yanked a zip tie from his pocket and secured Lamar's feet. Then he dragged him toward Lamar's police car. He opened the trunk, hauled Lamar into it and slammed it shut.

Heart racing, he jumped in the driver's seat, started the engine and sped back toward the farmhouse and his family.

Lamar had stolen years of their family's life together. He refused to let him take another minute.

Chapter Twenty-Four

Melissa closed her eyes in prayer as Lucas drove toward the Hawks' main house. *Dear God, please let Dex be okay.*

She opened her eyes and glanced over her shoulder, hoping to see Dex, following them. But nothing...

"Are you okay?" Dex's father asked.

She nodded, although she wouldn't be okay until she knew Dex was safe.

"You remembered everything?" Melissa asked.

He nodded. "I'm Steven Hawk. My family... I lost them..." His voice cracked. "They think I abandoned them?"

Jim Smith was Steven Hawk. That had been a shock.

Compassion for Dex and his family filled her. Detective Lamar had deceived Dex. He had to feel betrayed.

She squeezed Steven's hand. "They love you and never stopped looking for you. They'll understand."

Lucas slowed to a stop by the stable, out of clear sight of the house. His brothers Harrison and Brayden were waiting, both looking worried.

"Stay in the car, Melissa." Lucas turned to his father. "You, too, Dad."

Steven shook his head. "No way. I lost my family once. I'm not going to let anyone hurt them now."

Tears blurred her eyes at the determination and love in

his voice. She searched for Dex again as Steven and Lucas climbed from the car.

A gunman stepped from inside the farmhouse onto the porch. He was standing guard, on the lookout for trouble.

Was there another man with the family? Were the foster girls inside?

Lucas and his brothers and father hovered together by the stable. They shared an emotional moment as Harrison and Brayden realized their father was standing in front of them. Brief hugs went around.

But there wasn't time for a big reconciliation yet. The family in the house were in danger.

Finally a car sounded in the distance, and she glanced back and saw the detective's car flying down the road.

Nerves ricocheted through her. Was Dex or the detective driving?

DEX FLEW DOWN the road to the farmhouse, his pulse hammering. At least Melissa was safe. But his mother, the foster girls, Charlotte and whoever else was inside… maybe Honey and the baby, and Mila and her little girl, Izzy…everyone the family loved and cared about was in that house.

Dex spotted his brothers and his father by the stable, then searched for Melissa. Thank goodness she was in Lucas's SUV.

He parked behind the stable, then eased around to the side where his brothers had met. Harrison and Brayden looked shell-shocked as they studied their father, but Lucas was laying out a plan of action.

"Backup is on the way," Lucas said. "Where's Lamar?"

"Unconscious but secure in the trunk of his car." Dex used the binoculars to gain a better view of the house. "I see one guy on the porch. There must be others inside."

Harrison raised a brow, but pulled his gun and checked it for ammo. "The question is how many?"

"We'll find out." Lucas handed each of them a small microphone to attach to their shirt collars and they quickly prepared for a team approach.

"Hold fire until we see what we're dealing with," Lucas said.

Dex and his brothers and father nodded agreement, then Lucas gestured it was time to move. They dispersed, hunching down and running toward opposite sides of the house to assess the situation.

Harrison eased around to the back, while he and Brayden moved to the sides of the house to look inside. Lucas and their father situated themselves behind a tree to watch the gunman on the front porch.

Dex peered into the living room. One gunman with a rifle standing guard over the family. His mother, the foster girls, Honey and the baby, Charlotte, Mila and Izzy were all crouched together on the sofa and chairs. The foster girls looked frightened, and had sidled close to his mother. Honey was patting little Steven on her shoulder, while Charlotte's face looked strained as if she was in pain. Mila sat beside Charlotte, stroking her back and talking in a low voice.

Dear Lord, was Charlotte in labor?

"Kitchen is clear," Harrison said over the mic.

"So are the bedrooms," Brayden said.

Dex swallowed the fear gnawing at him. He had to be calm. Save his family. "They're in the den. One gunman with a rifle. Mom, the girls, Honey and the baby, Charlotte, Mila and Izzy—they're all there."

Lucas cursed. "Anyone hurt?"

Dex didn't know whether to tell him his suspicions about Charlotte or not. "No. Scared, but everyone appears unharmed."

His brothers murmured sounds of relief.

"I'm going after the one on the porch," Lucas said in a

low voice. "Just keep watch and make sure there isn't an-other shooter outside or in another room."

"Copy that," Dex and his brothers murmured.

Dex kept his eyes glued on the family as the gunman paced back and forth in front of the women and children. Bastard. He deserved to die for frightening them.

Seconds later, grunts echoed from the front of the house. The gunman inside paused and jerked his head toward the sound, his gun raised. Dex wanted to burst through the window and tackle him, but that would be too dangerous. If the gun went off, someone could get hurt.

"One down," Lucas said a minute later. "Unconscious, tied up by the porch. Now for the inside man."

A shout echoed from the front. His father.

What the hell was he doing?"

"Dammit, Dad knocked on the door," Lucas said.

He was going to distract the second gunman, draw him out. But what if he got shot and died this time?

"Gunman heading toward the door now," Dex said. "Dammit, he has Mom with him."

The next few minutes raced by in a blur of action. "He's at the door with Dad," Lucas said. "Everyone move in."

Harrison and Brayden shouted they were storming the back, and Dex rushed in the side door through the hall to the den.

"He has Ava," Honey cried.

"I know, Lucas is at the door with them now."

Charlotte cried out in pain, and Mila stroked her hair away from her face. "She's about to have this baby."

Harrison burst in and raced to Honey and the baby while Brayden rushed to Mila. "Are you okay?"

"Yes, but I have a baby to deliver." Mila gestured to the girls. "Get some blankets and clean towels. Hurry!"

A gunshot sounded from the front. Everyone froze. "Stay here," Dex ordered.

Dex eased through the house to the front. The screened door stood open, a body on the floor of the porch. Lucas stood over it while his father stood by Lucas. "He's dead," Lucas said.

His mother was crouched against the wall inside by the door, shaking.

Dex put his arms around her. "It's okay, Mom, it's over. Everyone's safe."

She leaned against him, wiped her eyes and straightened. "Lucas, Charlotte's in labor," she shouted.

Panic flashed in Lucas's eyes, and he raced past Dex to go to Charlotte.

His father had stepped into the entryway, emotions straining his face as he looked past Dex at his mother.

"Ava?" his father murmured.

His mother's eyes flared with emotions. "Steven?"

He nodded, a tear slipping down his cheek.

His mother didn't hesitate. She dove into Dex's father's arms, and they kissed and hugged and cried.

Emotions overcame Dex. His father was home. His family was back together and safe.

Except the woman he loved was in the car waiting, alone.

RELIEF FILLED MELISSA as Dex walked down the porch toward her. Another car screeched up in the drive, and a female and male in suits climbed out.

Dex strode toward them, and Melissa slid from the vehicle. The male identified himself and the female as FBI agents.

"Agent Hawk called for backup," the female agent said.

Dex nodded, and Harrison hurried down the steps and crossed to them.

"We secured the scene and took two gunmen out," Dex said.

"Agent Hawk is a little busy right now," Harrison told the agents. "His wife is giving birth."

Melissa gaped at Dex. Charlotte was having her baby now?

"An ambulance is on the way." Harrison gestured toward the dead man on the porch and the unconscious man tied up on the ground. "So is the ME."

Dex pointed toward the detective's car. "Detective Lamar is inside the trunk, secure. He has a gunshot wound to the shoulder so will need medical aid."

Harrison explained about Lamar's involvement with the scam involving Baxter.

"Lucas filled us in when he called. We have agents at Baxter's ranch now," the male agent said. "We'll take care of Detective Lamar and the two gunmen."

Brayden rushed onto the front porch. "The baby's here!"

"Come on, Melissa." Dex tugged at her hand. "I want you to meet the family."

Melissa resisted a step. "It's family time, Dex. I'll just get a ride home."

"You're not leaving right now. Everyone is going to want to thank you for bringing Dad back to us." He pulled her hand, and she followed, nerves bunching in her belly as they stepped inside.

"Everyone's in the den with Charlotte and the baby," Brayden said.

Tears stung Melissa's eyes at the tender way Steven and Dex's mother were holding on to each other.

Steven was cradling a baby in a blue blanket, obviously Harrison and Honey's baby boy whom they'd named after him. Lucas hovered on the couch by Charlotte, a beaming smile on his face.

"It's a girl," Lucas said.

Charlotte looked up, blankets covering her as she held

the newborn to her chest. "We're going to name her Christine and call her Chrissy."

The Hawks cheered, and the young teens sang out the baby's name from the corner of the room where one of them bounced a little girl about three on her hip. That must be Izzy, Mila's daughter.

When the cheers settled down, Dex cleared his throat and introduced her. "This is Melissa Gentry. Without her, we wouldn't have Dad back."

"I didn't do anything," Melissa said. "He was looking for you all along, weren't you, Jim—I mean, Steven?"

Steven wrapped one arm around his wife and rocked his grandson in his arms. "You believed in me, Melissa. All those years I couldn't remember what had happened or who I was. I started to wonder if I was a bad guy. But you made me believe that I wasn't."

Melissa blinked back tears. For some reason, Jim—Steven—had felt like a father to her. Maybe that was why she couldn't believe anything bad about him.

The next few minutes were chaotic as the family hugged and congratulated Charlotte and Lucas. They also hugged and thanked her.

Still, she felt like an outsider with this close-knit family. They needed and deserved time alone to celebrate Steven's homecoming.

She told Dex that she needed to go the shelter and meet April so they could reopen.

"I'll drive you," Dex offered.

She shook her head. "No, you need to be with your family. You all have a lot of time to make up for."

Emotions brimmed in Dex's eyes. "I don't know how to thank you, Melissa. You saved our family and brought Dad back to us."

She blinked back tears. She didn't want his thanks. She wanted his love.

But she bit her tongue to keep from admitting that, and asked to borrow his car instead. Dex handed her the keys, and their fingers brushed.

A tingle rippled through her, and she tried to memorize his touch. It would probably be the last time she'd feel it.

Tears blurred her eyes as she climbed in his vehicle and started out for home. Her heart was breaking.

This was the very reason she didn't get involved. The reason she'd moved so much. The reason she shouldn't have fallen in love with Dex again.

He belonged here with the Hawks. They had eighteen years to make up for.

She wasn't part of this family and never would be.

Time for her to pack that suitcase and move on.

Chapter Twenty-Five

Dex didn't want Melissa to leave, but the ambulance arrived for Charlotte and the baby, and Harrison was dealing with the agents. Inside, his family was still reeling from the fact that Steven Hawk was alive.

And home.

Lucas and Steven hugged in an emotional moment as the medics loaded Charlotte and baby Chrissy to transport to the hospital. Mila assured them everything was fine with mother and daughter, but still wanted routine tests run on the baby.

"Dad, you should get checked out, too," Dex said.

"I'm fine." Steven waved off his concern. "My memories are back. And I'm home."

"I hate to leave right now," Lucas said to Steven. "We've missed you, Dad. And I want to hear everything that happened to you."

"We have time," their father said. "I'm proud of you and your brothers, son. Thank you for taking care of your mother all these years." Their father wiped at his eyes. "Now, go with your wife and my granddaughter. This time, I'll be here when you return." He glanced toward the house. "As long as your mama still wants me."

"She does," Dex assured him.

Lucas hugged Steven again and hurried to join Charlotte and the baby while the medic examined Lamar. The agents kept him handcuffed and would escort him to the hospital to have the bullet removed, then a trial and prison were waiting.

Bitterness tasted ugly in Dex's mouth. Just what Lamar deserved.

When the agents and ambulances left, he and Harrison joined the family inside. His mother opened her arms and welcomed their father home as if their love had never died.

Dex wanted that kind of love. He thought he had it with Melissa.

Only she'd seemed anxious to leave.

Emotions warred inside him, but their mother wanted answers, so he and his father explained the events that had torn their father from the family all these years.

Then he and his brothers and mother spent the next few hours filling their father in on everything that had happened on the ranch, how the foster girls had come to live with them, how Harrison, Lucas and Brayden had met their wives. How they'd begun to develop the ranch into a working business again.

"We've only just begun," Brayden said.

Their father looked down at their mother, another tear slipping down his scarred face "I missed so much, so many years with you. And the boys growing up. I...don't want to miss any more time with you guys."

"Hawk's Landing is your ranch," Dex said. "Dad, we need you around here."

Their mother pressed a kiss to her husband's cheek. "Yes, we do, Steven. I've been lost without you. Tell me you're home for good."

"I am if you'll have me, if you'll forgive me..." his voice broke, emotions overtaking him.

Ava drew him into an embrace. "There's nothing to forgive." She placed her hand over her heart. "I never thought you abandoned us. Your place is right here."

More laughter and chatter followed, and drinks were poured to toast. But as they toasted the family, Dex felt an ache deep in his soul.

Someone was missing. Melissa. She belonged here with him.

His father cornered him by the bar. "I owe Melissa so much, Dex. If it wasn't for her generous heart, I might have never remembered and come home."

"I know," Dex said. "She stole a part of my heart, too."

"Then where is she?" his father asked. "Because take a lesson from your old man. Time is precious. Love can be taken away in a heartbeat." He glanced lovingly at his wife. "Some of us get second chances, though. If you love Melissa, go after her, son. Don't waste a minute."

Dex hugged his father, then pounded him on the back. "You're right. She belongs here with me." He gestured around the room. "With all of us. But I hate to leave you when you just got here, Dad." Guilt nagged at him. "I'm sorry for not trusting you. For believing Lamar over you."

Forgiveness blended with love in his father's eyes. "Don't waste time on regrets, either. You thought I was dead. And you had every reason to believe him. You were just a kid when Chrissy disappeared, and when I did, too. You don't deserve to feel guilty."

But he had. And that guilt had hindered him from allowing anyone to get close.

Only Melissa had wormed her way into his heart anyway.

His father was right. He couldn't waste any time on the past. Judging from the way his parents kept looking at one another, they needed some time alone tonight anyway.

He gave his mother a kiss and told her where he was going. She took his hand and ushered him to her bedroom.

Dex frowned, confused. Then she removed a ring box from inside the drawer of her jewelry box and handed it to him. "This was the promise ring your father first gave me when he proposed." She gestured toward the wedding ring she'd never removed. "Later he bought me a bigger diamond. You can do the same for Melissa later if you want, but for now, maybe she'd accept this."

Emotions clogged his throat. The fact that she was giving him her ring meant more to him than words. It meant she accepted Melissa into the family.

And why wouldn't she? Melissa was the most loving woman he'd ever known. She'd seen something in a stranger's eyes and trusted it when Dex had been too blind to believe. He'd lost faith...but Melissa had restored it and given him so much more.

Too emotional to speak, he thanked his mother with a kiss, then went through the kitchen and snagged a set of keys for one of the ranch work trucks from the hook by the door. Adrenaline pumping through him, he jogged outside and drove to the shelter.

Disappointment hit him when he realized Melissa wasn't there.

Maybe she'd gone home first. He spun the truck around and sped toward her house.

Time to tell her how he felt.

He just hoped she loved him in return.

TEARS BURNED THE backs of Melissa's eyelids as she tossed clothes into her suitcase. It was better this way. Better to move on and start somewhere fresh where she could forget about Dex and his family and how much she loved the darn man.

Grateful she didn't have any sentimental mementos sitting around that needed boxing up, she snatched the picture of her and her father and jammed it in her bag. Her clothes were rumpled and messy, but who cared?

She hated to leave Lend-A-Hand, but there were dozens of other shelters where she could work. Sure, she'd exhausted a few of them in Texas, but it was a big state. Maybe she'd move to the southern end. There were always people in need.

Helping others would enable her to forget about herself. She hated needing Dex. But she did.

Tears overflowed, and she swiped at them. She'd have to be satisfied knowing she'd helped him piece his family back together again. Maybe he could finally forgive himself for his sister's death and find peace now that his father was home.

She rushed to the bathroom and tossed her makeup bag and toiletries into her toiletry case, then hurried to set it by her suitcase at the door. She was just carrying it out to her car when the sound of an engine rumbled.

She froze, one hand on the handle of her luggage as a pickup rolled into her drive. For a second, fear caught in her throat. Had Baxter sent someone after her?

But the truck engine died, and Dex slid from the truck. He looked so handsome and tall and masculine and wonderful that she almost threw herself into his arms.

But he took one look at the suitcase in her hand, and his jaw hardened. "Going somewhere?"

Her stomach clenched. "I figured it was time for me to move on."

"Why?"

Her hand was sweating so badly she dropped the suitcase with a thud against the pavement.

"Why are you leaving?" he asked.

She shrugged. "That's what I do. I help at a shelter, then after a while move to where I'm needed more."

He stared at her, emotions warring in his eyes. "What if you're needed here?"

She exhaled. "April can handle the shelter."

He stepped forward, so close she inhaled his masculine scent. Lord help her, she wanted him. "I'm not referring to the shelter."

She swallowed.

"You're running," he said boldly. "And I want to know why."

Pain knifed through her chest. "I can't stay where I don't belong," she said. "People move on."

"Not when they have people who care about them. Not when they have family."

"The people at the shelters are my family."

"It doesn't have to be that way," he said. "The Hawks care about you, Melissa. My father thinks of you like a daughter. The rest of the family is so damn grateful to you for being kind to him and bringing him back that they want you to stay, too."

She jutted her chin in the air, her chest about to explode. "I don't want your gratitude, Dex. I did what I did because that's who I am. I believed in Jim, I mean Steven, and I'm glad I did. No one needs to feel indebted for that."

"I know, you did it because you have an incredibly generous heart." He inched closer. His breath was shaky, and his lips parted, his hand trembling as he reached for hers. "And this is not about gratitude."

Hope budded in her chest. But hope was dangerous. "Then what is it about, Dex?"

He pressed a kiss to her hand, a kiss so tender that her knees nearly buckled.

"I think you're leaving because you're scared. I understand that more than you know." His breath rushed out. "I understand what it's like to feel abandoned. To shut down and close yourself off from others because you're afraid of getting hurt."

She blinked back the tears, her pulse throbbing.

"But I promise you I will never abandon you." His gaze met hers, then he dropped to his knees in front of her, removed a ring box from his pocket and held it out.

"I love you, Melissa. I want you." His voice cracked as he opened the box. A thin silver band holding an oval shaped diamond glinted back at her. "I want you to be my wife."

"Dex—"

"The ring was my mother's," he said as he removed it from the velvet interior. "It was her promise ring, and she wanted you to have it." He swallowed. "*I* want you to have it as a promise that I'll always love you, that I'll never leave you." His voice wavered. "Later, I'll buy you a bigger ring if you want. You can pick it out—"

"I don't want a big ring," she said in a raw whisper. "I don't need fancy things, Dex. All I've ever wanted was a family. And…someone to love."

"We can have that love and family together," he said gruffly. He reached for her hand again and slipped the ring on her finger. "Just say yes, that you'll be my wife."

Her heart swelled with love, and emotions overcame her. Tears streamed down her cheeks as she nodded and whispered yes.

Dex swung her into his arms and kissed her deeply, and she kissed him with all the longing and love in her heart.

She'd been running all her life, afraid to get hurt.

From now on, the only place she was running was into Dex's arms.

* * * * *

THE
DARK WOODS

DEBRA WEBB

This book is dedicated to the outstanding police officers
and deputies in Winchester and Franklin County,
Tennessee. Thank you for all you do.

Chapter One

Sunday, March 24

Sasha Lenoir struggled to keep her smile in place as her lifelong friend Audrey Anderson showed the last of the guests to the door. The gathering after her grandmother's funeral was a tradition as old as time, and Sasha had managed to muddle through the event without embarrassing herself by bursting into tears. As the social requirements of the day drew to an end, however, her nerves had grown ragged and her wherewithal dwindled.

She needed to close herself away in a quiet room for a few hours to recharge, to collect her emotions and tuck them neatly away once more. She had spent many years sharpening her skills at controlling her reactions and feelings. Despite the pressure or the insurmountable odds, any crisis manager worth her salt would never allow the slightest crack in her carefully constructed veneer for the rest of the world to see.

But today had been different. Today was personal. The only remaining family member, besides her daughter, she had left in this world was now gone. Dead and buried. There was no one left to ask about her history.

No one to remind her of all she had overcome, become and could do in the future despite that history.

Life would never be the same.

Viola Simmons had been more than a mere grandmother. She had been mother, father, sibling, best friend, confidante, cheerleader and, most important, the keeper of the faith. Not once had she ever lost faith in Sasha or let her down in any way. The sweet, brave lady had believed in Sasha when she barely believed in herself. She had picked up the shattered pieces of their lives and soldiered on when she had every right to want to give up.

There was a gaping hole in Sasha's life and in her heart now.

"I should stay tonight," Audrey offered as she entered the drawing room once more. "You shouldn't be alone."

Sasha dredged up a weary smile for her old friend. "I appreciate everything you've done, Rey. I'm not sure I would have been able to pull this off to my grandmother's standards without you, but right now alone is exactly what I need to be."

Everyone close to Audrey had always called her Rey. Nicknames were a mainstay of Southern culture. When Sasha was a small child, her parents—even her grandmother—had called her Sassy. By age twelve, no one dared to do so—not without the fear of a black eye or a bloody nose. Only once in her career as a top crisis manager in New York City had Sasha's childhood nickname surfaced. She had quashed that errant leak in a heartbeat.

"Are you sure?" Rey's face lined with worry. "I really hate to go and leave you in this big old house all by yourself."

Sasha hugged her arm around her old friend's and guided her to the door. "You've done more than enough." They faced each other in the entry hall. "You handled the outreach to her friends. You went over my grandmother's wishes and arranged the entire service at DuPont's with hardly a nod from me. You organized the lovely gathering here afterward. You've gone above and beyond already. Go home, kick your shoes off and have a glass of wine—or two...or three. Snuggle with Colt."

They laughed together. But instead of sounding happy, it seemed sad. It was the end of an era and Sasha suspected Rey was thinking of her own mother, who wasn't getting any younger and whose health had been plagued by dementia. Time stopped for no one and it felt as if it was slipping away far too fast.

Rey sighed. "The service was beautiful. I know your g'ma would have been proud." Rey shook her head. "It's such a shame about Mr. DuPont. I can't believe a close colleague of his daughter's murdered him. I'm certain she must be completely devastated."

The news of the DuPont murder had rocked the small town of Winchester, Tennessee. DuPont Funeral Home had served the community for more than a hundred and fifty years. Edward had been the fourth generation DuPont undertaker. His daughter Dr. Rowan DuPont was now the fifth. Strange, Sasha realized, the DuPont family's history was littered with as much tragedy as her own. Rowan's identical twin sister drowned when she was twelve and a few months later their mother committed suicide. Worse, her mother hanged herself in the funeral home and Rowan was the one to find her.

"I was surprised to hear she'd decided to return to Winchester and take over the funeral home." Like Sasha, Rowan DuPont had carved out a good life and a successful career elsewhere. With her father's murder she had apparently made the decision to give up everything to come home and take over the family business. There was likely more to Rowan's decision than what the media had covered. Whatever her reasons, Sasha applauded her courage. It took guts to come home after a tragedy and to start over.

Particularly with the guilt of her father's murder hanging over her like a dark cloud.

"Life has a way of sending us down a different path sometimes," Rey said almost to herself.

Sasha inwardly cringed. Her friend was right; no one understood that stark fact better than Rey. A hitch in her career had brought her home to some immensely dark history of her own that just last month had surfaced for the whole world to see.

"I guess we never know what the future holds." Sasha chafed her bare arms with her hands, chasing away the sudden chill that came from deep within her bones. "Don't you find it odd that the three of us have suffered such similar tragic pasts?" Sasha shook her head. "Winchester is a small town and that's a lot of skeletons rattling around."

Rey made an agreeable sound. "I suppose every small town has its secrets."

"My grandmother probably knew them all." Sasha laughed, the sound strained despite her effort to lighten the moment. "No one was privy to more rumors and gossip than Viola Simmons."

Rey smiled. "There was something about her—an aura maybe—that made you want to spill your guts." Rey grabbed her handbag from beneath the table next to the door. "Don't forget I want to do a reflection piece on her. Everyone loved Vi. It'll be a great way to pay tribute to such an admired lady."

"She would be so honored, Rey." Sasha's grandmother would love the notoriety. "We'll get together next week and talk."

Rey paused, her hand on the door. "Does that mean you're hanging around for a few days longer than you first anticipated?"

Sasha didn't hesitate. She took the plunge. "I told my partners I would be gone for at least two weeks. If there's an emergency they know how to reach me."

"I am so glad to hear that." Rey nodded. "You should take your time and do what you need to do before you jump back into work." A frown tugged at her lips. "Will Brianne be okay with you staying so long?"

"She's having a blast with her nanny. The woman spoils her rotten."

"And," Rey pointed out, "you get some *me* time. I have a feeling that doesn't happen often."

"No kidding. I can definitely use it." Though, in truth, it was work that stole most of Sasha's time, not her precious daughter.

The two hugged for a moment and then Rey hurried to the street and the car she'd left there that morning. She'd arrived early to help Sasha get ready for the funeral. She was a good friend and Sasha genuinely appreciated her help. Three times each year Sasha had visited her grandmother—on her birthday in September, Mother's Day and at Christmas. She and Rey, on the other hand, had lunch at least every other month since Rey lived in DC—or at least she had until she suddenly rushed back to Winchester to take over the family newspaper late last year. Sasha would never in a million years have considered that Rey would move back to Winchester. Not after the way Sheriff Colt Tanner, her first love, had broken her heart when they were in high school. Not only was Rey back in her hometown, she and Colt were giving their relationship a second go. Sasha definitely had not seen that one coming, though she was immensely happy for her dear friend.

Maybe happy endings weren't a total myth after all. Certainly there was a theme going on with the whole homecoming thing.

Sasha had made her own happy ending far away from Winchester and without any help from the man she had fallen head over heels for when she was too young to understand what heartbreak was. She and Brianne were a strong, complete family. They would both miss G'ma but they still had each other.

Sasha closed the door and, out of habit, locked it. She'd lived in Manhattan for the past thirteen years. One didn't leave the door unlocked in the city. No matter that almost two decades had passed since she'd lived in Winchester, folks in her small hometown hadn't changed very much. Doors were still left unlocked more often than not and neighbors still checked on each other on a regular basis, which was the reason her grandmother had been found so quickly after her unexpected death. She hadn't come out for her newspaper. Viola Louise Simmons would never have left her newspaper lying on the porch until noon. A neighbor had noticed and knocked on the door to check on Vi, as her friends had called her.

A heart attack had taken her as she sat down for her morning tea. At eighty-three, no one could complain that Viola hadn't lived a long and productive life. Yet Sasha still grieved the loss, felt shocked at the idea that her grandmother was no longer here. She leaned against the closed door and surveyed the familiar surroundings. She had lived in this big old house from age nine until she went off to college and after that she'd spent holidays and summers here.

Growing up, this house had been more her home than any other place. Even when her parents were still alive, she was with her grandmother far more often than with them. Sasha pushed away from the door and moved along the hall, studying the family portraits and photos that had captured a place in time, curating the moment for all eternity. She stopped and stared at one portrait in particular, the last one of her with her parents before they died. Memories of the photographer urging Sasha's mother, Alexandra, to smile whispered through her mind. Her parents had both looked uncomfortable that day. But Sasha had been a kid, so she hadn't really noticed at the time. Two weeks later they were dead.

The remembered sound of gunshots blasted in her brain, making her jerk.

Sasha banished the haunting memories and walked to the kitchen. Maybe a cup of tea would settle her nerves.

She put the kettle on, lit the flame beneath it then reached instinctively to the pocket of her suit jacket and found nothing. She sighed. *Upstairs.* Her cell phone was upstairs. The device was as much a part of her as her two hands. It was never beyond reach…except for today. Out of respect for her grandmother she had left it in her room. Viola had hated cell phones. Rather than money, she had been convinced the invention of the cell phone was the root of all evil.

Sasha smiled as she took the rear staircase up to the second floor. The house was an early nineteenth-century American Foursquare. Sasha loved this place, but she wasn't sure what she would do with it. Her life was in New York and she couldn't possibly move back here. Never in a million years.

She found her cell on the bedside table in her old room. A text flashed on the screen. Sasha smiled as she responded, typing the words I miss you, too, followed by three kiss emoji. Her heart swelled. She was really glad Brianne wasn't angry with her anymore. Her daughter had been furious when Sasha told her she couldn't come to G'ma's funeral. She had school and Sasha wasn't sure how long she would need to remain in order to settle her grandmother's affairs. At least Brianne was speaking to her now. Five minutes after Sasha was out the door, her daughter was planning all the things she and her beloved nanny could do together. Twelve was a tough age. Sasha remembered it well.

Love you.

Sasha sent the text and tucked the phone into her pocket. Downstairs the kettle screamed for her attention. She could taste the bitter tang of the tea already. Her grandmother was a die-hard Earl Grey fan. Sasha compensated with an abundance of sugar and milk.

With a quick twist of the knob she doused the fluttering flame under the kettle. She grabbed a cup and the ceramic box where her grandmother stored her tea. She dropped a bag into the cup and grabbed a mitt to pour the hot water. While the tea steeped she went to the refrigerator for the milk and rounded up the sugar.

The doorbell rang, echoing its Westminster chime through the house. Hoping it wasn't another plant since the front parlor was full already, Sasha made her way to the entry hall. Rey had suggested the plants be donated to one or more of the nursing or assisted living homes in the area. First thing tomorrow a local floral shop was sending a van to collect the plants and divide them up among the three homes in the Winchester area. It was a good solution, one her g'ma would approve of. Sasha peeked beyond the drapes, didn't see anyone on the porch or in the drive. Frowning, she unlocked the door and opened it. Definitely no one on the porch or in the driveway.

When she would have turned away, she spotted the corner of a pink envelope sticking up from the mailbox hanging on the wall next to the door. Had someone dropped off a sympathy card? Maybe a neighbor who hadn't been able to make it to the service or to the gathering.

Sasha tugged the envelope from the mailbox, then went back inside and closed the door. Her name was scrawled across the front. She turned the envelope over, noted the bold *H* stamped on the flap. Her heart stumbled as she opened it. The single page inside was folded twice. Frowning, Sasha unfurled the page and read the brief note that went straight to the point and then the name signed across the bottom of the page.

There are things your grandmother should have told you...about your parents. We should talk. Arlene Holloway.

For twenty-seven years the world had believed Sasha's father had killed her mother and then himself.

Deep down she'd had questions, had doubts. But each time Sasha had broached the subject, her grandmother hugged her and said that sometimes bad things happened to good people. Her grandmother was like the policemen who came to her parents' house that night. They didn't want to listen to what a traumatized nine-year-old had to say. Two people were dead and nothing on earth was going to bring them back.

But Sasha remembered vividly what no one had wanted to believe.

She had heard at least one stranger's voice that night…maybe two. Voices that didn't belong to her mother or to her father or to anyone else she recognized.

Someone else had been in the house the night her parents died.

Chapter Two

Arlene Holloway was born and raised in Winchester. Sasha stood at the woman's front door as the sun dipped behind the trees and mountains that surrounded her hometown. Mrs. Holloway was—had been—Vi's best friend. Didn't matter that Vi was black and Arlene was white and that their childhood era had not been amenable to multicultural relationships of any sort. The two had weathered that storm and become stronger because of it. Through marriage and childbearing and widowhood Vi and Arlene had grown even closer over the years. Both had warned Sasha's mother nearly forty years ago how difficult life could potentially be if she chose to marry a white man. Alexandra had ignored the warning and married Sasha's father. Sasha had the dark curly hair of her mother and the pale skin and green eyes of her father.

More important, she had the determination and relentlessness of her grandmother. Both had served her well in the high-stakes world of celebrities and politicians where ruthless tactics and colliding egos were par for the course. Handling the high-profile issues of the rich and famous as well as the influential and powerful required a certain skill set, including fearlessness. The fearlessness as well she had inherited from her grandmother.

But for her parents, as predicted, life had been difficult and far too short.

Sasha knocked on the door a second time, and when the knob turned, her heart took another of those troubling tumbles. Was it possible that after all these years she might be on the verge of learning something new about what happened that night? If her grandmother had possessed some knowledge as to the events that unfolded that fateful night, why would she not have told Sasha years ago? The answer was easy—Viola Simmons would have done anything, gone to any lengths to protect her only grandchild. She firmly believed the past should stay in the past. Viola had wanted desperately for Sasha to move forward with no dwelling in a history that could not be changed.

But what if some aspects of it could change?

Why would Vi ignore that possibility?

The door swung inward and Sasha prepared to launch into her planned spiel about how she and Mrs. Holloway hadn't had the opportunity to properly catch up during the funeral or later at the graveside service or even at the gathering. She decided she wouldn't bring up the mysterious letter until the older woman did.

Except it wasn't eighty-five-year-old Arlene Holloway staring at Sasha when the door opened fully. It was Branch… Mrs. Holloway's grandson.

US Marshal Branch Holloway.

The boy Sasha had loved from afar since she was thirteen years old. The man she'd finally—after a decade of fostering a secret crush—made love with in his truck on the heels of having had far too much champagne at her five-year high school reunion.

The *man* who was the father of her twelve-year-old blond-haired, blue-eyed daughter.

A fact the man in question did not know.

That trademark grin spread across his handsome face—the same face she saw in her daughter every day. "Sasha Lenoir…aren't you a sight for sore eyes."

And just like that her heart melted and she wanted to lean into him the way she had that one night almost thirteen years ago. It would be so easy to cry on his wide shoulders after losing the only real parent she'd had. To lose herself in the warmth and promise of his arms and forget that she, like her grandmother had been, was on her own now, raising a child.

Except Sasha had far too much to lose to even think of going down that path. Her decision not to tell Branch about her pregnancy and the daughter she'd had nine months later had been based on fear and self-doubt during an intensely stressful time. She'd just graduated with her master's and had dozens of job interviews in front of her. Two months later she'd barely settled into her new career when she realized she was pregnant. Her life had already been far too complicated; she couldn't drag Branch into it. He was kicking butt and taking names in Chicago. There simply was no common ground for them to find for raising a child together. She'd made the decision not to tell him and her grandmother and Rey had kept her secret.

Now the decision seemed like the mistake it no doubt was. Brianne was missing out on the wonderful man who was her father and the still unmarried Branch had no idea what an amazing daughter he had helped create.

Remorse heaped onto Sasha's shoulders. What had she done?

She'd also caused her grandmother to keep that secret from her lifelong best friend. Her poor grandmother had taken that weight with her to her grave.

More guilt accumulated to the point Sasha almost sagged. But didn't.

All at once regret claimed Branch's expression. "I'm as sorry as I can be about your grandmother. I would have been at the funeral today but there was an emergency with a prisoner transfer."

Arlene had explained Branch's absence. Not that Sasha had really expected him to come to the funeral. They hadn't exactly been close friends back in school. He was two years older and had been too popular to have time for a mere human like Sasha and her friends. But he'd always been kind. Besides being incredibly handsome and spectacularly charming, one thing Branch Holloway had always been was kind. Fear abruptly clutched Sasha's heart. How kind would he be if he ever learned her secret? She had stolen a dozen years of his daughter's life from him.

She pushed the negative thoughts away. No one was better at keeping shocking secrets or neutralizing the rumors around those secrets than Sasha. They didn't call her the queen of spin doctors for nothing. As for her personal dilemma, she had made her bed; she would lie in it.

Steadying herself, Sasha produced a smile. "Thank you. I apologize for the unannounced visit. I was hoping for a few minutes with Mrs. Holloway." Sasha leaned to the left and peered past him into the cavernous foyer beyond. "Is she home?"

"She sure is. Come on in." The long fingers of one hand wrapped around her arm and ushered her across the threshold. "Gran and I have dinner together every Sunday. We were just about to sit down at the table.

We'd be thrilled to have you join us. There's always plenty to eat."

Sasha dug in her heels, stopping their forward momentum. "I couldn't possibly impose." Good grief, she had forgotten how early people had dinner around here. It wasn't even six o'clock.

"Nonsense. It's no imposition."

Before she could react to the statement, he'd taken her by the arm again and was guiding her through the house. Mrs. Holloway was beaming when they entered the dining room.

"Sassy, how sweet of you to come to dinner."

Branch pulled out a chair at the table and ushered Sasha into it. She managed a "Thank you." Then she propped a smile into place for the elderly woman across the table while Branch laid a setting for her. "It wasn't my intent to intrude. I came by to speak with you about—"

"Say grace, Branch," his grandmother ordered. "This girl needs to eat. She's as thin as a rail."

"Yes, ma'am." Branch shot Sasha a wink before sitting then bowing his head.

After the shortest dinner blessing she'd ever heard, he announced "Amen" and picked up the bowl of potatoes and passed it her way. "If you need anything at all while you're in town, you let me know. I'm sure you have your hands full."

"The hard part's over," Arlene insisted before Sasha could respond to Branch's offer. "The rest is as easy or as difficult as you choose to make it."

Funny, the older woman was far more right than she likely knew. "I appreciate the offer, Branch," Sasha said, her voice steadier than she'd hoped for. "My grandmother was very organized. She left specific instructions for everything."

Sasha nibbled at the food on her plate in an effort to appease her host and hostess. She listened avidly to their chatter about who had done what and the excitement of last month's organized crime case. Branch was still fielding offers for top assignments across the country but Arlene was hoping he would stay in Winchester.

Coffee had been poured and dessert served before Sasha had the opportunity to speak openly to Mrs. Holloway. Branch had excused himself to take a work call. Sasha wasn't sure how much time she had, so she went straight to the point.

"Mrs. Holloway, did my grandmother ever mention any second thoughts as to what happened to my parents? Did she feel satisfied with the police reports?"

Arlene stared at her for a long moment…long enough for Sasha to fear she'd shocked the poor woman.

"You received the note I had delivered."

Sasha nodded. "I did. I was quite surprised. You've never mentioned anything before."

"Your grandmother wanted the past left in the past. I felt her decision was a mistake but I held my tongue until today. Now it's time for the truth to come out, so long as you understand there will be consequences."

Sasha studied the older woman's face for some indication of exactly what she meant. "Certainly, I understand. I want the truth and I've always felt as if the truth was swept under a rug all those years ago."

There, she'd said it. It was past time she stopped pretending the truth didn't matter. It wouldn't bring her parents back but perhaps it would right a terrible wrong.

Arlene continued to stare at her, her blue eyes faded to a pale gray beneath the thick lenses of her glasses.

"Your grandmother never wanted you to pick at that ugliness. Are you sure you want to go against her wishes? She's scarcely cold in her grave."

Flustered and frustrated, Sasha held her ground. "Mrs. Holloway, with all due respect, you are the one who contacted me."

"I only made the offer—this is your journey to take."

Grappling for patience, Sasha asked, "Do you or don't you know what really happened?"

Arlene reached for her iced tea glass, took a long swallow. "I'm not sure anyone knows for certain but with the proper guidance I'm certain you could uncover the whole story."

"I'm thinking of hiring a private detective," Sasha confessed.

"A private detective?"

Branch's deep voice shook her. Sasha's attention swung to him. She hadn't realized he'd walked into the room. When she found her voice, she said, "Yes."

He pulled out his chair and dropped back into it, automatically reaching for his coffee. "Why do you need a PI?"

"She wants to know what really happened to her parents," Arlene explained. "She doesn't believe the police reports any more than I do."

Sasha cringed, as much at Branch's look of surprise as at Mrs. Holloway's words. "It's not that I don't believe the reports—I'm just not certain the investigation was as thorough as it could have been."

Branch nodded slowly. "I'm confident the investigators attempted to be thorough. Sometimes it's a matter of a failure on the part of the investigator and sometimes it's just a lack of communication. You were really young when your parents died—I can see how you would have questions now."

Sasha reminded herself to breathe. "I think you've nailed my feelings on the matter." She considered pointing out that she hadn't just shown up at his door with these questions. His grandmother had sent her a note. But she decided against that route for now. She had a feeling his grandmother had set them up for precisely this result. Sasha cleared her throat and pushed on. "With my grandmother's passing it feels like I need to settle my own affairs as well as hers. I would like to put the past to rest, I suppose."

"You can help with that, can't you, Branch?" Arlene suggested. "You're on vacation. What else have you got to do?"

He smiled patiently at his grandmother but the gesture didn't quite reach his eyes.

"No." Sasha shook her head. "I don't want to bother anyone. This is really something I need to do on my own. It's very personal."

His gaze rested on hers. "Gran's right. I'm on a long-overdue vacation and I don't have a lot planned. I can help you look into the case—if you feel comfortable with me digging around in your personal business."

If he'd said her hair was on fire she wouldn't have been more startled. Anticipation seared through her. Branch was a lawman. He would know how to conduct an investigation—that much was true. He would be able to spot the holes in the decades-old investigation. She could trust him. He would be thorough. His assistance would be invaluable.

What on earth was she saying?

She couldn't spend that kind of time with the man. There was too big a risk that he would discover her secret. Or that those old feelings that still stirred when she thought of him would be ignited all over again.

Either possibility was a chance she could not take.

"Perfect," Arlene announced. "I've always wanted to know what really happened. Out of respect for Vi, I kept my questions to myself. She never wanted to talk about it. I'm certain she was afraid of the consequences."

This was one aspect of the past Sasha had not considered. She knew in her heart that someone else was involved in the deaths of her parents. The fact that no one else seemed to feel that way and that her grandmother had been so opposed had prevented Sasha from pushing the theory over the years. But Arlene was right. If someone else was involved there would be consequences. That person or persons would want to keep the truth hidden as desperately as Sasha wanted to reveal it. Just another reason to be grateful she hadn't brought her daughter back to Winchester.

Finding the truth might be more dangerous than she had anticipated.

"When would you like to begin?"

Branch's deep voice drew her attention from the disturbing thoughts. *Breathe.* "I was hoping to start immediately." She blinked, realized it was Sunday evening only hours after her grandmother's funeral. "Tomorrow, I suppose."

He nodded. "I have a lunch meeting in Nashville tomorrow, but I can pick up the file and meet with you first."

"I would genuinely appreciate it." Anticipation lit inside her. This was really happening. "I can work with your schedule."

"I'll call Billy and let him know I'm picking up the file and we'll go from there."

Billy Brannigan was the Winchester chief of police. Sasha nodded. "Sounds good."

She thanked Mrs. Holloway for dinner and made her excuses for heading home without finishing her dessert. She wanted to spend some time going through papers and mementos at her grandmother's. Primarily, she wanted to put some distance between her and her teenage idol. Except just when she thought she was in the clear, Branch insisted on walking her out.

When they reached her car he opened the door for her and smiled; his expression looked a little sad. "I'm sure sorry about the circumstances," he offered, "but it's good to see you, Sasha. It's been a long time."

She wondered if he ever noticed that she carefully avoided him whenever she came home for a visit. Probably not. He was a busy man. She likely rarely crossed his mind, if at all. All these years, she had brought her daughter three times each year to see her g'ma and she had somehow avoided ever bumping into Branch. It was a miracle really in a town this small. And yet somehow she'd managed.

Doubt regarding the intelligence of this plan to investigate the past nudged her again. She at times second-guessed her decision about keeping Brianne a secret. But it was too late to undo that now.

All the more reason this was a really bad idea.

"It has been a while." She moved around the door, using it as a shield between them. "I'm usually only here for a couple of days when I visit. Between G'ma and Rey, I hardly see anyone else."

He nodded. "I hear you have a daughter."

Uncertainty whooshed through her like the flames from a roaring fire catching on dry kindling. She managed a laugh. "We really are behind. The daughter came into the picture ages ago."

He chuckled. "I didn't know you'd gotten married."

Her nerves jangled. "No wedding. The relationship was over before it began."

Before he could ask anything else, she threw out a few questions of her own. "What about you? Wife? Kids?"

The answer to both was no, of course. The idea that she knew this was intensely sad.

"No and no."

"Well, that's a shame, Branch. You don't know what you're missing. My daughter is amazing and brilliant. Being a parent is the best thing that ever happened to me."

Had she really just said that? Her heart swelled into her throat. Obviously she needed to go home. Today had been overwhelming and she was clearly not thinking straight.

"It's hard to be a parent without finding the right partner first." He winked at her. "I'm beginning to think I let the only one for me get away a long time ago."

The warmth that gushed through her was at once exhilarating and terrifying. "I'll see you tomorrow." Sasha dropped behind the wheel and closed the door before Branch could say anything else.

He watched as she backed from the drive and drove away.

Branch Holloway had always been incredibly charming. He hadn't meant what he said the way it sounded— the way her mind and body took it. Sasha was certain on that one. Being kind was one of his most well-known traits. It was as natural as breathing for him.

He hadn't actually meant that she had stolen his heart

and ruined him for anyone else. They'd had a one-night stand after years of her pining after him.

End of story.

At least, for Branch, it had ended there.

For Sasha, that night had only been the beginning.

Chapter Three

Monday, March 25

Chief of Police Billy Brannigan was waiting in his office for Branch's arrival. Billy had personally dropped by the archives and picked up the Lenoir file. He stood and extended his hand across his desk when Branch walked in.

"Morning, Branch. I thought you were on vacation."

Branch clasped his hand and gave it a shake. "I am. Just helping a friend."

Billy settled into his chair and tapped the file box on his desk. "This is everything we have. You looking for something in particular with this old case?"

Though Billy had been a senior when Branch made the team, they'd spent one year on the high school football team together. They'd been friends and colleagues most of the time since. Billy was a good man. He'd spent his life giving back to the community. Branch respected him, trusted him. He saw no reason to beat around the bush on the subject.

"You're aware Mrs. Simmons just passed away." Branch had spotted him at the funeral.

Billy nodded. "Viola was one of the people who insisted I step into the position of chief of police. She and

about a half a dozen descendants from the town found-
ers showed up at my door and practically demanded that
I take the mayor up on his offer. Until the end of her life
she still attended every single city council meeting."

"She'll be missed," Branch agreed. "You remember
her granddaughter Sasha."

It wasn't really a question. Even those too young or
old to remember Sasha Lenoir from when her parents
died, most everyone had heard about how she worked
with some of the biggest celebrities in the country.
Sasha had set the gold standard for turning around a
media crisis.

"I spoke to her for a moment at visitation on Saturday afternoon."

"She wants to go over the case, mostly to put that
part of her past to bed once and for all. There are a lot
of questions in her mind about those days. I'm hoping I
can help her clear those up. She mentioned hiring a PI,
but since I have some time on my hands I thought I'd
save her the trouble, see if we can't find the answers."

Billy nodded. "Understandable. She was just a kid
when it happened. I'm sure she has questions she wasn't
mature enough to ask at the time."

"From what I gather, her grandmother didn't want
her looking back, so they never talked about what happened. Now that she's gone, Sasha feels it's time to
open that door."

"I'm entrusting the case file to you," the chief reminded him. "All I ask is that you keep me advised of
anything you find contrary to the investigation's final
conclusions and return these files intact to me when
you're finished."

As chief, of course he wanted to be kept advised and
aware of any red flags. Any contrary conclusions re-

flected on his department. "Understood." Branch got to his feet and reached for the box.

"Look forward to your insights."

Branch exited city hall and loaded the box into the back seat of his truck. It was still fairly early, only eight thirty. He imagined Sasha was still operating on Eastern time. Since he didn't have her number he couldn't shoot her a text before showing up. He'd just have to take his chances.

When he reached the Simmons house, Sasha was sitting on the front porch. Like a number of other homes in Winchester's historic downtown, the Simmons home wasn't far from anything. On the other hand, the house where Sasha had grown up—where her parents died— was outside Winchester proper, deep in the woods on the family farm. His grandmother had often commented that she didn't know why they hadn't sold that place rather than allow it to sit empty and falling into disrepair. Maybe it had been too painful to make a decision.

He grabbed the case file box and headed for the porch.

"Good morning. Would you like coffee?" She gestured to a porcelain pot waiting on a tray. "I have blueberry scones. I made them this morning."

"You've been busy." He placed the box onto a chair and settled into the one next to it.

"I'm not the only one." She poured his coffee and passed the delicate cup to him. She placed a scone on a dessert plate and handed it along next. The china was covered in pink roses and looked far too fragile for a guy like him to handle.

"Thank you, ma'am." He felt kind of foolish drinking from the fancy little cup but the scone was far tastier than he'd expected. "This is not bad, Sassy."

She lifted her eyebrows at him and he winced. "My apologies. I guess I had an awkward flashback."

Sasha laughed. "Forgiven. But just this once."

"Whew. I was worried," he teased. "I remember you socking Randy Gaines in the nose. Bled like a stuck hog."

Her hand went to her mouth to cover a smile. "I always felt bad about punching him—not at that precise moment. After I'd had time to cool off. Eventually I apologized to him. I think it was like ten years later at our first class reunion."

She looked away and silence expanded between them for the next minute or so. It didn't take a crystal ball to comprehend that she was thinking the same thing he was. They'd had sex in his truck the night of her five-year reunion. Heat boiled up around his collar. He hadn't exactly shown a lot of finesse. Since that night he had wished a hundred times for a do-over. His gut clenched at the thought. Memories of how she'd felt in his arms, the soft sounds she'd made, the way her skin had smelled, echoed through him and his body tightened with lust.

"So, have you had a look yet?" She nodded toward the box, careful to avoid eye contact.

He polished off the last bite of his scone. "No, ma'am. I waited so we could do it together."

Their gazes locked and that same lust he'd experienced a moment ago flared again. She looked away. He reached for the box. He should get his act together. She'd just lost her grandmother and she was vulnerable. The last thing he wanted was her picking up on his crazy needs.

"Let's see what we've got."

While he removed the stacks from the box, she gathered their dishes and set them on the tray. Then she disappeared into the house. By the time she returned with glasses of ice water, he'd arranged the files in chronological and workable stacks.

"So what we have here—" he opened the first folder "—are the investigator's reports, the coroner's report, crime scene photos and the medical examiner's report." He studied Sasha for a moment. He wondered if she realized how difficult this was going to be. She had the prettiest green eyes and he loved all those soft curls that fell over her face and shoulders. She was a beautiful woman. He blinked, reminded himself to stay focused. "Are you sure you want to see all the grisly details?"

She stared at him, her eyes hot with determination. "I was there, Branch. I saw everything that night. Heard my mother's screams and my father's pleas."

He nodded. "All right, then." He opened the folder and spread the photos across the table. "Your mother was lying on the living room floor. She'd been shot twice in the chest." He read the description of her father's injuries. "Your father took—"

"One shot to the head. He was dead before he fell onto the sofa. Blood was everywhere." Her voice was hollow, distant. "I had to stand on the fireplace hearth to avoid the blood."

His chest ached at the image of her as a little girl, the pigtails he recalled so vividly and those big green eyes, standing alone and surrounded by a sea of red pouring from her mother's lifeless body. "There was no indication of forced entry. The responding officers had to break down the door to get inside."

Sasha stared at the photos. "I tried to wake them up, but I couldn't. Then I called 911. But I was afraid to unlock the door when they pounded and called out to me. I'm sure I was in shock."

Her voice had gone small, like the child she had been when the tragedy happened. The urge to take her hand and remind her that she was safe now tugged at his gut.

"How about we go over the reports and you tell me if you recall anything differently than the way it was documented."

She nodded and took the pages he offered. While she read over the reports, he studied the ME's report to see if either victim showed any indication whatsoever of a struggle. The ME noted wisps of Alexandra's hair having been torn out. So he—presumably her husband—held her by the hair rather than by the wrist or arm. No scratches or bruises on either victim. No alcohol or drugs found in her mother; her father had been drinking fairly heavily. The evidence reports showed a number of unidentified fingerprints found in the house. Not unusual. People had visitors. Visitors left prints. That alone didn't mean anyone besides the family or close friends had been in the house that night or any other.

Sasha laid the investigator's final report aside and took a breath.

"Thoughts?" He waited, gave her time to collect herself. This was hard. This was exactly, he imagined, why or at least part of the reason her grandmother had never wanted to take this journey.

"That night and then again about a week after…*that night*, I told my grandmother I'd heard another voice, maybe two in the house besides my parents'. She took me to see Chief Holcomb but there's nothing in the report about my statement."

"It's possible—" Branch hoped to convey this without being too blunt "—the chief didn't feel your statement was reliable enough to enter into evidence, particularly if it was days later."

She made a face that spoke of her frustration and no small amount of anger. "I suspected that was the case. I remember Chief Holcomb suggesting that I'd dreamed about that night and my imagination had added the voices in an attempt to divert guilt from my father. He urged my grandmother to take me for counseling and she did, but those sessions didn't change what I remembered."

Branch could see how Holcomb might have come to that conclusion. For an officer of the law, logic had to be first and foremost when looking at an emotional situation. Anyone could imagine the horror and pain involved with an event like murder, but that empathy could not dictate how an investigator tackled a case.

"Denial is a powerful emotion. It's possible what Chief Holcomb suggested was exactly what happened."

She stared at him for a long moment before shaking her head. "That's not what happened. I know what I heard. I was simply too traumatized at first to explain my impressions. I've lived with this for a long time, Branch. I know what I heard. Those voices have played in my thoughts and in my dreams for twenty-seven years."

"All right, then. Let's talk about the voices." Was it possible someone else was involved? Absolutely, and if he found even a speck of evidence to support that theory, he was going the distance with it. He shuffled the crime scene photos together and placed them back into the folder. There was no need to leave those gruesome images lying in front of her. "Let's talk about the voice or voices. What exactly did you hear?"

"I heard a voice and it wasn't my father's."

"And it wasn't your mother?"

"No. It was a male voice. Deep, really deep—and mean. I remember shaking when I heard it even though I didn't understand the words. Then I heard my mother crying and my dad pleading with someone to let her go. He kept saying *Please don't do this. Just let her go.*"

Her voice trembled with the last. "At what point did you hear the second unidentified voice?"

"When my mother started to scream, I heard another male voice. This one wasn't as deep. It sounded like he said *There's another way we can do this.* It's possible, I guess, that it was the same man, but I believe it was someone different from the first voice I heard."

Branch braced his arms on the table and considered her recounting. "Where exactly were you in the house?"

This was the point in the conversation when she shrank down in her chair, her shoulders visibly slumped, her eyes reflecting the remembered horror. "I was hiding under the stairs. When Mom and Dad argued I always hid in the closet under the stairs."

This would explain why she hadn't actually witnessed what happened. "After the gunshots, how long did you stay under the stairs?"

She shook her head. "I don't know. Minutes. An hour. Until it had been quiet for a really long time. I was too afraid to move."

Branch hesitated but then asked, "So there were sounds after the gunshots?"

She blinked. "Yes." She paused as if she'd only just considered that idea. "There were sounds. Footsteps." Her brow furrowed in concentration. "A door opened and then closed."

Branch found himself leaning forward. Every instinct he possessed told him she was telling the truth or at least what she believed to be the truth. "Were the footsteps heavy or light, a shuffle or more like a march or big steps?"

"Heavy, like the person walking was big."

"What about the door? Did he use the front door or did he exit through the back of the house?" If he remembered correctly, the staircase in the old Lenoir house was very near the front door.

"Not the front door. Farther away." She cocked her head as if trying to remember. "It must have been the back door." She suddenly nodded, the movement adamant. "Definitely the back door because I heard the squeak of the screen door, too. There was no screen door on the front."

"What happened after that?" It was important that he didn't lead her in a particular direction. Just a nudge from time to time to keep her going.

"I opened the closet door a little to try to see." She moistened her lips.

He watched, wished he hadn't. More of that foolish lust had his fingers tightening into fists.

"I didn't hear any more sounds and I couldn't see anyone, so I crawled out of the closet. I called for my mom and dad." She shook her head. "They didn't answer. So I got up and started to look for them. That's when I saw the blood." Her eyes grew bright with emotion. "I tried to wake her up. Got blood on my dress and shoes." She shuddered. "I ran to the sofa—to my dad—but there was a sizable chunk of his skull missing. I don't know how I remembered to grab the phone from the end table, but I did. I ran to the hearth and that's where I stayed until help came."

"Let's talk about what was happening in the days prior to that night." He needed to pull her away from that ugly scene. He would be talking to Holcomb about her statement. Her recounting certainly seemed credible to him. But she was an adult now. She'd had years to refine her memory. "Your parents were arguing, you said. Was the argument any more serious than usual?"

"My father had lost his job. Mother accused him of drinking too much. I think that's why he was fired. She was tired and angry. And under a lot of pressure at her job."

"Your mother worked at the municipal office."

"She was a supervisor at building inspections. The job came with a lot of stress."

He knew most of this because he'd grown up right here in Winchester with Sasha. The more they talked, the more he remembered. Looking at those photos of Sasha as a kid, a terrified, emotionally traumatized kid, tore him apart.

"I'll speak to Luther Holcomb. See if they had any leads relating to any other scenarios. Anyone who had it in for your dad or your mom."

She sat up straighter then. "Does that mean you believe me? You don't think I imagined the voices and the…?" She waved her hand in the air. "The other stuff?"

"I believe—" he chose his words carefully "—there was more to what happened than what we're finding in the reports."

"So what do we do now?"

"Now we start at the beginning of when any trouble began and we work our way up to that night. We put together the pieces we find until we discover the parts no one else has found before. We turn over every rock, we shake every tree and then we do it again until we unearth anything we didn't know before."

"But it's been so long." She pressed her fingers to her lips. "Do you think we can find the truth? Will anyone else remember?"

If Sasha's father did not murder his wife and then shoot himself, that meant someone else did. Branch could guarantee that person remembered what happened, and if Sasha's recall of the voices was accurate, at least one other person would remember, too.

"I don't know how successful we'll be but we can try."

She nodded, stood abruptly. "Thank you for agreeing to help me. You said you have a meeting in Nashville. I don't want to keep you."

Branch pushed to his feet, picked up his hat. "I'll call you as soon as I get back."

"I'll keep digging through all those reports and see what I can find."

He gave her a nod and she walked him down the steps, then waved as he crossed the yard to his truck. Whatever truth there was to find, he would help her find it.

He just hoped the truth turned out to be what she wanted to find.

Chapter Four

Sasha stood on the sidewalk surrounded by overgrown shrubs and knee-deep grass. It all seemed so small now or maybe it was only that the woods were swallowing up the yard and the house, ruthlessly invading all within its path. White paint once gleamed from the wood siding; now it was chipped and curled away like the skin slithering from a snake. Green moss had taken up residence on the gray roof. The house looked old and tired, broken-down.

This was the first time Sasha had set foot on the property since she was nine years old. Her fingers tightened on the key she had dug from a drawer in the mudroom. After Branch had left she'd gone up to her old room and dug out a pair of boots to go with her jeans. She'd added a sweater over her blouse and buttoned it to the throat. She'd started to bring a flashlight but then she'd remembered that the electricity and the water remained on for insurance purposes. Her grandmother had arranged for any necessary expenses related to the property to be drafted directly from her bank account. Beyond that step, she had washed her hands of the property.

Weeds poked through the cracks of the sidewalk and steps. Memories of drawing with chalk and play-

ing hopscotch sifted through her mind. She climbed
the steps and crossed the porch, boards gray with age
creaking beneath her weight. Unlocking the door took
some doing. The lock probably needed oiling. After a
couple of minutes of frustrated twisting and turning,
the tumblers gave way and the lock turned.

Darkness and dust motes greeted her beyond the
threshold. A memory of swiping the switch next to the
door prodded her to slide her hand across the wall. An
overhead light came on.

For a long time Sasha stood staring at the narrow
entry hall. It wasn't very large, perhaps seven by nine.
Dust was thick on the wood floor and the wool rug that
might be blue or gray. Some sort of pattern attempted
to emerge beyond the layer of dust but failed miserably. Cobwebs draped across the ceiling, making a path
over the chandelier with its two bulbs out of six struggling to light the space. A table sat against the wall, a
set of keys amid the layer of dust there. Above it a mirror hung on the wall, the glass like the windows, heavy
with years of buildup.

Deep in her chest, her heart hammered as if she'd
run miles and miles.

The worst was the smell. Decades of mustiness with
an underlying hint of copper. The stillness gave the
sense of a lack of air. It was hard to breathe. Sasha
drew in a deep breath that seemed to dissipate before
it reached her lungs. To the right was a small parlor
that her mother had used as a home office and straight
ahead was the living room, a hall, dining room and the
kitchen and a bathroom. The bedrooms and another
bathroom were upstairs.

If she kept going, only a few more steps, she would
enter the living room. Someone had cleaned up the

bloody mess. She'd heard her grandmother discussing it a few weeks after that night. Friends or neighbors had rid the place of all indications of the bad thing that had happened.

Bad thing.

A very bad thing had happened in this house. Sasha forced one foot in front of the other. As she entered the parlor, voices vibrated in her mind. Her mother crying...her father pleading...the other voices growling with such menace. Sasha stood very still; she stared at the staircase and the door that was hidden until you walked beyond the newel post. She'd hidden there so many times.

Her heart pounding harder and harder, she continued on, along the hall and into the kitchen, turning on lights as she went. It looked exactly the same save for the cobwebs and dust. The teakettle still sat on the stove, the red-and-white-checked mitt hung from a drawer pull nearby.

You'll be late for school.

Her mother always worried that Sasha would be late for school. Or that she wouldn't finish her homework or her breakfast.

The newspaper from their final morning in the house lay on the kitchen table where her father had left it.

She stared at the headlines from that date. Man Is Killed by Lightning Strike while Working on Barn Roof. New Hospital Construction Is Moving Forward.

Sasha walked through the dining room on her way back to the living room. This time she forced herself to take a closer look. The spot on the floor in the center of the room where her mother had fallen. The rug that had once been there had been taken away. The sofa was gone, as well. Her father's blood and brain matter had been sprayed over the upholstery. All that remained were two chairs with a table between them. The princess-style phone still sat on the table. Sasha had dragged its long cord over to the hearth that night to escape the reach of her mother's blood flowing across the floor.

Please don't do this. Just let her go!

Sasha blinked away the voices and moved toward the stairs. The runner was coated in dust. The steps creaked as she climbed upward. Her fingers trailed along the wooden banister the same way she'd done as a child. Her father had grown up in this house. His grandfather had built it. Her father had been a good man. Never raised his voice. Was always a gentleman with her or her mother. No one could understand what happened to his temperament. Surely losing his job had not turned him into a killer.

No. Sasha shook off the notion. Someone else had been in the house. Her father had not done this and it was time she proved it and cleared his name. Both he and her mother deserved justice.

Someone had murdered them. Sasha was certain of it.

Two doors on the right were the guest room and a bathroom; on the left was her room and then that of her parents. She walked through her parents' room first. The bed was made. Sasha crouched down and checked underneath the bed skirt on her father's side. His old high school baseball bat was still there. He had called it his security system. Anyone broke into their house, the security system was going off.

Sasha stood and moved to the other side of the bed. Her mother's heels lay next to the closet door where she'd come home that evening and shed her work attire. She always stripped off the suit and pulled on jeans and a tee or a sweater. Her father wore jeans and work boots all the time. His work as a construction superintendent rarely required a shirt and tie. They had been so different and yet so suited for each other.

At least until the last few weeks of their lives. Things had been tense. Very tense.

Even as a child Sasha had sensed the extreme tension.

Her mother's pearls lay across a small mirror on the dresser. Sasha fingered the necklace. Alexandra Lenoir had worn those pearls every Monday and Friday. She had laughed and said she wanted to feel special on Mondays and she wanted to be ready to celebrate on Fridays. The pearls were a gift to her mother from her father, Sasha's grandfather, when her mother was sixteen, the year before he died. They were the only piece of jewelry her grandmother hadn't had the heart to remove from the house. She'd wanted the pearls to stay exactly where her daughter left them.

Sasha stared at her reflection in the mirror standing above the dresser. Other than the lightness of her skin and the green eyes, she looked exactly like her mother. Same features and profile. Her mother had been a very beautiful woman.

She turned away from her reflection and walked out of the room and into the one that had belonged to her as a child. Her white canopy bed with its pink lace and mound of stuffed animals was heavy with dust. Posters of cartoon characters and butterflies dotted the walls. Her favorite doll was at her grandmother's. It was the only item Sasha had wanted to take with her.

Her grandmother had bought her an entire new wardrobe so she wouldn't have to be reminded of her former life if she didn't want to be. Looking back, she and her grandmother had both been in denial. They had looked forward, never once looking back, and pretended the bad thing had not happened. It was easier that way. They became a family unit.

No looking back. No looking back.

Sasha sat down on her bed and allowed her surroundings to soak in. The lavender walls and the hair bows on the dresser. Her mother had loved brushing and braiding Sasha's hair. Giggles and the sound of the brush stroking through her hair whispered through her mind.

Life had been good here all the way up until it wasn't. She should have looked back, should have cherished the memories rather than trying to forget them.

But her grandmother had wanted to protect her. How do you protect a child? You insulate her from danger, from harm.

The denial, the memories that refused to stay buried had haunted her. It was time to unearth them and learn the truth.

Sasha descended the stairs and rounded the newel post. She grasped the knob of the closet door and gave it a twist, opening the door. The closet looked even smaller now. Maybe two feet by three. The only thing inside the closet was dust. There had been raincoats as she recalled. She could only assume they had been moved during the processing of the house for evidence. After all, she'd been hiding in the closet.

Sasha stepped into the closet and pulled the door closed, pitching the tiny space into darkness. She squatted down, hugged her knees and allowed her bottom to slide down to the floor. Then she closed her eyes.

You had a chance to save yourself...

Her eyes shot open as the voice echoed through her. It was the man's voice—the one with the deep, menacing voice.

Please don't do this. Just let her go.

Gunshots erupted in the darkness.

Sasha bolted upward and pushed out of the cramped space.

She couldn't breathe.

She ran out of the house and across the porch, down the steps. *Deep breaths. Slow it down.*

Perspiration covered her skin.

She focused on her breathing, told herself over and over to calm down.

A panic attack had not managed to get the drop on her in ages. Not since she was a teenager.

She braced her hands on her hips and breathed. Her heart rate began to slow. Still the dense woods seemed to close in on her.

If you go down to the woods today...you'd better not go alone.

The old nursery rhyme murmured through her. She'd loved exploring the woods around their home when she was a kid, but after that night she had been terrified of the woods. She'd gone camping once with a friend and her family and suffered her first panic attack that night in the woods.

Pulling herself together, Sasha walked back into the house and turned out the lights and locked the door. She climbed into her car and backed away, the trees closing in on the place sticking in her mind as she drove back into town.

She had a feeling if she didn't find the truth soon it would vanish forever.

TAREK MARTIN STILL lived in the same house he'd bought when he and his wife married, the same summer Sasha's mother and father had married. The two couples had their daughters within two years of each other and both men worked at Kimble & Douglas, K&D, the largest construction firm in a tri-county area. Sasha's father, Brandon, had often joked that imitation was the purest form of flattery and that Tarek had been flattering him for years.

Mr. Martin was one of the few people who had stood by her father during the investigation. He had insisted that Brandon Lenoir would never hurt his wife. His insistence hadn't changed the coroner's report.

Burt Johnston, the same man who was county coroner now, had concluded murder-suicide, and the medical examiner's autopsy, though inconclusive, had not disagreed.

Sasha had almost called Mr. Martin before driving to his home, but she'd decided that surprise would be a handy element under the circumstances. Never allow one's adversary an advantage. An announcement that the daughter of your former best friend was going to pay you a visit after more than two decades was turning over a fairly large advantage.

She opened the screen door, it squeaked and she knocked on the door. A television blasted the laughter and cheers of a game show. When she knocked a second time a dog barked. Sounded like a small breed. Sasha allowed the screen door to close between her and the wood door just in case the dog made a dive for the stranger doing all the knocking.

The knob twisted and the door opened. The voice of the talk show host blared out around the big man filling the door frame. Tarek Martin was considerably heavier than he'd been the last time Sasha saw him and his hair was gray through and through; his face looked significantly craggier but she easily recognized him.

His breath caught and he hissed it out between his teeth. "Sassy Lenoir, as I live and breathe."

She opted not to call him on the use of her nickname. "Mr. Martin, how are you, sir?"

"Well, I'm fine." He reached to push the screen door open. "Come on in here, little girl." He hollered over his shoulder, "Edie, come see who's here."

The little white dog hopped around his feet, yapping madly.

Sasha dared to step inside, expecting a snip at her heels. But the little dog just continued to bounce and bark.

A woman, obviously his wife, wandered into the living room, drying her hands on her apron. "I swear, you look just like your mama, honey."

Sasha didn't remember Edie Martin. Her voice was vaguely familiar but her face drew a blank. "Thank you."

The older woman's mouth formed an O. "I am so sorry about your grandmother. We came to the funeral but we didn't get a chance to talk to you. It was so crowded."

Sasha nodded. "G'ma had a lot of friends."

"She sure did," Mr. Martin said. "Come on in here and sit down. Can we get you something to drink? Coffee or tea?"

Sasha shook her head. "No, thank you. I just wanted to ask you a few questions if you have a moment."

"Course." He gestured to the sofa as he and his wife claimed the chairs they obviously preferred.

"I suppose you're busy taking care of your grandmother's affairs?" Mrs. Martin commented.

"Yes, ma'am. There's lots to do."

Mr. Martin grinned. "You sure enough pulled that pop star out of the fire last month."

Sasha smiled, her first real one of the day. "Yes, I did." The pop star in question had really blown his image on social media recently. Sasha had turned the situation around for him and set him on a better track. It was up to him now to stay the course.

"Your grandmother was so proud of you. She was always talking about you everywhere she went."

"I appreciate you sharing that with me."

Mr. Martin's craggy face scrunched up. "You said you had some questions. You know we're happy to help any way we can."

Sasha squared her shoulders. "When my parents died, Mr. Martin, you were the one person who stood up for my father. You insisted he would never have done such a thing."

Mr. Martin shook his head firmly from side to side. "I stand by those words still. There is no way Brandon would have hurt Alexandra. No way in the world."

"No way," his wife echoed. "They were having some problems with him getting fired and all, but they loved each other. He wouldn't have hurt a fly, much less his sweet wife."

Sasha blinked back the tears that threatened. "I tried to tell everyone that myself, but no one listened." She swallowed the lump in her throat and pushed on. "Can you think of any reason anyone would have wanted to hurt either of my parents?"

"You see," Mr. Martin said, "that's the thing. Everybody loved those two. I mean you had your jerk who made some remark about the fact that your mama was black and your daddy was white, but that was rare. I honestly can't remember more than one occasion that it happened and that was years before…that night."

"Why was my father fired? The reports say he was drinking on the job."

He scoffed. "That's another thing that was stretched out of proportion. Yes, he'd had a couple of drinks, but he was not falling-down drunk. Your daddy wasn't much of a drinker in the first place. The real problem is he crossed the wrong person and that person was looking for a way to be rid of him."

"Who did he cross?"

"Dennis Polk, the crew chief at our site. Dennis didn't like your daddy. To tell you the truth, I think he had a thing for your mama and didn't like the man she chose. I think I heard something about her dating Dennis back in high school but that's pure hearsay."

"Whether she did or not—" Mrs. Martin took over from there "—your mama had no use for the man. He had it in for your daddy, and as soon as he got that promotion to crew chief, he found a way to get him in trouble." She shook her head. "But they were working that situation out. Your mama had a good job that included a health insurance plan. They had the house they'd inherited. There were no real money issues. I think your daddy just felt like he wasn't pulling his weight those last few weeks and that caused tension."

Words echoed through Sasha. Her parents arguing over his need to find work and to stop moping around. She pushed the memories away. "Is it possible Mr. Polk may have wanted to hurt my parents?"

Mr. Martin moved his hands back and forth as if to erase the idea. "Oh, no, not in a million years. Polk was a weasel, rightly enough, but he didn't have the guts to do anything like that. He was all talk." Martin laughed. "Still is, as a matter of fact."

"There was that drug operation," Mrs. Martin said. "Brandon came across it deep in the woods behind your house in that old shack. Remember?" She directed the question to her husband.

"I sure do. We told the chief about it and he looked into it, but those knuckleheads were long gone. Drifters, I think."

"I didn't read anything about that in the reports from the investigation."

"I know it was looked into," Mr. Martin countered. "I took Chief Holcomb through those woods personally. Showed him the shack and told him the whole story same as Brandon told me."

"What about my mother?" Sasha looked from one to the other. "Did she have any enemies who might have wanted to hurt her?"

Both shook their heads. "Folks loved her. She was always so helpful with the permits and zoning issues. Anytime anyone wanted a permit to build or change something on their home, they went to Alexandra first even though she was in planning and development. She did it right and she did it fair. None of that playing favorites or making things more difficult than necessary."

"Your mama was under a lot of pressure that year," Mr. Martin said. "Her boss had a heart attack and that left only her to oversee everything going on in the county and to keep up with all the inspectors. It was a difficult time. Especially with the hospital and the big-box store going up that year. It was a real mess."

Frustration inched up Sasha's spine. These were the people closest to her parents. If they didn't know of anyone who wanted to hurt one or both, who would?

"But there was no one related to her work who might have wanted to hurt her or have revenge for some action she'd taken or failed to take?"

More shaking of heads. Sasha felt her hopes deflate.

"Can you tell me where Mr. Polk lives?" She might as well talk with him, too. She had nothing to lose but time.

"Over at the Shady Pines nursing home," Mr. Martin said. "He had a stroke some years back and he can't get around too well, but he can talk. He's a little difficult to understand at times."

"I appreciate your help." Sasha reached into her handbag for a business card. She passed it to Mrs. Martin. "If you think of anything at all that you feel might be useful in my search for answers, please call me. I would really like to find the truth."

Mrs. Martin saw her to the door. Both she and her husband assured Sasha they would contact her if they recalled anything useful.

If she had to interview every single person who had known one or both of her parents, she intended to do so. Someone had to have seen or heard something.

Murder didn't happen without leaving ripples.

Chapter Five

The Shady Pines assisted living facility had been around as long as Sasha could remember. As a child her grandmother had brought her here to visit one of her teachers, Ms. Clements, who had been in a terrible accident. She had no husband or family, so she'd had to stay in this facility through her rehab. Three months later she was able to return home but she was never able to teach again. Ms. Clements had been Sasha's favorite teacher. She was the one to sit in the bathroom with her whenever she felt the need to cry that first year back at school after her parents died.

Sasha should visit her while she was in Winchester. Ms. Clements would love seeing photos of Sasha's daughter. She smiled to herself as she thought of all the things about her childhood that she needed to show her daughter…including the father her daughter didn't know.

The realization startled Sasha but there was no denying the truth.

She put her car in Park and shut off the engine. For years now she had been telling herself that she should talk to Brianne about her father. Her daughter had gone through that phase where she'd asked every other day about her father. Sasha had told her that he was a good man but that he didn't know he had a daughter. So far Brianne hadn't questioned her mother further but Sasha understood the time was coming. Her daughter was quickly going from a child to a teenager.

The truth was, how could Sasha be so intent on having the truth about her own childhood when she concealed her daughter's? She had been afraid to tell Branch. Not at first. At first she'd been certain he wouldn't be interested, so she had chosen not to tell him. Their one night together hadn't been about love or the promise of a future; it had been about need and happenstance. Neither was a good foundation for a relationship. She had told herself that Branch wouldn't want to be weighed down with fatherhood and at the time that was most likely the case.

Years later, on a visit to her grandmother, she had run into him again. He, too, was home for a visit and he had talked and talked about how exciting his work was in Chicago. He had been happy, focused singularly on his career. Again, Sasha had told herself that she had made the right decision. But then, two years ago her grandmother had shared Arlene's concerns about how lonely Branch was. He'd mentioned to Arlene that he worried that he'd waited too long to pursue a real relationship… that maybe a family wasn't in the cards for him.

Sasha had always intended to find a way to tell him, but time had slipped away. Her grandmother had never advised her either way. She'd said Sasha would know what to do when the time came.

"I'm still waiting for that time to come, G'ma."

She climbed out of her car, draped her bag over her shoulder and headed for the assisted living center entrance. After a stop at the registration desk, she wove her way along the corridors until she found the room belonging to resident Dennis Polk. Though the facility wasn't a five-star resort, it was certainly well maintained.

Sasha knocked on the door and a surprisingly strong male voice shouted for her to come in. She opened the door and stepped inside. The room was neat and spacious. Mr. Polk sat in a chair by a large window that washed the room in sunlight. His bed was made, a patchwork quilt folded across the foot, and a small arrangement of flowers sat on the bedside table. The television was tuned to a news channel.

Mr. Polk eyed her over the top of his reading glasses for a moment. His curly dark hair had gone mostly gray now. She vaguely recalled meeting him at a company picnic once. His tall frame was far thinner and his ebony skin sagged from his chin. But his eyes were bright and alert.

"Mr. Polk, I'm—"

"I know who you are." His words were a little rough and clipped but easy enough to understand. He closed his book and laid it on the window ledge. "You're Alexandra and Brandon's girl."

She smiled and moved a little closer. "Yes, sir. I am. I'd like to ask you a few questions if you have the time."

"I have all the time in the world, young lady." He gestured to the small sofa. "Please, join me."

Sasha took the offered seat. "I don't know if you heard, but my grandmother passed away."

"I heard." He nodded to the small radio perched on the table next to his chair. "I listen to the local talk show every morning. They always announce who's married and who's passed and so forth. She was a good woman and a lucky one. Her granddaddy made a fortune on a land deal when the dam came in and he bought his wife one of those stately historic homes. They were the first folks of color to own one. Did you know that?"

Sasha nodded. "I did." Her grandmother had told her the story when Sasha was just a child but she never spoke of it again. Viola Simmons did not believe in rehashing the past. She was a firm believer in moving forward without looking back and dwelling on the things that had already occurred. All the more reason Sasha needed to find the truth—whatever it was—and move on with her life. There was no future in dwelling in the past.

"I was in love with your mama. Did you know that?" His expression was a little sheepish now.

Sasha met his gaze and asked the question burning inside her. "Is that why you got my father fired from his job?"

His eyebrows shot up. "There were folks who believed that was the reason and I have to tell you that I certainly was looking for a reason to give him his comeuppance. But no, I didn't turn him in on account of how I felt about your mother. I turned him in because he came to the job site drunk. Drunker than a skunk, I'm telling you."

Hurt speared through her. She had wanted to believe otherwise. "My father wasn't much of a drinker." This she remembered quite well, which was why she'd held out hope that the story was wrong.

"That's true and that's also why I was so surprised that he came into work at six in the morning with alcohol on his breath and staggering. I took him off to the side and asked him what was going on. He got defensive and told me it was none of my business." Polk shook his head. "I surprised myself when after all that time of looking for a reason to get him into trouble, I felt sorry for him instead. I knew something wasn't right. Brandon Lenoir wasn't a drinker."

The ache inside Sasha eased. "Did he tell you what happened?"

"He and your mother argued over something. He wouldn't say what. He just kept repeating that there was nothing he could do. He couldn't fix it and that seemed to have him awfully upset."

"Do you have any idea what he meant?"

Polk shook his head again. "I don't. I tried to talk to him, to reason with him, but he was having none of it. I told one of the other guys to take him home and I warned your daddy to sleep it off and come back the next day. I'll be damned if he didn't take a swing at me. Knocked me flat on my back but good, I'm telling you. I thought he'd broken my jaw, but lucky for me the worst damage was to my pride." He shrugged. "I didn't have a choice then. I had to fire him but I told him when he got his act together to come back and we'd work something out. The next thing I knew, he and your mama were dead."

His tone and his downcast gaze told her he felt partially responsible. "Did you ever hear any rumors about what happened? Maybe an opinion that differed from the official conclusion?"

His faded brown gaze lifted to meet hers. "I heard lots of opinions but none of them were any truer than the one the police came up with."

Her pulse rate accelerated. "So you don't believe my father killed my mother and then himself."

Polk shook his head firmly from side to side. "There is no way on God's green earth that Brandon Lenoir hurt his wife. He loved her too much. He would've done anything for her."

Sasha took a much-needed breath, hadn't realized she'd been holding it as he spoke. "Then who killed them?"

"That's the question, isn't it?" He stared out the window for a time as he spoke. "I'm pretty sure they didn't have any enemies. In a small town you hear those sorts of things. Never heard any talk like that about your folks."

Sasha hesitated. Should she tell him what she remembered hearing? Why not? Maybe it would spur some lost memory of his. "I heard at least one other person in the house that night. It was a man, perhaps two. My father pleaded with him or them to let my mother go."

Polk's gaze locked onto hers again. "Did you tell Holcomb about that?"

She nodded. "Apparently he felt my statement was too little too late. By the time I could tell someone they'd already concluded the murder-suicide scenario based on the lack of evidence for any other theory. I can't really blame the police. You said yourself my parents had no enemies. There was no evidence to support what I heard."

"It's been twenty-seven years. Digging at it won't change nothing at all. Sometimes it's just best to let sleeping dogs lie." He reached for his book and opened it, started to read once more—or pretended to.

Sasha recognized the cue. He was through talking. She retrieved a card from her bag and placed it on the table next to him. "If you think of anything else that might help, please call me."

He gave a single nod but didn't look up from his book. Sasha left his room. How could everyone be so convinced her father would never do this and yet sit back and let the whole thing go as if it made no difference?

Outside she unlocked her car and slid behind the steering wheel. The question that haunted her now echoed in her brain.

What difference will it make? Dead is dead. Her grandmother had said those words to her once when Sasha was fifteen and demanding answers.

She started the engine, braced her hands on the steering wheel. What now? Who else should she interview? Years ago she should have demanded that her grandmother help her do this. Now the one person who had known her parents better than anyone was dead. How was she supposed to piece together this mystery without her grandmother?

Tears spilled down her cheeks. Despite her best efforts to contain the flood, Sasha surrendered. She laid her forehead against the steering wheel and let them flow. She hadn't allowed herself to cry—to really cry—since she got the call about her grandmother. She'd been too busy, too shrouded in disbelief to totally break down.

Apparently there was no holding it back any longer. She pawed through the console of the rental car looking for a tissue or a napkin, anything with which to wipe her eyes and nose. The more she searched for something to dry her tears, the harder she cried. By the time the stream had slowed, she was exhausted and weak with an odd sort of relief.

She finally found a pack of tissues in her bag. She cleaned up her face as best she could and took a long, deep breath. She would get through this. As much as she had wanted to have her grandmother around forever, that wasn't possible. But what she could keep for the rest of her life were the memories. Memories that she would pass down to her daughter.

Sasha put the car in Drive and rolled out of the parking lot. The most important thing she could do for the memory of her family was to prove her father's innocence and to see that the person who murdered her parents was brought to justice.

If that person was still alive. Twenty-seven years was a long time. He could be dead or in prison or in a nursing home.

But, if he was alive, he had gotten away with murder for more than a quarter of a century. It was well beyond time to rectify that wrong.

THOUGH IT WAS still hours until dark, the sun had dropped behind the trees, leaving the old Lenoir home place cast in shadow. Sasha parked in front of the house and climbed out. She had her cell for all the good it would do. Cell service in the area was sketchy at best.

She unlocked the house and tucked the key into the hip pocket of her jeans. First, she walked through the downstairs and turned on lights, chasing away a portion of the creep factor. It was impossible to shake the idea that the deep, dark woods that surrounded the house appeared to be closing in a little more each year. She should probably have a service come out and clear the yards back to the original boundaries.

Upstairs she noted a few dark spots on the ceilings. The roof was deteriorating. She had to make a decision about this place soon or it was going to collapse into a heap. Her grandmother hadn't cared. She never wanted to come back here. But Sasha had cried each time she spoke of selling it. Some part of her had hoped one day she would wake up in her bed in the room she'd slept in as a child. That her parents would be gathered around the breakfast table, smiling and wishing her a good morning.

But she was not a child anymore. All the hope and wishing in the world wouldn't bring her parents back. It was time she did what needed to be done.

That would mean clearing out her parents' things as well as her childhood possessions. She felt confident there was someone she could call to donate whatever remained usable.

But first she had to determine what, if anything, she wanted to keep. Her grandmother had left most all their worldly possessions right here in this house. There were photo albums and keepsakes. The family Bible and a million other things that Sasha needed to consider before walking away.

She started with her parents' bedroom. The bedside tables were first. She went through each drawer, her mind instantly conjuring a memory connected to each object she touched. From her mother's favorite lotion to her father's wallet. She thumbed through the contents of the wallet. On the very top inside was a photo of Sasha and her mother. It was worn from being stored in his wallet but the images of their smiling faces said it all.

Happiness.

What had happened to change that?

Another thought occurred to Sasha. She glanced around the room. Where was her mother's purse? She summoned the image. White leather trimmed, a sort of tan-colored bag, some straw-like material since it was summer. The end of June.

Sasha searched the closet, looked under the bed, and then she went to the single shared bath on the second floor. No purse. Downstairs, she started with the small mudroom off the kitchen. Her mother's sweater hung on one of the hooks near the door. A windbreaker that had belonged to her father was there, too. She checked the pockets. A piece of peppermint candy was in her mother's right pocket. Beneath the sweater was her purse. Her wallet was there. Staring at the driver's license photo made her stomach hurt. The pressed powder compact, a brush and lipstick cluttered the bottom of the bag. A receipt from the local grocery store dated two days before her death.

Sasha walked through the kitchen, checked under the table and in all the cabinets, though she couldn't see her mother storing any big secrets in the cabinets. Then she moved on to the dining room and living room. She checked under tables, behind chairs and in bookcases. No surprises.

The same in the entry hall. An umbrella stood in the corner.

Her mother's office was cluttered and as dusty as the rest of the house. Framed accolade after framed accolade filled one wall. Her mother had graduated from architecture school at the top of her class. She'd spent two years in Nashville working but then she'd fallen in love with Sasha's father and she'd come home to marry him and to start a family. It wasn't until Sasha was in kindergarten that her mother took the position with the city in planning and development.

Sasha surveyed the rolls and rolls of plans on her mother's desk. There were dozens of notes in a stack next to the phone and more on the bulletin board; all appeared to be about work.

One by one she scanned the notes on the bulletin board. All were related to upcoming deadlines at work. A stack of file folders waited on one corner of the desk.

Her mother had made notes on call sheets and forms attached to the folders. Most looked like copies, not originals. Sasha assumed she had a working copy at home and the originals at work. Her fingers stalled on the photos tucked under the glass on the desk. Sasha's green eyes and big smile beamed out from the one in the middle. There was another of her parents in a hug, their lips just touching. Her heart squeezed. How had two people who seemed to love each other so much and who had everything necessary for happiness ended up dead in such a violent, heinous manner?

Sasha banished the question and moved on to the drawers. She found her mother's peppermint stash. She unwrapped a piece of the red-and-white candy and popped it into her mouth. Still tasted okay. More work files and office supplies but nothing else.

A memory of her mother working late in this office flashed through Sasha's mind. Her position had been very stressful and demanding. But could it have had anything to do with her death? Sasha couldn't see how. She'd only been in the position for four years. Perhaps an outsider coming in and taking a top spot had caused some resentment. But was that enough motive for murder?

There was that woman with whom her mother had lunch occasionally. What was her name? Penny something. Sasha remembered her, mostly because she always seemed to be intense, so needy. She should find the woman and ask her about her mother's work. First, though, she had to figure out what the woman's name was. Her attention settled on the old Rolodex and she reached for it. Seemed like a good place to start looking for names.

She moved from *A* to *B* and so on, turning the wheel to the next letter. Still no Penny. Maybe she had the name wrong. Could be some other *P* name. Patty? Pricilla? Penelope?

The digital number on the phone snagged her attention. It was one of those old-fashioned phones with the built-in answering machine.

"Old as dirt." Sasha studied the device. The handset was cordless, so not entirely ancient.

A number 2 stared at her from the small window that displayed the total of stored messages on the answering machine. Sasha had no idea if the machine still worked, but the small button glowed red for answering machine on.

With nothing to lose, she pressed the play button. The first message was from the dentist's office, reminding Mrs. Lenoir that her daughter Sasha had an appointment the next day.

That appointment hadn't taken place for another month.

Another voice echoed in the room. The sound quality was a little scratchy but it was certainly clear enough to understand.

We need to talk, Alex. Call me as soon as you can. It's important.

The date-and-time stamp indicated the message had been left the afternoon of the day before her parents died.

Was this the woman who had been her mother's friend? Penny or Patty or whatever?

It's important.

Maybe this woman had the answers Sasha needed. All she had to do was figure out who her mom's friend was and then find her…assuming she was still alive. And that she was the woman who had left that message.

With nearly three decades having elapsed, anything could have happened.

Chapter Six

It was almost dark by the time Branch reached the Winchester city limits. He had tried to call Sasha since he passed the Tullahoma exit but she hadn't been answering. He just kept getting her voice mail. Since he had promised to catch up with her as soon as he was back in town, he headed to her grandmother's house.

He'd done a lot of thinking on the drive back from Nashville and none of it was about the offer he'd been made in the meeting. The promotion and the opportunities available in Nashville were a far cry from the future he could expect in Winchester and still he hesitated.

As crazy as it sounded, he had sort of grown accustomed to the slower pace in Winchester and being around family and old friends. But the Nashville offer was one he'd been hoping would come his way for a long while now. He'd been certain the trouble in Chicago early last year had set his career back at least a decade. Last month's high-profile takedown had launched his career back up to where it belonged.

As gratifying as the offer was, at the moment he couldn't keep the Lenoir case off his mind. There was more to what happened twenty-seven years ago than was in the pages of those investigation reports. Maybe it was all the years of his grandmother shaking her head and commenting about what a travesty the investigation into the case had been.

She had insisted that Brandon Lenoir would never have murdered his wife. The question was, why hadn't Viola Simmons demanded the case be reopened? She had kept quiet and allowed the police to do their job, whatever the outcome. Not once had Branch ever heard his grandmother mention Mrs. Simmons's thoughts on the matter. Maybe Mrs. Simmons believed his grandmother spoke loudly enough for both of them. But he had watched the elderly lady go after councilmen in city council meetings. He'd witnessed her speaking on behalf of the lack of opportunities for young black women in the area. When Viola Simmons believed in something, she went the distance.

Why hold back when it came to the murder of her own daughter?

It just didn't fit.

He parked in front of the Simmons home and made his way to the door. He knocked twice. No answer. No sound inside. Sasha's rental car wasn't in the driveway or on the street. She had said she would be reviewing the reports. Maybe she'd found something she wanted to follow up on. He sure wished she had kept him informed. He would have to talk to her about the need to stay in touch. Going off on her own wasn't a good idea. She could run into trouble and he'd have no idea what happened.

He called her cell again and this time it went straight to voice mail.

For the next half minute he considered what he would do if it was his history he was attempting to dissect and correct.

First, he wouldn't have screwed things up with her

all those years ago. He'd been attracted to her since high school but she had completely ignored him. She'd always been busy with her friends. Always had a boyfriend hanging around. No surprise there. Sasha was the prettiest girl in school. The biggest stumbling block had been his grandmother. She had warned Branch about doing anything that might in any way take advantage of or hurt Sasha. She had been through enough, his grandmother cautioned.

And he had. He'd done exactly what his grandmother told him…until that fall Sasha showed up for a high school reunion. If she had been pretty growing up, she had become a stunningly beautiful woman. Just looking at her had taken his breath. That one night, thirteen years ago, had turned him inside out. He hadn't managed a serious relationship since. Oh, he'd had plenty of dates, but none that had gone beyond the physical. He hadn't met anyone who made him want more.

Work had consumed his life. And he had been exceedingly good at his job. Then he'd made the mistake of his life by getting involved with a witness and she'd lost her life because of his error. That wasn't entirely true. He had been cleared of wrongdoing related to her death, but deep down he would always feel that if he'd done things differently maybe he could have seen what was coming.

He would second-guess himself on that one for the rest of his life.

Clearing his head of the troubling memories, he decided to check the old Lenoir place. It was possible Sasha had decided to have a look around in the house without him. Not that he could blame her. There was no better way to put herself in the middle of the past than by going back to the scene of the crime.

The Lenoir house wasn't that far outside Winchester proper, still in the city limits but nestled deep in the woods off South Shephard and Gem. The area was densely wooded and the old place had been abandoned since Sasha's parents died. Mrs. Simmons refused to allow the property to be sold or rented, or even maintained.

Weeds had encroached on the long driveway, making it narrower. Cracked and broken asphalt aided the weed coup. He breathed a little easier when he spotted Sasha's rental car parked near the house. He had no more appointments for the next few days, which left him free to focus on this investigation. And her.

He shook his head, reminded himself that he had to look at this as a case—not as a personal venture. This was not about spending time with Sasha—well, maybe it was in part—it was about finding the truth. There was an aspect of the case he needed to find an opportunity to present to her. As much as she wanted to clear her father completely of any fault in what had happened, Branch worried that wouldn't be possible. One of the two victims, either her father or her mother, was involved on some level. People rarely got murdered in this manner—planned and executed—without some degree of involvement.

First thing, they needed to set some ground rules. Although he had no reason to believe either of them was in danger related to this exploration of the past, it was best not to take any chances. If they learned someone else was responsible for her parents' murders, that person in all probability would not want his secret revealed.

If that person was still alive.

Branch wanted to remain objective on this case but he was having a difficult time doing so. Maybe because of his grandmother's certainty, maybe simply because he wanted a different ending for Sasha.

He thought of her daughter. Was there still a connection between her and the girl's father? She hadn't mentioned a relationship with the man but it was more likely than not. After what Sasha had been through losing her parents, he felt confident she would want her daughter to have a relationship with both her parents if possible.

He walked to the door and knocked. It was quiet inside. He glanced around the overgrown yard. He would call the lawn service his mother used and have them come over and work on the property. Sasha would potentially want to put it up for sale now. He wasn't sure it would pass any sort of inspection considering the condition of the roof and the siding, but all those things could be repaired. It could be a nice place again. A little TLC would go a long way.

He reached up to knock again and the door opened. She started, stared up at him in surprise.

"You didn't answer your phone." He removed his hat, held it with both hands, mostly to keep them busy since his first instinct was to reach out and touch her.

She frowned. "The service is really bad out here. Sorry. I guess I should have sent you a text to let you know where I'd be."

"How's it going?"

"I haven't found anything earth-shattering." She shrugged. "Anyway, come in. I can't offer you any refreshments because there's nothing here."

He followed her through the entry hall and then into a room to the right. Her mother's office. Sasha went around behind the desk and sat down. She pushed a button on the phone. "Listen to this."

He listened through two messages. The first was an

appointment confirmation; the second was from a female who urged Alexandra to call her. "Do you know the caller?"

She shook her head. "I tried to review the numbers on the caller ID but they're no longer available. The only reason the messages are still there is because it's one of those old answering machines with the cassette tape."

"The voice doesn't sound familiar to you?"

"It's too scratchy or low, maybe both. I know Mother had a friend, Penny or Patty. Something like that. I've been looking through her Rolodex and her notes. I haven't found a reference to a female with a name that starts with *P*."

"Rolodex? Really?"

The hint of a smile peeked beyond her obvious weariness. "Believe it or not, there are people in this world who would die protecting their Rolodex. For a businessman or woman who's been around since before contact lists and smartphones, a Rolodex is sacred."

She gave the Rolodex wheel a spin; the alphabetized cards tumbled around the wheel. "I can ask my grandmother if she remembers anyone in particular who was friends with your mom."

Sasha's gaze lit up. "That would be great. I considered calling her but I thought I'd exhaust my other options first."

"Frankly, I'm surprised the phone and the answering machine weren't taken into evidence."

"That was my first thought," she agreed. "It feels like the investigators had made up their minds and simply didn't bother looking for evidence."

He wasn't prepared to go that far just yet, but he had to admit that there was a lot that had been missed. Then again, hindsight was twenty-twenty.

"Why don't you give me a tour—if you're up to it." Branch had been here a few times growing up, but he never paid much attention to the layout of the house. He'd always been focused on the green-eyed princess who lived here.

"Sure." She pushed away from the desk and stood. "Obviously you can see this was her home office. She worked a lot of long hours and she didn't like spending so many away from Dad and me. So, she brought homework from the job nearly every day."

They moved into the living room and she walked him through the scene though he already had a good grasp from the crime scene photos. The closet where Sasha had been hiding was literally less than a dozen yards from where her parents had died. God Almighty. No child should have to go through that kind of trauma.

The kitchen and dining room were next. Branch stared out the rear windows at the gathering gloom. "Do you remember exploring those woods as a kid?"

"I do. There was an old shack. Rey and I used to use it for a playhouse. We spent hours pretending to clean and cook."

He wondered if that was the same one where the drug cookers had taken up residence during the time frame when the Lenoirs died. He would look into the exact location. "You never ran into anyone out there?"

She shook her head. "Never."

As they walked back into the living room, Branch studied the scene once more. The living room was located about midway between the front door and the back. If there was someone else in the house and they went out the back, as Sasha recalled, then they must have cut through the woods to get to where they had parked.

Otherwise they would have had to go around front and to the main road and risk being seen by neighbors.

"How far through the woods until you reach another road?" he asked.

"Not that far. The woods are dense and there's probably a lot more undergrowth now since no one's been keeping it tramped down. For an adult running, maybe fifteen minutes. As a child it took a little longer."

Branch would follow up on where the shooters might have parked and, if they were lucky, someone who still lived nearby had seen someone. It wouldn't have mattered twenty-seven years ago because apparently no one was looking for a killer beyond the husband.

"Have you gone through the bedrooms?"

"I poked around a little. No serious digging."

Her arms went around herself as if she were cold and needed to protect herself from potential harm. She was tired and not entirely comfortable here, no matter that she wanted to appear strong and capable.

"Did coming here prompt any new memories?"

That was the real question. She hadn't been in this house since the night of the murders. It was possible seeing everything with new eyes had nudged one or more hidden memories.

"Nothing important that I didn't already know. There were two men in the house that night besides my father. I heard their voices. I'm almost certain there were two distinct voices." She shook her head. "My father didn't do this, Branch. No matter what the reports say and no matter how bizarre it sounds after all these years. My father did not kill anyone."

The thing was, he believed her.

Chapter Seven

Sasha chafed her arms to chase away the chill. Branch watched her so closely, his blue eyes seeming to see right through her. She wanted him to see her strength and determination but at the moment it felt as if all he saw was her fear that she wouldn't be able to prove what she believed in her heart.

And what if she was wrong?

No. She refused to believe her father had done this. Her entire life she had known, without doubt, that he was innocent. Now she had the opportunity to prove it and she was extremely fortunate to have Branch offering to help. Local law enforcement would lend far more credence to his investigation of an old case than to that of a member of the family—particularly the daughter determined to prove her father's innocence.

"Why don't we call it a day?" Branch glanced around. "You've taken in a lot today. Maybe let it filter tonight and start fresh tomorrow."

Not until that moment did Sasha realize how incredibly tired she was. It was as if his words somehow prompted her to relax, to stand down from the fight. "Good idea. I am unreasonably exhausted."

"I'll take you to dinner," he announced. "You can

give me your thoughts on today's effort and I'll give you mine."

If she was smart she would pass. If she was smart she would go directly home, take a shower and hit the sack.

If she was smart she would recognize how very precarious this cliff upon which she had perched herself really was.

But she wasn't smart when it came to Branch Holloway and the past they shared.

"I'm not really dressed for going out." *Good job, Sash.* At least she tried, despite the idea that she felt herself leaning toward him, waiting for him to give her one good reason why her manner of dress didn't matter one little bit.

"The Back Porch is a great pub just off the town square." He looked her up and down, her skin heating with the move that even in an innocent moment like this one exuded sex appeal. "Nothing fancy, but great food."

There it was, the excuse she needed. "Well then, let me lock up here."

He followed her to the kitchen, where she locked the back door. "We can drop your rental off at your grandmother's and you can ride with me, if that's okay. No need to take both vehicles. Parking is sometimes at a premium."

She glanced at him. "Sure."

He trailed her back to the front door; she turned off the lights as she went. They stood on the porch while she locked the front door. No matter that it wasn't completely dark yet, it was utterly dark on the porch. The dense woods blocked the fading sunlight from reaching this far. She thought of all the times she had chased the looming shadows across the yard. She had never once been afraid here…not until that night.

When she was loaded in her car, he settled his hat into place and gave her a nod. "See you at your grandmother's."

Sasha gave him an answering nod. She told herself to smile but somehow being in the dark with Branch left her unable to do so. She rolled away from the gloomy house and the woods that held it hostage, and breathed a sigh of relief when she reached the main road. She felt as if she hadn't managed a deep breath since she set foot in that old house. All the dust, she told herself.

Layers and layers on top of the memories…the pieces of her life.

The drive to her grandmother's home was wrought with building tension. Hard as she tried not to, she had worked herself into an emotional frenzy by the time she parked in front of the house. She should have better control than this.

He hopped from his truck, skirted the hood and opened the passenger-side door for her.

Control? Ha! This was Branch Holloway. She'd never had any control when it came to him.

She climbed into the truck and he closed her door. All through her teenage years she had been besotted with him and he had barely acknowledged her existence beyond the Sunday lunches their grandmothers had shared. He slid behind the wheel of his truck, that big black cowboy hat of his lying on the seat between them. Of course, they'd run into each other outside school. Their grandmothers had been best friends. But he'd been two years older and always busy with football or being the most popular guy in school.

Sasha had been reasonably popular as a teenager. There were several difficult years right after her parents died but those may have been more about her inability to interact than about anyone else. She'd crept into a shell for a while. What child wouldn't under the circumstances?

A furtive glance in his direction had her gaze lingering there. He'd always had that perfect square jaw. The kind of face—particularly his lips—romance novel heroes were written about. Her daughter had those same lips as well as his blond hair and blue eyes. Brianne was the female version of Branch Holloway. So many times Sasha had wanted to tell her…had wanted to get out her old high school yearbooks and show off the child's handsome father.

But fear had kept her from doing so. Sasha, the woman who was fearless in every other aspect of her life, was terrified of what she had done and it was too late to fix that huge misstep.

Funny how she was here now, spending time with Branch to try to rectify a part of her past, and she was keeping this life-altering part of his from him.

He would hate her when he learned that truth.

Her stomach roiled. Any appetite she had possessed vanished. What was she thinking? Allowing him to help her with this investigation would only make him feel used in the end. This had been a very bad idea.

Branch parked at the curb across the street from The Back Porch. Sasha recognized the corner shop. It had been an old antiques store the last time she was here. Now it was a happening place from all appearances. Lights were strung over the sidewalk on both street-facing sides of the establishment. Beyond the big windows tables were filled with patrons. Waitresses were running around with laden trays.

The passenger door opened before she realized Branch had gotten out of the truck and walked around to her side. He held out his hand and helped her down. She tugged at the hem of her tee and wished she had taken the time to change. He was right in that the place looked very casual, but she felt dusty and rumpled after plundering through her mother's office for so long.

"I can't say for sure what'll be on the menu tonight, but I can tell you that anything you order will be excellent."

She glanced at him, produced a smile. "Smells great." The aromas emanating from the screened entry doors had resurrected her appetite.

He smiled and her heart reacted. She looked away. She spent her days and weeks managing other people's personal and professional crises and she couldn't keep her own ancient history under control? How sad was that?

Pull it together, Sash.

Branch opened the door and the music washed over them. A recent country hit, strumming through the sound system and through her. Inside, the floor was rustic, reclaimed wood as were the walls. A bar ran the length of the far wall. Every stool was occupied. Branch spoke to the waitress who looked up at him as if she was a mesmerized fan and he was her favorite rock star. Then she directed them to a table. It was tucked into a dark corner and Sasha was thankful for the out-of-the-way location.

The waitress took their drink orders; Branch suggested the house specialty—their craft beers. Sasha could use a beer to settle her nerves. Maybe she would sleep better, as well. Last night had been a battle with the covers all night. She'd awakened more tired than when she went to bed.

When the waitress returned with their beers, they

ordered burgers and fries. Brianne would be appalled. She would strictly eat only healthy food. Sasha sipped her beer and relaxed. She loved that her daughter was so independent and strong-minded.

"How did your meeting go?" They had spent most of their time together talking about her and her parents; she felt bad that she had asked so few questions about him and his life.

He stared at the beer in his glass. "Great. It went great. They made me a terrific offer for a position in Nashville—a promotion." He shrugged. "The whole thing went better than I expected."

Sasha laughed. "Wow. I have never heard a guy sound so down-and-out over such good news. Is this your excited face?"

He stared at her for a long moment, that mask of uncertainty not shifting the slightest. "I'm undecided. To tell you the truth, I like being close to my family. It's an unexpected development, that's for sure."

He sipped his beer and Sasha bit back the words she wanted to say. Branch was a good guy. He recognized that his parents and his grandmother were getting older and he felt compelled to stay close. This was just another perfect example of what made him so sweet. She, on the other hand, felt like scum. She hadn't once considered that it might be better if she moved closer to her grandmother. She was completely focused on her career and on her own life and that of her daughter.

"You should do what makes you happy, Branch." She turned the frosty beer glass round and round, kept her gaze focused on the rivulets of condensation sliding down the sides. "Too many people rush after the brass ring and lose out on happiness."

"Are you speaking from experience?"

Oh, damn. She'd said too much. She might as well confess now. "I have to say that I've considered the idea that I should have been here for my grandmother. I was the only family she had left and I was not around." If she'd hoped that confessing would make her feel better, she had been wrong.

Even after she'd found out she was pregnant, Sasha had been determined to forge her own life. She'd wanted to go far away from here and become someone else. Not the daughter of a man who had killed her mother and then himself.

"My grandmother always said your grandmother was very proud of you. She was very happy about your success. So don't go beating yourself up for something that wasn't real when she was alive and damned sure isn't real now. You're feeling guilty for a nonexistent issue."

She laughed. *God, if he only knew.* "So what are you, a shrink?"

He shook his head. "No. Just a guy with experience in the blame department."

No matter that she told herself she didn't want to know, she found herself asking, "What happened?"

"I broke protocol. Got involved with a witness and she died. My superiors cleared me of any blame in her death but that didn't seem to matter up here." He tapped his temple. "I still felt responsible. The two-week suspension for breaking protocol didn't seem like punishment enough."

"So you punish yourself by second-guessing whether or not you deserve this promotion."

The waitress arrived with their food before he could respond. Sasha poured a pool of ketchup on the edge of her plate and dragged a French fry through it. She nibbled the salty goodness. If she were completely honest she would admit that she devoted herself entirely to work and to her daughter because she didn't feel as if she deserved a personal life outside the relationship with her child. She lost that right when she gave up everyone who had been there for her during her life before college.

Her gaze drifted to the man across the table. Mostly because of him and how she'd left him out all these years.

They ate. Laughed at silly moments from high school. Shared the ways they had struggled to build their careers. When she'd devoured all she could hold of the best—bar none—hamburger she'd ever eaten and half a plate of fries, as well as a second beer, she asked the question that had been burning in the back of her mind for years.

"Why no wife or kids? And don't give me that ridiculous answer you gave before about letting the only one for you get away."

He shrugged. "Hey, it's true." He sipped his ice water. No second beer for him since he was driving. "How was I supposed to fall in love with someone else when you stole my heart when I was fifteen."

She rolled her eyes. "That is completely not true and certainly no answer."

He pushed his plate away. "I guess I just never ran upon anyone who made me want that kind of relationship. What about you? What went wrong with your daughter's father? The two of you aren't still together. Maybe you let the only one for you get away, too."

Fear pounded in her veins. "We were never together." She stared at her plate, tried to think what to say next. "I… I screwed that one up. He was a good guy but he's…he's out of the picture." She met his gaze then.

"I made a mess of everything and my daughter is pay-ing the price."

A frown of concern lined his handsome face. "There's nothing you can do to work things out? He doesn't sound like such a good guy to me if he's not interested in having a relationship with his daughter."

Sasha felt as if she couldn't breathe. She had to change the subject. Now. "I visited the guy who fired my dad. Polk, Dennis Polk."

Branch angled his head, studied her face for a long moment. Then picked up on her cue, her change of sub-ject. "What did he have to say?"

"He didn't fire my dad permanently." She explained how Polk had tried to handle the situation. Her tension eased a little as they drifted back onto safer ground. "The interesting thing was, he doesn't believe my fa-ther killed my mother either."

She also told him about her conversation with the Martins. A brief pause was required while the wait-ress cleared their table and asked about dessert, which they both declined. Branch insisted on paying. Another point of contention. She could not have him paying for her meals as if they were on a date. *This was not a date.*

"You were busy today." He leaned forward, braced his forearms on the table. "I'd like you to keep me in-formed of where you are and what you're doing from now on. Just to be safe."

She stared at him for a long moment, hoping to as-certain the motive for the statement. "Are you or Chief Brannigan concerned with my activities?"

Branch held up his hands. "No way. I just want to know you're okay." His arms dropped back to the table. "We have to face the fact that if your father didn't do this, someone else did. Whoever that someone else is, chances are they don't want us learning their secret."

It was a valid point. Certainly the idea had crossed her mind but she had chosen not to be put off by it. "What if that person or persons is dead?"

"Then we probably have nothing to worry about but we're talking about cold-blooded murder. A well-thought-out-and-executed set of murders. This was no impulse kill or robbery. It was planned carefully and carried out mercilessly. That tells us a number of things. First, someone powerful may have been involved—as in someone who paid hired professional thugs to do the dirty work. Or someone close to your family who knew the details of their daily lives and who could get in and out without being caught."

Planned and executed. She reminded herself to breathe. He was right. The images conjured by his words made her stomach clench and the taste of the burger she'd eaten turned bitter. Their deaths had not been about a robbery. Nothing had been missing—at least nothing of which anyone was aware. Certainly not money or jewelry or the usual valuables.

"Let's exchange contact information."

Once their cell numbers were added to each other's contact list, she asked, "So what do we do now?"

"We create a list of potential suspects. Anyone who was involved in the lives of your parents, either professionally or personally. Someone who had something to lose if a particular event occurred." His broad shoulders lifted and fell in a slight shrug. "We can probably rule out Polk. If he was in love with your mother, it's unlikely he would have killed her. The more reasonable path would have been to try to get your father out of the way."

"We might as well list everyone living in Winchester at the time." She rubbed at her forehead. The idea was overwhelming. "This is a small town, Branch. Everyone knows everyone else."

He nodded. "True. But not everyone has something to gain at the expense of someone else. This is what we need to find. What did your parents know or have that was worth killing for?"

She shook her head. "I should have made my grandmother talk about this. She refused when I was growing up. She said it was too painful. But I should have pushed the issue in recent years. Now she's gone."

Sasha rested her face in her hands. This was too much. Too, too much.

"Hey." Long fingers wrapped around one of her hands and tugged it away from her face. Blue eyes zoomed in on hers. "We'll figure this out. One step at a time. If you look at the big picture it can be overwhelming."

She dropped her free hand to her lap and told herself to pull her hand away from his but her body refused to obey. The sensation of his long fingers encircling hers made her feel safe and warm and not so lost and alone in this misery.

"We're going to look at this one piece at a time. We'll start with their personal lives. We dissect each piece. Were there financial issues? Had your grandmother been helping financially? I'll talk to my grandmother and see what she knows—if anything—that might help."

"Why are we starting with their personal lives first?" As a crisis manager, Sasha knew the value of a marketable commodity. For most people that was their professional lives. Certainly with celebrities the two often intertwined but the concept was the same. No matter that her grandmother liked to laughingly disagree, money—or the lack thereof—was usually the root of real trouble.

"This was up close and personal. Not a drive-by or a long-distance kill. Up close. Personal. There was intense passion behind these murders."

Sasha stared at him for a long moment; her hand felt cold despite the feel of his skin against hers. "Is that why the police were so convinced the killer was my father?"

Branch nodded. "In situations like this, it's almost always the husband."

"But not this time."

"I firmly do not believe your father killed your mother," he agreed.

There was a *but* coming. She could see it in his face, hear it in his voice.

"*But* there's a strong possibility the reason they both ended up dead is because of something your father knew or had done. This would be why he pleaded so for her life. He didn't want her to die for something he had done."

She drew her hand away from his, his skin suddenly burning hers. "I see your point, but I'll reserve judgment until we have more facts."

Sasha had spent her entire life believing her father was innocent. She wasn't about to throw him under the bus from a different perspective at this point without substantial evidence.

"Reserving judgment is warranted," he acquiesced. "We should both keep an open mind until we have all the facts—or as many as we can dig up."

"All right." She clasped her hands together in her

lap. "Are you certain you have the time to devote to this case? I know you're on vacation and obviously you have a decision to make."

Sasha stopped herself. What was she doing? Could she really spend the next several days working so closely with Branch without resurrecting those old feelings? Of course not. She was already struggling. Instead, she should be trying to figure out how she was going to tell him about Brianne. She had waited a very long time to find the truth. She didn't want to screw it up now.

What a mess she had made.

He started to answer her question but she held up her hands to stop him. "I'm sorry. I shouldn't be asking you to do this. You've been far too kind and giving already. This isn't your issue. It's mine. You have a life and I shouldn't be dragging you into my problems."

He chuckled but there was no humor in the sound, more a sad weariness. "First, I offered to help because I would very much like to be a part of resolving this case. Second, I have nothing else I need to do except make that career decision in the next few days about where I go from here. Seriously, I am totally available."

"Still," she argued, "this is too complicated, too personal…"

"I want to do this, Sasha. It means a lot to me. Your family means a lot to me."

She wished he hadn't said those words. Tears brimmed on her lashes before she could stop them. "I don't have any extended family left, Branch."

He grinned. "You have your daughter and you have me and my family."

"You're right. I'm feeling sorry for myself and I should get over it and get the job done."

He winked. "That's what I want to hear."

He stood. "Come on. I'll take you home. We have a lot to do tomorrow."

The drive to her grandmother's house was quiet but it was a comfortable silence. Sasha felt content with the decisions they had made. When he'd parked in front of the house and reached for his door, she stopped him with a hand on his arm.

"Now *I* have some ground rules."

He nodded. "All right."

"I don't need you to walk me to the door and I can open my own door." When he would have argued, she held up a hand and went on. "It's not that I don't appreciate it, but it's not necessary. Also, I pay for my own meals."

He made a face. "You're being unreason—"

"No exceptions. Tomorrow I pay since you paid tonight."

He held up his hands in surrender. "Fine."

"I don't mind keeping you informed of where I am—it makes sense. But I am a strong woman, Branch. I am completely capable of taking care of myself."

He nodded. "Got it."

"Thank you." She reached for her door. "Good night. I'll see you in the morning."

"Good night."

She climbed out of his truck, closed the door and walked straight to the front door without looking back. He didn't leave until she had unlocked the door and gone inside. She supposed she couldn't complain about that part.

Inside, she leaned against the door and closed her eyes to slow the spinning in her head. She really was in trouble here. She wanted Branch Holloway in a completely selfish way.

Sasha had developed a reputation for never giving in or giving up. She was relentless. Other than her time with her daughter, she had no personal life. Honestly, she could not remember the last time she'd been intimate. She wasn't an idiot. She understood the core issue at play here. Years of depriving herself had made her weak, had caused her to be vulnerable.

This was not a good time to be vulnerable.

But Branch made her want things she shouldn't want. All he had to do was walk into the room. He didn't even have to look at her. The very act of breathing was somehow sexy on him.

"Idiot."

Sasha pushed away from the door, locked it and headed upstairs. She needed to hear Brianne's voice, and then she intended to have a long hot bath and to get some sleep.

Whatever else tomorrow brought, she had to be prepared for spending time with the man without making a mistake that would impact her daughter.

She'd already made one too many of those.

Chapter Eight

Tuesday, March 26

Sasha's eyes opened.

It was still dark. She reached for her cell on the bedside table.

2:06 glowed from the screen.

She closed her eyes and told her brain to go back to sleep. It was too early.

The whisper of a sound, the slide of a rubber sole across a wood floor, fabric swiped against a painted wall. Just a little swoosh.

Her eyes flew open again.

This time the darkness closed in on her, squashing the air from her lungs.

Heart pounding, she sat up, grabbed her cell. Her fingers instantly poised to enter 911.

Wait. She needed to take a breath and listen. Ensure she hadn't dreamed the sounds. She struggled to calm her racing heart and to quiet the sound of blood roaring through her veins.

The squeak of a floorboard…another soft whisper of a footfall.

Someone was definitely in the house.

She tapped Branch's name in her contact list as

she hurried soundlessly across the room. Holding her breath, she opened the closet door. Thank God it didn't squeak. She burrowed as deeply inside as possible, pulling the door soundlessly shut behind her.

"Hey—" Branch's voice echoed sleepily in her ear "—what's up?"

She turned her back to the door and whispered, "Someone is in the house."

"Hang up and call 911. I'll be right there."

She did as he asked and tried to flatten herself against the back wall behind the clothes from high school that still hung in her closet.

The dispatcher came on the line with her practiced spiel. Sasha gave her address and situation.

"Officers are on the way to your home, Ms. Lenoir. Where in the house are you?"

"Second floor, third door on the left. I'm in the closet."

"Good. Are you armed?"

Another brush of sound. This one on the stairs.

"What?" she murmured.

The dispatcher repeated the question.

"No." What she would give for a weapon. "Wait." Sasha used her free hand to feel through the darkness until her fingers tightened on the item she hoped to find. "I have my baton."

It was the baton she'd used in junior high. Just over two feet long and with a classic star ball on each end. A whack to the face or chest or private area could disable a man.

As long as he didn't have a gun.

Her fingers tightened around the baton.

Pounding echoed through the house.

Sasha's heart nearly stalled.

"Sasha! It's Branch. I'm coming in."

The door was locked. How would he get in?

"The police are turning into your driveway now, Ms. Lenoir."

Sasha tried to think. "US Marshal Branch Holloway is at the front door. I called him first. Should I go down and let him in?"

"Stay where you are, ma'am."

"Sasha!"

She couldn't just stay hidden like this. She opened the door and eased out of the closet. The moonlight coming in through the window had her blinking after being in total darkness for several minutes.

Standing very still, she listened for sound. Besides Branch's pounding she heard nothing else.

She burst out of her room and rushed down the stairs. "I'm coming."

A crash in the kitchen froze her feet to the floor.

For a single second she wanted to run after the sound. Good sense took over and she rushed to the front door instead and unlocked it for Branch.

"Are you all right?"

"Yes. I heard something in the kitchen just now."

"Stay close behind me."

Sasha fell into step right behind him. He flipped lights on as they went. Once in the kitchen he stopped. She bumped into his back.

"The back door is standing open," Branch said.

Sasha leaned past his shoulder, saw a uniformed police officer coming through the wide-open door. She had locked that door. She was certain of it.

"My partner's going over the yard," the officer said. "Are you clear in here?"

"I'll make sure. You take the exterior."

The officer disappeared into the darkness. That was when Sasha saw Branch's weapon.

Her breath caught.

Branch reached back with his free hand and gave her arm a squeeze. "I want you to stay close behind me while we look around inside. I'm confident the intruder is gone but let's not take any chances."

It wasn't until they had cleared the dining room and family room as well as the powder room that she realized she had dropped her cell phone. It lay on the floor at the bottom of the stairs.

She grabbed it. "I don't think he came upstairs. I think that was his intention but your pounding on the front door stopped him."

As they climbed, Branch asked, "Do you have reason to believe the intruder was a he?"

"Well, no. I'm just assuming."

"He didn't speak or make any sounds?"

"I heard the sound of his clothing brushing the wall or a piece of furniture and the whisper of his shoe soles on the floor."

"What woke you up?" He entered the first bedroom, the one her grandmother had always used for a guest room.

"I guess the sound of him moving about downstairs. I thought I imagined it, so I tried to go back to sleep. Then I heard it again. Really soft sounds."

They checked each room and found nothing.

"Now let's have a look downstairs and see if anything is missing?"

"Okay."

One side of his mouth hitched up into a grin. "Nice weapon."

Her fingers loosened slightly on the baton. "One of the girls on my team knocked a guy out with her baton."

He laughed. "I think I remember hearing about that. Gave him a concussion, didn't she?"

"That part was a rumor, I think."

"Marshal Holloway, I'm coming in."

Sasha turned toward the front door as it opened and one of the officers stepped inside. Since Branch was armed, the officer announcing his intentions was a smart move.

"We have a secondary scene outside."

Sasha wasn't certain what the term *secondary scene* meant but she was confident it wasn't a good thing.

"Stay inside with Ms. Lenoir and I'll have a look."

"Excuse me," she protested. "I would like to see this secondary scene, as well."

Branch looked to the officer, who said, "The yard is clear, Marshal."

"Take a second look around inside," Branch suggested. "Ms. Lenoir and I will talk to your partner outside."

"Yes, sir."

"Stay close," Branch cautioned again.

She followed him outside, down the steps and around the corner of the house. Obviously this secondary scene was in the backyard. The other uniformed officer was waiting near the porch.

"The perpetrator entered through the rear door," the young man, who couldn't be more than twenty-five, said. "There's evidence the lock was disabled."

"Good work, Officer Gabrielle. What else did you find?"

Gabrielle shone his flashlight onto the wall near the far end of the porch. Words had been spray-painted on the siding.

You were supposed to die that night...

For several seconds Sasha could only stare at the words; they wouldn't assimilate in her brain... Then suddenly they did. Her heart bumped against her sternum.

"I think you can safely say that you've kicked a hornet's nest," Branch announced.

Where's the kid? the man with the deep voice demanded.

At a friend's. She's not here. Her mother's voice. Terror pulsed in every syllable. *She's a child. She doesn't know anything!*

Sasha turned to Branch. "Whoever left that message was in the house that night. He knows I was supposed to die, too, but my mother told them I was at a friend's."

A sinking feeling had her knees going weak. Sasha steadied herself. At least now there was no question about what happened that night and it was no longer only dependent upon her unreliable memories. This was evidence.

Someone had murdered her parents.

DAYLIGHT HAD ARRIVED by the time the evidence collectors had come and gone. Sasha had made two pots of coffee and dragged out the leftover pastries from the gathering on Sunday evening.

She stood in the backyard staring at the words that had been sprayed with red spray paint. *You were supposed to die that night...*

Why did it matter to her parents' killer if she lived or died?

What could she have possibly known that counted for anything?

Had she seen the killer before? Was it someone she knew when she was a child?

She needed more coffee. In the dining room the pastries were mostly gone but there was still coffee. She'd had to set up in the dining room since the kitchen was a crime scene.

Crime scene.

She shuddered. No one should have to go through something like that twice in a lifetime. In New York she had a security system. Maybe she should have one installed here.

Should she sell the house at the same time she sold the Lenoir home place?

She hadn't really thought that far into the future. She had to talk to Brianne. This was her legacy, too.

Sasha poured the coffee and went back outside via the front door. Halfway around the house she ran into Branch and another man wearing a cowboy hat. Wait— she knew him. She just couldn't place his face.

"Sasha, this is Chief of Police Billy Brannigan."

She extended her hand. "I remember you. You played football for Tennessee."

"I did." He gave her hand a quick shake.

All of Winchester had celebrated when he made the cut. "Did your forensic people find anything useful?"

"Well—" he pushed his hat up a little and settled his hands on his hips "—it's too early to tell just yet, but I did want to speak with you about the case you and Branch are investigating."

Sasha glanced at Branch.

"We should talk inside," he offered.

Sasha led the way to the family room. She closed the French doors to the dining room as well as the door to the kitchen. She turned back to the two men waiting for her attention.

"Why don't we sit," Brannigan offered.

"Of course." Sasha hadn't had nearly enough sleep. Her brain was hardly working.

They settled around the coffee table, Branch on the sofa with her, Brannigan in the chair directly across from them.

"Ms. Lenoir—"

"Sasha," she protested.

"Sasha," he amended, "it's clear you've awakened a sleeping bear."

That was one way to put it. "It's also clear that my father didn't kill my mother or himself."

"I certainly believe we have justifiable cause to officially reopen the case."

Sasha barely restrained a cheer.

"We've established more than justifiable cause, Chief," Branch argued. "We've proven reasonable doubt in the initial findings. If there were any questions, the message outside should have alleviated those."

Brannigan nodded. "I agree, but I also understand that there are plenty of folks who like to stir trouble. It's possible someone you've spoken to—" this he said to Sasha "—has decided to give legs to your case. Folks were divided twenty-seven years ago. There were those who believed your daddy was guilty and those who were certain he was innocent. Your digging around in the past is the perfect opportunity to turn the tide of things in the direction they believed was the right one to begin with."

As much as Sasha wanted to dispute his assertion, his conclusion was reasonable and logical. Even in a small town people took sides in controversies, especially those that involved lifelong members of the community and murder.

"What're you suggesting we do moving forward?"

Branch asked, his tone as pointed as his expression. He obviously wasn't happy with where this was going.

Sasha spoke first. "Chief, I respect your thoughts on the matter but I have every intention of continuing my search for the truth. I'm well aware that as long as I don't break any laws or cause any obstruction of any sort that I can do as I please."

Branch turned his hands up. "I'm on vacation and I intend to help her do exactly that—in a completely unofficial capacity, of course."

Brannigan looked from one to the other. "Well, I won't waste my time trying to talk you out of it. I will, however, need the case file back so I can reopen the investigation."

"Do we have time to make a copy?"

Brannigan's lips formed a grim line. "It was one thing when this was a cold case, Branch. This is now an official police investigation. I can't have copies all over the place. We should step back and do this right. You know the drill as well as I do. Whatever we find, we don't want a simple technicality to cause trouble in the courtroom."

"I understand," Branch conceded. "The case file is at my house. I'll have it at your office before noon."

Sasha wanted to argue with him but decided to save her frustration for when it was just the two of them. A united front was what she needed right now. She was an outsider, no matter how many years her family had resided here. Branch was one of them and he was a member of law enforcement. Besides, the case file wasn't at his house; it was here. She trusted that he had good reason for not sharing that information with the chief.

In the end, they would figure this out, with or without the file.

"Thanks, Branch. I'll make sure Cindy is on the lookout for it. I'll have a meeting with my detectives and get the ball rolling and I'll keep you informed as well as I can."

"I appreciate it, Billy."

Brannigan stood and settled his hat back into place. "Thank you for your cooperation, Ms. Lenoir." He nodded to her and then to the other man. "Branch."

Branch followed him to the front door. Sasha strained to hear anything one or both might say.

"Keep an eye on her, Branch," Brannigan warned. "Obviously there is some danger here. I'm not sure she understands how complicated this could get."

"I'll keep her safe," Branch guaranteed. "A situation like this morning won't happen again."

When Branch returned to the family room, Sasha opened her mouth to protest having to turn over the file without a copy but Branch held up his hand for her to wait. He went back to the entry hall and checked out the window. When he returned to where she waited, he kept his voice low.

"We have a few minutes before Billy will become suspicious. Where's the case file?"

"In my bedroom. I put it in the closet." She shrugged. "Just in case."

"Good idea."

As they climbed the stairs, she whispered to him, "If he won't allow us to make a copy—"

"We can't make a copy but he didn't say anything about taking photos."

Sasha smiled for the first time today. "Smart thinking."

At the top of the stairs he paused, held her gaze. "I've been doing this a while. Never count me out."

She would know never to do that again. "Thanks."

During the next few minutes they snapped pics with their cells. Every page, every photo. Sasha's stomach churned as she took care of the crime scene photos. When the last one was complete, Branch repacked the files into the box.

"I'll tuck this back in your closet and pick it up on my way to Billy's office later today."

She nodded her understanding. Before she could ask what was next, he said, "Pack a bag. You're not staying here alone anymore."

"Where are you suggesting I stay?"

"You're staying with me." He carried the file box to her closet, deposited it on the floor and covered it with the same throw she'd had over it.

For a moment she only stared at him. He couldn't possibly think she would stay with him at his house... *alone.*

"I know what you're thinking." He tapped her on the temple. "Don't fight me on this, Sasha. Besides my grandmother, I'm the only one who's completely on your side in this."

"I can stay at a motel or at the inn." She wasn't actually sure of what establishments still operated in Winchester. Good grief. She could not spend time under the same roof with him. Not the way he was suggesting.

"Look. This is not some plot to take advantage of you. You can stay at my grandmother's if you prefer. I just don't want you alone at night—anywhere. We can use the evenings to go over what we find and compare notes and thoughts. We'll spend most evenings together anyway."

So maybe he had a point. "You have a guest room?"

"I do. You can take my room since it's upstairs. I'll

take the guest room downstairs. There will be an entire floor between us."

Now she just felt foolish. "Well, all right. I'll pack a few things."

"Good." He nodded. "I'll get out of your way."

Somewhere downstairs the sound of her cell phone ringing pierced the air.

Sasha headed for the door. "That's my phone."

"You pack. I'll get your phone."

She nodded. "Thanks."

With her smallest suitcase opened on the bed, she started layering in sleepwear and clothes. She groaned when she realized she'd been running around all morning in a nightshirt. At least she'd had the good sense to pull on one of her grandmother's sweaters once Branch had arrived.

"What a night," she grumbled.

"Mom?"

The sound of her daughter's voice reverberated up the stairs. Sasha's heart nearly stopped.

"I'm not your mom, but I'm taking the phone to her. Hold on a minute."

"Who are you?"

Sasha winced. That was her daughter's interested tone. She probably thought— Sasha shook her head. She didn't want to go there.

"I'm US Marshal Branch Holloway, an old friend of your mom's."

He walked into the room, grinning from ear to ear.

Sasha reached out; her hand trembled in spite of her struggle to keep it steady. "Thanks."

He placed the phone in her hand, her daughter's pic filling the screen. Her blond hair and blue eyes exact duplicates of his.

"I'll be waiting downstairs."

Sasha nodded. Not trusting her voice. When he'd left the room she took the phone off Speaker and said, "Hey, baby."

"Who was that?"

Sasha collapsed onto the bed. "An old friend, sweetie. He's helping with all this stuff that needs to be done." She had not told her daughter about her search into the past. Until she had some evidence one way or another, there was no point sharing any of this with anyone beyond official personnel. Though, technically, she did have some evidence now.

"Mom, he sounds hot. You should live a little. I'm doing a Google search on him right now."

Sasha's mouth went dry. "You know how photos on the internet are never like the real person."

"So when are you coming home?"

Sasha managed her first deep breath since her phone rang. "Next week, I hope."

"I don't understand why I can't come there. There was a death in the family. I can make up the homework and tests."

"We'll talk about that later in the week."

"OMG, he is straight fire."

"Why aren't you on your way to school?" Her heart was hammering again.

"Okay, okay. Chill. I won't be late."

In the background Sasha heard Avery's voice urging Brianne to hurry before she was late. Saved by the nanny!

Thank God.

"I'll talk to you after school, sweetie."

"Okay. Love you!"

"Love you, too."

The call ended but Sasha's heart didn't stop pounding. Her daughter had seen a photo of her father.

Branch had seen a photo of his daughter.

Sasha was running out of time and someone had threatened her life.

She stood. She couldn't control precisely how the investigation of this case went, but she could still navigate the other. She would not leave her daughter in the dark the way her grandmother had left her.

All she had to do was find the right moment to tell her the truth. First, she needed to tell Branch.

Chapter Nine

Arlene Holloway had come to her grandson's house as
soon as she heard the news. She also insisted on throwing together a late breakfast. Sasha tried to help but the
eighty-five-year-old woman shooed her away. So while
Arlene prepared eggs and toast and bacon, Sasha and
Branch discussed where to go next with their investigation.

"Come and get it!"

By the time they wandered into Branch's kitchen,
Arlene had already arranged her own plate and was
stationed at the head of the kitchen table.

Sasha had been certain she couldn't eat. Not after all
that had happened this morning. Apparently her emotional reaction had been a little delayed. By the time
they had driven from her house to Branch's, she was
trembling and feeling weak-kneed. She hated feeling
frail, hated even more for anyone to witness the episode.

"That's the way it always worked for me," the older
woman had said. "I was always the one who could keep
it together during a crisis, but then when it was over I
fell apart."

Weathering crises was Sasha's brand. No one was
better, but she had definitely had trouble holding herself
together after they left her grandmother's home. Sasha

understood the reason this situation was different was because it was personal. At work she was dealing with other people's crises. This was profoundly private and it went all the way back to her childhood.

"I've been thinking about what you asked me," Arlene announced, her attention moving from her freshly emptied plate to the man at the other end of the table.

"Did you think of anyone?" Branch asked.

Sasha looked from him to his grandmother.

"Your mother," she said to Sasha, "had lots of friends. She was a very busy lady, all about work, so she didn't do a lot of socializing. But there was one friend she lunched with fairly regularly. Vi and I sometimes ran into them at the diner."

"Is her name Penny or Patty?" For the life of her, Sasha could not recall the name. She was glad Branch had remembered to ask his grandmother.

"Not a Penny or a Patty. That's why I had to do some thinking. The name was wrong. It's Leandra Brennan. Her friends called her Lenny."

"Lenny." The name clicked. Sasha nodded. "That's it. Is this woman still alive?"

"She is. Still lives in the same house and works at the same job. Her house is over on North High Street. Six-oh-six. You probably won't find her at home on a workday though. She's Jarvis Packard's personal assistant."

"Jarvis Packard?" The name wasn't familiar to Sasha. She'd been gone a very long time.

"The biggest land developer in the Southeast," Branch said. He pushed his cleaned plate away. "His company is involved in any major project that happens in the area."

"Where're the Packard offices?"

"Over on South College," Arlene said. "You can't miss it. There's a huge sign."

Arlene scooted back her chair and stood. "Now you two get on about your business and I'll clean up here."

"Gran," Branch argued, "you've already done too much."

"Your mama told me to take care of you while she and your daddy are on vacation."

"I don't think she intended for you to cook for me," he protested as he took his plate to the sink.

Sasha followed with her own plate and fork. She loved hearing the two bicker. It was so cute to see the big fearless marshal concede to his little old grandmother. Sasha rinsed the dishes and tucked them into the dishwasher. Arlene wiped the table.

"You planning to visit Lenny?" Arlene asked.

"I am," Sasha confirmed. "If she was my mother's closest friend, perhaps she'll know if there was something unusual happening around the time of the murders."

It felt suddenly odd to speak about the murders in such an investigative manner. Twenty-seven years had elapsed since that night. Sasha had long ago come to terms with the pain of shock and loss. The events of that night had left lifelong wounds with deep scars. But she had chosen to move forward despite the trauma.

Now those emotions resurfaced with the same raw ache she'd felt as a child.

"I can go with you," Branch offered.

Arlene sent him a frown. "I doubt she will want to talk in front of you. Heavens, Branch, you know better than that. If the woman knows anything, she's far more likely to tell her friend's daughter than some lawman."

"She has a point," Sasha agreed.

"I'll follow you there on my way to see Luther Holcomb."

"Luther?" Arlene pushed the last chair into the table. "He was convinced your daddy did the killing, Sasha. He refused to see that night any other way. I remember arguing with him but it did no good whatsoever."

This was the part that nagged at Sasha. All her adult life she had ignored this aspect of the past but now it was simply impossible to ignore. "Why didn't my grandmother argue with him? Why didn't she fight for the truth?"

Arlene seemed to shrink into herself—as if the question had shaken her. Sasha immediately felt contrite for her poor choice in words.

"I think she wanted to protect you? The longer the investigation dragged out, the harder it was for you to move on. Like she said, *dead is dead*. No amount of hollering and screaming and making a fuss was going to bring her daughter back."

Sasha considered for the first time how painful her mother's death must have been for her grandmother. Alexandra had been Sasha's mother, but she had been Viola's only child. Sasha couldn't fathom even the concept of losing her own daughter.

"I can understand how she wanted to put the hurt behind her—behind the both of us." She pushed the painful thought away and turned to Branch. "I guess we should get started."

He nodded. "I need to talk to Luther," he explained, "before the official investigation shuts him down to those not part of that investigation."

"We'll connect after our meetings," Sasha said. She

could do this part on her own. Besides, they could get a lot more done going their separate ways.

He pointed a finger at her. "I want to know where you are at all times. When you leave one location headed to another, I want to know."

"I expect the same," she tossed back at him.

He grabbed his hat and settled it into place. "You got it."

"Thanks for breakfast, Mrs. Holloway." Sasha gave the lady a hug.

She patted Sasha on the back. "Your mama would be very proud of you."

The words haunted Sasha all the way across town. Her grandmother had told her often enough as a child that her mother would be proud of her, but Sasha hadn't considered how her mother would feel about her reopening this investigation.

"The truth is what matters," Sasha said aloud as she turned into the parking lot of the Packard building.

She watched Branch continue on South College. Sasha wasn't sure where former chief of police Luther Holcomb lived now. Her attention settled on the six-story building with the huge *P* on top that had not been here when she was a kid.

Sasha climbed out of the rental, tucked the strap of her bag on her shoulder and headed for the main entrance. She couldn't be sure if this Lenny person was at work today, if she was out of town on vacation or tied up in back-to-back meetings, but Sasha had to try.

Inside, the elegant lobby was massive with towering ceilings and a wall of plants behind the elegant reception desk. The other three walls were tinted glass. Sleek tile floors, combined with all the glass, gave the lobby a cold feel. The neatly arranged pit of leather seating didn't help.

Cold and austere.

Sasha was glad she'd chosen a gray sweater to wear with her jeans today. She didn't exactly look professional but she did look casually comfortable. She'd tucked her long, curly hair into a clip.

When the receptionist ended her call and looked up, Sasha smiled. "I'm here to see Leandra Brennan."

A practiced smile that didn't quite reach her eyes slid into place. "Do you have an appointment?"

"No," Sasha confessed. "I'm only in town for a few days and I thought I'd drop in. I'm Alexandra Lenoir's daughter. If you would just tell her I'm here."

"I can call her office and see if she's available," the receptionist offered.

"Thank you."

Rather than sit, Sasha wandered to the far side of the lobby where a freestanding glass wall featured ongoing and upcoming projects. A new mall in Tullahoma. A hotel near the interstate. A medical complex by the Winchester hospital. Packard was apparently involved in anything big in the tri-county area.

"Ms. Lenoir—" the receptionist's carefully modulated tone reached out "—Mrs. Brennan can see you now."

Surprised but thankful, Sasha went through the steps. She provided her driver's license and stood still for a photo. Then she was given the code for the ride upstairs. On the elevator she entered the code and the doors automatically closed and the car bumped into motion, stopping on the top floor.

As cold and austere as the lobby was, the top floor was anything but. Thick carpeting, rich wall colors and lavish furnishings. Another receptionist looked up from her desk and smiled.

"Please have a seat. Mrs. Brennan will be with you shortly."

"Thank you."

Sasha settled into a plush upholstered chair and worked on relaxing. She wanted to appear calm and intelligent, not emotional and desperate. This could be the step that made all the difference in discovering the truth she so badly wanted to find. If she had harbored any reservations about this endeavor, she certainly did not after last night's intruder. Someone knew what she was doing and that someone was worried. That had to mean something.

You were supposed to die that night...

Had her grandmother feared for her own and Sasha's lives? Was that why she hadn't pursued a different conclusion from the official one reached by the police department? Her grandmother had been a very intelligent woman. She would have realized that nothing added up. The concept that Viola Simmons might have been afraid shook Sasha. Her grandmother had always appeared so brave and strong.

But everyone had his or her breaking point. Sasha could not imagine surviving the loss of a child. Arlene was right. Viola's entire focus would have been on protecting Sasha.

Whatever it took, she would find the truth—for her parents and for her grandmother. Sasha's grandfather on her mother's side had died before Sasha was born, so she had never known him. She had heard stories that he was a shrewd businessman, which was why her grandmother had never had to worry financially. Her father's parents and sister had moved away after the murders.

Sasha had never once heard from them. She supposed they had been too devastated. But she had been a child and they shouldn't have abandoned her.

She had considered contacting them but she'd never pursued any search. If they hadn't cared about what happened to her, then she'd just as soon leave well enough alone. Unless they had information about what had happened?

Why would they not have stayed and fought for justice if they believed her father was innocent? Or had some proof?

Why hadn't someone done the right thing?

"Sasha."

Sasha looked up at the sound of the woman's voice. The red hair and blue eyes instantly triggered memories of her mother and this woman—a younger version of this woman—huddled over magazines and talking about decorating.

She stood and extended her hand. "Thank you for taking the time to see me, Ms. Brennan."

The woman nodded. "Let's go to my office."

Sasha followed her down the hall and into an office with a massive window; though the view of South College and the parking lot wasn't that spectacular, it did allow lots of light. The furnishings were elegant and numerous accolades lined the walls.

Brennan loosened a button on her suit jacket and settled into the chair behind her desk. She wore her hair down over her shoulders as she had decades ago. The gray streaks reminded Sasha just how much time had passed.

"Please—" the older woman gestured to the chairs opposite her desk "—have a seat."

Sasha perched on the edge of a wingback. Suddenly

she felt nervous. Perhaps it was foolish but she felt as if what this woman had to say could be a turning point in her search for the truth.

"You look well," Brennan said. "I was sorry to hear about your grandmother. She was a kind and gracious woman."

"Thank you. It was a blow." There was no other way to put it. Losing her grandmother had shaken Sasha's world. Perhaps that was why she was here as much as for any other reason.

"I hear you've made quite the name for yourself in New York." Brennan smiled. "Your mother would be proud."

Sasha nodded, the burn of emotion suddenly attacking her eyes. She really needed to get a hold on herself. "I'm good at what I do."

"And you have a daughter. I understand she's quite the dancer. I'm sure you have your sights set on Juilliard."

Sasha wanted to ask if Brennan had remained close with her grandmother but it didn't feel right. Why wouldn't her grandmother have mentioned talking to Brennan?

"She does," Sasha allowed. "Personally I have my hopes set on Columbia or Princeton."

Brennan nodded. "Sometimes things don't turn out the way we expect."

There was a sadness in her eyes and her voice as she said the words.

"No one knows that better than me," Sasha agreed. "One day my life was the perfect nine-year-old's world and the next my parents were dead. Murdered."

Brennan blinked. "It was a tragedy."

"My mother was worried about something those last

few days of her life," Sasha lied. She actually had no recall of her mother being upset about anything except her father's job issue. "You were helping her. I remember you calling and leaving her a message."

Fear or something on that order flashed in the other woman's eyes before she schooled the reaction. "Perhaps you didn't know that your parents were having a difficult time. Your father had lost his job and they were arguing a lot. I tried to be there for her but I'm afraid I failed her miserably. If I'd had any idea Brandon would go that far I would have done something. The fact is, I was out of town on business for days before and after... that night."

"Is that why the police didn't interview you?" It seemed strange to Sasha that the police would not have interviewed the victim's best friend.

"I suppose so. Why do you ask?"

One aspect of Sasha's work that she was particularly good at was reading her clients. It was extremely important that she recognize when one was lying. It wasn't that she took only clients who were honest and aboveboard—that wasn't the case at all. But she didn't take clients who lied to *her*.

Leandra Brennan was lying.

"Oh." Sasha frowned. "I guess you haven't heard."

Brennan frowned as if she had no idea what Sasha meant.

"Chief Brannigan is reopening the case. New evidence has come to light that suggests my father was innocent. In fact, the same person who murdered my mother murdered him, as well."

Blink. Blink. Shock. "What new evidence?"

Sasha sighed. "I'm afraid I'm not at liberty to discuss it. I can tell you that someone broke into my grandmother's house last night and left me a threatening message. It wasn't pleasant. The chief feels that's all the more indication that the new investigation is on the right track."

Sasha hoped the other woman wasn't so good at ferreting out untruths because she had just woven an elaborate tale that was only partly true.

Brennan put her hand to her chest. "That's terrible—about the break-in, I mean. I'm glad you're all right. What kind of message did the intruder leave?"

Sasha held her gaze for a long moment, mostly to drag out the tension. "He said I should have died that night. I guess the killers didn't realize I was hiding under the stairs and heard everything." She shook her head. "There were two of them in the house. It's a shame Chief Holcomb didn't listen to me all those years ago or my parents' killers wouldn't have gotten away with murder."

"I had no idea." Brennan's words were cold and stilted.

"No one did. But now they're going to know. Because I won't stop until I find the truth. Actually, I'm hoping you can help me."

Brennan looked startled. "How would I be able to help you?" As if she'd only just realized how her words sounded, she added, "Of course I will be happy to help any way I can, but I'm not sure how that's possible. It's always been my belief that Brandon was the one…and as I said, I was out of town."

Sasha stood. She reached into her bag and pulled out one of her cards. "I'm certain if you think about it, something will come to you. I still have your message to my mother the day before she was murdered. You were worried—you wanted to warn her about something. When you remember what that something was, call me. Please."

She placed her card on the desk and turned away from the woman's stunned gaze.

Sasha had a feeling she'd just shaken the lion's cage. A roar of a reaction would be coming.

Good. That was the point.

She rode the elevator down to the lobby and walked out of the building. She could almost feel Brennan's eyes on her as she climbed into her rental car.

All she had to do now was wait for the domino effect.

Chapter Ten

Luther Holcomb no longer lived in Winchester proper. After he retired four years ago, he divorced his wife and moved out into the woods in the middle of nowhere. He spent most of his time fishing or hunting.

Branch supposed a man who'd spent his life being a cop had the right to do whatever he wanted when he reached sixty-five without getting himself dead. Now, as Luther approached seventy, it seemed he rarely even came into town anymore.

Branch parked his truck and stared at the cabin directly in front of him. Was this what happened to a man who spent his life focused on catching criminals? Luther and his wife never had children and then after all those years they just walked away from so many decades invested in a marriage. Had they been living separate lives all along anyway? Branch knew lots of lawmen who did exactly that. The lives they led with the badge were the ones that consumed their existences. Their wives and kids had their own lives. Once in a while—like birthdays and holidays or graduations— those two lives intersected.

Branch didn't want that kind of life. Maybe it was the idea that he was barreling toward forty but he didn't want the family life he hoped to one day have to end up a casualty of his career. He wanted what his parents had. He wanted what his grandparents had shared.

He thought of Sasha and her daughter. What kind of life did they have together? Without the girl's dad in the picture? Her daughter—Brianne—had looked nothing like Branch had expected. He'd expected her to have her mother's dark hair and green eyes but she'd been blonde with blue eyes. Before he could stop his mind from going there, he imagined Sasha with some New York City hotshot. His gut tightened with envy.

A rap on the glass made him jump. His attention whipped in that direction to find Luther staring at him.

"You gonna sit in there all day?"

Branch couldn't believe he had allowed the old guy to sneak up on him. He opened the door and climbed out. "Hey, Luther, how are you doing?"

"Well, I'm still above ground, so that's always a good thing."

"Can't argue with that."

"Is this an official visit?" Luther eyed him speculatively.

"Kinda sorta." Branch closed the truck door and leaned against it. "Is that okay?"

Luther shrugged. "Sure. Why not? I just made a batch of shine if you're interested."

Branch shot him a grin. "I've had your shine before, Luther." He pressed a hand to his stomach. "I don't think I should go down that path today."

"When did they start making you guys so soft?" The older man laughed as he led the way into his house.

Branch followed, removing his hat at the door. "They like us to keep a clear head these days."

Luther grunted. "Is that supposed to make you better lawmen?"

"Presumably." Branch glanced around at the sparse furnishings and then at the bulletin board with its big calendar and all those crossed-out blocks. "You lining up your fishing calendar?"

"Oh, yeah." Luther poured himself a little shine in a mason jar and gestured to the seating area. "Sit. Tell me what you're up to, Mr. US Marshal."

Branch settled in the nearest chair. "Technically, I'm on vacation, but I'm helping a friend. You remember the Lenoir case?"

Luther collapsed into an ancient recliner. He knocked back a slug of his drink and then nodded. "How could I forget? It was an ugly mess. That poor little girl was shattered."

"That poor little girl is all grown up now," Branch commented, "and she wants to know what really happened that night."

Luther's gaze narrowed. "You think there was something wrong with the way I conducted the investigation?"

Branch had expected a bit of defensiveness. It was human nature. "No, sir. I reviewed the reports and I think you did everything you could with what you had to work with at the time."

The tension in Luther's expression relaxed marginally and he indulged in another shot of homemade liquor, winced at the burn.

"I actually just have one question."

"What's that?" Luther set the mason jar down. "The scene was cut-and-dry. Easy to read. A blind man couldn't have missed the clues to what happened that night."

"Almost too easy," Branch noted. Then he asked his

question. "Why didn't you put the little girl's statement in the file?"

Luther's eyebrows reared up. "You mean the one she came up with a week later?"

Branch didn't miss the guy's skepticism. "She insists she mentioned it the night her parents died but no one was listening."

"Let's take a minute and go over what I had," Luther suggested, "if you have the time."

"I have the time." Obviously Branch had struck a nerve. Not surprising. No lawman ever liked having one of his cases called into question.

"Brandon Lenoir got fired for drinking on the job. His blood alcohol level that night, by the way, was point one, well over the legal limit of impairment." Luther flared his hands. "Do the math. Taking into consideration his size, that means he had at least six beers or drinks in the couple of hours before he died. He didn't have a reputation for drinking, so I'm thinking that level of alcohol was unusual for him. People do crazy stuff when they're inebriated—especially someone not accustomed to being in that condition."

There was no denying that assessment. "So you're convinced Brandon Lenoir did this? No matter that he had no violent tendencies and from all reports loved his wife."

Luther shrugged. "Every killer starts somewhere. Many of them were never violent before their first kill. Sometimes people just snap. When he realized what he'd done, he killed himself."

"Why didn't he kill his daughter?" Branch countered. "He had to know where she was. If he wanted to kill his family, why leave her alive?"

Luther picked up the mason jar and had another

swallow. "We explored the possibility that his wife was having an affair, but we found no evidence of infidelity—on either side."

"So basically they were a happy family with no serious problems. In fact, losing his job wasn't a major blow to their financial stability."

"Maybe it was a pride thing," Luther offered.

Branch wasn't buying it, particularly after last night. "You didn't answer my first question."

"The victim's advocate urged Mrs. Simmons to take the child to a psychiatrist. I did the same. She made an appointment immediately and the psychiatrist's report indicated the girl's story was something her mind conjured to make her feel better—a defense mechanism. What else was I supposed to do? Pursue a lead on a voice or voices that didn't exist?"

Branch couldn't deny the conundrum the man had faced. "You know my grandmother is still convinced Mr. Lenoir didn't kill his wife."

"She made her feelings known well enough." He laughed. "She complained louder than Mrs. Simmons."

"Did you consider why Mrs. Simmons kept so quiet? Is it possible she was afraid for her granddaughter's safety?"

This suggestion got the man's attention. "Did she tell her granddaughter that?"

Branch shook his head. "Nope, but someone broke into Mrs. Simmons's house last night and left a message for Sasha. *You were supposed to die that night.*"

"I guess word has gotten around that she's looking into the case. Some folks don't like the past being dug up."

"Unless they have something to hide, why all the fuss?"

"You got a point there, Marshal." He tossed back the last of his shine. "Let's talk off-the-record."

"This entire conversation is off-the-record," Branch reminded him. "I'm on vacation and anything I do or say is strictly coming from just me."

"No one really believed Brandon Lenoir would kill his wife, but stranger things have happened. The evidence was clear. There were powder burns on his hand. No indication of forced entry. No evidence of foul play anywhere on the property."

"But," Branch argued, "I'm guessing it was the psychiatrist's conclusion that Sasha had made up the voices that convinced you to close the case?"

"If I have to pinpoint one thing, yeah. It was his report."

"Why isn't that report in the case file?" Seemed strange to Branch to leave out the primary reason for his conclusion.

"Mrs. Simmons didn't want any record of her granddaughter having emotional issues. I guess she was afraid the conclusion would haunt her in the future. I figure that honoring her wishes was the least I could do under the circumstances."

"Can I pass the psychiatrist's name on to Sasha? If he's still practicing she may want to meet with him."

"Sure. It was Dr. Bruce Farr. His office is across from the hospital. He doesn't see many patients anymore. He's some big-deal board member at the hospital these days."

Branch stood. "Thanks, Luther. I appreciate your help."

Luther pushed to his feet, gave Branch's hand a shake. "I'm not so sure I helped."

"If you think of anything else that might be useful, I would appreciate a call." Branch reached into his pocket and pulled out one of his cards.

"Sure thing." Luther took the card. "Bill called me. He wants to meet later to do this same thing."

Branch wasn't surprised. "It might be better if you don't mention I was here."

Luther grinned. "I never kiss and tell."

Branch was back on the main highway before his cell service kicked in again. He pulled over to review a couple of text messages from Sasha. She had met with Leandra Brennan and learned very little. Chief Brannigan wanted to meet with her, so she was headed to city hall. Branch sent her a message explaining he'd met with Luther and intended to follow up with the shrink who had examined her, and then the coroner.

She promised to call him as soon as her meeting with Brannigan ended.

Branch drove back to town and took the turn that wound around by the hospital. Dr. Farr's office was a brick building directly across the street. Branch pulled into the small lot and climbed out. He settled his hat into place and walked to the entrance.

The door was locked. The office hours posted on the door showed Wednesday through Friday from one to four. There was an emergency contact number but Branch preferred catching the man in person to question him. He didn't want to give him a chance to prepare answers or to blow Branch off.

He moved on, heading to the veterinarian's office on Decherd Boulevard. The drive took only a few minutes. Burt Johnston had been the county coroner for about forty years. He also operated two large veterinarian offices. By trade the man was a veterinarian. Though he mostly oversaw the operations from a distance these days, folks still considered him the top vet in the area.

Didn't seem to matter to anyone that he also pronounced their deceased loved ones.

A technician waved Branch through. He found Burt in his office. Branch knocked and was summoned inside.

"Well, if it's not our celebrity US marshal. You chasing down another big mob element here in Winchester?"

Branch laughed. "No, I think we've cleared all that up."

Burt gestured to a chair. "What can I do for you today, Branch?"

"Tell me what you remember about the Lenoir case. Anything that stood out as a question for you?"

Burt shook his head. "It was a pretty straightforward situation." He shook his head again. "That poor child was the worst part. She was crying at the top of her lungs. Until we got her grandma there, it was a nightmare."

"Did you see anyone near the house that night who shouldn't have been there? Maybe someone who was there to see the show?"

Crime scenes were like car accidents—people often went out of their way to see.

"Not that I can recall. Two of Luther's boys got there first. Officers Kenyon and Lacon. When I arrived, Kenyon was in the front yard puking his guts out and Lacon was trying to calm the kid down."

"No neighbors or code scanners showed up?" Some folks listened to the police scanners and rushed to the scenes of crimes. The internet had made the uploading of photos and videos for titillation a way of life.

"The officers were there. I came next. I was already in the area when I received the call. The ambulance was right behind me and then Luther brought up the rear."

"As you know," Branch ventured, "Viola Simmons passed away and her granddaughter is in town settling her affairs. She has a lot of questions about what happened and she'd like to have answers to those questions while she's here. She's waited a long time to put this behind her. I've offered to help her find those answers."

"A lot of people weren't satisfied with the conclusions from that one, and frankly, I was one of them."

In Branch's opinion, having the coroner a bit skeptical was saying something. "Looking back, is there anything you would do differently today?"

He appeared to contemplate the question for a bit. "I would have sent a team through the woods a second time. They did a search that night but I would have done another at daylight. Luther didn't think it was necessary. He had the case nailed shut already. Personally I think the decision not to do a second search might have been a mistake. I'm convinced ignoring the little girl was one. I don't know that either issue would have changed anything, but better to be safe than sorry. Especially since the child said she heard voices besides her parents' in the house that night."

Branch frowned. "You certain about that? There are some who believe she never mentioned the voices until about a week later."

"You'd have to ask Luther to be certain, but I recall her saying something along those lines that night. Course, I was pretty focused on the bodies, but I'm reasonably sure I didn't hear wrong. In fact, I told Chief Brannigan the same thing this morning."

It appeared Brannigan was on the same track. No real surprise. "Thanks, Burt. I'll talk to Luther," Branch assured him.

The problem was, he already had.

Chapter Eleven

City hall looked basically the same as it had when Sasha was a child except for the metal detectors and the bag search. She'd come here with her grandmother once or twice after her parents died. Her grandmother had always gone into the chief's office while Sasha sat in a chair in the small lobby with the secretary or assistant to the chief.

She sat in a similar chair now. The upholstered chairs were different from the ones that had been here when she was a child but the polished tile floor was the same. The nondescript tan walls were the same. A couple more framed photos of officers who had lost their lives in the line of duty had been added to the one blue wall.

Sasha wasn't anticipating anything new in the chief's investigation of her parents' deaths. He'd only decided to reopen the case a few hours ago. Of course, there was the chance they had discovered some piece of evidence at her grandmother's house related to the break-in. Frankly, she was grateful for any support on the case. She hadn't expected to garner this much attention.

"Ms. Lenoir," the older woman behind the desk said, "the chief is ready to see you now."

Sasha stood and the door across the small room

opened. The chief stepped out to greet her. "Thank you for coming, Ms. Lenoir."

Sasha thanked the secretary and entered the chief's office.

"Do you have some news for me, Chief?" She watched as he closed the door behind them.

"Actually, I have a few questions for you." He gestured to the pair of chairs in front of his desk. "Please, have a seat."

Sasha settled into one of the chairs and waited for the chief to do the same on the other side of the desk.

He leaned forward, scanned his notes. "I met with former chief of police Luther Holcomb and the county coroner, Burt Johnston. Both remembered the Lenoir case quite vividly. The trouble is I got conflicting stories about you from the two of them." Billy's gaze fixed on hers. "I know it's been a long time and that memories cloud with time, but this is one of those things that shouldn't be difficult to recall."

"How can I help, Chief?" Strange, Branch had the same two men on his list this morning. She wondered if he and Brannigan had run into each other.

"There seems to be some question as to when you actually mentioned hearing other voices—besides your parents'—in the house that night."

A frown tugged at her brow. She was surprised by this particular question. "Chief Holcomb didn't include a statement from me in the official case file. He didn't feel my statement was credible. Are you saying you think that was a mistake?"

"Before we talk about my thoughts, did Chief Holcomb explain his reasoning for that decision?" Brannigan asked.

"There was some question as to why I didn't speak

up earlier and the psychiatrist who evaluated me seemed to feel I was making up the whole story." Hurt and anger twisted inside her. She had been telling the truth. If everyone had listened to her then, maybe the investigation would have been conducted differently. Her grandmother had been so upset by Sasha's reactions to the sessions that she had refused to take Sasha back to see the man. At the time, Sasha had been glad. The doctor had made her feel strange, as if she were lying, and she had been telling the truth.

"I've tried to contact Dr. Farr, the psychiatrist who evaluated you, but he seems to be unavailable. The dilemma I have is that according to Burt Johnston, the coroner, you were talking about the other voices that very night, which directly conflicts with what Chief Holcomb says. Obviously, someone made a mistake. I just need to figure out which one is correct."

Sasha searched her memory of that night, tried to find a moment where she remembered speaking about the voices to someone amid the macabre activities happening around her. She remembered her parents' motionless bodies…the blood everywhere…the anguished screams of her grandmother…the uniforms of the officers and the men from the ambulance. Sasha had felt as if she was in an odd bubble lingering all around the insanity but not quite inside it.

"Chief, parts of that night are a complete blur. I was in shock. Traumatized. If I was talking, I'm sure I said something about what I heard. The problem is, I can't actually remember speaking. If my grandmother was here…"

But she wasn't. Viola Simmons was gone. And with her, any information she had possessed about that horrendous night.

After so many years, how could Sasha hope to ever really know the truth? So many who might have known more were either dead or in bad health or simply no longer remembered.

Brannigan nodded, his expression filled with concern. "I've known Luther and Burt my whole life. They're both good men and neither would purposely misdirect a case. I would trust either one with my life. That said, one of them is wrong. Is there anyone else who would have been close enough to you and your family to know the details of that night?"

There was only one person. "Arlene Holloway. My grandmother and she were best friends. She might be able to help."

"I'll drop in on Mrs. Holloway. Thank you for coming by, Ms. Lenoir. Whatever you believe, I want to get to the bottom of this the same as you do."

"Thank you, Chief. That means a great deal to me."

As Sasha left the building, she noticed Leandra Brennan at the security desk in the lobby. The older woman spotted Sasha at about the same time and their gazes locked. Sasha held her gaze until her mother's old friend Lenny looked away. What kind of friend withheld potential information that might be able to cast new light on an old tragedy?

"The chief's office is directly that way, ma'am."

Sasha turned, walking backward and watching the Brennan woman as she strode toward the chief's office. Funny, there was no statement in the case file from her mother's best friend. Sasha wasn't a cop or a private investigator, but she could not see how that was right under any circumstances. Anyone close to her parents should have been interviewed. It simply didn't make sense. Brennan had insisted that she was out of town and nothing she knew was relevant, and apparently Chief Holcomb had taken her at her word.

A huge mistake, in Sasha's opinion. The woman was definitely hiding something.

Outside, she stood on the sidewalk and stared at the fading afternoon sun. She had been back in Winchester since Thursday evening—mere hours after she received the call about her grandmother. Friday Rey had taken care of all the funeral arrangements and Sasha had gone through photo albums and boxes of her grandmother's stored treasures. It wasn't until sometime Saturday that the reality sunk in. Her grandmother was dead.

Sasha climbed into her rental and drove the short distance to the cemetery. She hadn't been back there since the burial on Sunday. Right now she just needed to go back. To be near her grandmother.

She drove to the section of the cemetery where the family plot was and parked. The breeze kicked up and she shivered. Growing up, she'd never liked cemeteries. She would never forget watching her parents' caskets lowered into the cold ground.

A part of her had vanished that day. She hadn't seen that little girl since.

She walked over to the family plot, which was quite large. Simmonses had been buried here for several generations. Sasha sat down on the bench her grandmother had had installed near her parents' graves. The double headstone sat right next to the double one for her grandparents.

There was still enough space in the plot right next to her parents' for another double headstone. Would she need a double? She hadn't even come close to the altar or even moving in with a significant other.

It was just she and Brianne.

Sasha studied the date on the headstone that belonged to her parents. She suspected that her grandmother had only buried them next to each other for Sasha's benefit. Looking back, what mother who actually believed a man had killed her daughter would want him buried in the family plot for any reason—even to appease her nine-year-old granddaughter?

Had Viola really believed the official conclusions?

So many aspects of the tragedy were contradictory. So many pieces didn't properly fit into place.

But was she looking for a reason to believe her father was innocent? Had someone else been doing the same thing when they broke into her house and left that note?

Now she was really grasping at straws. She reminded herself that Branch Holloway and Billy Brannigan would not be poking around in the case unless they suspected something was amiss.

Several headstones away, she noted a blonde woman wearing a dark sweater. Arms hugged tightly around her slim body, she stood staring down at a wide granite marker. Sasha watched her for a moment, sensing she should recognize her. The breeze pushed the hair back from her cheek and Sasha realized who she was. Rowan DuPont, the undertaker's daughter. She'd buried her father in this cemetery barely a week ago. Like Sasha, she was alone now—except Sasha had her daughter. But the last of her ancestors were gone. Somehow the realization made the loss all the more difficult.

She checked her cell. Nothing from Branch yet. She should go back to the house and look around some more. The memories had really been coming inside that old house, and as difficult as it was to be there, this—*venture*—was about revisiting the past. More often than not the truth was not comfortable.

Discomfort she was prepared for.

Sasha called her daughter as she walked back to her car. There were more questions about Branch and more teasing. Deep down it pleased Sasha that her daughter thought he was good-looking. She'd had a great day at school and only had one more test this week. She could leave for Winchester tomorrow afternoon and spend the rest of the week. Sasha managed to talk her out of that one. She promised to text good-night.

When the call ended Sasha was halfway across town before she remembered to text Branch with her change of plans. She had promised to keep him informed of her whereabouts. Not that she was opposed to doing so; she'd simply forgotten. After her late-night visitor, he was right about keeping in touch. When she made the turn onto the long narrow driveway, she braked long enough to send the text. Then she rolled the quarter of a mile to her childhood home.

This late in the afternoon it was almost dark on the porch. Sasha unlocked the front door and flipped on a light. She'd spent a lot of time in her mother's office when she was here before. No need to pilfer around in there today.

She climbed the stairs, turning on lights, watching the dust motes float through the air. Bypassing her own room, she walked into her parents' room. This time, rather than look through drawers, she went to the closet and started digging through pockets and bags. Her mother had owned a dozen or more handbags. Sasha fished through each one and found nothing. She ran her hands into each pocket on each pair of pants and blouse or dress. Not one thing. Not a scrap of paper, a business card or even a piece of lint.

Viola had taken most all her daughter's jewelry, except the pearls, to her house and put it away for Sasha, so there was nothing in the jewelry box. That left only one unexplored space—the bathroom. Of course, the original investigation had checked for drugs and anything that might be considered contraband.

Sasha checked each item in the bathroom. Every bottle of makeup, stick of deodorant and jar of liquid soap. There was nothing that should not be there. Nothing unexpected. She turned toward the door, her gaze landing on the tissue box on the back of the toilet. No point leaving a single stone unturned.

She picked up the box and pulled out tissue after tissue, allowing them to fall onto the closed toilet seat. Obviously she was losing it. Rolling her eyes, she started to put the box back and then she noticed the blue on the white tissues. Sasha picked up the one on top.

Major structural flaws.

She dragged another from the box. It, too, was marred with blue ink.

Material will be stressed beyond its strength.

Then another. *Monumental failure at some point in the future.*

And the next. *Don't know what to do.*

Sasha's heart was thundering by the time she reached the last tissue in the box.

Can't tell Brandon.

She wasn't sure what this meant but it had to be important. Why else would her mother hide the notes in the bathroom tissue box?

Sasha could imagine her mother sitting alone in this bathroom, worried and afraid, and making notes to herself…or to anyone who might find them.

Cold seeped into Sasha's bones. The idea of her mother being afraid twisted her heart.

She pulled her cell from her pocket and checked her screen. Why hadn't Branch responded to her text?

A red exclamation answered the question. Message failed to send.

A scan of the top of the screen explained why. No service.

She hit Try Again with the same result.

"Well, damn." Maybe the service would be better outside. She shoved the tissues back into the box and stowed it under her arm.

The house was utterly silent. No humming refrigerator sound. No soft purr of the heating or cooling systems. No ticking clock. So when a creak splintered the air Sasha froze in her tracks.

There was no gun in the house. No weapons that she was aware of… Maybe a knife in the kitchen.

But she wasn't in the kitchen.

Then she remembered the security system. She rushed to her father's side of the bed and dragged the baseball bat from under the skirt.

Her heart pounding, Sasha placed the box of tissues on the nightstand and gripped the bat with both hands. Moving slowly in hopes of not hitting a squeaky spot in the floor, she eased out of her parents' room. She made it to the hall without a sound. Downstairs the intruder wasn't so careful. He had just entered the kitchen.

Could it be the same guy from last night?

She was halfway down the staircase when the tread beneath her right foot creaked.

Sasha froze.

Silence seemed to explode all around her and yet there was utter stillness, utter quiet. It was the blood roaring through her veins that sounded like an explosion.

The crash of the back door banking off the siding

jolted her into motion once more. Sasha ran for the kitchen. As she reached the door that stood wide open, she spotted a male in dark clothes and a dark cap disappearing into the woods.

She hesitated for only a moment. Long enough to hit Try Again and then to send Branch another text.

Intruder!

Sasha shoved her phone into her pocket and ran for the woods, the bat held at the ready. "Stop!" she shouted.

When she reached the woods she scanned the trees, caught a glimpse of a dark shape fading into the shadows.

She hurried in that direction. "Hey! What do you want?"

Her voice reverberated around her, bouncing off the trees.

She ran until she stopped seeing glimpses of the fleeing man. Then she skidded to a stop.

Her breath heaving in and out of her lungs, she surveyed the gloom. Nothing. And it was so damned quiet. Frustrated and feeling completely ridiculous, she started to turn around. Branch would be furious when he found out what she'd done. She'd run toward the trouble rather than away.

Not smart, Sasha. Even if she did have her father's baseball bat.

The corner of something rustic and out of place captured her attention.

Wood and metal.

The shack. Sasha cut through the dense underbrush, following a now hidden path that she knew by heart.

Her jaw dropped as she stared at the dilapidated

structure. The shack was maybe eight feet by ten and perhaps seven feet tall. Her father had told her it was at least a hundred years old when she was a little girl.

This had been her playhouse by the time she was seven years old and knew how to sneak through the woods without her mother or her grandmother knowing she'd disappeared. She had come here nearly every day.

She reached for the old door. It wasn't a real door. Just a bunch of boards nailed together and hung on hinges. The wood was rotting around the edges of the door and the hinges squeaked when she pulled it open. Wood banged against wood as the door plopped against the exterior of the shack.

Inside she blinked to hasten the adjustment of her eyes. There were cobwebs and dust. Lots of dust like in the house.

Against the far wall was a blanket. A discarded soft-drink can and a bit of other food trash. Had someone been staying here?

No, wait. The layer of dust on everything suggested no one had been here in a very long time.

Sasha stepped into the small space and picked up a potato chip bag. She searched until she found the expiration date: one year after her parents died.

Whoever had been staying in here could very well have been here when her parents were murdered.

Why had no one checked this shack?

The more she learned about the investigation the more convinced she became that the chief of police at the time had not wanted to unravel the facts. Suddenly aware that she was contaminating a potential crime scene, she eased out of the shack. Bat gripped firmly in her hands, she surveyed the woods around her. Clear.

She headed back toward the house. She'd just passed the tree line when a hand snagged her arm.

Sasha tried to swing the bat, but he held her tight.

Her scream rent the air.

Chapter Twelve

Branch.

It was only Branch.

Sasha dragged in a breath, tried to calm her racing heart.

"What the hell happened?" He glanced around the overgrown yard. "There was an intruder? *Here?*"

She had made it back to the yard. Branch had obviously just arrived and spotted her barreling out of the woods. The other man—person—was gone. "There was someone in the house with me. When he heard me he ran. I..." She moistened her lips, braced for his disapproval. "I followed him into the woods, but I lost him near the shack."

Branch visibly restrained his frustration. She watched the struggle play out on his face. "Did you get a look at his face?"

She shook her head. "He wore dark clothes and a skullcap."

"How tall was he?"

"Average." She shrugged. "Medium build, maybe a little on the thin side."

Her knees were slightly weak now with the receding adrenaline. She steadied herself and braced for whatever he had to say next. No doubt a lecture on common sense or something along those lines.

He looked away for a moment, his hands planted on his hips. She had a feeling he had planted them there to prevent shaking her. Now that she thought about it, maybe she needed to be shaken. She had come here—to this desolate place—alone. After last night she should have known better.

She hadn't been thinking. Sasha was accustomed to being strong and fearless. This sort of uncertainty was not the norm for her.

"What's this about a shack?"

So maybe she was going to skate through this without a raking over the coals from Branch. "When I was a kid I played there. My father said the shack was really old, like a century old or more. It looks as if someone was staying in there."

He frowned. "In the shack?"

She shook her head, then nodded. She wasn't making sense. "Not today, but back when the murders happened. Come this way—I'll show you."

He hesitated at first but then he relented and started forward with her.

"Point the way," he said, "and stay behind me."

"Yes, sir." She gave him a little salute. He shot her a look that said he was not playing.

Sasha guided him back to the shack with only one wrong turn. When she'd stumbled upon it a little while ago she'd been chasing the intruder and she hadn't been thinking. It had been twenty-seven years since she'd visited this shack.

She spotted a flash of rusty metal roof to their left. "There it is."

They moved through the overgrowth of saplings and

brush until they were standing beside it. The squatty primitive structure looked smaller with Branch looming nearby.

"Did you go inside?" he asked.

"Yes. For a moment."

He pulled the door open and used his cell as a flashlight to illuminate the interior. It was darker now, the setting sun withdrawing its feeble reach through the dense trees.

There was the blanket she'd seen and the food refuse.

"The chip bag shows an expiration date the year of my parents' deaths." She pointed to the bag, now wishing she hadn't walked inside. "It's possible someone was staying here when my parents were murdered. There could be prints or other evidence."

Branch leaned inside, surveyed the space more closely with the aid of the flashlight app. "The dust on the floor looks undisturbed before today."

Yes, she had made a mistake. "Whatever's in here could still be useful, though, right?"

Her desperation was showing. No one hated that kind of slip more than her.

"It could. Absolutely." He withdrew his upper body from the shack and put through a call on his cell. "Hey, Billy, we have a new development over at the Lenoir property."

While Branch explained recent events to the chief of police, Sasha surveyed the woods, hoping she might spot the man who had sneaked into the house. He had to have seen her car parked in front of it. If he knew she was there, why try sneaking in? Had he hoped to get a drop on her? He hadn't appeared to be armed—or even after her, for that matter. He'd run away. Was he only watching her? Or was he like her, searching for something that would lead to the truth?

"I wasn't able to talk to that shrink," Branch said, drawing her attention back to him. He propped one shoulder against the side of the shack to wait. "He apparently doesn't operate by his posted business hours."

"Brannigan couldn't reach him either."

There was something else she'd forgotten: to brief him on her meeting with Brannigan. They would have gotten around to it eventually, she felt confident. At his prompting, she explained the differing statements from Holcomb and Johnston as well as the idea that Brannigan seemed intent on getting to the bottom of the discrepancy.

"Unfortunately my memory of events after I came out of the closet that night is not reliable." She chewed at her lip and considered whether there was more she should be telling him. "And I saw Leandra Brennan going to the chief's office as I was leaving."

"Burt told me the same thing about that night," Branch said. "He feels Luther closed the case too quickly. Burt wasn't happy with the limited search around the property or the fact that Luther blew off your assertions. But then, Burt is the coroner. He's not a detective. Still, I agree with him. This—" he hitched his head toward the shack "—is a perfect example of why a more thorough and expansive search should have taken place that night. Nothing may come of this, but it should have been done back then."

Sasha didn't remember Luther Holcomb well enough to reach any sort of conclusion on this news, so she asked, "Is there any chance Holcomb was part of the cover-up?"

Branch's lips formed a grim line for a long moment

before he spoke. "I don't think so. There have never been any rumors about his work or about him. He had a stellar reputation when he was chief and no one has suggested otherwise. Course, I was gone for a lot of years. I'll talk to Billy and see what he thinks. Billy worked with him until he retired four years ago. If we have reason to be concerned about his actions in the investigation, Billy will know."

Sasha felt suddenly immensely tired.

For twenty-seven years she had been waiting for the truth about what happened to her parents. She had put off pushing for that truth as long as her grandmother was alive because it was too painful for her. She had told Sasha this only once when, at sixteen, Sasha had demanded she hire a private investigator. When Viola had tearfully begged for Sasha to put that part of the past behind her once and for all, she'd had no choice. She could not bear to hurt her grandmother.

Now she understood a little of what her grandmother did not want to face. It was overwhelming and frustrating and painful all at the same time. Those in law enforcement—like Branch—trying to help were so incredibly important to the probability of success. Now the chief of police and the coroner were involved. It was finally, really happening, and Sasha was drowning in all those overpowering emotions.

"We should walk back to the house," Branch offered. "Or Billy's officers will be swarming the woods after us."

Over the next hour Brannigan arrived and was escorted to the shack by Branch, and then the forensics unit was called. The part that made the chief of police so happy was the fact that the intruder hadn't appeared to be wearing any gloves. Until he asked, Sasha hadn't considered whether the man had or not, but when her mind replayed him running away, his hands were bare.

Maybe this was the break they needed.

EVENING HAD GIVEN way to night and it was well after dark when Branch insisted on driving her home.

"There's nothing else we can do here," he told her.

He was right, except a part of her wanted to stay as long as there was still activity going on, but she relented. "There's something in the house I need to grab first."

Branch followed her to the back door. She retrieved the box of tissues and declared she was ready to go. Branch didn't question the move. During the drive she thought of the things her mother had written on the tissues. Had she been brainstorming? Trying to work out a path to take some sort of action? Had she hoped that someone would find her notes?

How could they possibly?

By the time they reached Branch's house, Sasha felt agitated. Had her mother been in some sort of trouble? Who had known? Why hadn't someone helped her? Was this why the woman who had been her best friend pretended she knew nothing? Had she abandoned Sasha's mother when she needed her most? What had her father known? Was this situation related to his work at a major construction company?

Sasha closed her eyes for a moment. How in the world could she possibly find the answers after all these years?

"You okay?"

She opened her eyes and turned to Branch. They were parked in his driveway and he sat behind the wheel watching her.

"I'm not sure." She stared forward. "I'm really not sure at all."

"Let's go inside, have a bite to eat and tackle this one piece at a time. I think you're feeling inundated because of all the questions and all the possibilities."

He was right. She nodded. "Okay."

On the porch, she held tight to her box of tissues while Branch unlocked his front door. He flipped on the lights and inhaled deeply. "You smell that?"

Sasha stepped inside and took a deep breath. "I do. Smells like roast and fresh-baked bread."

He shoved the door closed, gave the lock a twist. "My grandmother has been here. She was afraid I wouldn't feed you right."

Sasha had to smile. "Well, it smells heavenly."

They followed the aroma into the kitchen. Arlene had left a note on the island.

Dinner is in the oven. Make sure she eats.

Sasha laughed out loud then. "I think we can make that happen."

"I'll get a couple of beers," Branch offered.

"I'll check the oven." Sasha left her bag and her box of tissues on a chair.

Branch had a nice house. It wasn't a new build but it was recently renovated. His kitchen was particularly stylish with modern appliances. The casserole dish in the oven was covered in aluminum foil. Sasha settled it on the stovetop and removed the foil. Potatoes and carrots and a roast. Looked as good as it smelled. On the counter was a basket filled with freshly made rolls.

Two bottles of beer landed on the counter then and Branch grabbed bowls and spoons. They filled their bowls and settled around the island. The roast tasted just as amazing as it smelled. The rolls melted on the tongue and the beer was the perfect contrast to all the smooth, rich tastes and textures.

When Sasha couldn't eat another bite, she pushed her bowl away. "Your grandmother is an amazing cook."

"She is." Branch pushed his bowl away, too. "She spoils me."

"I suspect this is something else you'll miss if you move to Nashville."

He nodded. "No doubt. Course, there's always Sundays. My grandmother feeds everyone on Sundays. The whole Holloway crew."

Sasha needed to start traditions like that. She and her daughter only had a couple. Traditions, even small ones, were important to future bonding. One day her daughter would be all grown up and have a family of her own. The thought terrified Sasha. She glanced at Branch, who was putting their bowls into the dishwasher.

This was another past wrong that Sasha had to make right. Soon. Very soon.

"I asked Billy if he could share any information about his interview with Leandra Brennan. He couldn't."

Sasha paused in her work covering the leftover roast. "But he did call her into his office about the investigation."

Branch nodded. "He also called her a hostile witness, so she didn't come in voluntarily."

Sasha shook her head. "I just want to know the story there. Arlene has no idea?"

"I asked her if she remembered any issues and she didn't. She says your mom and Brennan weren't really that close."

Surprised, Sasha started to question him further but she suddenly remembered the box of tissues. "There's something I need to show you."

She retrieved the box of tissues and went back to the island. Claiming a stool, she placed the box on the counter.

"I think we might need another beer," he said with a curious glance at the box.

"Good idea."

He grabbed two bottles from the fridge and joined her at the island.

"I searched everything in my parents' bedroom. As I was finishing up, I realized this was the one place I hadn't looked." She tapped the box. "So I pulled the tissues out, thinking something might be hidden inside—I guess I've watched too many movies. At any rate, this is what I found."

She spread the tissues with blue ink across the counter.

Major structural flaws.

Material will be stressed beyond its strength.

Monumental failure at some point in the future.

Don't know what to do.

Sasha's heart started that painful squeezing again when she read the last one.

Can't tell Brandon.

"You're certain this is your mother's handwriting?"

Sasha nodded. "Positive."

"Then it looks like we have ourselves a starting place."

Sasha met his gaze. "You think the murders were related to one or the other's work?"

"I was leaning in that direction already, but this makes it pretty clear." He searched her gaze. "Your mother was responsible for approving plans and architectural drawings for every building that was constructed in this county for as long as she held the position. Any issues with the plans would have been flagged by her office. These—" he tapped the counter near the tissues "—are the sorts of issues developers don't want to hear about."

"Are you saying someone could have wanted to stop her from doing her job?"

He nodded. "That's exactly what I'm saying."

Sasha put a hand over her mouth so he wouldn't see her lips trembling.

"I'm sorry. I didn't mean that to sound so callous."

"No." She put her hand over his, almost jumped at the soft zing that sparked between them. "You've been nothing but helpful and a great friend. I couldn't have done this without you, Branch."

With his free hand he reached up and stroked her cheek with the tips of his fingers. Warmth spread through her. "I'm grateful for the opportunity to do the right thing." He let his hand fall away but didn't draw from her touch. "I shouldn't have left the way I did."

She frowned, not understanding what he meant. Then she realized he was talking about the morning after their one-night stand. She held her hands up, withdrawing contact. "We were young. It was…"

"Thoughtless," he argued. "I had to be back in Chicago but I should have delayed my flight and at least spent some time with you."

If either of them had anything to be sorry for, it was her, but she couldn't bring herself to confess. She just couldn't go there right now. She needed his help. How selfish was that?

"You didn't do anything wrong, Branch."

He gave her a nod. "We can agree to disagree. For now, let's start a list of possible suspects."

She blinked. Okay, so they were back on the case now. Good. "You go first."

"Leandra Brennan."

Sasha was surprised. "Really?"

He gave an affirming nod. "She still works for the same developer. One of the largest, most powerful ones in the Southeast."

"Okay."

He came up with paper and a pen and they started their list.

She liked being shoulder to shoulder with him as they jotted down the names. She liked his smile and the sound of his voice.

She liked everything about him, actually.

Her daughter was right. He was hot.

Slow it down, Sash.

Right now she could without question say that Branch was a really good friend. Whatever happened after this, it had to be a slow build toward total honesty…and hopefully forgiveness.

She would need his when he had the whole truth.

Chapter Thirteen

Wednesday, March 27

Branch had just poured the coffee when Sasha appeared in the kitchen. He'd had a hard time sleeping last night, as much because she was sleeping in his bed as because of the case.

"Morning." He set a mug of steaming brew on the counter in front of her. "I hope you slept well." Toast popped up in the toaster.

"I did." She picked up the mug, cradled it in both hands. "Actually, I slept better than I have since I arrived." She sipped her coffee.

"I'm glad." He turned his own cup up to prevent saying more. He hoped she felt safe in his home…in his *bed*. He wanted her to feel safe with him. "I thought we could talk about the list over some toast."

They hadn't gotten very far on their list last night. *Brennan* was the only name scribbled there so far. He'd been toying with a few others. He'd already put in a call to Billy about pulling records to find out what planned developments Sasha's mother had been working on the final year of her life. There would hopefully be notes in the records if any of the developers or builders had given her any trouble or if any issues had cropped up with the properties during construction or later on.

"Toast would be perfect."

He slathered butter on both pieces, placed each on a small plate and offered one to her. "Jelly?"

"No, thanks." She nibbled a bite. "Perfect."

He devoured his in a few bites, washed it down with coffee.

"I've been thinking about Leandra Brennan." Sasha dabbed her lips with a napkin. "I sent a text to Rey—you know Audrey Anderson at the newspaper."

He nodded. "I know her, yes." Audrey Anderson had been accidentally instrumental in the resuscitation of his wounded career. The remains buried in the basement of her newspaper had set off shock waves from here to Chicago. Not to mention, a highly sought after federal witness had been hiding amid the Mennonite community in Franklin County and Audrey had helped shake him loose.

"I realized that Brennan is about the same age my mother would be if she were still alive," Sasha explained, "so I asked Rey to check her extensive resources to see if the two attended school together. Well, you know Rey—thorough is her middle name. She sent me a very long text this morning. The two went to school together from kindergarten through high school graduation. They were accepted into the same college from which they both graduated, and they were married the same summer—they were each other's maid and matron of honor."

Branch had never been married or even engaged, but even he understood the maid and matron of honor thing was a big deal. "So they were *really* close."

Sasha nodded. "*Really* close. The big difference was

children. Mother and Daddy had me a few years after they were married. Brennan didn't have her first child until the year my parents were murdered. She had a son that fall and then another one two years later. The thing is, I couldn't understand why I didn't really remember her. You would think friends that close would have done more than have the occasional lunch together. I would expect shopping sprees, picnics and barbecues, and maybe even family vacations, but I don't recall anything like that involving Brennan."

"You should ask Arlene," Branch offered. "Maybe there's more to the story that she didn't mention."

"There has to be. It's too strange." She picked up her mug again. "I mentioned to Rey that the murders might have been related to trouble with one or both of my parents' workplaces, so she did a little digging there, too." Sasha touched the screen of her phone, forcing it to light up. "On my mother's side there were several small issues with zoning and site developments, as well as architectural review setbacks, but only a few were noteworthy. The big-box store that opened on the boulevard was one. The drama played out in the courtroom before an agreement was reached. The extension at the auto manufacturer facility created a little commotion in the community. There was some question as to whether the adjoining property was properly zoned. But it was the William Richards Stadium that generated the most buzz. Apparently my mother was embroiled in a major battle over design issues that failed to meet code. According to Rey, it got really ugly in the media and in the city meetings."

"That was the year before, though, right?" Branch remembered his father commenting that the stadium might not happen because of some sort of design flaws.

"It was."

Branch added the stadium to their list. "We can get the developers' names for both the stadium and the big-box store. Anything on your dad's side?"

"There was some issue with the hospital." She shrugged. "The construction company he worked for was contracted to complete some part of the project and then midway into the project they pulled out. Rey said her father did an editorial piece on the disagreement but otherwise there was no mention of the trouble in the papers. Whatever happened, it was settled fairly quietly."

"The hospital would be a Packard project. Brennan works for Packard." Now, there was an interesting connection. "I almost hate to say it out loud, but I can see Packard being involved with murder." Branch surprised himself with the announcement. Maybe it was because his father despised the man, Jarvis Packard. Whatever the case, Branch couldn't help seeing him as a scumbag—a rich one, but a scumbag nonetheless.

"Beyond the connection with Brennan, why would you feel so strongly about Packard? Is there something else I should know?"

"Something my father said on several occasions when I was a kid." He should ask him about it. "He said a man was only as good as his word and Jarvis Packard's word was as worthless as sand in the desert."

Sasha nodded. "That's fairly worthless."

Branch laughed. "In my father's opinion, anyway."

Their gazes caught and for a long moment they looked at each other. It was one of those moments when you didn't know whether to speak or to act. Either one seemed like a risk to what came next, and yet the urge to do the latter was nearly overwhelming. Branch went with the former.

"This is not the time, I get that, but I want to kiss you more than I've wanted to do anything in a very long time."

For another endless second she only stared at him. Then she smiled. "I'm having trouble with that, too. I'm sure we shouldn't—"

Before she could say more, he leaned across the counter and kissed her. She tasted of coffee and felt like silk. He hesitated, their lips still touching, and when she didn't pull away he deepened the kiss. He wanted to walk around this damned island and pull her into his arms. He wanted to carry her to his bed and make love to her. He wanted to do it the right way this time.

A cell rattled against the counter with a lively tune and Sasha drew away. "That's my daughter. I have to take this."

She rushed away, but not before Branch saw her touch her lips and draw in a sharp breath. He wondered if her lips were on fire the way his were or if her heart was pounding as his was. He should have gone after her all those years ago. He'd never wanted anyone the way he did Sasha and he'd kept it to himself all this time. For no other reason than so he could focus on his career, and just maybe there had been a little fear involved.

His dad and his grandmother had warned him often that there were more important things in life than one's career. He'd had to learn that the hard way.

When he'd shaken off the lingering lust, he made a call to Billy and brought him up to speed on what he and Sasha were thinking.

"I can do some checking. See if Packard has had any issues since then. Any lawsuits or code violations. You know," the chief of police pointed out, "it's always easy to finger the bully—the one everybody expects to be bad. But it's not always the bully who does the bad stuff."

Branch shut off the coffee maker and rinsed the carafe as the man spoke. "You've been here all these years and I've been out of the picture until recently. If we're putting the number one pushy developer aside for the moment, who's your runner-up?"

"Keegan and Roark, they built the stadium. They wanted in on the hospital deal—according to my daddy. They intended to make a huge donation and have a wing named after them, but Packard wouldn't have it. He didn't want their money. Some long-ago bad blood, the way I hear it."

Branch had a funny feeling Billy was feeding him all this information for a reason. "Not that I don't appreciate the heads-up," he confessed, "but I have to say, I'm surprised you're sharing all this with me, Chief. Is there something I should be reading between the lines?"

A few seconds of silence elapsed. "This is all speculation, Branch. I don't have a speck of evidence. I can't exactly investigate a problem that doesn't exist. As you well know, that's not the way it works in law enforcement. Someone has to break the law before I can investigate. On the other hand, a guy working off-the-record—on vacation, let's say—can poke around to his heart's desire as long as he doesn't break any laws."

Someone had warned Billy to back off.

"I guess there are folks who don't like to see the city waste resources on a cold case."

"Especially when the fingerprints found in a certain shack lead to a man who went missing twenty-seven years ago and eventually ended up as a long-term resident in a psychiatric facility."

Branch's instincts perked up. Oh, he remembered the case. "Are we talking about Packard's son Devlin?"

"Bingo."

That was one case Branch doubted anyone would forget. Devlin Packard had come home on spring break the same year Sasha's parents died. Before the week's end, he had abruptly disappeared. Months later, when he was found, the guy was strung out on drugs. The word was he never recovered. "Devlin would be what? About forty-seven or -eight now? The last I heard, he was still in an assisted living facility of some sort."

"He was, until he walked out about three days ago. No one has seen him since."

Tension coiled inside Branch. "Was he the one staying in the shack when the Lenoirs were murdered?"

"He's been in there at some point in the past and I'm guessing he was the one in the Lenoir house when Sasha was there. Maybe even in the Simmons house the other night. The timing would fit."

"Is he dangerous?" Worry gnawed at Branch's gut.

"No violent tendencies. Always the ideal patient. Then he just ups and walks out. His daddy has a whole posse of his security minions out looking for him."

Sasha walked back into the kitchen. Branch would have to find a way to convince her to stay close, particularly after this news.

Good luck with that.

"Anything else?" Branch asked. Sasha had her handbag. Obviously she was ready to go. The second intruder had done little to deter her. But then, he couldn't blame her. She had waited a long time for the truth.

"That's it for now. Watch your step, Branch. Something is wrong with this case and I can't quite put my finger on it. I had no idea so much had been swept under the rug. By the way, thanks for the heads-up on Leandra Brennan. She didn't have much to say but she knows plenty. I'll be watching her. I'm hoping when she realizes I'm not pushing this case back into a drawer, she'll come around."

"I'll touch base with you later today." Branch severed the connection and settled his full attention on Sasha. "We may have an ID on the intruder."

"That's great."

He briefed her on the latest from Brannigan. The news only seemed to create more questions rather than provide answers. Branch was feeling the same rising tension.

One step forward, two steps back.

"Why would Packard's son have been staying in the shack?"

Branch mentally ran through a couple of scenarios. "It's possible he was involved with a drug dealer on that side of town and happened upon the shack by accident. It was empty, so he made himself a home. I remember my parents talking about his disappearance. The rumor was he had some kind of breakdown."

"But you said he had shown no violent tendencies, so it's not likely that he committed the murders."

"There's always a first time," Branch countered. "The truth is, if he went over the edge in some sort of psychotic break, he may have done some very violent things and have no recall of the events. This would explain why Packard has kept him locked away all this time."

Even as Branch said the words, he thought of Billy's suggestion that the bad guy was not always the obvious bully. But maybe this time the glaringly obvious bully was the bad guy. Sometimes bad guys liked hiding in plain sight. The boldness of the move gave them a sense of power.

Sasha squared her shoulders. "I intend to track down Dr. Farr today. I want to know why he concluded that I made up the voices. I want to know what else he said in his report. In fact, I believe I have the right to demand a copy of his report."

Branch thought of her daughter and realized that Sasha was the only family the girl had left since her dad was not in the picture. "I'm not sure you going off on your own is such a good idea, Sasha. Your daughter is counting on you to come back home when this is over. Any risk you take is a risk to her."

Sasha held up her hands. "I'm a good mother, Branch. I always consider my daughter's needs first." When he would have tried to explain himself, she added, "I am perfectly capable of driving across town to Dr. Farr's office on my own. I've done pretty well so far."

The woman lived in a major metropolitan area. She was accustomed to taking care of herself in far more risky environments than this one simply due to the nature of her work. She obviously knew how to handle herself. But they were just getting started with this case and a media-binging pop star with a bad attitude was vastly different from a cold-blooded killer. Things could escalate quickly.

"I let you talk me into going our separate ways yesterday and you got into a dicey situation," he reminded her. "I don't think we should go down that same path again today. And for the record, I'm certain you're a fantastic mother and very capable."

"Okay." Sasha exhaled a big breath. "Let's compromise. I'll track down the shrink while you do whatever it is you need to do, and then we'll meet up to see what we have." Before he could utter his protest, she urged, "I will go only to the man's office and to the hospital looking for him. Nowhere else."

"No going back to your old home place or to your grandmother's house without me. Basically no going anywhere you might end up alone and cornered."

"You have my word."

He nodded. "All right, but I want to hear from you every half hour."

She rolled her eyes. "Fine. And what about you? What will you be doing?"

"I'm going to the office where your mother worked and see how difficult it's going to be to get into their archives. Most of the files are public record, so we'll see."

"You think it was Packard, don't you?"

The lady was far too perceptive.

"I think Packard probably has more motive than anyone else simply because of the sheer number of projects he was and is involved with."

"Whoever was responsible," she said, her voice overly quiet, "he had something to hide. Something my mother knew about. But there haven't been any epic fails of structures or roads or anything like that, which seems to negate the entire idea."

"Maybe he's gotten lucky until now. The trouble might be just around the corner or coming in the next decade. But we know there was something. Something big enough to kill for. And if he killed once to keep his secret, he won't hesitate to kill again."

She was backing away from him before he could talk himself out of allowing her out of his sight. "We'll catch up as soon as I've spoken to Dr. Farr."

Branch grabbed his keys and his hat. "I'll follow up with Brennan while I'm at it."

She glanced at him, clearly surprised by that move.

"Now that the chief of police has rattled that cage," he explained, "I'm hoping she'll be a little more cooperative."

Billy's hands had been tied to some degree. Branch didn't have that trouble.

"She has the answers we need," Sasha insisted. "I'm certain of it."

One way or another Branch intended to find out.

Chapter Fourteen

Sasha met Rey at the diner for an early lunch. The toast she'd had with Branch was long gone. A Cobb salad was just the ticket. She decided to forego the dressing and just enjoy the rich ingredients and a glass of sweet iced tea with lemon in honor of her grandmother. Viola Simmons had loved sweet tea.

"I did some additional research on Devlin," Rey said. She stabbed a forkful of her greens. "He's a resident at Mountain View, a private resort-like facility in Sewanee. No hardship there, I can tell you. I did a piece on the services they provide. Only the very best. I'm surprised he walked out of such a posh environment. Mountain View is known for top-notch patient care."

"Do you know his diagnosis?" Rey was good at ferreting out information. However, Sasha wasn't sure if what she was asking with that question was something she could learn without doing so via some illegal avenue. There were some things even the best investigative reporter couldn't uncover. The HIPAA Law was generally a brick wall when it came to protecting the privacy rights of patients.

"A distant cousin who visits him occasionally tells me it's schizophrenia and drug addiction. He can't stay on the prescribed meds and off the nonprescribed ones, so he can't stay healthy, thus the long-term residency. He long ago made the choice to become a permanent resident rather than deal with life outside those insulating walls."

"I guess he changed his mind since he walked out of the place a few days ago."

Rey added a packet of low-calorie sweetener to her tea and gave it a stir. "The family's not talking about his abrupt departure but I hear the father's security team is scouring the countryside for him. You think he's your intruder?"

Sasha nodded. "I do. I think he left the note and that he was the one staying in that old shack when my parents were murdered."

"Wow." Rey's eyes rounded. "That could potentially mean he witnessed what happened that night. It's possible that's what sent him over the edge. The timing is about right."

"Someone knows what happened. Leandra Brennan, Devlin Packard—someone knows." Sasha sighed. "I just have to persuade one of them to talk."

Rey studied her a moment. "How's it going with Branch? I've wanted to ask but…"

Sasha's grandmother and Rey were the only ones who knew who Brianne's father was. Both had sworn never to tell, though her grandmother had warned on numerous occasions that she felt Sasha was making a mistake.

Her grandmother had been a smart lady. Sasha *had* made a mistake.

"It's going well. He's a great guy and…" She shrugged. "I see every day that I'm here how I misjudged him. I should have listened to my grandmother."

"And me," Rey reminded her. "I always believed

Branch would have jumped in with both feet to help with his child."

Sasha shook her head. "I was just so young and I had so many plans. I didn't want to throw away my dreams for married life. I was on fire to make my mark."

"No one said you had to get married." Rey smiled. "Anyway, you certainly made your mark, my friend."

Sasha laughed, the sound weary. "I definitely have." She shook her head. "But you know how it was back then. Branch would have expected us to raise her together. His family would have expected the same, plus a marriage. Certainly my grandmother would have. I can see my shortsightedness now, but at the time I could only see the future I had planned and it wasn't here, Rey. You know that. We both wanted out of this town—the sooner the better."

Rey sank back into the booth. "You're right. After what happened between me and Colt, I couldn't imagine ever coming back, much less ending up with him again under any circumstances."

Sasha felt her lips curl into a real smile. "It's amazing is what it is. You two are great together. I'm glad you came back and ended up a couple again."

"The same could happen for you," Rey suggested.

"I'm afraid my situation is a bit more complicated with a daughter who already believes she owns the world. I can't bring myself to pull the rug from under her." Sasha shook her head. "I can't bear the idea of her hating me for the decision I made."

Rey reached across the table and squeezed Sasha's hand. "You'll know what to do when the time comes."

"Hope so."

Her forearms braced on the table, Rey leaned forward. "As for this investigation, when we figure out what your mom and dad had on Packard, we're going to take him down. I, for one, can't wait. He's always been an arrogant son of a gun."

"What if it's not him?"

"Then it'll be someone like him," Rey argued. "There are some people in this world to whom human life means nothing. To kill someone standing in the way of their ultimate goal is like swatting a fly. Whoever did this, we're going to ensure he pays."

"Branch said he planned to visit my mother's office—her former office—and dig around. Find out who was doing what that year."

"Branch is a smart man," Rey said. "I'm doing a little digging in that area myself. Between the two of us, if there was something going on, we'll find it."

"There were a lot of big projects during that time frame. The stadium, the hospital."

"That decade changed the face of this city," Rey agreed. "At least one of them created a lethal ripple. We just have to figure out which one."

She made it sound so easy.

Sasha checked the time. "I should go. I'm staking out Farr's office. I intend to catch him today. If he doesn't show I'm going to his home."

Rey grinned. "Let me know if you decide to go to the man's house. I've always wanted to see inside that lake mansion of his."

"You're on," Sasha assured her.

They paid their checks and parted ways on the sidewalk. Rey walked back to the newspaper office and Sasha climbed into her rental and headed for Farr's office. It was near the hospital, only a few short miles away from where she was. She made the necessary turns around the downtown square and then drove past the towering Packard building. The hospital was only a couple of miles beyond that iconic structure. Though the hospital was certainly not Packard's biggest development in terms of money, it was the most prestigious. Directly across the street from the hospital stood a row of boutique medical suites, one of which Farr used as an office. Sasha parked in the lot that flanked the cleverly decorated Victorian-style buildings.

To her surprise the entry door for the one on the west end was unlocked. An alarm chimed somewhere beyond the lobby as she walked inside. The interior was elegantly decorated and well-appointed. Four chairs and two Duncan Phyfe tables, along with a magazine rack, made up the tiny lobby. Distinguished-looking artwork adorned the walls. There were two doors, one to the left marked Restroom and one at the rear marked Dr. Bruce Farr. Evidently he did not have a receptionist or secretary. Sasha crossed the room and had just raised her hand to knock on the door carrying his name when it opened.

Dr. Bruce Farr blinked behind the thick lenses of his eyeglasses. "May I help you?"

"Dr. Farr?" She asked the question though she knew it was him. She had done a Google search. Though tall and distinguished in stature, his hair had grayed and thinned to near nonexistence. His skin was mottled, making him look even older in person.

"Yes, I am Dr. Farr, but I'm not taking new patients. I haven't taken new patients in nearly thirty years. I would be happy to recommend others in the area."

"You're retired, I know," Sasha said. "You serve on the board at the hospital and you continue to see a handful of longtime patients but otherwise you're retired."

His brow lined in heavy ruts. "What is it you want?"

"My name is Sasha Lenoir," she said, feeling immensely proud to inform him of this fact. "I'm here to discuss the evaluation you conducted when I was nine after my parents were murdered."

For several long seconds he stared at her. During most of those Sasha was convinced he would refuse to answer. But then he said, "I remember the case."

"Good. I have questions for you, Doctor."

Once more, he stared at her for an extended time. Just when she had decided he would say he didn't have time, he gestured to his office. "Very well. Please join me in my office. I don't have an appointment for a few minutes. I'll answer what I can until then."

He turned and walked deeper into his office, leaving the door open for her to follow. Sasha instinctively glanced over her shoulder before going inside.

"Close the door, please."

She did as he asked and then crossed the room to his desk. He indicated the lone chair waiting on her side of the desk and she sat. What remained of his once dark hair was completely gray. His eyes were a matching shade of pale gray, cold and unforgiving. She had clips of memory related to him, but none that were complete. Most were nothing more than pieces. Snippets of conversation. Him asking questions. Him staring unblinkingly at her.

"What would you like to know, Ms. Lenoir?"

"You concluded that I was making up the voices I heard the night my parents were murdered. I heard those voices, Dr. Farr. According to the county coroner, I spoke of them that very night and I told the chief of police about them a few days later. I know what I heard. Why would you insist they were my imagination at play?"

He held her gaze a long moment. "You were a very frightened and traumatized little girl. You cannot trust your memories from that painful time."

It wasn't necessary to be a shrink to know someone who had in part witnessed the murder of her parents would be traumatized and frightened. "Of course I was, but my memories are very solid from that night. You were wrong, Dr. Farr."

"You are entitled to your opinion, Ms. Lenoir, but my professional opinion hasn't changed. If you've come here to try to change my mind, I'm afraid you've wasted your time."

"Actually, it's irrelevant to me whether I change your mind, Dr. Farr. My question is, who paid you to conclude I was lying? I know it was someone with a large personal stake in the matter of whether or not my story held up in court. Perhaps Jarvis Packard or Seth Keegan. Maybe Hadden Roark."

For a moment he looked stunned, as if he couldn't believe she had voiced her accusations by listing names, or perhaps because she had hit the nail on the head, so to speak.

"You're grasping at straws, Sasha. May I call you Sasha?"

Now he was just patronizing her. "No, you may not." She laughed. "As for my grasping at straws, perhaps when my search for the truth began, that was true. Not anymore. Now I have proof."

The tiniest hint of uncertainty flared in his eyes before he could school the reaction. Oh, yes, he knew plenty about that night, just as she suspected Leandra Brennan did.

"I'm certain if you possessed proof of what you believe, you would be sitting in the chief of police's office rather than mine."

"Actually, Chief Brannigan believes me, too," she countered. "In fact, he has reopened the case. Additionally, Marshal Branch Holloway is looking into the case, as well. Everyone knows my parents were murdered. It's time for you to speak up while you still can. I feel confident there are options for a man in your position, Dr. Farr."

She was overstepping her bounds, she knew, but the words tumbled out.

"Maybe you're simply having trouble letting go of the past, Ms. Lenoir." Dr. Farr nodded as if privy to some knowledge she did not possess. "Your mother had a similar issue, which seems to be why she could not let go of the best friend who caused her husband to stray. Such self-destructive behavior." Farr stood. "I'm afraid that's all the time I have, Ms. Lenoir. I wish you the best of luck in your pursuit."

Scarcely restraining the fury smoldering inside her, Sasha removed a business card from her purse and placed it on the man's desk. "Call me—or Chief Brannigan, if you prefer—when you decide you want to tell the truth, Dr. Farr."

She walked out of the office and climbed into her rental. If she had ever been more angry and frustrated, she had no recall of the event. She drove around for a few minutes, considered going to visit Leandra Brennan again. Branch had said he was following up on her, so Sasha drove on. Besides, she didn't trust herself to speak to the woman right now. Not after what Farr said.

Was it possible the arrogant man was correct? Had her father cheated with her mother's best friend? This didn't make sense and yet it explained why she would keep her ongoing friendship with Brennan away from her family life. This was the reason Sasha didn't recall any outings with Brennan.

"What were you thinking, Mom?"

The idea that she'd forgotten to demand a copy of Farr's report barged to the front and center of her thoughts. Anger roared inside her again. Probably he would insist all records that old had been archived or destroyed. What difference did it make? Whatever he'd said in the report was lies anyway.

She circled the cemetery and then drove to her grandmother's house. She'd fully intended to drive on past but a car parked in the driveway had her turning in. She parked beside the vehicle and rested her attention on the older man standing at the front door of the house. He looked back at her, obviously startled.

Though she had promised Branch she wouldn't come here or go anywhere else she might get trapped alone... she wasn't alone. There was a man standing on the porch. Sasha opened the door and climbed out.

"May I help you?" Since she didn't recognize the man, he likely didn't recognize her.

"Sasha?"

So maybe he did recognize her. "Are you lost?" She closed the car door and started up the walk, taking her time.

He shook his head as she approached, whether in answer to her question or in hopes of making her stop, she couldn't be sure.

"You won't remember me." He adjusted his eyeglasses. "My name is Alfred Nelson. My friends and coworkers called me—"

"Al." Sasha remembered her mother referring to Al. They worked together in the city planning office.

He nodded. "We need to talk, Sasha."

"All right." He looked harmless enough. He was old and frail, his body stooped. There was no telltale bulge in the pockets of his khaki trousers, and that was about the only place he could possibly be concealing a weapon. "Let me unlock the door and we'll go inside."

She reached into her purse and fished for the key. The house was no longer a crime scene, so they could go inside. She unlocked and pushed the door inward, then invited the older man to follow her inside. The house was cool and dark. She flipped on lights as she went. She turned to offer coffee but he had hesitated in the entry hall. He stared at the framed photograph of Sasha with her parents. It was the last one done with her parents before their murder.

"You have to stop digging into the past." His gaze shifted from the photo to her. His look was not menacing. More tired and resigned than anything.

"Why would I do that, Al?" She moved slowly toward where he stood. "I want to know the truth. Do you know what really happened that night?"

"What you're doing..." He stared at the photo again. "What you're doing is dangerous and she would not want you to be in danger. She would have done anything to protect you."

"Who killed my parents, Al?" She stood toe to toe with him now, her gaze insistent on his. He knew something—maybe everything—and she needed to hear the whole truth.

"I tried to convince her to let it go, but she refused." His gaze settled on the photograph once more.

Sasha frowned. Had this man been more than a coworker to her mother? "Were you in love with my mother, Al?"

His gaze clashed with hers, his eyes growing wide behind his glasses. "I loved her, yes, but not like you think. She was like a daughter to me." A smile touched his lips. "She was so young when she first came to the office but she had big plans. She worked harder than anyone else, so no one was surprised when she received promotion after promotion."

"Did you know about her friendship with Leandra Brennan?"

"They were like sisters growing up." He shook his head. "But Lenny took advantage of their friendship. She wanted what your mother had but her marriage was a mess. Their friendship was not a healthy relationship for Alexandra. I warned her about that, too."

"But she wouldn't listen because she loved my father," Sasha guessed. "She loved Lenny, too, so she tried to keep their relationship on some level."

"Lenny was like the snake," the man said. "The snake was cold and hungry and begged for help. Pity and kindness for his plight allowed a young girl to turn a blind eye to the fact that he was a snake. When he bit her, he reminded her that she had known what he was when she picked him up."

"Lenny was the snake," Sasha suggested.

Al nodded.

"Why were my parents murdered?" she asked, unable to breathe for fear he would stop talking.

"Because the snake was too smart. I've said too much."

He turned toward the door. Sasha couldn't allow him to leave without explaining what he meant.

"Wait." She put a hand on his arm. "You say you loved my mother like a daughter. If that's true, then why won't you help me? All I want is the truth."

He stared at Sasha, his eyes filled with regret. "The truth won't change anything."

He reached for the door again. "Don't my parents deserve justice? The truth can give me that if nothing else."

"It's too late. The truth might eventually allow for justice but it won't give you peace, Sasha. It will only bring you pain. There are some evils that are too big to stop."

Sasha followed him out the door. When he had driven away she locked up and climbed back into her rental and drove. She drove until she reached the hospital and then she pulled over and stared at the sprawling compound.

This was the biggest project her mother had been working on. This was a Packard project. Devlin—the man who had most likely left her that message and sneaked in on her twice—was a Packard. And Leandra Brennan—aka the snake—worked for Packard.

It had to be Packard.

He had her mother and father murdered to stop them from exposing something he wanted to hide.

All Sasha had to do was find that something.

Chapter Fifteen

Sasha turned into Branch's driveway right behind him. She had driven around for an hour. Unable to bear the uncertainty, she had gone to Branch's grandmother and asked her about the rumors. Afterward, Sasha had driven around some more before she'd finally stopped and sent Branch a text. He'd called and sent her a couple of texts by then but she hadn't been ready to talk.

She wasn't sure she could now.

Everything felt wrong. She had been so certain the truth would help her to put the past behind her once and for all but that wasn't happening. The more she dug, the more questions and uncertainties she uncovered. Her parents' lives now felt skewed and off-kilter. Where was the happy childhood she had dreamed was real all these years?

Was this why her grandmother had refused to go down this path?

Had she known that hurt and disillusionment were all that waited for Sasha at the end of this journey?

She should have come to Winchester, buried her grandmother, closed up both houses and then walked away without ever looking back.

Branch climbed out of his truck and turned in her direction. A smile spread across his handsome face.

Weakness claimed her and she barely held back the tears. How in the world was she supposed to make any of this right? She had built a career spinning other people's mistakes and she had no idea how to turn her own life around…how to tell her own truth.

How could she be disappointed in the skewed truth of her parents' lives when her own truth was way off-balance?

Did anyone get it all right? Of course not. No life was flawless. There were ups and downs and turnarounds in every life.

It was what you did with those deviations and bumps in the road that mattered.

Sasha climbed out of the rental car and walked straight up to him. "I'm not sure I can handle the truth anymore."

He pulled her into his arms and hugged her. Sasha closed her eyes and lost herself in the scent and feel of the man. He ushered her inside and closed the world out.

"You need a drink." He guided her to the sofa and left her there.

Her entire being felt bereft at the loss of contact with his. He was wrong. She didn't need a drink. She needed his body wrapped around hers so thoroughly that it was impossible to tell where one of them began and the other one ended. She wanted to lose herself in him in that way. She didn't want to think. She only wanted to feel.

He thrust a small glass of amber liquid in front of her. "Drink it. You'll feel better."

She didn't believe him but she drank it anyway. Scotch. She shuddered with the burn of it sliding down her throat. "Thank you."

Branch sat down in the chair across the coffee table from her and knocked back his own shot of Scotch. He placed his glass on the table and then settled his hat next to it. He ran his fingers through his hair and set his attention fully on her. "Tell me what happened."

"The reason I don't remember my mother's best friend is because they never saw each other outside the occasional lunch. Leandra Brennan—Lenny—and my mother grew up together. They went to college together, got married the same summer. They were best friends—like sisters. Until something happened between my father and her. According to Arlene—"

"You talked to her today?"

Sasha nodded. "She said my grandmother never wanted me to know any of this, so they kept my mother's secret. There was a big barbecue when my mother was pregnant with me. Lenny and her husband were fighting and everyone was drinking except my mother. Anyway, at some point that evening my mother caught Lenny and my dad kissing. Arlene said Mother would never elaborate if there was something more going on than just two drunk people doing something stupid. But she and Lenny stopped being friends for a long while. Apparently they had only recently started having the occasional lunch together right before my parents died."

Branch shook his head. "It's easy to forget that our parents are mere humans, too, and they've made mistakes."

Sasha stared at the empty glass in her hands. "I was a child when they died. My every memory is of these perfect people who were above mere human mistakes. I don't even remember ever being scolded. All the memories other than the night they were killed are sweet and cherished and perfect."

"Just because you discovered a painful truth doesn't mean all the happy truths are no longer real or relevant."

She placed her glass on the table and wrung her hands. "I found Dr. Farr. He refuses, of course, to change his opinion of my story. He, apparently, was aware of my father's infidelity, which makes me wonder if it was such common knowledge why I hadn't heard of it before."

"Maybe it came out in the investigation but wasn't necessarily common knowledge."

"Maybe."

"Or," Branch offered, "maybe your grandmother suggested that Luther look into Alexandra's former best friend because of what had happened."

Sasha nodded. "You're probably right. G'ma would likely have considered the possibility. I know I certainly would have." She looked to Branch. "Did you talk to Brennan today?"

"I did." Branch stared at the floor a moment. "She came up with an even crazier story. In fact, she broke down into tears and blubbered her way through most of it. She explained how she and your father had been having an affair and your mother found out and intended to divorce him and take everything. She thinks your father intended to have her killed and things went terribly wrong."

"Are you serious? She said those things?"

He met Sasha's gaze. "She did. She claims she was trying to put her marriage back together but that he wouldn't leave her alone. She and your mother were having secret lunches to discuss how to handle the situation."

Sasha shook her head. "I don't believe it. I would remember that kind of tension."

"At one point you did say they were arguing more during those final weeks."

She had said that. "It was about work. I remember distinctly that he thought she was working too much and she complained that he needed to find a new job."

This—all of this—grew more confusing by the moment.

"Wait." She had almost forgotten to tell him about Alfred Nelson. "I spoke to Mr. Nelson, the man who worked in the office with my mother. He was knocking on the door of my grandmother's house when I drove past, so I stopped and talked to him. He urged me to stop digging around in the past. He said it would only hurt me the way it did my mother. He alluded to how Brennan betrayed my mother."

"At least it sounds like everyone has gotten their story straight."

He was right. Farr, Brennan and Nelson were all suddenly spouting basically the same story. "Seems rather convenient."

Branch nodded. "It does. I think maybe we need to take today's influx of information with a grain of salt."

"Nelson also said something like there are some evils too big to stop. Do you think he was referring to Jarvis Packard?"

"Packard would certainly fit the description."

Sasha shot to her feet. She couldn't sit still any longer. "This is just too much. I don't know why my grandmother didn't simply explain the situation to me once I was an adult. I shouldn't have to be doing this." She crossed the room and stared out the window.

Branch moved up behind her. Her body reacted instantly. How she would love to turn around and fall into his arms.

"You don't have to do this, Sasha. Knowing the truth—whatever it might be—won't bring your parents back. It won't make you feel any better about the fact that your grandmother didn't want to talk about it. It won't change anything unless it helps to put a killer behind bars."

"And clears my father's name," she reminded him.

"If you want to clear your father's name and find justice for your parents, then you have to do this. Otherwise, you don't have to go down this path. No one will fault you if you decide you've had enough."

He made it seem like such an easy decision.

"It's not that simple," she argued.

"It's never that simple," he agreed.

She turned around, her body so close to his she could feel the heat of his skin beneath his clothes. "Why are you helping me?"

It wasn't what she'd intended to ask when she opened her mouth but it was what came out.

He frowned down at her. "Why wouldn't I help you?"

"That's not an answer."

He searched her eyes as if the motive for her demand might show itself, but she couldn't let him see that what she wanted was to push him away. To stop this thing before it was completely out of control. While they could still look back and call what they'd shared the past few days nice, a friend helping a friend.

"I told you I've always wanted a do-over. I've wished more times than I can count for an opportunity to spend time with you again."

Sasha thought of all the lies she had discovered...all the confusing things that didn't add up. Was that the legacy she wanted to leave her daughter? A box of untruths and a trail of uncertainties.

She grabbed Branch and pulled his face down to hers. She kissed him with all the hunger and desire strumming through her. A minute from now he would never look at her the same. A minute from now he would know the one truth that mattered more than all the others.

His arms went around her and he pulled her against him, deepened the kiss, taking control, and she wept with the knowledge that this would be the only time.

When she could bear the sweet tenderness no longer, she pushed him away. When he released her, his eyes glazed with need, she crossed the room, found her bag and pulled out her cell phone.

"What's going on, Sasha?" He watched her, worry in his eyes now. He understood something was very, very wrong.

Something besides her murdered parents and their secrets. Besides her dead grandmother and the truths she chose to take with her to her grave. Besides the urgent need still roaring through her body.

"I've never wanted a do-over of that night, Branch."

He stared at her, confusion clouding his face. "I don't understand."

"That night was amazing." She smiled, swiped at an errant tear that escaped her iron hold. "It was the night I had waited for since I was thirteen years old and first fell madly in love with you."

He smiled, his own eyes suspiciously bright. "I remember thinking that if you would have me I would be the happiest guy in the world, but I always thought you had other plans."

His confession hurt more than she wanted to admit. How could they not have known? Had they been too busy running away from their lives here that they couldn't see each other clearly?

"I did and that was my mistake. I couldn't stop running toward the future long enough to see what was right here in my present. I had all these big plans. I was going to make my mark, make a name for myself. I was never again going to be the orphaned girl who lost her whole world. I was going to be someone who mattered."

"First—" he took a step in her direction "—you were always someone who mattered. To your grandmother. To my family. To *me*."

More of those damned tears flowed down her cheeks. "But I couldn't see that. I allowed the need to prove myself to rule my life and I made a terrible, terrible mistake. One I'm certain you won't be able to forgive me for."

He reached up and tugged a wisp of hair from her damp cheek. "I'm fairly certain you have nothing to worry about on that score. Whatever you did or didn't do when you left, you don't owe me an explanation. I'm here for you now and I'll be here for you tomorrow. I want to be a part of your life—a part of your daughter's life."

Sasha stared at him, her entire being aching. Her fingers tightened around the phone full of pictures of her precious daughter. "She's *your* daughter, too."

The kaleidoscope of evolving emotions on his face took her breath. He went from shock to amazement and then to anger.

"What do you mean?"

"I mean, the one time we were together Brianne was conceived. I didn't know until weeks later and…"

And what?

She made the decision not to tell him. She chose to go on with her life and to not look back.

"Why didn't you call me?"

His voice was hollow. That, too, would change in a moment. "My grandmother said you had accepted a big promotion in Chicago. I had that job offer in New York. The timing was just wrong."

"Timing?"

Now the fire was in his tone. He was angry. She didn't blame him. She deserved whatever he decided to throw her way.

"I should have told you." She took a breath. "I promised myself I would a thousand times, but it never felt like the right time, so I never did."

The entire scene had taken on a dreamlike quality. Sasha felt uncertain of herself and at the same time completely at peace with the decision she had made.

She had told him. At long last. Regardless of what happened next, she had done the right thing.

He looked away, shook his head. "I need some air and to think."

She nodded. "I understand."

He walked out of the room. Moments later she heard the back door close.

She tapped her contacts list and put through a call to Rey. "I need to talk to you."

Five minutes later Sasha had left a note for Branch, telling him that she would spend the night with Rey, and then she left to give him the space he needed to come to terms with her announcement. Her soul ached as if she were driving away from that night all those years ago all over again.

She and Branch had made love and then they'd walked away from each other without ever looking back.

They had both made a mistake, but hers was the far more egregious one.

REY MET HER at the Lenoir house.

As much as Sasha would love to lose herself to a bottle of wine, a buzz would not help. She needed to keep her mind busy—to focus on something until she could bear to properly consider what she had done.

Branch knew he had a daughter now.

Now she had to tell Brianne. Maybe it would be better to bring her here and to do the introductions in person.

"What's the plan?" Rey glanced around the dusty old house. "I've got pizza and wine ordered. We have about half an hour before it arrives."

"Pizza and wine?" Since when did the two pizza places in Winchester deliver wine?

"Brian is bringing us dinner. Don't worry—he's not staying. He and his love have plans. He's just dropping off the food and a few other things we might need."

Brian Peterson worked with Rey at the newspaper. He and Rey had been best friends in school and later it had been the three of them. As close as Sasha and Rey always were, there had been a special bond between Rey and Brian.

"I'm afraid to ask what kinds of things."

Rey shrugged. "Nightshirts, sleeping bags, toothbrushes. Just a few necessities."

Sasha was really grateful for good friends like Rey and Brian.

She instantly chastised herself for leaving Branch out. He was a good friend, too. She hoped they would be able to be friends again.

"So." Rey turned to her. "What's the plan?"

Sasha started to say that she had no plan, but then she realized she had a very important plan. "I want to take this place apart."

Rey made a face. "Define *take apart*."

"I want to look inside and under everything. If it's here, I want to find it."

Another of those strange expressions twisted Rey's face. *"It?"*

Sasha nodded. "I have no idea what it is, but we're going to look until we find it—unless you have objections."

Rey shook her head. "None. Except maybe I'll text Brian and add gloves to the needs list."

"Good idea." Sasha smiled. She didn't have to see it to know it was sad; it felt sad. She felt sad. But this was the first step toward moving forward. She did not want to leave this painful black cloud hanging over her daughter's life.

Her daughter deserved happiness.

Her daughter deserved to know her father.

Branch deserved to know his daughter.

And Sasha intended to have the truth—whatever it turned out to be—and justice for her parents.

Chapter Sixteen

Branch knocked on the door of his grandmother's home and waited for her to answer. He usually called before showing up just to make sure she was home, but this time he couldn't bring himself to make the call. He needed to see her in person. He needed to see her face when she answered his question.

Eighty-five-year-old Arlene Holloway opened the door. Branch reminded himself of her age and her station in his family. He reached for calm. Upsetting this woman was the last thing he wanted to do and in his current state he didn't completely trust himself to make good decisions.

"Branch, is something wrong?"

He hadn't called and he always did. "Yes, ma'am. I'm a little upset. May I come in?"

"Well, of course." She drew the door open wide and shuffled back out of his way. "Is Sasha all right? Where is she?"

The sweet little old lady craned her neck to see through the darkness beyond the door.

"She's with Rey Anderson."

Arlene nodded. "Rey's doing a fine job with the newspaper. Far better than her uncle Phillip ever did. He was too busy chasing the widows around town."

Branch smiled in spite of the circumstances. His grandmother always knew how to put a smile on his face, even when she wasn't trying. "I hear he went down to Florida for spring break."

"Spring break?" she grumbled as she locked the door. "He looks like a spring break. The man needs to find a hobby that doesn't involve chasing skirts."

Branch knew better than to encourage her. "I have some questions I need to ask you, Gran."

She stared at him from behind the thick lenses of her glasses. She blinked. "Do we need a stiff drink to make them go down easier?"

"Possibly." No point pretending.

"Have a seat over there." She gestured toward the living room. "I'll round up Walker's bourbon."

His grandfather had been dead for ten years and his grandmother still called the stash of bourbon she kept his. Branch knew for a fact she'd purchased a new fifth of bourbon at least twice in those ten years. Most of the time she had Branch's father pick it up. It wouldn't be proper for her to be seen in the liquor store, much less buying something. She shuffled over to the sofa, two sipping glasses and the fifth of bourbon clasped in her gnarled hands. She poured, passed a glass to him and lifted the other to her lips.

When they'd downed a swallow, she looked him square in the eye and asked, "What happened?"

"Did you know Sasha's daughter was my child?"

Since Sasha left, she had sent him a dozen photos of Brianne via text, some going back to when the girl was a baby in diapers. The younger photos were like looking at candid shots of himself as a kid.

Every time he looked at the photos he felt a punch to his gut. How the hell had this happened? Why would

Sasha have kept a secret like this from him? For a dozen years no less.

He should have gone after her.

"I had my suspicions," Arlene confessed. "But I never knew for sure. Vi never said a word—I imagine because Sasha told her not to. It was like what happened to Sasha's parents. We never discussed it. I tried once and she said no and that was that. We respected each other that way, son. When you get older you realize how important that one thing is. When your loved ones vanish one by one and your health goes by the wayside, you still got your self-respect and the respect of your good friends—if you're lucky."

Branch shook his head. "Part of me wants to raise hell. She kept this child from me for twelve long years."

"Would that fix anything?" she asked. "Make you feel any better?"

He downed his bourbon, winced at the burn. "Not likely on either count."

"Well, there's your answer. If I had my guess, she kept this information from the girl, too. She's going to have herself enough trouble explaining that decision. She won't need any trouble from you on top of that. I think a little patience is in order. And maybe some understanding. She was young and terrified. She's already done all the hard work. Now all you have to do is enjoy. She's a beautiful girl and, from all the things Vi told me about her, smart as a whip to boot."

Branch nodded. "We'll figure this out."

Arlene smiled. "I think you already did."

"I think you're right."

He had a daughter. A beautiful daughter who was smart and who deserved the best dad he could be.

"I guess I should call the folks."

"You might want to have another sip of that bourbon first. Your mama has been pining for a grandchild for years. She will be over the moon."

His cell vibrated and he slid it from his pocket in case it was Sasha. He checked the screen and frowned. Not Sasha. "Hey, Billy, what's going on?"

It was a little late in the evening for the chief of police to be making social calls. Branch braced for trouble. He'd had a text from Sasha not an hour ago, so hopefully all was well with her.

"Hey, Branch, I've got a situation you need to have a look at."

Oh, hell. "What's the location?"

"Alfred Nelson's place. Looks like a suicide but there's a strange note."

"On my way."

When he stood and tucked his phone away, his grandmother frowned up at him. "You have to go?"

"Yes, ma'am. Thank you for the advice and the drink." Though it was a good thing he hadn't taken more than a sip.

"Not to worry, son. I'll finish it off for you." She shot him a wink.

Branch gave her a hug, her body so frail beneath his big arms. "Love you, Gran."

"Love you. Now you be nice to Sasha. She's had enough troubles in her life. She deserves good things and she's just given you a miraculous gift. Enjoy it. Don't fret over how long it took her to get around to giving it."

"Yes, ma'am."

On the porch, he settled his hat into place and headed for his truck. His grandmother was a very smart lady.

ALFRED NELSON LIVED ALONE. His wife had died four years ago. According to Burt Johnston, who knew everyone in the county, Al, as his friends called him, had been instrumental in Alexandra Lenoir being hired in the planning and zoning office. He'd also gone to bat for her big promotion two years later. Though he had worked in that office for a half a dozen years before she came along, he had not possessed the degree he felt the supervisory position deserved. He had insisted that Alexandra was the right person for the job.

It appeared that at some point after lunch today he had decided to end his life. He'd tied a length of clothesline around the ceiling fan and made a noose. Then he'd climbed back up the ladder, put the noose around his neck and stepped off the rung. The ladder had been knocked onto its side by his swaying body.

But before he'd done all that, he'd written a note to Sasha, explaining that her parents' deaths were his fault. He hadn't really meant for everything to turn out the way it had, but he'd made a terrible, terrible mistake. He'd gone to their house with the intention of killing Brandon Lenoir and taking Alexandra far away to be his. He had wanted to have her all to himself for a very long time. But things had gone wrong and a struggle over the gun had taken Alexandra's life. He'd then killed Brandon Lenoir and attempted to make it look like a murder-suicide. His voice was the one Sasha had heard that night. It was all him.

"What do you make of his confession?" Billy asked, his tone heavy with skepticism.

"About the same thing you do, I suspect." Branch shook his head. "This would mean that Alfred was the intruder, and we both know he was in no physical condition to be running through the woods, much less to break into anyone's home. When Sasha spoke to him today, he warned her to stop digging and that some evils were too big to stop."

The strangest part of the entire scene were the empty file drawers in his home office. Any personal or professional papers he had kept were gone.

"Someone is tying up loose ends." Billy watched as the coroner's two assistants removed the body from the scene.

That was the part that worried Branch. "I should talk to Sasha about this before she hears some other way."

"Devlin Packard is still missing," Billy warned. "I don't know if this is his work—frankly, I don't think so—but he's part of this somehow. I've got this feeling that his disappearance and all this are not just coincidence."

Devlin was another of those pieces that simply refused to fit into a slot, like long-missing puzzle parts that were too faded and misshapen to go into place. Yet it was instinctively understood that those pieces belonged in this particular puzzle. There were apparently a whole slew of secrets among the players from twenty-seven years ago and each of those secrets fit together somehow.

"Did you talk to Leandra Brennan again?" Branch wondered if Billy had gotten the same story he did.

"As a matter of fact, she was very forthcoming about her relationship with Sasha's mother and her father. Brennan thinks that during the time she had the affair with Brandon that Alexandra was involved with Alfred." Billy hitched his head toward the body bag. "Perfect timing for her to offer up that previously withheld information. Funny how that keeps happening."

Branch shook his head. "Give me a call if you learn anything new."

Billy gave him a nod. "Will do."

From the Nelson residence, Branch drove to the Lenoir house. Sasha had told him that she and Rey were spending the night there. He wasn't happy about the idea but at least she wasn't alone.

The porch light was on as he climbed out of his truck. He walked past Rey's car. Sasha had left her rental at Rey's. The backyard was completely dark. He wasn't happy about the idea that someone could get all the way to the house from the woods without being seen. For insurance purposes Viola had kept the power and water turned on to the old house, but she hadn't exactly ensured the maintenance was taken care of. Sasha needed to bear that in mind.

He knocked on the door. Half a minute later it opened and Rey beamed a smile at him.

"Branch." She opened the door wide. "Come on in."

He followed her inside and Sasha appeared at the bottom of the stairs. "Hey."

He gave her a nod.

"I'll get back to work." Rey flashed Sasha a smile before bounding up the stairs.

"Is everything okay?" Sasha asked, her expression as uncertain as he felt.

"Billy called. Alfred Nelson is dead."

"What happened?"

"He appears to have committed suicide. He left a note addressed to you."

He repeated the contents of the note and she immediately started to shake her head.

"He insisted that he thought of my mother as a daughter," she argued. "He helped her get the job, pushed for her promotion—both of which sound more like what someone would do for a daughter. I didn't get the impression that he was lying to me or that his feelings were anything other than platonic. This doesn't make sense."

"None at all. And, by the way, in her statement this afternoon to Billy, Leandra Brennan just happened to recall a possible affair between Nelson and your mother."

"We're too close." Sasha's gaze locked with his. "They're worried, so they're attempting to cover all the bases. They hadn't counted on me remembering anything from that night. They thought they'd shut me down."

"They still could."

She looked away. "I'm being careful. Rey is here with me."

"Promise me you won't take any chances, Sasha. I don't like that you're here instead of at my place."

"I'm grateful you feel that way, Branch. I honestly didn't know what to expect after you learned the secret I've kept all these years."

"The decision you made was as much my fault as it was yours," he said. As much as he wanted to be angry, that was the truth of the matter. "If I had behaved differently, you might have felt more inclined to be forthcoming. Either way, what's done is done. We should go from here, not dwell in the past."

She hugged him and for a moment he couldn't move. Maybe it was the shock of her sudden display of affection. Finally, he hugged her back. Whatever else they were, they were friends. They had a daughter. There were a lot of things that needed to be worked out, but this didn't have to be one of those things.

When she drew back she crossed her arms over her

chest in a protective manner. "We're going through everything in the house. If there's anything else to find, we plan on finding it tonight."

"Keep the doors locked and stay on alert. Billy thinks someone is tying up loose ends."

The idea made way too much sense and Branch did not like it one little bit.

She nodded. "We will."

"Call me if you need anything. I'm only eight or nine minutes away."

"I'll call if we need anything. I promise."

As much as he had hoped she would ask him to stay, she didn't. She needed space and time. He understood that. Still, this was not the best time to want distance.

But Rey was here.

That was the only reason he was able to climb into his truck and drive away.

Even then he didn't feel particularly good about it.

Nine minutes later he was in his own house and ready to call it a night, though he doubted he would sleep a wink.

Notification that he had received a text message had him reaching for his cell. The message was from an unknown number. A New York area code. Not Sasha. Her name and number were in his contact list.

He opened the message and read the words.

So, I hear you're my dad.

His heart surged into his throat.

Sasha had told her.

He hadn't anticipated that happening so fast.

Yes. I apologize for the delay in being around. As long as you let me, I plan to make up for it.

Holding his breath, he hit Send.

He didn't breathe again until another text message appeared.

I can handle that.

He smiled and typed a quick response.

Great.

Then he called his parents.

His mother answered on the second ring. "Is everything all right, Branch?"

"Everything's fine," he assured her. "I know it's late, but this couldn't wait."

Chapter Seventeen

Thursday, March 28

It was barely daylight when Sasha awakened the next morning. She and Rey had stayed up far too late going through drawers and boxes and closets. She'd spent a lot of that time talking to Brianne. She'd at first thought she would wait until she was back home to talk to her in person, but considering her grandmother had just died and the rest of what was going on, Sasha had decided a live video chat was the perfect compromise.

Brianne had taken the news in stride. She'd been waiting a long time to learn the identity of her father. Sasha was grateful for her patience and her understanding. One of her first requests was for his cell phone number. Branch had let Sasha know that Brianne had contacted him.

Sasha was particularly thankful that Branch was handling the news so well. For years she had worried about how this would all go down. She should have known her daughter would handle the situation well. Brianne was a very well-adjusted and confident young girl. Sasha was very proud of her.

Branch was a lucky guy to get a daughter as awesome as Brianne.

Sasha ventured into the kitchen. Rey had brought wine and bottled water but she hadn't thought of coffee. Sasha needed coffee badly. She could probably run into town and grab coffee and muffins or something before Rey was up The woman had been like a mini tornado last night. They'd gone through nearly everything in the house. There was nothing else here—nothing that helped with the case, anyway.

So much had happened the past couple of days. There was no question now about whether her parents were murdered or not. They were. Several suspects had come to their attention. Leandra Brennan, Alfred Nelson, Jarvis Packard, Seth Keegan and Hadden Roark. Then there was Devlin Packard. But Sasha had him pegged as a witness rather than a killer.

She grabbed her purse, the keys and her phone and eased out the front door. Locking it behind her, she dropped her phone into her bag.

"You should have listened to me."

Sasha whipped around to face the voice.

She recognized the face from her Google search. Devlin Packard stared at her, his eyes wide with fear or uncertainty—perhaps insanity.

Her first thought was to scream. She resisted the impulse.

"Devlin." She reminded herself to breathe. "I'm glad you came back. I've been trying to find answers. I could use your help."

He stared at her, his expression trapped somewhere between fear and distrust.

"Would you like to come inside? I was going for breakfast. I can bring you back something to eat."

She prayed he was hungry.

He grabbed her by the arm. "You have to come with me now."

Her bag and keys hit the floor.

Fear surged into her throat. Now would be the time to scream. But if she did, any trust she had built with this man would vanish.

Could she trust him not to kill her?

She reminded herself he'd had opportunities before and he hadn't killed her.

He moved faster and faster across the backyard. Dew on the knee-deep grass dampened her jeans. She stumbled in an effort to keep up with his long strides. They hit the tree line and she realized where they were going. The rising sun was abruptly blocked from view by the dark woods.

"You were living in the shack when my parents died."

He yanked her closer as if he feared she might try to take off.

Sasha allowed him to draw her nearer and she didn't fight him. He needed to sense that she trusted him. If he had seen something—if he knew anything about what happened that night—she needed him cooperative.

Her heart was pounding hard by the time they reached the shack. He pushed her through the door and followed her inside, leaving the door standing open, perhaps for the meager light. Still, the interior remained in near-total darkness. She wished she had her phone for the flashlight app.

"You shouldn't have come back asking questions. Big mistake. Big mistake." He was agitated, shifting from foot to foot, shaking his head.

She wrapped her arms around herself and tried to remember what she had seen inside this shack. An old quilt. Some trash.

"I just wanted to know what happened to my mom and dad." She said this softly, quietly, like the child she was when her parents died. Strange, no matter how many years had passed, she still felt like a hurt and lonely child when she allowed herself to be transported back to that time.

"They'll kill you just like they killed them." He leaned close to her. She fought the urge to shudder. "That's why I came back."

"Thank you." *Keep him talking.* Rey would wake up and realize she was gone. She would call Branch.

"I found out you were back and digging around. You should have just buried your grandma and gone back to the big city. You shouldn't have started asking questions. I knew they'd find out and do to you what they did to them."

"Who?" she asked. "Who hurt my parents?"

He shook his head again, moved toward the door, stared outside as if he feared someone might have followed them. "They're dead. Can't bring them back."

Was he talking about her parents?

"We should call the police and tell them what really happened," she urged. The more agitated he grew, the more nervous she felt. But he knew something. She was certain.

He swung around and glared at her. "Are you crazy? The police can't stop them. No one can."

Fear swelled inside her. "You're right. I don't know what I was thinking."

For a few seconds it was so quiet she could hear him breathing, could hear the blood sweeping through her veins.

"Your mother let me stay here because she felt sorry for me. She was nice to me."

"Were you in trouble?"

He glared at her. "I was always in trouble. I couldn't do anything right."

"So my mother was helping you." Sasha mustered up a smile. "She liked helping people."

He shook his head again, so hard it couldn't have been comfortable. "She shouldn't have helped me."

"Do you think they hurt her and my dad because she helped you?" If her heart pounded any faster it would surely burst from her chest.

"They think I don't know but I do." He looked outside again. "They're coming for me. I'm too tired to hide from them anymore. I can't keep running."

Sasha looked outside. "Who's coming?"

"I have to show you before they come. I might not get another chance."

Sasha didn't see or hear anyone. But if he had something to show her it could be important. "Okay."

He went to the farthest corner of the shack and pawed around on the floor.

She had the perfect opportunity to run. His back was to her. She was standing next to the door. He was several feet away. But she needed to stay...to see what he intended to show her.

He stood, turned around and moved toward her. "I kept this. They don't know about it. I wanted you to have it."

He handed her a wad of papers. "If they find them, they'll take them and then you'll never have what you need."

"I'll keep them safe," she promised. Her hands shook as her fingers wrapped around the pages.

The distant sound of a voice jerked their attention to the door.

"They're coming," he murmured.

He shoved the door closed and turned to her. "Stay away from the door. They're here to kill us."

BRANCH WAS JUST about to walk out the door when his cell vibrated with an incoming call. He didn't recognize the number but it was local. "Holloway."

"Branch, this is Rey. Sasha is missing. Her purse and keys were lying on the porch but I can't find her. There are some guys here—they look like SWAT or something. They want to search the property."

Branch was already climbing into his truck. "Do not allow them to search the property. Call Colt and Billy. I'm on my way."

Branch had a feeling the SWAT types Rey meant were some of Packard's security force, and they had no jurisdiction beyond the Packard facility and certainly not on private property. Unfortunately he doubted a little technicality like that had ever stopped them.

It took him six minutes to drive to the Lenoir house, and Franklin County Sheriff Colton "Colt" Tanner's truck was already there.

Rey was on the porch.

"They're in the backyard!" she shouted, pointing around the corner of the house.

As Branch rushed around the corner of the house Billy's truck roared into the driveway. Branch didn't slow down. Rey would send him in the right direction.

Colt had stopped the four-man team dressed in black and armed to the gills at the tree line where the backyard faded into the dark woods.

All four men in black seemed to track Branch's movements as he approached.

"US Marshal Branch Holloway," he called out, identifying himself. "Chief of Police Brannigan is here, as well. You gentlemen are trespassing."

"Morning, Branch." Colt nodded. "I was just explaining to these fine gentlemen that this is private property."

"We have reason to believe our employer's mentally unstable son is in those woods. He may present a danger to himself and to others. We have orders to take him back to the hospital."

If he was here, Branch knew where he had gone. "Sheriff, if you and the chief will babysit these gentlemen, I'll have a look around."

Colt gave him a nod and Branch walked into the forest. He barely restrained the need to run until he was out of sight of the security team. Then he ran like hell. When he spotted the shack, he slowed down, stayed in the cover of the dense foliage.

Quietly and straining to hear any sound, he moved closer.

He couldn't be sure if the man was armed or not. Rather than risk going in, he called out. "Sasha, it's me. You in there?"

"Branch!"

Shuffling and muffled sounds told him that Devlin was with her. He held himself back when he wanted to rush inside and rescue her. He couldn't do anything that might get her hurt…or worse.

"He's my friend," Sasha said.

Branch eased closer.

"I can't protect you," a male voice growled.

Branch wrenched the door open. "I can protect her." He looked from the man who whirled to face him and then to Sasha. She looked unharmed but shaken. "I can protect you both," he said to the man he recognized as Devlin Packard.

Packard shook his head. "They'll kill us if they get the chance."

Branch thought of the assault rifles the men in black had been carrying.

"Stay in the shack and lie down on the floor." He looked to Sasha. "You, too."

Sasha quickly obeyed. She grabbed the man by the hand and pulled him down, too. Branch took a position in front of the door. He called Billy. "I'm at the shack and they're both here. He's terrified of the guys in black. He thinks they've been sent here to kill him and Sasha. We need to get these two out of here and back to city hall."

Thirty-five minutes were required to clear the area. Branch sweat blood every second of every minute. Knowing the kind of powerful man Packard was, he could have several four-man teams combing the woods. Branch kept expecting to be overtaken from one direction or the other.

When Billy and his officers arrived to escort them out of the woods, Branch took his first deep breath.

"The security team has been relocated to city hall via the sheriff's department."

Branch was glad to hear it. He opened the door and held his hand out for Sasha. "It's clear."

As soon as she was out of the shack she went up on tiptoe and whispered in his ear. "Don't treat him like a prisoner."

Branch nodded and offered his hand to the man still lying on the floor of the shack. "It's okay to come out now, Devlin. No one is going to hurt you."

The man took his hand and pulled himself up. He looked around as he stepped out.

"This is Chief of Police Brannigan," Branch explained. "He's going to make sure we get safely out of the woods so we can explain what happened."

Still looking uncertain, the man nodded.

ANOTHER HALF HOUR was required to get everyone transported to city hall. Devlin Packard was settled into an interview room and a court-appointed attorney was on his way. They were trying to move fast, before Jarvis Packard showed up and started to swing his weight around.

Billy, Sasha and Branch stood over the conference table and considered the drawings Devlin had given her. Several of the drawings showed a woman watching through the windows of a house. Sasha presumed it was her childhood home and that the woman was her mother. The other pictures showed men in black looking in those same windows. Sasha thought of the men in black who had shown up to take Devlin. Were these Packard's security thugs in the drawings? Why would they be looking in the windows of her childhood home?

She shook her head. "I'm not sure what any of this means."

"I think I am." Branch picked up his cell phone and tapped on the screen. Then he turned to Billy and said, "Sasha needs to see Devlin. He wouldn't talk to you, but he'll talk to her."

"I think he will," Sasha agreed. "If there's any chance he can explain what this means, it's worth a shot."

"We can try." Billy opened the door. "You and I can watch from the observation room."

"That'll work," Branch agreed.

Billy led the way to the interview room. Branch passed his cell phone and the drawings to Sasha. "Ask him if the woman in the drawings is this woman."

Sasha stared at the image on the screen: Leandra Brennan's face from twenty or so years ago. The photo was from a feature article in the local newspaper. She had noticed it when she'd done an internet search on the woman. Sasha thought of the woman's accusations and renewed fury whipped through her. Then she suddenly understood what Branch was thinking. Their gazes locked and she nodded her understanding of his instructions.

Bracing herself, Sasha entered the interview room and sat down at the table. "Do you need anything to drink or to eat, Devlin?"

He shook his head, the jerkiness of the motion warning her he was still agitated.

"I think we've figured out what you've been trying to tell us, Devlin." She placed the drawings on the table in front of him. He looked from one to the next, the pages faded with time.

"Is this the woman you were watching and drawing?" She showed him the image on the screen of Branch's cell phone.

He nodded, the movement frantic. "She's not a nice person."

"Did she hurt my parents?"

He shrugged. "She only watched. The men—" he tapped another of his drawings "—they are the ones who hurt them."

"You're sure about that?" Sasha reminded herself to breathe.

He nodded. "My father always stopped people who got in his way."

Sasha forced her trembling lips into a smile. "Thank you, Devlin. That helps a lot."

When she had reclaimed the drawings and walked

out of the room, she stared at Branch. "He identified her. Why was she watching my family?"

But she knew the answer. The affair, or whatever it was that had happened between Brennan and Sasha's father.

"Two of my officers are bringing her in now," Billy assured her. "The moment Devlin identified her, I ordered a unit to pick her up."

"What about Packard?" Branch asked.

"I have my best detectives headed to his house now."

Was this really happening? Would Sasha finally know the truth?

TWO HOURS DRAGGED BY. Sasha was keenly aware of every second.

And finally Leandra Brennan confessed. With Branch at her side, Sasha watched from the observation room via the one-way mirror.

"He loved me more than her but she wouldn't let him go. I tried to do the right thing since she was pregnant. But then I saw him again years later—after he lost his job. We ran into each other. He was drinking and I helped him get home. I knew after that day that he was still in love with me. So I decided to make it happen."

"How did you do that?" Billy asked.

"I knew Mr. Packard would never allow anyone to get in the way of his hospital plans. So I set her up. I made her believe that Packard was taking shortcuts. I gave her altered site plans. I made Mr. Packard believe she wanted money." She laughed. "For such a brilliant man he bought the story hook, line and sinker. He ordered his men to take care of her." She frowned. "Brandon wasn't supposed to be home that night. He was supposed to be with me. Only Alexandra and Sasha were supposed to die. But he got in the way and I lost him. If Sasha had died that night, no one would ever have known."

Sasha couldn't listen to any more. She left the observation room.

The idea that her mother had died because her best friend wanted her husband made Sasha sick. She would never know for certain how guilty her father was in the whole mess, if at all. But she did know that her father had tried to protect her mother in the end. That meant something.

Branch stepped into the corridor. "You hanging in there?"

Sasha shrugged then nodded. "I think so. I just need some time to think."

"Rey is waiting to take you home with her. I'm staying here until I'm sure Packard and his minions are all accounted for and arrested."

"Thank you, Branch. I couldn't have done this without you."

He gave her a nod. "We'll talk soon."

He was right. They did need to talk. *Soon.*

Chapter Eighteen

Monday, April 1

Sasha stood in the backyard of her childhood home and stared at the woods. As a child she had loved this place. She had explored every inch of those woods. She turned back to the house. It was a shame for it to continue to fall even further into disrepair. The house could be a home for a family. She would contact a Realtor and a contractor to get started with the cleanout and renovations.

There was a lot of work but it was time to move on from the past.

She had decided to keep her grandmother's house. It felt more like home than this place, or any other, for that matter. Besides, how could she part with the home her grandmother had loved so much? She couldn't. She would pass it down to her daughter when the time came.

Though she had reached a number of decisions, there were more to make.

The breeze shifted, wrapping her in the cool morning air. She hugged her arms around herself. She had taken an extended leave of absence from her firm. Brianne would finish her school year online. Together they would spend the summer exploring their options.

Jarvis Packard had lawyered up and was denying any knowledge of the story Leandra Brennan had told. Not that Sasha had expected him to own his part in the deaths of her parents. Brennan had also insisted that Packard had ordered Alfred Nelson's death, as well. Unless Brennan had proof of her allegations, there was a very good chance Packard would walk away unscathed. Sasha was grateful to know the truth finally and she felt confident Brennan would spend a very long time in prison for her heinous deeds.

Brennan had conspired to end the life of Sasha's mother—her former best friend. Brennan had wanted Sasha's mother's life for her own. The cost had been irrelevant.

Sasha shuddered. She was extremely grateful to Devlin Packard for helping to reveal the persons responsible for the murders of her parents. She might never have known for certain without him. He was headed back to his posh resort-like rehab facility. Sasha wished him well.

More important, Branch had stood with her through this journey into the past. He was the real hero here.

The sound of a vehicle arriving drew her attention to the house. Speak of the devil. That would be Branch. She walked around front and watched as he climbed out of his truck. As he moved toward her, anticipation fizzed in her belly. She would never tire of watching him move or hearing him talk. He smiled. Or seeing him smile.

"Morning."

"Good morning." They met on the front walk. It was actually visible now. Branch had sent the lawn service that took care of his grandmother's property to tame the jungle around this house.

"Billy called," he told her. "Dr. Farr cut a deal with the district attorney. He's going to testify that Jarvis Packard gave him a position on the hospital board of directors in exchange for his expert testimony about you."

Sasha pressed her fingers to her mouth. She had known Farr was lying. When she found her voice again, she asked, "Will his testimony make the difference we need?"

He nodded. "Packard has an entire legal team, but I think Farr's testimony will make the difference."

"This is really good news." Sasha felt immensely relieved. "Thank you."

Silence lingered between them for a moment. When Sasha could bear this new anticipation no longer, she asked, "Did you make your decision?"

He nodded. "I did."

She held her breath. She had no right to expect Branch to alter his life plan for her or for Brianne.

"I'm staying in Winchester."

Relief whooshed through her. "I'm sure your parents and your grandmother are thrilled."

"They are." He grinned. "To be honest, I'm really happy about the decision. It wasn't an easy one to make but it feels right."

"I'm glad."

He held her gaze for a moment. "Good to know."

They were dancing all around this thing between them, but right now neither of them could emotionally afford to go there. They both needed time.

"I've taken a leave of absence to take care of things around here, so I'm not going anywhere for a while either."

"Sounds like a smart plan."

His tone was guarded. Was he worried about where

they went from here? Frankly, she was definitely worried but they had other considerations—like a preteen daughter.

"I think so. I want to stay close—at least for a while. Give you a chance to get to know your daughter."

The anticipation that lit in his eyes made her heart skip a beat.

"I'd like that a lot."

Sasha nodded. "Good, because she can't wait to meet you."

Brianne was giddy with excitement. She couldn't wait to learn all about the other half of her family.

A grin peeked past his guarded facade. "The feeling is definitely mutual."

Branch and Brianne had spoken by phone every day. As soon as the plane landed yesterday she'd wanted to drive straight to his house, but Sasha had insisted on her taking a moment to acclimate herself.

"Would you like to come in and say hello in person?"

He nodded. "I would."

They walked up the front steps together. He reached to open the door and she hesitated. "I wondered if you might like to come to dinner tonight. Brianne and I are cooking."

"Name the place and time."

"Seven, at my grandmother's?"

He gave a nod. "I'll be there."

He opened the door and Sasha walked in ahead of him. Brianne was loping down the stairs.

"Hey, sweetie, this—" she gestured to the man next to her "—is Branch."

Brianne stood on the bottom step for a long moment while she took in the real-life man who was her father. Branch broke the ice by stepping forward and extending his hand. "It's very nice to meet you in person, Brianne."

She put her hand in his and gave it a shake. "Nice to meet you."

"Brianne and I were about to take a walk. Maybe you'd like to join us."

"Sure."

They walked back outside and wandered across the yard. Sasha hung back to watch the two of them together. It was amazing how much Brianne looked like her father. Sasha had known but it was so much more evident in person. She also understood that this fledgling relationship would not be so easy every day. Right now her daughter was in the honeymoon phase of this new discovery. There would be bumps in the road along the way, but for now they were both committed to building a solid relationship. Sasha was immensely grateful things were progressing so well.

The dark clouds that had hung over her life for so very long were gone.

Moving into the future had never looked brighter.

Even as the thought whispered through her mind, Branch turned back to her and smiled.

If there had been any question in her heart, she now knew with certainty that this really was home.

Whatever the future held, Branch and Winchester would be a part of it.

* * * * *

LET'S TALK

Romance

For exclusive extracts, competitions
and special offers, find us online:

f facebook.com/millsandboon

🐦 @MillsandBoon

📷 @MillsandBoonUK

Get in touch on 01413 063232

For all the latest titles coming soon, visit
millsandboon.co.uk/nextmonth